THE SNAKE DOCTOR

Odie Hawkins

authorHOUSE®

AuthorHouse™
1663 Liberty Drive
Bloomington, IN 47403
www.authorhouse.com
Phone: 1-800-839-8640

Published by AuthorHouse 2/28/2013

ISBN: 978-1-4817-0933-0 (sc)
ISBN: 978-1-4817-0934-7 (e)

Library of Congress Control Number: 2013901075

Any people depicted in stock imagery provided by Thinkstock are models,
and such images are being used for illustrative purposes only.
Certain stock imagery © *Thinkstock.*

This book is printed on acid-free paper.

Cover and author's photo by:
Zola Salena-Hawkins, www.flickr.com/photos/32886903@N02

Cover Model/Entrepreneur: Rashid Bahati, www.wix.com/rbahat5/leaddogent

Dedicated to the first African Tarzan

CHAPTER 1

"I think my great grandfather Kwame was the first person I had ever known, personally, to die. I was ten years old. What do you know about death, what do you think about death at that age?

I had seen dead animals here and there, but a dead person is a totally different thing. Great grandfather was one hundred and four when he died, of "natural causes." One hundred and four seemed to me to be as old as a human being could be. Doing the math, I imagined him having ten lifetimes plus four years before I was born. He was old when he died, but he never seemed to be that old when he was alive.

"Kofi, tell me what you learned in school yesterday?"

He was always asking me about school, about how I felt about this 'n that. And he would sit there in his favorite chair and give me his complete attention. That was one of the things I liked about visiting him, he was always interested in what I was interested in.

"So, you want to be a snake man, huh?"

That's what he called a herpetologist, a person who studies snakes, snake behavior. He was the first one in our family to find out about my interest in snakes.

One hundred and four years old. I stood at the side of his casket and stared at his profile. He seemed to be sleeping. He died of "natural causes." That one puzzled me for a bit. I asked my father about that, I was always asking questions about something or another.

"Dad, if great grandfather died of "natural causes," what would an "un-natural cause" be?"

"Well, a bullet through the head would be somewhat unnatural, don't you think?"

I thought my Dad and his Mom and Dad, my paternal grandparents, were some of the smartest people on the planet. They had <u>original</u> answers to any question I asked them. Granddad Kofi and Grandma Nzingha were as busy as two middle aged people could be, with their bookstore, but they always had quality time for me, no matter how busy they were.

"What's on your mind, young man?" That was the way Grandfather Kofi and Grandma Nzingha usually set me up.

Mom's parents, my maternal grandparents, Minerva and Harvey, were quite different. It wouldn't take a genius to figure out that they were much more involved with things, with material stuff, rather than ideas.

They always gave me presents; they're always giving me presents, things. I love them both very much, but there are times when I wish they would back away from the gift shop. Mom told me – "That's the way they are, Kofi, that's the way they've always been."

Mom and Dad, they named me Kofi after granddad and because I was born on Friday, are/and have been the checks and balances in my life. Dad, the filmmaker/writer/producer/director. Mom, the writer.

Like I said earlier, I was always asking questions about one thing or another. And I have to give them, Mom and Dad, my grandparents (Dad's side) credit for encouraging me to ask questions.

"Grandson, if you don't ask questions, people will assume that you know everything just like all of the rest of the young folks."

My great Grandfather had a very dry sense of humor, so dry it would make your cheeks pucker before you smiled. I had the questions and they had the answers, or as Dad must've told me a zillion times.

"If I don't have the answer to your question, we'll go to your mother. And if she doesn't have the answer, we might have to go to the library."

I could count on one of my parents to supply me with answers to the most naïve, most esoteric questions, except for my father, when we got to snakes. I was always very interested in snakes for some reason. I couldn't explain where my interest came from, but it was there, full blown.

I was fascinated by snake lore, the unusual – mainly evil history of snakes, how they mated, the ways they hunted for their food but more than anything – their poisons.

I knew, for example, that the venom from various snakes like the king cobra was being used to treat various neuromuscular disorders.

Ten years old and I was seriously thinking about a career in herpetology, specializing in the creative, scientific use of snake venom to deal with Parkinson's, fibromiligia, Alzheimer's, stuff like that.

I was more than a little bit surprised to discover that my Dad wasn't 100% behind me.

"Why herpetology, son?"

What could I say?

"I don't know why, Dad, it's just something I'm interested in."

"Well, son, it's natural to be interested in a lot of things when you're ten years. Why don't you feel around a bit, explore a few other career fields before you settle into one specific groove?"

I nodded in agreement, but his attitude really puzzled me. Dad was usually so open to whatever I flung at him. If I came to him and told him I wanted to go sky diving, scuba diving, drive a truck for a living, and become a doctor, nurse, veterinarian, chef, whatever, he was always open to the idea. It took me a loonng time to find out why he wasn't enthusiastic about herpetology."

· ℘℃ ·

FATHER KOJO

"I would've been blind to not see that Kofi was interested in snakes from the time he could crawl. It would've been really hard for me to explain to him, to anybody why I didn't want to encourage his interest in snakes.

My Dad, the bookstore owner, noticed Kofi's interest in snakes and was always giving him books about snakes, on his birthdays, for Kwanzaa, whenever. I was really in a bind.

I mean, how could I tell my Dad, my son, my wife, about my deal with Asiafo the Wizard? And how a snake came to be the main character in the piece.

I must've done a flash back about Asiafo the Wizard and the deal I made with him, for years. I'm forty-six years old now, a successful writer-producer-director, got all of the goodies I think I want. And it may all stem from a deal I made with a guy in a forest in Ghana, twenty years ago.

Just for the record; my parents sponsored me to a trip to the

Motherland, to Ghana West Africa, when I was eighteen years old. Maybe they saw it as a "rite of passage" kind of thing.

In any case, I went to the "con-ti-nent," as my grandfather Kwame used to call it. In our Africentric family it was ordinary for one family member or another to be making a trip to Africa, every year. Sometimes, it would be family groups.

"Don't allow them to lock you outside of Africa, Kojo, they've been trying to do that ever since they brought us over here."

That's what my grandfather used to say, at least once a week. And my Mom and Dad weren't far behind him.

"Kojo, you have to <u>think</u> about Africa, it has to be a part of your consciousness, otherwise you'll be caught up in this negative bag that so many of our young, and some not so young African-American sisters 'n brothers have been swept into. And we're not just simply talking about the ones who go around calling each other "nigggahs.""

My family was a rock bed foundation for my Africanity and I bless them for that. My first trip to Ghana was a blast! All I need to do is sit still, daydream for a hot minute and I'm back in Africa. The trip would've been a huge success if I had only done two things, met Comfort Lartey and Grace Vivian Hlovor.

Eighteen years old, hormones racing like fire engines. I'm sure, if it hadn't been for the packages of condoms that Mom and Dad insisted that I carry, I would've had at least two pregnant young women in Ghana.

Yeahhh, Ghana, Africa really opened my eyes to a lot of stuff. I got a chance to see, to experience what effect, for example, colonialism had on the African psyche. Never will forget the billboard with the blonde Jesus on Danquah Circle, the subservient ways many Africans behaved whenever any European showed his face, the poverty, the malaria.

"Kojo, when you get to Africa, to Ghana, you'll have a few people attempt to make you feel inferior, feel bad because you're an African-American. Don't buy into it.

Some Africans have an almost "Japanese attitude towards us."

"Woww, Dad, you're a lil' too far ahead of me – a 'Japanese attitude'?"

"Sounds crazy let me explain. Some, many Japanese, even today, blame the victims of Hiroshima and Nagasaki for their misfortune, for being in the wrong place at the wrong time, kharmically speaking. That's the 'Japanese attitude' some Africans have toward us, the Africans in the Diaspora. If your kharma had been correct, you wouldn't've been carted off into slavery. That's like blaming the victim for being a victim.

Hopefully you won't find as much of that attitude as your mother and I found, the first time we tripped to West Africa."

I could honestly say that I didn't find the "Japanese attitude" to be as strong for me, as it was for my parents. But I still felt tinges of it. I mean, why weren't we given a Diaspora welcome, instead of being directed to go stand in line with "the rest of the Obruni, the Europeans?"

That really put a wild hair up my ass for a few minutes. I asked, because I always asked, whatever – "Why aren't Africans from the Diaspora given more preferential treatment? After all we're returning to our ancestral home."

I got a few fuzzy answers and one realistic reply. The realistic reply came from Comfort Lartey, one of the young women I had seduced on my third day in the section of Accra called Osu.

"Kojo, you must look at this from our perspective: it doesn't matter that you are <u>not</u> fair skinned and that you do <u>not</u> have curly hair. What matters is that you do not know which village your ancestors came from, and more importantly, where they are buried. What matters is that you do not speak the Ga, Twi, Adangme, Nzema, Ewe, or any of the other languages in Ghana here."

"Would I receive greater acceptance if I spoke Ga, Twi or Ewe?"

"Probably not. I mean, at the end of the day, a language is just a language. It's the culture above and below the language that counts. It's not about color, it's about culture."

"So, you're saying that I could never claim my African roots, no matter what I did?"

"I didn't say that. I'm just saying that the culture makes you a Ghanaian, a Nigerian, a Fon, or whatever.

There are some Lebanese born in Ghana here who are more African that you could ever be. We call you Obruni because that's what you are; if you walk like a duck, squawk like a duck and act like a duck, then we must call you a duck.

Understand me well, Kojo, there is nothing personal about this. You walk like an American, you talk like an American, and so we call you an American. So, what's wrong with that?"

"There's a whole lot wrong with that. Number one, it just kicks my African side completely to the kerb."

"You say?"

"Forget about it, Comfort, it would take about four years of African-Caribbean-South/North American studies for you to understand what I'm trying to explain. Are we still going to see the Ghana National Dance Ensemble this evening?"

"Yes please."

There was an awful lot about that six weeks stay in Ghana that turned me on my ear. I knew, when I got on the KLM flight back to Los Angeles at Kotoka Airport, that I wanted to return to Ghana."

·   ℘℃   ·

CHAPTER 2

"Eight years later, after four years of battling the racist bastards in the U.S.C. Film School – "Sorry, Mr. Brown, we just don't have an authority who can validate your thesis/film short, your claim that there were African explorers in the Polynesian/Melanesian islands. We'll have to ask you to pick another subject area."

"They came before Columbus, Van Sertima …"

"Mr. Brown, the Film committee can definitely appreciate your desire to … uhh … focus on unknown African presences here and there, but we must insist that your subject areas pass certain benchmarks. This new subject area, 'They Came Before Columbus,' for example. We don't have any hard evidence to substantiate your premise …"

"In other words, you can't find a White PhD. who is willing to admit what I'm saying is the truth. And you won't accept the credentials of the African-American historians that I've submitted – Ivan Van Sertima, Dr. John Henrik Clarke, Dr. Diop and all the rest."

Four solid years of arguments, debates, disagreements. At one point, midway into my junior year, I was half a finger snap from slapping the shit out of two of my racist-snakedog-asshole instructors, turning a desk or two over, calling most of the people in the Film school a sack load of motherfuckers, and stomping off to Brazil, or the Congo, or somewhere.

Mom and Dad sat me down in the library, our serious conference room, opened a bottle of Harvey's Bristol cream, and quietly, coolly spelled the past, the present and the future out to me. Now that I think back on it, I have the feeling that they had carefully orchestrated their talk with me. Dad came first with the past, Mom laid out the present, and they took interwoven shots at my head with the future.

"Now Kojo, let's make this clear and simple. We can't allow you to drop out of school because of racism. Personally, I think that would be a slap in the face of all your ancestors, all of those brothers and sisters who struggled, gave their lives for us, for you to be able to get to where you are.

I'm sure you'll have to agree with me when I say we told you so. We told you, from Day One, that this place has a racist foundation. So, you can't tell us that you thought you were going to go to this institution and find a level playing field.

The lessons of the past have taught us that this place and its institutions have deep reservoirs of racism. You hear what I'm saying?"

What else could I do but sip my sherry and nod in agreement.

"From time to time the reservoirs seem to be at a lowered level, especially when there's a large scale war. Or some other national crisis that forces the usual suspects to reach out for all the colored hands and bodies they can find. But as soon as the dark cloud passes – things tend to return to what they were.

Don't misunderstand me, what I'm saying – racism is, has been, and probably always will be a thread in this society's fabric. The reason why? Because the usual suspects would have to do three radically different things; number one, they would have to tell the absolute truth about how the Europeans cheated, stole and took this land away from the Indigenous people. Number two, they would have to tell the absolute truth about the role that the African importees/slaves played in the development of this "New World." Number three, they would have to be willing to share the power. And, as you know, that's something they've never done and they're not very likely to do it any time soon."

Mom slid in right after Dad said, "Soon."

"Kojo, think about it. Films/movies are the audio/visual aids of this time. Film/video/T.V./VCR, all of this stuff has ulterior objectives. I and your father haven't been to a movie in years. Why? 'Cause they're not making films/movies for people like us, for thinking people.

They can give us a bunch of gobble de gook gender/demographic/age crap about movies being made only or the fifteen-thirty-five year old market. Or whatever they choose to call it. The truth of the matter is that they've cornered a herd of non-thinking people and decided to force feed them chewing gum for the eyeballs and the emotions, bubbled up stuff that explodes on cue and completely lacks substance. That's what makes your presence on the scene so desirable and necessary."

"Kojo, don't you understand what your mother is saying?"

What else could I do but nod and sip? My Mom and Dad were spellbinders. They could whip my ass with their logic harder than any other weapon in their arsenal.

"Kojo, let me follow up with what your mother was saying. We need you, son. We need to have the alternative perspective your eyes and your sensitivities are going to bring to the scene."

"It's never been easy, Kojo, never. I can't think that any conscious African-American woman has ever given birth to a child, male or female, and thought, well now, that's done, they've got it made. No my son, it's never been that way with us. We've always been forced to think – what can I do to put a firewall up for this boy, this girl? 'Cause I know the virus is lurking everywhere."

"What your mother says is true Kojo. And that goes for the African-American man also. It doesn't give you a good feeling to know that you are the father of a son/daughter who is going to be pounded on by the society that this child is born into."

"You're a filmmaker, Kojo, a person who has the vision to turn some of this racist craziness around, a person who can give America a different slant on itself."

"Kojo, I think you have a sacred obligation on your shoulders. Look, you might have to endure a lil' racist nonsense/bullshit for a lil' while. And that's regrettable, no doubt about that. But the sacrifices you make will benefit a while slew of people who are coming after you. And make no doubts about it, there are bunches of 'em waiting in the wings. The question they will be asking is – did Kojo make it?"

"Kojo, I think your mother has basically put the whole thing in a nutshell, so I'm not going to belabor the point. All I would like to suggest to you, finally, is that you put your personal agenda; goals, ego, on ice for a lil' while longer.

We're not asking you to bow down and kiss anybody's ass or anything like that. We're just asking you to put racism into its proper perspective and keep on stepping!"

What if Harriet Tubman, Henry "Box" Brown, Mary McLeod Bethune, George Washington Carver, Dr. Martin Luther King, Marcus Garvey, Dr. John Henrik Clarke, Obama, and God only knows how many others, had decided – Hey! This racism is too heavy for me I gotta give up!"

Maybe the sherry was a contributing factor, but I left our family conference feeling energized. Shit? I was Kojo Bediako Brown, son of Kofi and Nzingha Brown, what right did I have to give up? To surrender?

It was no contest from that point on. I went on a satirical/historical charade that completely messed my academic screeners up. In rapido succession I made requests to do fifteen-minute student films about the Scottish discovery of chit-lins, the European discovery of a tribe of Kalahari people in Eastern Europe who had lost their way, due to the effects of global warming. The African-American pimp and how he came to be. I used visual subliminals to suggest that African-American pimping, at the street level, was a subversion of the African-American's place in American life.

Some of the people at USC grew to hate my guts for twisting their comfortable little shit around, but there were others (they've asked me not to reveal their names) who gave me lots of encouragement. In any case, I survived my junior year doubts and climbed up out of the USC Film School cess pool, smelling like a rose.

It didn't take long at all for me to get a whole bunch of assistant director/second unit director/associate producer gigs. I was a USC Film School grad and the Powers-That-Are gave me some brownie points for having endured, persevered, and stuck it out.

"So, Kojo, unusual name – we see here that you're a USC Film school grad …"

I did it all; instructional films, industrial films, anti-AIDs films, whatever. In every case I made it my business to tweak it with my own special sense of style, to put on that "Kojo Touch." Over the period of four years, I was in a very good spot. I set up my own production company. I was preparing myself to explore the outer perimeters of the creative, lucrative world.

"Kojo, remember – artists may start off being hungry, but they don't have to <u>stay</u> hungry. Dig it?"

It was time to go back to Africa again, to Ghana, to feel <u>that</u> feeling again. I was twenty-five, a good age to be. So, the minute the window opened I flew.

Ghana, in the forms of the two sisters I had dealt with during the course of my first trip, had changed radically.

Comfort Lartey and Grace Vivian Hlover were as different as proverbial day and night, when I first met them at the wise ol' age of eighteen. Comfort was about as radical as the Ghanaian circumstances would allow her to be.

"I don't care what the Europeans say! It's all a crock of crap!"

Grace was at the other end of the pole.

"Think about it, Kojo, if the English had not come to Ghana, we would still be having tribal wars and worshipping fetish gods."

I can't say what happened because I wasn't there to see how the change had occurred, but <u>A Change</u> had occurred. Comfort, the radical bohemian had become a religious nut, a conservative.

"Kojo, I can't do with you what we used to do because Jesus wouldn't like that."

"If you don't tell Him, I won't tell Him and everything will be cool."

"You are blaspheming and you may be forced to pay for your transgressions by spending an eternity in Hell."

As my lawyer friend, Horace Hennessey Harper, used to say – I absconded from Comfort "without any malice aforethought, forthwith." Grace took up the slack.

"Oh Kojo, I am so pleased that you have returned."

She made me feel like the prodigal lover. It didn't take me long to find out that an Older African-American brother, thirty-five maybe, had been on the scene during our interim/separation.

"Charles introduced me to jazz music."

I couldn't/wouldn't allow myself to have jealous pangs or anything like that. After all, when I split back to America, we hadn't signed a mutual romantic agreement or anything like that. We had made some real good love, no doubt about that. But we hadn't created a foundation for anything.

In some ways it made things better between us. I hadn't told her any lies and she hadn't offered me any false hopes. We fell into each other arms and offered each other lots of emotional space. I wasn't simply in Ghana for her, I was in Ghana for the sake of being in Ghana.

She understood that. That's why I wound up spending time in a village called Tsito. Chee-toe.

"So, my African-American man, you want to go to see how life is, in the village, eh? Well, you shall have your wish. Give this note to my Auntie Eugenia, in the village called Tsito."

So, that's how I wound up spending a week in the village of Tsito. And making the acquaintance of Mr. Asiafo, the Wizard.

But first, a few words about the village called Tsito. Unless something incredible has changed in the last few days, you're not likely to find the place on any map anywhere, not even in Ghana.

It's in the northeastern section of the country, somewhere between here and there, about twelve-fourteen hundred people. It's unusual in the sense of having a young population, as well as an old population. It's one of those places where all of the young people have <u>not</u> jumped up and gone to the big city.

"Why should I leave Tsito (Chee-Toe)? I love this place."

It would be hard for me to figure out what there was to love in Tsito. There were only two taps of running water in the whole village and sometimes, when the dry season, the Harmatan comes, the water stops flowing. During the rainy season, from May-September, the place is like a mud hole.

There is no telephone service. Someone told me, while I was there, that they had two telephones at one time; "but something happened to spoil them and we are waiting for repairs to be done."

People grow their own food; corn, beans, okra, plantains, mangos, sugar cane. And they raise chickens and pigs. There is a forest surrounding Tsito, which supplies wild game, mostly "bush meat" and deer.

The people are relatively healthy, but there are no "extras," no luxuries. Tsito is not the place to go if you want to see bright lights and dancing girls. I went there because I wanted to experience the <u>real</u> Ghana.

Accra, Kumasi, Tamale, the "big cities" are just like big cities everywhere – over populated, dirty, unhealthy.

"So, my African-American man, you want to go to see how life is in the village, eh?"

Those were Grace's words and her note to her Aunt Eugenia in Tsito was my passport to the primitive life. And my meeting with Asiafo."

· ℰℛ ·

GRACE VIVIAN HLOVOR

"Of course I knew that Kojo had another girlfriend when he came to Ghana here, the first time. It was no big thing. We were very young, he was an exciting experience for me, a wild African-American boy, and he was nice to me.

When he went back to America, I thought I would never see him again. We exchanged letters, birthday cards, that sort of thing, but we did not make great promises to each other. He came back for another visit after an eight-year absence.

In the interim, going right along with my life, I met another African-American guy. Charles Howard was an arts entrepreneur who had set his sights on becoming a man with serious money. He saw Ghana, West Africa, as an untapped source of wealth.

"Grace, your country has so much to offer the world. I would like to see a film industry developed here, one that would create and export world class films to the world. I would like to have at least four Ghana Dance Ensembles on tour in Europe, Asia, and the US. I would bet you even money that many people would get a big kick out of seeing some of the great traditional plays, the things about the supernatural and all that."

Charles was an older man. Well, I was nineteen and he was thirty when we met, so I guess I can say that he was "an older man." He introduced me to African-American jazz, to fine foods, sophisticated people, and the good life. If I had to compare the two, I would say that Kojo was a wild, free spirit, full of himself, a creative mind.

Charles was rather laid back, more focused on the material aspects of life. I have to feel that the gods, Dadi Togbe Wo, were very gracious to me, to have allowed both of these beautiful men in my life.

I was quite surprised to hear that Kojo was coming back to Ghana after eight years. I was not under any illusions. I didn't know if he was coming back to spend time with me, or with the other one. Ghana is small-small and everybody knows everything about everybody.

Charles was in London, fortunately, to do business during the time Kojo was visiting. And I felt no compulsion to tell Charles anything about Kojo. Nor did I feel any need to say a lot about Charles to Kojo. I did let Kojo know that there was a man in my life and I let it go at that. I knew he was sophisticated enough to deal with the situation.

Honestly speaking, I felt deliciously wicked. I was having a chance to have my cake and my pie too.

I was somewhat annoyed with Kojo for wanting to take a week away from me, to go to a remote village, "to experience the real Ghana." I had no idea he would go to Tsito and become involved with that awful creature in the forest, that man-thing called Asiafo.

I knew something of Asiafo from the stories that had been passed down to me from my elders: the story of how Asiafo and his mother were caught having sexual relations. The mother was burned alive in her hut as a witch; the boy cast out into the forest to die.

The story of how, somehow the boy managed to survive and develop incredible powers. These stories were already old when I was a small girl. Some say that a few people who had very serious problems went to Asiafo, and he helped them solve their problems.

I cannot say if this is true or false. My Auntie Eugenia and those who live in Tsito have always spoken of Asiafo as an evil-spirit-demon-thing. And I accepted their opinion, based on the history of the man. Who else but a demon could go into the forest, alone, and, live for many years?

Now, my African-American man meets with this creature and comes back to Accra, talking about some kind of "deal" he has made with this … this person."

· ℰℭ ·

CHAPTER 3

KOJO

"I wasn't raised in a conventionally religious household. My Mom and my Dad made it quite clear, early on, that they could offer me some spiritual advice, and they were totally comfortable with the idea of me becoming a Christian, Muslim, Jew, Buddhist or whatever.

Dad laid it out for me more than a few times.

"I rejected Christianity and Islam outright, the minute I found out that both of them sanctioned slavery. I don't care what people say that Christ said. Or that people say that this is what Muhammed said. All I can go on is the hard evidence of what these so-called Christians and Muslims have done, what they <u>are</u> doing. It would be damned near impossible for me to go sit up in a church somewhere and sing 'Amazing Grace' and all the rest of that stuff, knowing what I know. Ditto for bowing down to Mecca five times a day, knowing what I know about the Arabian slave trade."

"I'm right at your father's side on this one, Kojo. I have a lot of issues with <u>all</u> of the major religious when it comes to the position and the role of women, Black, White and whatever. It seems to me that <u>all</u> of the major religions have relegated women to some lil' room over there. Islam is usually pointed out as the worse offender, but I don't think they're any worst than the Hindus, the Buddhists, the Jews or the Christians."

"So, what do you guys believe in, what's your religion?" I was about twelve at the time.

"Go 'head, Nzingha, you tell him you're pretty good at this."

"Look at whose talking …"

My parents were always enjoying kidding each other.

"Well, o.k., I'm the designated hitter, huh? Let me explain it to you this way, Kojo. We are proud African-Americans and we feel that the spiritual systems our ancestors had when they were brought here are good enough for us."

"So, that's what your altars are all about?"

Dad clapped me on the back, a big smile on his face.

"Give the man a kewpie doll for his powers of observation." Mom had a serious expression on her face as she continued with her "explanation."

"We don't believe any religion or spiritual system on Earth is any better than any other, they're all flawed because they are practiced by human beings. But we feel closer and more in tune with the vibes that come down to us from our ancestors.

All you have to do is just think about it for a moment … would you rather believe in something your ancestors believed in, or would you rather believe in something that your conquerors, the people who enslaved your ancestors, forced them to believe in?"

"That's not a difficult choice."

Now Dad was the one with the serious expression.

"That's the way we felt about it. We felt it would be truer to the spirit of who we are, and where we came from, to pay homage to the spirits of our ancestors, rather than pay lip service to some stuff that had been force fed to our ancestors."

"I've had a helluva time trying to make my mother and father, your Grandma Minerva and Granddad Harvey, understand where we're coming from. But it really doesn't matter, I love them and they love me. And, at the end of the day, that's all that matters."

It wasn't too long after that conversation that I created my own family altar/shrine. Hard to explain how I felt, but it was definitely a good feeling. My Mom and Dad were pleased as punch.

"You got to understand, Kojo, we don't feel, we didn't feel that it was the right thing to do, to superimpose our ideas, our way of worship on you."

"But I have to say, as a mother, it gives me a warm feeling to know that you've decided to follow in our footsteps."

"The thing to do now is study the African spiritual systems. Become intelligent about what you believe in. As you probably know, as a result of the African Diaspora, there are African spiritual systems all over the planet. You may find a lil' bit of this one inside that one, or vice versa. But one of the central points they all hold to is this – you must make the proper sacrifice for what you want. In Yoruba, they call it an ehbaw."

By the time I made my second trip to Ghana, at the old age of twenty-five, I had made ehbaws all over the place. I have to believe that my ehbaws were well received because I had received just about everything I had prayed for.

However, as a writer-producer, with my own production company – Kosmic Muffin Productions – I still lacked the millions that I needed to make that break out film. This is where Asiafo comes onto the set.

Despite the inconvenience of village life in Tsito, I didn't feel depressed or anything. And the morning that I met Asiafo in the forest definitely lifted my spirits, my morale and my expectations.

I had taken a walk in the forest, something that Grace's Auntie Eugenia, my host, couldn't clearly understand.

"Kojo, you are going to walk in the forest? O why?"

"Uhh, for exercise, Auntie, for exercise."

I can still see the puzzled look on her face. With all of the work to be done – washing, chopping wood, cooking, cleaning, planting, sewing, hut building, carrying five-gallon cans on your head, etc.; who needs to exercise?

It took about two hundred yards away from the village for me to find myself in the Equatorial rainforest. I had grown up on "Wild Kingdom," "Nature," "Animals of the World," so I wasn't freaked out about anything. I wasn't afraid of giant snakes dropping down onto my shoulders from the overhanging tree limbs. Or that I was being stalked by man eating leopards.

The forest was like a great, green, tree shrouded cathedral. There were monkey sounds here and there, bird calls, but mostly an immense silence. I inspected a large fallen log, tapped on it to make certain that the snake, or snakes, would know that I was about to straddle the log. I must've sat there for ten minutes or so before I smelt this incredible aroma.

It was not a smell, a will o' the wisp thing; this was an aroma, a kind of rich, wildflower perfume. I've never smelled anything like it since then.

Maybe the closest aroma I can think of is when you go to some place where skunks have been.

The aroma seemed to drift around my head, like the thin, blue smoke from a good Cuban cigar. I slowly turned to my left and as I turned, the man in my peripheral vision made a lightning move and wound up sitting, straddled on the log, a yard or so, in front of me.

I didn't know who he was because I hadn't been told anything about anybody named Asiafo, at that point in time. We must've sat there, studying each other for about five minutes.

The first thing I noticed about him, after acclimating myself to this exotic aroma that seemed to seep out of his pores, was how incredibly healthy he looked. He was a dark chocolate colored man and his skin actually glowed with health. He wore a large tree leaf on his uncombed hair, a cowrie shell necklace and a grass skirt. No weapon, just a bright gleam in his black eyes.

He was an African man, no doubt about that. But he seemed to be more a creature of the forest than anything else. I made a snap decision, to allow him to speak first, which I immediately forgot about. What if he doesn't speak English? What if he can't speak at all?

I spoke in a low tone, as softly as I could, but my voice still sounded too loud in that place.

"Do you, can you speak English?"

He cocked his head to one side as though he was trying to determine where my voice came from, and nodded yes, yes. We were still studying each other, two laboratory specimens mounted on a fallen log.

He was relaxed, cat like. I recalled the fantastic movement he had made to sit in front of me. He was at ease, relaxed now, but I knew he could be cobra quick if he wanted to be. How old? I could only guess. He had the slim physique of an 800-meter man, but his eyes were bright and old.

"Who are you?" I felt compelled to ask him.

"I am called Asiafo," he answered quietly.

Asiafo. It didn't mean anything specific to me, it was just a name. Really interesting person, really interesting situation. There seemed to be no need for us to start babbling at each other, the way a lot of people do when they first meet.

"And you?" he asked.

"My name is Kojo Brown, I'm from America."

He nodded, taking that piece of information in. And then we smiled at each other. And started laughing. I don't know why. Maybe the scene of the two of us straddled on this log struck a mutual funny bone.

"Asiafo, where do you live? I haven't seen you in Tsito."

"I do not live in Tsito, I live here." He made a sweeping gesture with both arms. I had to grip the log with my legs to keep from falling off.

"You live here – in the forest?"

He nodded yes yes. He didn't say a lot, but when he spoke it seemed that each word had a different accent. I couldn't place the accents. It wasn't the usual Ghanaian up-down tonal pattern. I had never heard anyone speak like Asiafo.

Zoom – Close up – Pan the forest – Another Angle. I started shooting my film right then and there – "Asiafo in the Forest." He looked at me with an amused expression on his face. There was something about his expression that made me feel that he knew what was on my mind.

"Asiafo, do you know what I'm thinking right now?"

He laughed, a short, high pitched laugh, a hyena laugh. That jarred me a bit.

"You are making pictures of me, of this." Once again his sweeping gesture.

"So, how do you know what I'm thinking?"

"Because your eyes tell me."

"My eyes reveal what's on my mind?"

He made his familiar nod yes yes. This was absolutely fascinating to me. What kind of training, how could he speak with such certainty about what was on my mind?

"Well, I know they say that the eyes are windows to the soul, or something like that, but I look in your eyes and I have no idea what you're thinking."

He shrugged eloquently, as though to say – well, I can do it and you can't. So what? And that's the way we left it for a few beats. I enjoyed the pace of our "conversation." There was no frenzied you say – I say you ask – I answer sort of thing.

He didn't say a lot but whatever he said was right on the button.

"Asiafo, you can call me Kojo, if you like?"

He nodded yes yes pleasantly. We didn't shake hands; we simply exchanged neat little bows. He made his hyena laugh again. He obviously had a different sense of humor.

"Asiafo, a little while ago you said, 'You are making pictures of me, of this.' And it's true; in my mind's eye I was creating a film about you, about this." I did his sweeping arms gesture. He edged forward on the log, giving me his full attention, inviting me to speak.

"I know there's never been a film made about an African man living in the forest alone. Uhh, you are out here by yourself, aren't you?"

He nodded yes yes. I was becoming familiar with his gestures.

"We've had pictures of White guys with loin clothes on, swinging through the trees, doing all sorts of idiotic stuff. But we've never seen a Black man, an African, living the natural life."

He smiled shyly.

"So, you want to do the Asiafo story, eh?"

"Yes, I want to do the Asiafo story, my grandfather's story, a realistic story of the Middle passage, the story of how the human being came into existence in East Africa, the stories of the connections that the Africans and the Indigenous peoples in North and South America made, how it happened.

I want to peel back the layers of bullshit and show the real deal." He had touched a nerve with his question and I was off and running.

"Which one of your stories would you like to picture first?"

I had to give that some serious thought for a long minute. He waited patiently, staring straight into my face. Which "picture" would I like to "picture" first?

"I have written a script called "My Grandfather's Eyes," it's the story of a man who lived a full, rich, colorful life, went through a lot of changes, made a positive impact on a lot of folks and died at the age of one hundred and four. We didn't mourn my grandfather's death, we celebrated his life. He was a wonderful man, a great spirit. That's the picture I would like to make first."

"So, why don't you do it?"

It was my turn to laugh. Evidently he didn't know all there was to know about the movie business.

"Why don't I do it? Well, the major problem is, as usual, money. It costs a lot of money to make a picture, if you're going to do it right."

"How much <u>money</u>?" Funny the way he said it made it sound like leaves from a tree. Or scraps of paper.

"Millions."

"Millions? How many millions?"

This was becoming very interesting. What next? Above the line and below the line costs? Distribution? Advertising? Point shares?

"I think I could do it on a shoe string, let's say five-six million, minimum."

He tilted his head back for a few moments, as though he were gazing at the tree tops around us, or maybe doing some sort of calculations.

"Come back to this place tomorrow, Kojo, at the same time, I think I may be able to help you."

And like a snake's tongue flicking out, he was gone. I sat on the log a few minutes longer, tempted to laugh out loud, but chilled out the urge, knowing Asiafo was watching me from somewhere.

"Tomorrow, same time, same place?" I spoke aloud to reaffirm our appointment. Asiafo's "yes" seemed to come from opposite places. Maybe he was a ventriloquist.

I strolled slowly through the forest. A half naked man in the Equatorial rainforest was going to help me secure financing for a movie. Or at least he said he might be able to do it. It didn't really matter either way. The idea of it was mind blowing.

· ℰℛ ·

CHAPTER 4

"Aunt Eugenia was wringing her hands and showing all of the distress signs that mothers, aunts, show about delinquent kids.

"O Kojo, you have been gone a long time, I was worrying that you would be lost."

"No, Auntie, I wasn't lost ..."

"Come, I have prepared your chop."

"It ain't bush meat, is it?"

She smiled at my joke. After four days of her generous hospitality and her delicious Ghanaian food we could smile at the memory of the first meal she had served me – "bush meat." It only took a few bites from this small hind leg to realize that I was gnawing on a large rat, "bush meat." It wasn't bad, just a bit unsettling. I dismissed my squeamish cultural bias and ate the damned thing as though I had been eating "bush meat" all my life. But I couldn't fool her.

"No more bush meat for you, Kojo, we have banku and okra stew."

I did the culturally correct thing and rinsed my right hand to dig into a bowl of sumptuous okra stew. It could've been gumbo file without the shrimps. Aunt Eugenia sat across from me on the low wooden table in front of her neat little three-room hut. She watched me eat; making little sounds to let me know that there was more banku and okra stew if I wanted more. She didn't eat with me. That was a cultural thing to do.

"Auntie, would you like to take some chop with me, it's delicious."

She smiled and shook her head no no. I was reminded of Asiafo nodding up and down yes yes. She brought me a small wooden bowl with water and a sliver of soap to wash my hands, a piece of cloth to dry my hands after I had eaten two bowls of banku and okra stew. She was pleased with my appetite.

I leaned my back against the hut wall, belly full, watching village life go on around me. Goats eating cardboard, dried banana leaves, bits and ends of whatever they could find. Children playing, as always. And women, young and old, washing, sewing, and hauling water and other things on their heads. The elder men sat under a large tree at the edge of the village, sipping palm wine and discussing village business. All surrounded by rainy season mud. "So, Kojo my son, how did you find it in the forest?"

I loved that, that "Kojo my son" thing; it had a beautiful family ring to it.

"Auntie, I met an unusual man in the forest ..."

She looked like she was going to keel over from shock.

"What does this man call himself?"

"Asiafo."

"Oooooohh!" She stood up and did a little circular dance, holding her right hand over her mouth. I just stared at her; I didn't know what to think. After a couple more circles, she beckoned me to follow her into the hut. We had never sat in the hut together. Since the first day she had gone to one of her relatives to spend the night and left me in the hut alone.

She gestured for me to sit on one of the stools in the hut as she dug down into a large straw bag hanging on the far wall. She brought out two glasses and a fifth of clear liquor. She sat on a stool across from me, poured both of us big slugs of liquor.

"Auntie, what is this?"

"Akpeteshie," she announced and started a series of serious libations. Each time she dribbled a bit of the liquor on the ground, she said what must've been prayers. It was in Ewe, it had a gorgeous feel to it, but I couldn't understand a word. Finally, she tilted the glass up and swallowed the rest of the akpeteshie. I tried to do the same thing, which seemed to be the proper thing to do, but I was only able to swallow a large sip. They called akpeteshie "the poor man's gin," but it was stronger than gin.

"Auntie, you seem to be disturbed about something."

She poured more akpeteshie into her glass, made three more libations and prayers before she spoke to me.

"Kojo my son, you have met this wicked one, Asiafo, in the forest. I have offered prayers for you ..."

Asiafo, wicked? He didn't seem wicked to me. As a matter of fact he seemed like a pretty nice dude. I mean, after all, he was talking about helping me get the bucks to make "My Grandfather's Eyes." I had already come up with a working title for my script.

"Auntie, I don't understand. Why do you say Asiafo is wicked?"

"He is a witch!"

I took a big sip of akpeteshie. I had to be cool about this. The word "witch!" sounded so, so medieval, I had to remember that I was in a small village in Ghana, in the middle of nowhere, and there was a lot for me to learn abut the scene.

"Please, Auntie, tell me – what makes him a witch?"

She took a big slug of her drink and stared down at the earth floor, looking embarrassed.

"You ask, I will tell you. When I was a small girl in this village, this wicked man was banished from the village and cursed for knowing his mother."

I stared at her. Village people were so into Biblical things. For "knowing" his mother. And thus did Onan "know" his brother's wife.

"Are you sure he 'knew' his mother?"

"They were caught by two of the elders."

I felt a warm thud hit the bottom of my stomach. Maybe it was the akpeteshie or maybe it was the information she was giving me.

"So, he was cursed and banished to the forest. How long ago?"

"It was at least forty years now."

"And what happened to his mother?"

"She was a witch and she was burned in her hut."

That sounded like excessive punishment, on both counts, but I didn't live in Tsito, and I couldn't pass judgment on them.

"How old was Asiafo when he was banished?"

The old lady took a moment to count back, she reminded me of my grandfather, who could never be rushed to say anything.

"He was twenty years ... eh heee, twenty years."

The guy that I saw today didn't look a day older than forty.

"Auntie, the man I met in the forest today didn't look like a sixty-year old man."

24

"He has learned great powers in the forest from the forest spirits. Maybe he has learned how not to become old. We know that he has many powers."

"Can you give me an example?"

"You say?"

"Can you tell me about something he has done, that shows some of his powers?"

She pursed her lips and furrowed her brow, thinking. I could sense her reluctance to talk about Asiafo, "the wicked man," but I could see that the akpeteshie had loosened her up a bit.

"Eh heee, this man who lived in our village had a wife who died. The man did not want her dead, so he went into the forest and found the wicked one and paid him to bring his wife back from the dead."

The sounds of the village seemed to go away for a moment. He brought somebody back from the grave.

"How much did he charge to do what he did?"

"The man did not pay money."

I couldn't quite figure out what that meant and decided not to press the issue.

"Can you think of anything else?"

"It is said that he has learned to disappear, to fly like a bird, to become a tree or a snake."

"And you think these things make him wicked?"

"There is much more. They say he can read the mind and see into tomorrow."

"Wowww!"

"And he is wicked because he hates everyone ..."

"Well, I think that's pretty easy to understand. His mother was burned alive and he was cursed and banished to the forest. I think anybody would be pissed."

"You say?"

"I can easily understand why he would be annoyed."

"Many in the village wanted to kill him, his mother and all of their family members."

"Does he still have family here?"

"They went away many years ago."

"So, now let me get this straight – a man was cursed and banished to the forest forty years ago. He gets help from the forest spirits to develop great powers and he is wicked because he hates everybody."

She stood, swaying a bit, and poured another dollop of akpeteshie into her glass, slugged it down.

"Six people of this village have gone to him to ask something of him and when they didn't make the proper payments on time they were never seen again."

"That's wicked."

"Eh heee, he is wicked. I warn you."

I watched the old lady shuffle out, slightly tipsy. I remained in place, trying to put it all together. I could see a helluva film in all of this, if I could determine which point of view would be the most effective: Aunt Eugenia's, Asiafo's, mine, someone else. And if all of the seams could be sewn so that the stitching wouldn't show. But somehow the problem would remain ... how could I make anyone believe that this was the 21st century?

·   ℘ℭ   ·

I forced myself to eat the onion/tomato/fish stew; sprinkled with the grits like corn they called gari. I was anxious to keep my appointment with Asiafo, the "wicked man."

Immediately after chopping I made an oblique move to get away. The old lady was sharp. She peeked my get away from around the corner of her hut.

"Kojo my son, you are going for a walk in the forest? I have warned you."

"Everything is cool, Auntie, everything is cool."

I checked my watch – 9:30 a.m. – and the sky. It looked grayish, like a little rain was on the way. No matter, I had an appointment to keep. I thought I had taken the wrong path until I came across the log.

Good. I'm in the right place. I straddled the log, wishing that I had brought a bottle of water with me. The humidity was stifling.

The hair on the back of my neck stood up when his hand reached over my left shoulder with the top of coconut lopped off. I tried to control my shakes as I took the coconut and drank the sweet liquid from it. I couldn't figure out why Asiafo was sitting behind me.

"Thank you, I was really thirsty."

"You are welcome."

I turned to pass the coconut shell back to him, to discover that he was sitting in front of me.

"You really get around, don't you?"

He nodded yes yes, took the coconut, smashed it on the log and gave me a large chunk of the meat to eat. Delicious, sweet. We chewed on the fresh coconut meat for a few beats before he spoke.

"So, now you know all about me."

Once again that fright wig feeling shot up the back of my neck. He hadn't asked a question, he had made a blunt statement. Now what?

"I know what one person has told me, I don't know your story."

"She told you the correct story."

His expression didn't change. There was no body language to indicate that he felt ashamed, remorseful or evil. The sudden shrill cries of a flock of birds filled up the word space between us.

"You've been living here in the forest since you were banished."

"Yes."

I stared at him. No wrinkles, no bags under his eyes, not an ounce of fat, all of his teeth, serene looking.

"Asiafo, may I ask you a few questions?"

"Do you want to get wet?"

"No, I don't want to get wet."

"It's going to rain in a few minutes."

He slipped from the log and gestured for me to follow him. Six people, Auntie said, had gone to see him for some reason and when they didn't make the proper payment they were never seen again. Well, I hadn't asked him for anything and I didn't owe him anything, so I felt I was cool.

After about five minutes of fast walking we came to a small clearing. There was a large hut made of broad banana leaves in the center of the clearing.

It was a scene right out of the documentary about the Ituri Forest people, the so called Pygmies, except that his banana leaf hut was larger. Ten seconds after we ducked inside the rain sloshed down.

"Woww! We made it just in time. How did you know?"

He cut my idiot question to pieces with a sharp glance.

How could I live in the forest this long and not know when it's going to rain?

Asiafo started a small fire in a hole in the center of the hut with flint sparks and dried moss. I felt like someone who had been taken back to the Beginning. He lit two wicks floating in two oil filled half coconut shells. He fed the fire with a few twigs and then, larger sticks of wood. The interior suddenly had a warm, hospitable atmosphere. He gestured for me to sit on a beautifully carved stool. If he was a "wicked man" then he certainly had an eye for beautiful things.

I stared at the vine-contraption animal traps hanging on the foundation poles of his hut, the woven baskets, the leaf shade hats, the hand fashioned tools. We sat on our stools, looking at the fire, listening to the drum-thunder beats on the roof of the hut.

"You wanted to ask me questions."

I had almost forgotten what I wanted to ask, a bit overwhelmed by the atmosphere. He was focused. What did I want to ask him?

"What happens when you get sick?"

He smiled at me in a patronizing way.

"I don't believe in sickness."

"I don't either, but let's say a mosquito bites you and you get malaria."

"I have medicine."

"You have a medicine for malaria?"

He gave his familiar yes yes nod. There was such a definite way he nodded yes yes.

"You have medicine for AIDs, cancer, the common cold?"

"I don't have these things here."

"But you do have medicines to treat them?"

"Yes."

I gazed into the fire for a long, thoughtful moment. Where the hell am I? Where is all of this? Can I make a film out of it?

"You want to make a picture of this?" he asked in a soft, sweet voice. I stared into the eyes of a man who could read minds and was obviously clairvoyant; I had no doubts about it.

"Yes, if not this, then other films that would change minds and attitudes, films that would be wonderful, reasonable, sensitive, intelligent."

"You spoke of these pictures before."

The rain seemed to be pounding on the leaves like down-stroking fufu sticks. We were silent for a few minutes.

"It is possible for you to have the millions you need to do your picture." He said quietly.

Once again, I stifled the urge to laugh. A half-naked man, making fire with sparks, living in a banana leaf hut in the middle of the Equatorial rainforest, tells me that it's possible for me to have the millions needed to do my film, fulfill my dreams.

"How do I get these millions?" I asked politely. I didn't want to sound skeptical.

"Come back to the log tomorrow, I will have the answer for you. The rain has stopped. Come, I will guide you back to the log."

I stood up feeling light headed. My problems were over, solved, I had nothing to worry about. The forest dripped raindrops from its leaves, the ground was gooey and there was a heavy, dank funk on the air.

I followed Asiafo back to the log, tried to stop where he stepped, bend under the branches the way he did, to blend into the forest. He literally disappeared when we got back to the log. O well, I'll see him tomorrow.

"Yes," his voice echoed from a place above my head, "tomorrow, same time, same place." And then that crazed hyena laugh. God, who taught the man how to laugh like that?

I held my wrist watch up to check the time. 10:45 a.m. No, that couldn't be right. I listened to my watch, an expensive time piece. It was ticking like a metronome. It's got to be later than 10:45 a.m. Something strange going on here. I can't believe all of what just happened only took 45 minutes? The meeting, going to his hut, the rain, all of that in 45 minutes. He spent the rest of the day holding his watch to his ear from time to time.

·   ℘ℂℜ   ·

I spent the day carefully reviewing every moment I had spent with Asiafo. I wanted to make absolutely certain that I was not indebted to him for anything. He had offered to help me; I had not made any requests or demands.

I wanted to be certain that I wouldn't be number seven on the list of people who had disappeared.

·   ℘ℂℜ   ·

CHAPTER 5

Auntie Eugenia was not happy about my lil' treks into the forest. Or, as the Ghanaians would say, "She was quite annoyed with me."

"Kojo my son, you are walking into the forest again this morning?"

"I need to do the exercise, Auntie, to burn off some of the calories from your delicious chop."

I could feel her eyes on my back as I eased away for my third meeting with Asiafo.

"I have warned you," she called after me.

I pretended not to hear and kept on stepping. I was surprised to see Asiafo leaning against the log, a chewing stick in the right corner of his mouth. I took careful note of the time – 9:30 a.m.

I strolled over and leaned against the log facing him. He used the licorice flavored stick to brush his teeth for a moment or so before he looked directly at me. It was Freeze Frame for ten long seconds.

"You will have what you want, your wish be fulfilled. You will have the millions needed to make your picture."

My heart felt like it was going to thump out of my chest. Millions, that's what the man said

"You do believe me, don't you?"

"Yes, I do believe you."

Was I being hypnotized? No, I felt in control of myself. Now what? Asiafo started to walk away.

"Asiafo?"

He stopped, but didn't turn around.

"Yes?"

"What do I have to do for this money?"

There it was, that hyena laugh. And then, as though he was reciting a speech or giving a recipe for a dish.

"I will arrange for you to have a visitor, the visitor will come four times a year and it must be fed. You understand?"

"Yes, I understand."

"I must warn you that the success or failure of what you want to do will depend on how well it is fed."

"That's no problem; we got lots of food in America."

"Very good. Do what has to be done and you will have what you want."

He started to walk away again. I felt a sense of panic.

"Is that all? I mean, that's all I have to do?"

"Oh, there is one more thing. When you return to your country, you should be married within three months."

"Three months? Married?"

The chess game was on. Which move should I make? What move could I make? Millions for my film and all I had to do was feed somebody four times a year. And get married.

"Asiafo, I accept the conditions. One last question; what do you get out of this? I mean, why are you making this possible?"

"Because I want to."

And then he was gone. I felt that I had been left in a huge, green walled room. The forest seemed to be booming with silence. I stood in place for a few moments; feeling emotionally drained and then started my trip up the path back to the village.

When I reached the path I turned to wave at someone I couldn't see – "Goodbye, Asiafo. And thank you."

The forest suddenly erupted with Asiafo's hyena laughter. What did he find funny about that? Or maybe he wasn't really laughing in the way I understood laughter. O well …

·   ℘ℂℜ   ·

Auntie Eugenia and the rest of the village seemed to be a different place when I returned. Auntie was reserved, aloof, and almost cold to me. Some of the villagers, who had formerly been cordial to me, were distant now. Some of them even frowned at me when they saw me walking through the village after the evening meal.

I had obviously blown it. I felt their attitude was unfair. Even if they knew I had gone to see Asiafo, I didn't feel that I had done anything wrong. What did I do to them?

I caught Auntie as she was getting ready to make her nightly getaway.

"Uhh, Auntie, I'd like to talk with you."

She stood in place; her arms folded under her breasts, and gave me a stern look. I felt two feet tall.

"Auntie Eugenia, I know you told me to be aware."

"Yes," she spoke in a sharp tone, "yes, I told you to be aware." And walked away from me. Now what?

I went into the hut, searched in the woven basket for the akpeteshie bottle, settled on a stool and took a long swig.

Damn, what the hell is this all about? All of the village sounds that had once sounded so interesting had an ominous tinge now. And I couldn't understand a word of Ewe. Another big swig of akpeteshie.

Be cool, don't panic, I told myself. You'll be out of here Monday afternoon. Monday afternoon, two days away.

What if Joshua, the taxi driver who drove me here, doesn't come for me? I broke into a paranoid sweat. How in the hell could I get out of this place?

A couple hours later, some kind of scraping sound brought me out of a deep, akpeteshie sleep. What was that? Were the villagers stacking wood around the hut to roast my ass, like they had done Asiafo's mother?

The hut suddenly seemed too small. I sat on the side of my cot, trying to put a game plan together. No matter what happened, I was going to go down fighting. An owl hooted. Didn't owls mean death?

·   ℘℃ଔ   ·

"Kojo! Kojo!"

It was daylight and I had a vicious hangover. I staggered to the door and let Auntie Eugenia in.

"Kojo, you locked the door?"

"O sorry, it's just an old fashioned city habit."

She gave me a curious look, sniffed the liquor residue on my breath and began to tidy up the hut, as usual.

"I have taken wattah for your bath."

"Thank you, Auntie."

So, that's the way we were going to do it, pretend that everything was just the way it was. I draped myself in my bath towel and walked around to the outdoor bathing stall. I could look over the enclosure at the villagers going about their business.

Saturday. After my bath I took awhile to put on my T-shirt, shorts and sandals. I knew I had to keep my wits about me. Auntie called.

"Kojo, your breakfast chop!"

"I'm coming," I answered automatically and checked myself. Poison, that's the way they would do it. Auntie Eugenia? Well, shit, she believed in witches and stuff like that.

I got angry at myself for thinking such negative thoughts about the kindly old lady. But I couldn't shake this paranoia off.

"Oh, Auntie, I'm really not hungry just now. I'll have something later."

She glared at me, both fists mounted on her ample hips.

"But you should eat, 'specially after the akpeteshie."

She blindsided me with a big smile, but that wasn't enough.

"Auntie, you're absolutely right, but not now I'll have something a lil' later."

The big smile was erased by the returning glare.

"So, now you are going to walk in the forest?"

I hadn't thought about it, but yeah, that sounded like a good idea.

"Yes, I'm going for a walk in the forest and I promise I won't talk to strangers."

The big smile returned.

"That is good, that is good. Your chop will be here when you return."

I grabbed a quart bottle of water and started walking. I didn't want to go anywhere. I had a hangover and I was hungry. But I also felt the need for a little space between me and the situation.

What could I do in the forest? I didn't want to go anywhere. I had a hangover and I was hungry. But I also felt the need for a little space between me and the situation.

What could I do in the forest? I didn't want to go too far. My stomach was grumbling like an old man. Maybe I should've eaten before I decided to take my walk. Too late now.

I took my time, exploring, studying things. I walked in a big circle around the village, keeping the sounds to my left as points of orientation. I felt no need to get lost.

After an hour I was soaking with sweat, time to go back "home." If the vibe had been somewhat negative when I started off on my walk, it was downright hostile now. Some people actually turned their backs as I walked in their direction. Auntie pointed her finger at the covered wooden bowls of food as though I was a dog.

I had to drink water and I had to eat. I had to take a gamble that Auntie Eugenia wouldn't poison me, that she wouldn't want to report the news to Grace that I had died in Tsito, of poisoning.

I ate, I drank, and I slept, wandered around, killing time. The midday siesta, when nobody did any thing that was unnecessary because it was so hot and humid, was the best time of all for me. I sprawled on my cot; sweat trickling off of my brow like somebody was pouring water on my head.

I wondered what Asiafo did in his cool little banana leaf hut during the midday heat. I did a mental review of the conditions/stipulations of the contract I had made with Asiafo. Feed a visitor four times a year. Marriage? Well, fortunately, I had someone that I had been thinking about marrying, but we hadn't gotten to the urgent level yet. I could imagine the expression on Akosua Ferguson's face when I popped the question. I would definitely have to keep my dealings with Asiafo out of the picture.

I couldn't imagine any woman being pleased because a wizard in the forest had said, "You should be married in three months."

· ∽୧ର୧ ·

Saturday seemed to last forever. I took long walks. I did three hours of the midday siesta. I wrote letters. I tried to read a book. And, of course, I ate Auntie Eugenia's food. If I was going to be poisoned, I felt it was better to be poisoned by her than to be burnt alive.

If Saturday lasted forever, Sunday was an eternity. I had never done any time, all blessings and thanks to Mom and Dad plus dumb luck, but I had friends who had gone to the joint for various stretches of time. One of my friends, an ex-coke dealer, had served five years, described what it felt like to be about to be released from prison.

"Kojo, you would have to be there to truly understand what the vibe is. Each minute is a sixty-second eternity, and there are times when you find yourself counting the minutes. No good, you could drive yourself nuts doin' shit like that. So, you begin to focus on the hours. And that's just as bad, because the hours become sixty-six thousand million seconds. Or some shit like that. You know what I'm sayin'?

I've seen dudes who had done "big time," on the verge of release after doin' years, years o' time with no sweat. And then they get down to the weekend before e-man-ci-pation. And they damned near lose it, damned near go crazy; developed nervous twitches, ulcers, all kinds of anxiety shit."

I wasn't exactly experiencing last minute "stir crazy fever," but I was definitely feeling anxious as a motherfucker, a word I had never heard in Ghana here.

Two p.m. I was feeling quite antsy. Don't tell me this guy is going to leave me stranded here. He was supposed to "collect" me at noon. Trying to kill off my tension, I took a final stroll through the village and was surprised to see that people were being cordial again. What a moody bunch.

Auntie Eugenia quietly explained the emotional switcheroo to me.

"Yesterday, in church, Reverend Donder told the people to behave themselves. He told us that you are not of our traditional beliefs – eh hee! – That you are not bound by our taboos, that you could not make a problem for us."

"Problem? What kind of problem?"

She did her little head down, embarrassed look.

"Ohhh, if you were of the village and you met with Asiafo there would be no problem. You are, after all, an obruni. If we had dealings with Asiafo, we might have to do sacrifices to take the bad spirits away. Are you getting me?"

"I think so." Of course I was pissed about the obruni labeling, me, a European?

The driver finally pulled in at three p.m.

"O, sorry sah."

I couldn't say what I felt like saying – you sorry-ashhole-chickenshit-motherfucker. How dare you not be on time? But I had to remember that I was in Tsito, in a distant/nowhere village in Ghana and that he had remembered to come for me. Even though I hadn't paid him for the return trip, yet.

I had left Auntie 300,000 cedis on her stool inside the hut for being so nice to me. I knew that she would be a rich woman for the rest of the year with that amount of money. And yes, she had been a gracious hostess, despite the Asiafo thing.

She felt like a stick of wood in my arms when I hugged her goodbye, but then I remembered that that wasn't considered good form in Tsito, for men and women to embrace in public. I was pleased to put the village behind me. I had spent my week there and gotten a helluva lot more than I bargained for. Back to Accra, back to Grace, my time in Ghana was winding down.

·   ℰ℧   ·

GRACE

"I am so annoyed with you; I want to knock you about. Kojo, I'm surprised at you. You go to a small, backwards-thinking village for a few days and allow them to turn you around the bend. Come on now, they're just a bunch of superstitious village people."

"Well, how about Asiafo? How do you explain him? How do you explain away somebody surviving in the forest, alone, for forty years?"

I couldn't explain that and I didn't try, but I did try to make him see the absurdity of talking about a half-naked man in the rainforest, promising him financial aid if he did "the right thing."

"Kojo, it's one of the oldest stories in human history – man makes a deal with the supernatural to get what he wants."

"Grace, if you knew Hollyweird the way I know it, you would be damned happy to get financing for your movie, no matter where it cam from, or how it got there."

And that's basically the way we left it, I didn't think it would make a great deal of sense for me to try to force him to "sit up," as we say it in Ghana here.

After all, he was a lovely boy and he had given me a beautiful time. Why should I clutter up matters by acting bitchy?

We spent three gorgeous days together and made two great promises when it was time for him to get on the plane.

"We will write each other once a month and we will be brutally honest with each other. Agreed?"

"Yesplease."

And then he was gone, back to the place where they invented milk and made money.

·   ℰℭ   ·

CHAPTER 6

Akosua Ferguson, the woman back home.

The loooonng trip back to the land of "milk and money" gave me lots of hours to think about my bride to be. Akosua Ferguson. Lots of heart and soul. How do you go about bucking the wishes of a couple Right Wing Thinking Negrocentric parents, all the way to changing your name from Cynthia, or was it Debbie to Akosua, and telling the folks that they could stick the inheritance, the homes, and all the rest of it up their asses, if they didn't like what she was about.

Akosua Ferguson, a novelist, a lovely woman, full of good vibes, independent thinking. We've had a thing going on for two years and I've never even introduced her to my folks.

Marvina, Jackie, Margo. Beautiful, but basically empty. Marvina wants a new car every year and someone to share her credit card debt. Jackie lives in a dream world. Margo is too hung up on her looks to really care about anything or anyone but the creature in the mirror.

Akosua, I owe you an apology. What in the world have I been thinking about? I've been taking you for granted. I need to have my ass kicked.

I felt pin pricks of anxiety. How is she going to take it when I ask her to marry me? What if she says no? Should I tell her about Asiafo? No, don't do that; she'll think I'm nuts.

AKOSUA

"After two years, Kojo and I had evolved into something that might be called 'a comfortable relationship.'

I knew a lot about him, his work, and his dreams. And he was definitely in tune with where I was coming from. I had spent a number of weekends in his Los Feliz apartment, and he had spent a few weekends in my Echo Park house, which meant we were 'way past the one night stage stuff. Sometimes, after a good Italian pasta and a few glasses red wine, we would become a bit more passionate than usual, but did that mean we were desperately in love? Well, maybe not desperately, but I felt we were in love.

We definitely shared a sense of humor. Case in point: I picked Kojo up from LAX when he returned from Ghana.

We stopped at Palermo's for a couple glasses of red wine to celebrate his return. Went to his apartment and took a very intimate joint shower, a prelude to … he popped under the covers and dropped off into immediate sleep. Of course, we laughed about it for days. It was certainly a matter of jet lag, but he was a little concerned about his masculinity for a few beats.

"What do you think, Akoś, you think I need some ginseng or something?"

"No, lover, I think you need a good night's sleep."

He was much more positive and definite about this film he was going to make.

"Akoś, I've had the idea to do this for a long time. 'My Grandfather's Eyes' might be considered my tribute to my grandfather. I'm going to do it."

"I hate to be the one who says the dirty word – money?"

"It's coming, it's coming."

He was just as positive about this other project. He made his "pitch" exactly one week after his return. We had been invited to his family's home in Compton for a family gathering; his "pitch" came the night before the event. We had massaged each other's bodies with fragrant oils and made slow motion love for long moments. Later, we curled up in each other's arms.

"Akoś," he whispered, "I want you to be my wife."

All I could think of saying was something inane; like, "Don't you think this is a bit sudden?"

He stroked the side of my face and laughed out loud, "Hahhhahhah, I knew you would say something like that, I just knew it."

"And did you prepare an answer?"

"Yes, I did." He got very serious on me. "These past two years have told me everything I needed to know about you, about us, and that I want to spend the rest of my life with you."

"Kojo, please don't misunderstand me. I do love you, you know that. But marriage is a Big Step."

"I know, I know."

There was a dead silence for a few beats.

"Kojo, are you sure this is the time for us?"

"Yes, this is the time for us."

"You sound pretty definite about this."

"I've never been more definite about anything in my whole life."

"Let me think about it for a couple days?"

We sealed the agreement with a kiss, and turned over to sleep. Or at least he did. It took me abut ten minutes to come to my senses. Mrs. Akosua Ferguson-Brown. This beautiful brother wants to marry me – he wants me to become his wife, to live happily ever after and all that. We were going to be one of the hippest couples on the planet. Kojo, the creative filmmaker-producer-writer-director. Akosua Ferguson-Brown, screenwriter-novelist. I could just see us traveling, having a grand time. I reached over and squeezed him so hard I thought I had bruised his ribs.

"Kojo, I've given it a lot of thought. Yes, I would like to become your wife, I would like to become Mrs. Kojo Bediako Brown."

"Well, that didn't quite take two whole days I'm glad to say."

I wish I could've filmed the relieved expression on his face."

· ℰℭ ·

KOJO

"Akosua took a big, fat weight off of my head. I don't know what I would've done if she had refused my marriage proposal because I didn't have a plan B.

Her acceptance the night before our family gathering really put the icing on the cake. I had the delicious job of whispering to my Dad and Mom; "Dad, Mom, Akosua and I are going to be married."

"When?"

"Soon, we haven't set the date yet."

It took all of my restraints to keep both of them from becoming "Town Criers" – "Kojo's getting married! Kojo's getting married!"

If they had done that, the celebration would've started right then and there. Uncle Amen, Aunt Deborah, Uncle Kwabena, Aunt Rose, Uncle Kalo, Auntie Afiya, first cousins: John, Ernest, Freda, Pokua, Asavia, Eve, Fatima, Kwasi, second cousins … and on and on.

I come from one of those large, tight knit families that are seldom written about, talked about or shown on television. Akosua was delightfully surprised.

"And here I am, thinking that my Nigerian gelé and outfit was going to be too colorful."

"I think what you're looking at is largely my grandfather Kwame's creation. Ever since I can remember he insisted on everybody wearing African clothes at family gatherings – "I don't want to see any bastard Euro-clothes at our family get-togethers, it just doesn't seem right for African-Americans to lynch themselves, with suits and ties inside the family circle." And so it was.

"Kojo," Akosua whispered to me at one point, "Do you know what I had to go through to force my Mom and Dad to call me Akosua?"

I suppose the blank look on my face said it all.

"I'm looking around at your family and everybody has an African name. Nzingha, your mother, Kofi, your father, these uncles and aunts. How did that happen?"

"I really can't say, it took place before I was born. But once again, I think we could trace the thread way back, beyond my grandfather. That's the effect Elders can have on a family/clan, if they have their stuff together."

Mom and Dad lured us away from the family circle for a lil' private Bristol Cream sippin' in the library.

"Show me a home without books and I'll show you an ignunt bunch of folks in a house." That was one of my Dad's favorite sayings.

41

"Akosua, we have all five of your books in our bookstore and we're proud and happy to have you become a part of our family."

"Thank you, uhh, Mr. .."

"Please, you're my son's bride-to-be; that makes you my daughter now. You should call me Dad."

"Thank you, Dad, thank you. Mom, thank you…"

Mom, Dad and Akosua clicked. By the time we left they had started talking about how many grandkids we were going to have, and what names we were going to give them.

On the drive to her house in Echo Park, she started crying.

"Hey, what is this? You're supposed to be happy."

"I am happy, Kojo, I am happy … that's why I'm crying. But I'm also crying about my mother and father. I wish they were more like your folks."

"Well, people have to be who they have to be."

"I know, that's why I wish they were more like your parents."

"When will I have a chance to meet them?"

"I figure we could go over this Sunday, we may as well get it done and over with."

"That bad, huh?"

"You'll see …"

· &⁊♋ ·

HARVEY AND MINERVA

"I was wearing this vanilla colored, double breasted Italian suit, backed up by a cold blooded Panama straw hat and some hand made beige Moroccan loafers. No matter what, my prospective in-laws would never be able to say that I came for lunch at their place looking like an orphan.

I wasn't intimidated at the idea of meeting them, I just felt vaguely pissed at the idea of spending such a beautiful day dealing with a couple fuddy duddies.

Akosua, the objective novelist, had given me solid character sketches of her parents and a little run down on their lifestyle.

"Dad has been hiding behind the daily newspaper for years. He doesn't like confrontations. He's a very complex man, definitely not a wimp, but he'll do anything to avoid a confrontation, 'specially with Mother.

Mother is sneaky. She will go around behind you to get what she wants. She had me going for awhile, 'til I figured out how to ignore her whining and conniving.

My Father and Mother both come from upper middle class backgrounds, teachers, attorneys, and professional people. They've both made their own money; Father, as an architect, Mother, as the owner of four exclusive boutiques. They think of themselves as being "semi-retired."

They've tried to give me everything they thought I wanted, with the accent on "things." And I love both of them dearly, but there are times when I wish they would put the accent on love, warmth, caring, rather than "things."

"Talk about things. Let's start with their house; one of those grand ol' things that silent movie stars used to own in Santa Monica, four blocks from the beach.

We were met by the family maid, Dolores.

"Ola Dolores, come le va?"

"Bien, señorita, muy bien."

"Damn, sweet thang, I didn't know you could speak Spanish."

"I get by."

We were escorted through huge rooms with plastic covered sofas, a fireplace that looked large enough to roast a cow. Rooms filled with very expensive knick knacks from all over the known world. Akosua winked at me and pinched my butt. Finally, we came to a back terrace/veranda that was about twenty yards wide and fifty yards long. And a great, green rolling lawn beyond that looked like a section of the Augusta Golf Club.

"Father likes to practice his putting," Akosua whispered to me as we negotiated our way past a couple filigreed tables and chairs. Predictably, Mr. Ferguson was folding his newspaper up and Mrs. Ferguson was standing regal tall, looking for all the world like a fiftyish version of Dianne Carrol.

"Father, Mother, this is Kojo Bediako Brown, my husband-to-be. Kojo, my parents, Mrs. Minerva Ferguson and Mr. Harvey Ferguson."

They both stared at me as though I had just stumbled off of an alien planet. I reached out to do the correct thing, a little bow, a handshake. Their hands were like limp rags.

"Aku-sowah, did we hear you correctly, dear?" Her mother probed sharply.

"About what, Mother?"

"About this, this young man being your prospective groom?"

"Yes, Mother, my husband-to-be, that's his official title until we tie the knot."

Mr. Ferguson didn't say a word, he simply gestured for us to sit down. They dynamics were fascinating. Akosua and her mother were close to fighting a knock down-drag out with only a few words being exchanged.

"Well, I must say, this certainly comes as a big surprise. Doesn't it, Harvey?"

Poor dude, he looked like he wanted to run off and start practicing his putt or something.

"Uhh, yes, yes, it certainly does come as a big surprise."

We endured a small, awkward window before Mrs. Ferguson opened up.

"Are we in a hurry to get married, or am I just imagining the unimaginable?"

"If you're asking me if I'm pregnant, the answer is I don't know yet." The awkward window narrowed. Mrs. Ferguson's eyes narrowed and she looked like she wanted to throw something at her daughter. Mr. Ferguson looked down at his newspaper.

"Well, we can discuss all this later. Mr. Brown, would you care for something? We'll be having lunch shortly."

Akosua popped in – "Yes, that's a wonderful idea, Mother. Dolores, tragamelos dos bottellas de Bohemia. Hay Bohemia?"

"Si, Señorita, pronto," came the answer from the kitchen.

"Ako-su-ah insists on speaking to the servants in their own language."

It was my turn.

"Doesn't sound like a bad idea to me, Mrs. Ferguson. After all, we are in California, which used to be a part of Mexico. And, depending on relative birth rates and politics it may be Mexican again."

There, the battle lines were firmly drawn. An icy curtain settled across the tale as the maid delivered two frosted bottles of Bohemia. Mr. Ferguson signaled to the maid, "Bring me one of those too. Minerva, are you having something?"

"I don't drink beer," she snapped. "Dolores, bring me an iced tea."

Akosua pinched my thigh under the table and stifled a sarcastic smile. I took it all in. This way of being family was completely new to me. The beer was deliciously chilled. A few pregnant moments passed as we sipped and watched Mr. and Mrs. Ferguson look uncomfortable.

"Uhhh, Mr. Brown?"

"Please call me Kojo, Mrs. Ferguson. And you too, Mr. Ferguson."

"Yes, of course, Ko-jo. So, our daughter tells us that you two want to get married."

"Father," Akosua broke in, "I told you that we were <u>going</u> to get married, not that we wanted to get married."

"Ako-su-ah, must you interrupt your father like that?"

Mr. Ferguson looked like he wanted to push his head into his shoulders.

"Yes, Mother, I must interrupt my Father like that, because he needs to be corrected."

Once again the icy curtain dropped. Mrs. Ferguson decided to do a flanking movement/attack.

"Uhh, Ko-jo, Ako-su-ah has told us that you're a brilliant writer-director-filmmaker ..."

Akosua tilted her head back and slugged half her beer down. She was definitely enjoying herself.

"Yes, it's true, I am."

The sour expression that sucked Mrs. Ferguson's cheeks in made me smile.

"Well, I must say, Ko-jo ... you're <u>quite</u> modest. Have you done anything noteworthy?"

I did a monotonic recitation of my credentials; starting with the first film I made, a Super 8, hand held job about women who had followed their men onto Skid Row – "I was a sophomore in high school" – all through my USC Film school days, up to my present project – "My Grandfather's Eyes."

Akosua beamed at me and called out ... "Dolores, dos mas, por favor?"

"Si, Señorita."

Ma and Pa Ferguson slumped a bit as we sipped our cold Bohemias. We had 'em on the ropes.

"Ko-jo, I hope you don't think I'm being intrusive, but I'd like to know one thing."

"What's that, Mr. Ferguson?"

"Why do you want to marry our daughter?"

I hesitated for a split second, on the verge of laughing, before I dive bombed his feeble question.

"Mr. Ferguson, Akosua is a treasure. She has brains, she knows how the world works, she's beautiful and she has two great parents. What more could a man ask for?"

Mrs. Ferguson coughed into her napkin and I think she was contemplating another flank movement when the maid announced, "Lunch, she is ready."

Delicious tamales, enchiladas, refried beans, rice, guacamole salad and more Bohemias. Mrs. Ferguson was determined to slip a jab or two in, even if she was on the ropes.

"Ko-jo, I'm sure you come from a good family."

"The Best!" I snapped at the ol' snob. Bullshit time was over.

"Yes, of course. I was about to say – in good families, the business of marriage is taken quite seriously."

Akosua groaned.

"Ahh Mother, give us a break already, please?"

After three Bohemias I was feeling quite up to whatever the sister had on her mind.

"No, please go on, Mrs. Ferguson … speak your mind."

"Well, it seems to me," she caught her husband's downcast eyes for moral support, "that a suitable period of time should have been set aside for a proper engagement."

"Mrs. Ferguson, Mr. Ferguson, I can assure you we have been firmly engaged for the past two years." I gave Akosua a sly wink.

"But we weren't informed, where is the engagement ring?"

"You weren't informed because our engagement only concerned the two of us, period. And so far as rings and all the rest of that Eurocentric nonsense, who needs it? The important thing is a heart to heart commitment, not a ring commitment."

The Fergusons stared at me as though I had slapped them in the mouth.

"Are you saying that it's Eurocentric to have an engagement ring?" Mr. Ferguson rumbled.

"Yessir, I think so. As well as this charade we're going through right now. If matters were really going to be handled properly, responsible Elders in my family would've contacted responsible Elders in Akosua's family, gifts would've been exchanged and so on and so forth.

But this is America and, for better or worse, we are African-American and things are different for us here.

Akosua has accepted my proposal and we're <u>going</u> to be married. There's really no need for us to sit out here on such a lovely day, antagonizing each other over a done deal."

Akosua gave me that sly look that said it all. Keep it up, baby, keep it up, Mother's loving it.

"Well, I must say, Ko-jo, you do seem to know what you're about."

"Yes, Mrs. Ferguson, I do know what I'm about, I've known since I was ten years old."

"Fine, I'm glad to hear that. It really puts my mind at ease to know that we can give our approval for your marriage to Ak-ko-sua without any reservations whatsoever. Don't we, Harvey?"

Mr. Ferguson looked slightly bewildered by his wife's turn around, but nodded in agreement anyway.

Akosua laughed out loud and chugged her beer. I smiled at the ol' fox.

"Now, then, now that we've solved that sticky little problem. Have you set a date?"

"No, Mother, not yet."

"Don't worry, Mrs. Ferguson, you'll be the first to know what were going to do and when we're going to do it."

"That takes a load off of my mind. Ah-ko, how do you say – bring more beer?"

"Mas cervesas, por favor."

"Dolores! Mos sir-vases, por fa-vour."

"Si, Señora," the maid answered giggling at Mrs. Ferguson's lousy Spanish.

Forty-five minutes later, after the cheeky cheeky kisses and limp handshakes, Ko-jo and Akosua drove away, trying to maintain straight faces. They both exploded with laughter at the first intersection.

"Ko-jo, did you see the flip flop that lady did?"

"Your mother is a very clever lady, if you can't beat 'em – join 'em!"

· ℰℛ ·

CHAPTER 7

"Dear Kojo,

Just a note. I know you're probably up to your neck with projects, things to do. More power to you, brother.

Ghana hasn't been the same since you left. I'm saying that for many reasons, the main one being the fact that I miss you a great deal. That may come as a big surprise from someone who is supposed to have an upper lip as stiff as mine.

But I remember that we agreed to be completely honest in our communications with each other. Onward. My office staff has shown a greater appreciation of my presence since your departure (smile) and life in Ghana here continues. I hope you had a pleasant trip back and that you'll remember to drop me a few lines, whenever you have the time.

Love, Faithfully yours,
Grace

P.S. Went to visit my Auntie Eugenia in Tsito last weekend and she told me to remind you to be aware, to be careful. It all sounds rather mysterious to me."

Kojo folded the letter in half, unfolded it and stared at the gracefully slanting curves of Grace's handwriting. Dear, dear Grace. And then tore the letter into small pieces. We can communicate, but there's no need to keep the communications.

·   ☙ ❧   ·

The car was loaded with the bare necessities, a few sandwiches, water, changes of clothes, shoes.

"A lot of people trip off to Mexico like they're on safari through the Sahara. Whatever we don't have we can buy en route."

"I'm in your corner, Kojo, all the way."

San Bernardino, straight through the Imperial Valley, kicking off into Yuma, Arizona for the first leg. Arizona sprawled in front of them, a sun struck city on an adobe platter. They were going to cross over into Nogales, Mexico from Nogales, Arizona. The air was blast furnace dry, the sky blue with flecks of clouds, the road clear for fast driving.

"I'm glad we left in the morning, the evening traffic makes me feel mentally ill at times."

"Yeah, I know the feeling."

They traveled without making unnecessary commentary; a casual point at some unusual rock formation. Or a full fledged – "Look at that!" – as a coyote chased a rabbit across the highway at twilight.

Kojo, the first driver, announced, "Time to chill, we've done a good day's journey."

"Where in the world are we?"

"This is the fantastic little place called Gila Bend."

The Gila Bend Motel was desert dusty but clean and they had showers in each cabin.

"Jest put 'em in a week ago, enjoy your stay, folks."

They showered, changed clothes and strolled out into the desert directly behind the motel.

"Kojo, you know this is the first time we've traveled together."

"What about that weekend in Morro Bay?"

"Where we went to breakfast, back to bed. Lunch, back to bed. Dinner and back to bed, for a whole weekend."

"Hahhhahhhah … I guess you wouldn't call that real traveling, would you?"

The distant howl of a wolf, or was it a coyote, startled them. Akosua pressed a little closer to his side.

"You kinda forget that there are still wild things in the world. Why don't we go back to the motel?"

"Scared?"

"Not at all, I just feel the urge to tell you a bedtime story."

· ℘℃ ·

The morning cool desert wind whispered into the open windows of the car. Kojo didn't like air conditioning; it made him feel that he was living in an artificial environment. Akosua was driving, looking cool and glamorous behind her big black shades.

A right turn at Tucson and southward to Nogales. They hadn't talked about Kojo's film idea or the outline for Akosua's next book. They just felt the urge to drift along at sixty-five miles per hour, gradually shaking off the frenzied tempo of the city they had left the day before.

Kojo studied Akosua's aristocratic profile. Thank God I love this woman, it would really be a drag to have to marry someone you didn't love.

Nogales straight ahead and then the other side. Akosua dealt with the customs people in her academic Spanish.

"Okay, Señor Brown, we can drive into Mexico now."

"That didn't take long."

"A little honest corruption goes a long way. The mordida, the 'little bite' is supposed to be passé, but no one seems to be willing to refuse a twenty dollar 'gift.' That gentleman over there, the one with the cigar and the pregnant looking tummy is a professional fixer. We have insurance coverage, which means practically nothing, visitor's permits, and the whole enchilada. Vamos."

"I'm impressed, my lady!"

"Like I said, a little honest corruption goes a long way."

The great Sonoran desert opened up in front of them. Highway 15, hot, dry and windless.

"Wowww, coming through Arizona is like heading into the mouth of the furnace, this _is_ the furnace."

"You got that right. We'll have to go through here for a stretch before we can get over to the ocean at Guaymas."

Miles of sandy earth, relieved by splashed splotches of desert blooms, and other, more unbelievable sights.

"Kojo, did you see those children? Where can they possibly be going out here?"

He stopped the car and backed up a couple hundred yards. Four boys and three girls, the oldest about ten years old. The children stared at the couple in the car.

Akosua asked them if they could give them a lift. She was certain that – "Queres ustedes un viaje?" conveyed the proper message, but their gestures were unmistakable.

The children smiled shyly and the oldest boy pointed his finger at a distant point and nodded, "No, gracias."

Kojo offered them small bottles of water, but they would only accept one.

"Gracias," the spokesman said and tipped the brim of his small sombrero.

"De nada," Akosua responded as they slowly geared up again.

"Where do you think they were going?"

"Where do you think they were coming from, that's the big question."

· &)C& ·

"Ahhh, the sea. I feel like an ancient explorer or something. Look at that beautiful water."

"Yeahh, Guaymas, after all of that desert. They made 'Catch 22' down here, that mad think piece with the crazy guy ... whatwashis name? Alan Arkin."

Kojo drove up and down a few of the main streets to give Akosua a feel of the place.

"Hasn't changed much since I was here last, years ago. A little more touristy than it was. Let's hope they have a vacancy in 'La mar.'"

No. 102, "La Mar." They showered in water that had been funneled from the ocean on the back patio.

"Now, that's what I call a salty bath. Akoś, shall we dress for dinner?"

"But of course."

They had the "La Mar" dining room to themselves, dressed in their wrinkled, but spotless white outfits.

"Huachinango a la Vera Cruzano for two, por favor."

"Si, Señor."

"Kojo, I thought you couldn't speak Spanish."

"I know how to ask for fish in about six languages."

The large, firm fleshed fish drizzled with succulently fried onions, pimientos, olives and dill tasted as though it had been plucked out of the sea minutes before.

"Mmm, I'd forgotten what fresh fish tastes like … mmm."

Fresh red snapper, chilled bottles of Carta Blanca. They strolled out onto the pier in front of the hotel after dinner, taking in the sight of the precision diving pelicans, the far flung twinkling of distant stars. He stood behind her, his arms circling her waist, nuzzling her neck.

"Akoś, I love you, do you know that?"

She made a slow, wordless turn, held his face in her hands and kissed him.

· ℰ)Ȣ ·

They sang old songs driving south, a few miles from the sea coast. They paused to have finger sized tacos and cold bottles of Moctezuma in towns that seemed too small to have a name.

"What do they call this place?"

"If they called it anything other than 'this place' it would be too much."

Kojo was delighted to discover a sense of humor in Akosua that he hadn't been exposed to before. It was dry and sharp, but not acidic.

"It's too bad more of our people don't travel to Mexico the way we're traveling, they might not miss the concrete slave ships as much as they think."

Akosua admired Kojo's way of coping. There was always a positive spin happening.

We're stranded in the middle of nowhere? No problem, help will be arriving soon.

The car won't start? It must be hungry for affection.

"My Dad has always preached that nothing is a real problem if your mindset can find the proper frequency."

"What's our destination, or do we have one?"

"Interesting that you should ask that. I wanted to surprise you by just coming to a dead stop in the town called Huatabampo."

"Huatabampo, sounds like a beautiful destination."

Huatabampo, population, a few thousands, Toltec and Spanish spoken.

They drove slowly through "the downtown area," circled the miniature plaza and two of the town's ten policemen, who smiled and waved at them going the wrong way on a one way street.

The Huatabampito Hotel, on the curved beach, curved gently for two miles. It was midmorning when they arrived and there was no sign of a desk clerk to register them. Kojo signed them in, took the key for #6 and they unloaded.

"Eventually someone will show up to collect our money, you can count on it."

They quickly changed into shorts and T-shirts to stroll along the beach. The water that lapped at their ankles was warm as blood and filled with shrimp, porpoises, and Portuguese men of war, large and small manta rays, and millions of brilliantly colored fish.

They sat in the low tide shallows, gazing out onto a horizon that was so blue it looked like a painting.

"Akoś, I want you to help me put a script together."

"I thought you'd never ask."

It was the beginning of a creative surge, they both felt it.

"I don't want it to interfere with your work."

"It won't. And I think the dividends will be well worth the effort."

"Good. Here's what I have in mind. I'm calling it a silent film, but it won't be silent in the old fashioned way. The tentative title is, 'My Grandfather's Eyes.'"

"Mmm, I like that. You've spoken abut it."

"I haven't worked the complete story out in my head yet, but I know what some of the elements will be: I want African-American satire, the stuff we her in some of the old blues singers, serious realism, our story, not history, edu-tainment, a cross sectioned look at what we're about, what we've accomplished.

I want to peel back some layers and take a look at some stuff that hasn't been considered before. When I say it won't be a silent film in the ol' fashioned sense of the word, that doesn't mean we won't be using subtitles, transitional music, stuff like that. The problem I'm concerned about is what kind of main story and sub-stories will be strong enough to hold the piece together."

"I can see the problem. Let me think on it."

"Camarones! Camarones! Camarones!"

The sight and sound of the little gray haired man with a huge sack draped across his back startled them.

"Woww! Where did he come from?"

"This is Mexico, lady; wherever there's a customer you'll have someone selling something."

They bought a pound of the finger sized shrimp for two dollars. The vendor explained that they would go well with "cervesas frias."

"Akoś, he's right. I'm going to run into town for a minute to pick up some beer and a few other items. Want anything else?"

"Sounds like we're going to need some note pads and a few more ballpoints."

"Be back in a bit."

She watched him jog away, feeling suddenly lonely on this gorgeous, foreign beach. We haven't been out of each other's sight in days. Maybe he felt the urge to be alone for a little while.

She strolled, nibbled on a few shrimp and thought about the proposed script.

"My Grandfather's Eyes." Yeah, I can get into that. We can take a serious look at perspectives that most American movies ignore, have ignored. Even now, whenever there are older African-Americans in movies, they're either treated like antiques or off brand jokes.

I can see ways to bring in the African-American women's point of view. Well, one of them anyway. He talks about the silent film era and how it demonized Black men. We weren't even thought about way back then.

After an hour of serious thinking and digging her toes into the warm sand, she strolled back to #6. Mr. and Mrs. Ferdinan Chavez and their six stair-step children greeted her as she walked into the cozy little lobby of the Huatabampito Hotel.

"Welcome, Señora, welcome. We were not here to greet you and your husband; we were attending a birthday party for my sister in town. Please, whatever you desire, please call upon us. This is my wife Ana, my son Juan, my son Felipe, my daughter Carlota, my daughter Juanita, my son José and my latest daughter, Carmen. My name is Ferdinan Chavez."

She liked them. The wife was Mexican-rural woman-shy. The man was macho proud of himself and the children resembled brown eyed cherubs. They stared into her mouth as though she had released a stream of gold when she greeted them in Spanish. The gringa speaks our language.

"And your husband, he also speaks Spanish?"

"Only when necessary."

Kojo returned an hour later, a six-pack of Pacifico beer in hand, looking amused and distracted. Akosua introduced him to the Chavez family. The amenities over, everyone melted into their own niches. The children went up and down the beach capturing crabs and doing the simple things that children do.

Papa Ferdinan dozed away in a hammock and Mama Chavez assembled a collection of spices that drifted through the small hotel like a seductive perfume. The beer was cold and the shrimps were warm and crunchy, a perfect first course.

"I don't know what the sister is cooking, but I think I'm going to eat seconds of it."

They sprawled in the deck chairs on the veranda of the hotel, the sole tenants, note pads at the ready, enjoying the lush vibes of the afternoon.

"What took you so long, Kojo? I thought they had deported you or something."

She detected an elfin, mischievous gleam in his eyes, "Just trying to find the coldest beer in town, that's all." An hour later the youngest Chavez came to tug gently at Akosua's hand, whispering, "Ahora, la cena."

"I think she's telling me that dinner is ready."

They raced to their room for a change of T-shirts.

"As good as it smells, it's got to deserve a change of T-shirts."

The five-table sized dining room on the enclosed patio was opened to them. Papa Ferdinan wished them "Buen provecho!" on his way to the beach with a long bamboo fishing rod. And, as soon as they were seated, Mama Chavez marched in with a beautifully painted clay pot, brimming with seafood.

"What is it called, Señora?" Akosua asked.

"It is called Sopa de Huatabampito," she answered proudly.

Steak firm cutlets of red snapper, paper thin slices of squid, chunks of turtle meat, stewed tomatoes, olives, onions, shrimps, small corn tortillas and chilled bottles of Pacifico.

"Kojo … mmm … you ever tasted anything this good in your whole life?"

"Only one thing," he replied deadpan.

The stew/soup was served in soup bowls and the small tortillas were replaced as soon as the stack was decimated. They sipped the cold beer, washing down the stew/soup and bit chunks from their tortillas. Mama Chavez peeked into the patio-dining room from time to time, to make certain that they were enjoying her food. She was not disappointed. Forty-five minutes later they surrendered to drum tight bellies, and sat smiling at each other, satiated.

"Akoś, how do you say – That was a helluva meal."

"Gracias, Señora, un buen provecho!"

"Gracias, Señora Chavez, un buen provecho!"

The Chavez children cleared their bowls from the table as they waddled out of the patio.

"Kojo, let's take a little walk."

"Good idea."

The skylights at twilight were rainbowing a collage of purples, blood reds, orange, blues and amber. They strolled on the beach, their arms linked around each other's waists.

"I want to get some of this in our first film, this sense of the romantic that we're never given credit for having. It's always about hump-thump sex next with us, according to the usual suspects."

"You're right; I'd love to see this kind of scene in an African-American film."

They passed Ferdinan Chavez casting his line far out into the waves. He held up two large red snappers for them to admire.

"Un buen provecho!" Kojo called out to him. Papa Chavez laughed.

A soft blooming night, the gentle lapping of the Gulf coast water against the beach followed them back to their sanctuary. The lamps in their room were dim but serviceable.

"How about the ending of the film? How do you see that?"

"I see the ending as the beginning."

They were beginning to work out intellectual shorthand, the result of imaginative minds in sync. Kojo was going to supply the bulk of the substance and Akosua was going to add to that, as well as helping to create the form. They exchanged ideas and made future plans before drifting into dreamless sleeps.

· ❧ ❧ ·

CHAPTER 8

Akoś! Akoś! Wake up! Wake up!"

"What?! What's wrong?!"

"It's almost nine o'clock!"

She gave him a curious look and snuggled back under the sheet. *What's with this man? Doesn't he know we're on a vacation?*

Kojo shook her gently by the shoulder and kissed her in her right ear.

"Akosua, sweetheart, please wake up, I need your help with something."

She responded, just as he knew she would.

"What is it, baby?"

"C'mon, I can tell you on the way to town."

A puzzled frown furrowed her forehead, watching him dash into the shower. *What's going on here?*

She popped into the shower just as he was toweling off, a half dozen questions on the tip of her tongue.

"Akosua, don't worry, I'll answer all of your questions – just hurry up, please!"

He laid her pearl white skirt and pink, embroidered, long sleeved sheer blouse across the bed.

"Uhh, I didn't know what color panties you were planning to wear today."

The Gulf breeze and the inland desert wind splashing in her face pushed her into a fully awake state. Kojo was driving a little faster than usual. *He wants me to help him do something? Oh, probably something having to do with Spanish. But what's the rush?*

He slipped into a parking space in front of the most imposing building in Huatabampo, the City Hall. What?

He checked his watch for the tenth time.

"Great, we're on time, got five minutes to spare."

He held her hand tightly as they dashed up the five steps into the City Hall. He seemed to relax, once they were inside the building. He pointed to a door at the end of the corridor. The Mayor's Office.

She could see the outlines of a number of people through the opaque glass as they approached the door. He opened the door and an animated group of people burst into smiles and applause.

"Kojo," she spoke in a small voice, "What is this?"

He held both of her hands and stared into her eyes, "If you consent to be my wife this morning, the Mayor is going to say the words and these other gentlemen are going to Mariachi us down the street to the Floridita Café for a wedding breakfast with champagne." Akosua burst into tears.

"Does that mean yes?"

After the binding words, the bonding kiss, a discreet distribution of pesos to the Mayor and the Mariachis, they floated out of the office with a license that certified that they were now husband and wife.

"We'll have to get a U.S. validation on this …"

"Whatever. So far as I'm concerned I am now Mrs. Akosua Ferguson-Brown."

Five doors away from City Hall they entered La Floridita Café. The owner, a golden skinned, plump woman with thickly coiled braids, smiled them to a corner table where two bottles of Piper Heidseck were sticking out of a zinc bucket, covered with chunks of ice.

"The breakfast is now, Señor Koho?"

"Si, Señora, now."

Akosua kept dabbing at her eyes, trying not to cry.

"Kojo, when did you do all this?"

"Yesterday, when I came to get the beer."

"But, but how? I mean, your Spanish is …"

"My Spanish is below average, but this makes up the difference." He held a thick wad of pesos under the table. Akosua smiled.

"Yeah, guess you got a point."

Huevos rancheros, refried beans and creamed spinach.

"I had to convince the lady that we didn't want the chorizo-sausage. She had problems with that for a few minutes."

"The spinach is delicious with the eggs and beans."

Customers wandered in and out, were informed of the reasons for the celebration at the corner table, and smiled in their direction. Midway into the second bottle of Piper Heidseck.

"Kojo, burp! Where did you find Piper burp! Heidseck in Huata burp! Bampo burp!"

"The Mayor's brother is 'Mr. Fixit' in town. As you once said – a little honest corruption goes a long way."

An hour later they made a shaky start from the curb but leveled out just past a donkey loaded with bundles of hay. They drove slowly, carefully, feeding on each other's vibes.

"Kojo, you've just given me one of the most beautiful mornings of my life."

"Let's try to see if we can extend that through the rest of our lives."

He stopped the car in the middle of the road to kiss her.

· ஓ∞ ·

By the time they arrived at the Hotel Huatabampito, the Chavez clan had been informed, via the small town gossip/chisme system, that they had just been married.

The Chavez's were obviously pleased with their guests and with the fact that they were now renting a room to an authentically married couple. Mrs. Chavez announced, "I will bake a small cake for Mr. and Mrs. Koho."

"Gracias, Señora."

It was dawn and they had made the decision the night before to begin their day with a walk on the beach, prior to beginning the drive back to Los Angeles.

"Akoś, I see the film as almost a collage, which is one of the reasons why I want it to be relatively silent. I've always been impressed by how well the Japanese, especially, and African dudes like Sembene, for example, use the silence in their films. The collage effect will give us a chance to weave in a number of themes. You ever listen to Indian music?"

"I have, with you."

"Well, think about the big sound you get from sitar and the sarod, and then all of those sympathetic strings."

"The sounds that shimmer."

"Exactly. Shimmer is a damn good description. I see 'Grandfather's Eyes' in that way. Sometimes I think dialogue is overused in American movies because people need to hear some noise. For example, if we were shooting this scene, I would only want to hear natural sounds – the waves lapping at the beach, bird calls, and the winds. I know it'll make our jobs harder, but I'd like for you to keep that in mind when you start writing."

"Because the economy of word usage will entail a greater need for selectivity."

He hugged her to his chest.

"I couldn't've said it better."

They meandered, paused to watch porpoises at play, to pick up interesting looking stones, to envelope each other in wordless hugs. She held her ring up to the light.

"Yesterday, about this time I was Akosua Ferguson. Today I'm Akosua Ferguson-Brown, your wife. And I feel very good about that." They made a gentle-meditation turn and started back to the hotel, each of them loaded with thoughts.

"I'll have to break the news gently to Mother and Father. She'll pretend to be close to a heart attack, no matter what."

"I'll have to figure out a way to prevent my Mom and Dad from giving us a Big Celebration. It'll be hard to make them understand that this trip to Mexico was another way for us to get to the drawing board."

Now then, I've done the first thing; I've made the first step. But I didn't feel that I have done it as an obligation. I think I would've probably married Akosua anyway, I think.

Mama Chavez welcomed them with a fish roe and egg breakfast.

"We'd be fat if we stayed down here longer than a week."

After the breakfast and heartfelt handshakes with all of the Chavez's, it was time to head back to "El Norte."

Akosua took the wheel for the first lap, "We've got about four days to get back, let's make every hour count."

· ℘℃ℛ ·

Guaymas came too soon. A late lunch at "La Mar," a small nap on the beach.

"Kojo, I hate to talk in clichés, but this whole thing seems like a dream."

"I was thinking that too. I think it's what we need, from time to time. Reality can be sickening."

"I heard that."

Ciudad Hermesillo gave them an opportunity to buy a small bucket, fill it with a bag of ice cubes and six cans of Tecate. They popped open iced beer whizzing through the blast furnace heat of the Sonoran desert. The glare of the sun and the dry heat kept them in a state of thirst. They stopped for more beer and ice, dumping the empty beer cans in a filling station trash can.

"I can think of a time when I would have thought that drinking beer and driving was quite gauché, quite gauché."

"My, my, Mrs. Ferguson-Brown – what language! Quite gauché, indeed!"

It was too hot to laugh; they simply smiled at each other.

"Yes, gauché, a perfectly legitimate way to say in French, wrong."

"Just goes to show you how relative things are."

Ten minutes down the road, in a gleaming sandy place speckled with hard scrub desert vegetation, Kojo tapped Akosua on the shoulder.

"Please pull over, the beer wants out."

"You got to pee?"

"Well, if you want to be gauché about it."

She slowed to a stop on the shoulder of Highway #15, stretched and got out to flex her legs. The moaning of the motor was off, the desert air hot and dry. Kojo waved and walked fifty yards away from the road.

He smiled at himself, a bit tipsy from a full afternoon of iced beer drinking. Stupid how fastidious people can be. Why would I have to walk his far from the road, from Akosua, to take a leak?

The figure squatting in the shade of a barrel head cactus looked like a strange animal. The figure grew to full size as he walked closer.

Asiafo …

"She is a lovely girl."

Kojo nodded numbly. It didn't seem possible that this half-naked man from Africa could be squatting in the middle of the desert, speaking to him. No, there's no one here, I'm hallucinating. Kojo rubbed his eyes carefully, to clear them for a closer look at the mirage twenty yards in front of him. When he removed his hands from his eyes, Asiafo was gone.

Yeah, just what I thought, too much heat and beer. He urinated in the sand and turned to fined Asiafo leaning against a scrubby little bush, twenty yards away.

"You must now remember to feed the visitor who will come."

Kojo's mouth was dry, his tongue felt thick and heavy, and he was beginning to feel a headache.

"How will I know..?"

"You will know. It will come four times a year, feed it and things will go well."

Kojo nodded, feeling drained of energy. Asiafo disappeared, like a desert mirage. Kojo stood in place for a long moment, his eyes fixed on the place where the man had stood a moment before. He walked slowly to the spot and bent down to study the prints in the sand.

The print was of a large snake. The weaving pattern was unmistakable. I was talking to Asiafo, a man, right here. And now I'm looking at the print of a snake's body. He was here, he spoke to me. I spoke to him.

Akosua was swabbing her face with a wet terry cloth towel when he got back to the car.

"Kojo, how long does it take to pee? I thought you had been bitten by a snake or something."

"Nope, nothing like that, just a very full bladder. Here, let me share that towel with you."

He got behind the wheel, joking with Akosua, pretending a humor he didn't really feel. He looked up into the rear view mirror as they pulled away, to see Asiafo standing in the middle of the road, offering him a military salute.

· ༄ Cৎ ·

The evening breeze was a merciful hand fanning cool air on them. Kojo drove by instinct, his mind wandering from subject to subject. A half naked man in the Ghanaian Equatorial Rainforest promises me that I will be able to make the films I want to make, the money will be there.

Why does he do it? He says he is doing it because I asked him for help and he has the Power. And I get on my horse and charge into the sunset, primed by the promise.

The only thing I have to do is get married within three months. He smiled at Akosua's sleeping profile. And feed a visitor four times a year. Four times a year for how long? Well, what the hell difference does it matter? If I had to feed a stranger four times a year for four years, that would only be sixteen meals.

Asiafo does have supernatural powers, no doubt about that. Anybody who can disappear, who can trip from continent to continent, must have some kind of power. He felt the urge to wake Akosua up, but vetoed the idea.

No, this is between me and my patron. My patron, yes, I guess that's the best description I could use.

When the brothers and sisters come to this meeting in September, I'm gonna lay something on them that will be so heavy that they'll want to stick with me 'til the bitter end.

What makes me think of stuff like this? The scattered lights ahead indicated a town, or a village was ahead.

"Kojo," Akosua whispered in his ear, "Let's spend the night here."

"I was just about to whisper the same thing to you."

The Hotel California, two avenues east of the "Panama Restaurant" offered them a shabby, but clean second floor room, with a shower that dripped warm water only.

"Hotel California? There's irony in here somewhere."

"Or maybe sarcasm."

A drippy shower, clean sheets, pillow talk.

"Kojo, we haven't talked about a lot of things."

"Let's talk."

"Well, we haven't talked about babies, children."

"I love 'em."

"You mean that? You want to have babies?"

"Only one at a time, please. Why do you ask me that?"

"Because I flushed my birth control pills down the toilet yesterday morning."

· ℘℃℞ ·

They put a working schedule together driving through Arizona. They also put a living pattern together at the same time.

"Well, the obvious move is to my place, I have the house."

"My lease has six months to go but I'm sure my landlord will let me break it, they're really sweet people."

"I know, I've met them. O.k., that'll work. As a matter of fact that's a good idea. It'll give me time to have a couple walls knocked out to give us more working space."

Plans. Plans. Plans. Plans for a script, a home life, careers, for future dinners, trips to Mexico again, a series of books stressing the need for everyone to understand Africanity/Africentricity.

"Kojo, how do you want to break the news to our parents?"

"Well, for mine, it'll be simple. I'll stick my head in the door, announce that we're now husband and wife, and run before they start having an ALL FAMILY CELEBRATION."

Akosua looked glum. "I wish I could say it was going to be that way with my folks. I can almost hear the anguished screams from Mother. And my Father grumbling betrayal of trust or something."

"Don't sweat it; I'm on your side. Don't look now but we just crossed the border into LALAland."

The familiar landmarks and freeways began to appear.

"Kojo, there's just one important item we haven't discussed, concerning the film. Where's the money coming from to set up an office, get the phones in, the office equipment, stuff like that."

"That's a big hurdle I have to jump over."

"Well, I've got $38,000 in savings and the equity in the house."

"Akoś, I love you for even making the offer, but that's not the way. One of the things they taught us at U.S.C., that made lots of sense to me; never use your own money to finance a project unless you absolutely have to.

Don't worry about the funds, I got irons in the fire."

She smiled at the confident thrust of his chin. My husband.

Bumper to bumper traffic/Friday evening.

"Welcome back to the parking lot."

They had decided to give themselves the weekend to be together a little longer, to map out the future without any interruptions.

"Wouldn't it be wonderful if this weekend never ended?"

"We can try to keep it going as long as possible. Why don't you come over to my place? It'll keep you away from your Mother's messages for a little while anyway."

· ℰℭ ·

Sunday bloomed sunny and humid. Harvey Ferguson felt cool and collected, starting from the front page of the Los Angeles Times to the comic strips.

"Harvey, dear, aren't you going to put something on? They said they'd be here at two."

"Minerva, it's only 11:30."

"Yes, I know, but you do want to make a good impression, don't you?"

"Well, not two hours ahead of time."

"Oh please, Harvey, don't be so, so snobbish. We're going to be meeting the parents of this young man that Ak-ko-su-a has fallen in love with."

"So, what should I do, Minerva?" Damn, a man can't even finish reading the newspaper."

"Change into something snazzy – why not your blue blazer?"

"It's a bit warm for that, don't you think?"

"Perhaps. At any rate you can't sit here in your golf shorts, reading the newspaper, expecting guests."

"And why not?"

Minerva Ferguson cocked her head to one side, her serious listening posture. Maybe Harvey was going through a middle age-crisis-rebellion period. She made a mental note to monitor his behavior a little more closely.

1:55 p.m. in the afternoon, hmmm, punctual people, not a bad way to start off.

The Browns strode up the tree shaded driveway, laughing, exchanging good vibe-laughter. Mrs. Minerva Ferguson cut them off at the pass.

"Welcome, you must be Mr. and Mrs. Brown."

Kofi and Nzingha Brown looked at each other with mock surprise.

"We must be," they chorused. And then formally introduced themselves – "Nzingha Brown – Kofi Brown."

"I'm Minerva and this is my husband Harvey."

They stood, looking at each awkwardly for a moment, before shaking hands.

"Uhh, please, please have a seat. Would you care for something? Tea? Fruit juice? Beer?"

"Fruit juice sounds fine."

"Dolores!"

They sat on the terrace/veranda, the Fergusons looking uncomfortable, the Browns, amused.

"Nzingha? Kofi? Those are names like the one my daughter has adopted."

Nzingha Brown and Kofi Brown exchanged rapid glances. Was this the Euro-Africentric world gone bananas, or what?

The car braking in the driveway announced the newly weds. They rushed onto the veranda, kissing and hugging their parents.

"Sorry, we're late guys."

"No big thang."

The Fergusons exchanged understanding eye codes. It's alright to be late – hmmm…

"Fruit juice? I think I'd like to have something a lil' spicier. Dolores!" Akosua called out, "Hay cervesas?"

"Si, Señora." Dolores had kept up with the trend of events, in her limited "Ingles."

"Hay dos botellas de Bohemia, por favor."

Mrs. Ferguson spotted the gold bank on Akosua's ring finger, took a deep breath of air and leaned back in her chair. There was something so theatrical about her motion that it focused attention on what she had noticed. Akosua decided not to play past the moment.

"Well, I guess we may as well come out with it, which is why we asked for this joint get together. Mother, Father, Mom, Dad, Kojo and I got married in Huatabampo, Mexico last week."

The Browns embraced them and offered sincere congratulations. "We knew you two were up to something!"

Minerva and Harvey Ferguson stared at each other, trying to figure out what to say, and who should say it. This was the first "elopement" either of them could ever recall on either side of their family trees.

Harvey Ferguson finally cleared his throat … "Ako-suah, Kojo, we wish you two young people all the happiness in the world."

Akosua hugged her father and stared a question mark at her mother. Mrs. Ferguson responded immediately.

"And I second that motion. I knew I had made the right choice the minute I met your son. Where did you get married?"

"In a little Mexican town called Huatabampo."

"Sounds so romantic. This calls for a celebration of some sort. Dolores! For favour, bring the two bottles of champagne here, they're in the vegetable bin of the fridge."

"Si, Señora."

Kojo and Akosua stared at her mother, shocked to see her reaction.

"So, now that we're all one big happy family, when do we get our first grandchild?"

Nzingha Brown initiated the laughter and it became contagious. Kojo and Akosua laughed with relief, their parents with joy.

·   ℘ℭ   ·

CHAPTER 9

They had split the script into two parts. He was dealing with the disharmony, the grief of the African Holocaust/Diaspora as a series of small stories within the big story.

"The scope of the thing is too huge for a ninety-minute film. I'm trying to scale it down to human terms, to make it understandable for people who can't imagine the genocide of millions over a four-hundred year period. And yet, maintain the enormous scope of the madness."

Akosua was working on part two, showing how a super psychic glue was used to prevent the disintegration of the Africans who were exported.

"What forces can you identify that would serve the purpose of preventing total disintegration of the African psyche, of the Africanity in us?"

"Well, spirituality is one of the major factors. I'm speaking of African spirituality, not Christianity, or Islam or any of the other foreign systems that invaded Africa.

I'm having my eyes opened by studies that pinpoint the vitality of the African spiritual systems/branches. It's called Vodun/Voodoo in Haiti, Candomblé in Brazil, Santeria in Cuba, Shango in Trinidad, Obeah in Jamaica, the Religion or Yoruba in the U.S., an interlocked spirituality that exists wherever there are African people.

I'm putting an emphasis on the spiritual thing. And, of course, the roles that women have played in helping us retain our souls. We got work to do."

They paid Grandfather Kwame a two-hour visit to discuss the African-American genius for pushing Nihilism into a distant corner.

"Now don't get me wrong, you two. I'm not going to come right out and say that we were spiritually stronger in the old days. I can't honestly say that. What I can say is that the floods that cause erosion are deeper now. Maybe it's got something to do with global warming. In any case, I can see that a lot of our young people have just given into, given themselves up to substances and garments, that is to say, 'pleasure' and 'adornments.'

They block out matters that they think will cause them any kind of deep thinking. I don't honestly know, it may have something to do with how cleverly the White guys who run America have manipulated the obstacles in front of them, behind them, around them.

In ancient times, in my day … hahhah, we knew exactly what the deal was. We had two simple choices to make, either survive and thrive, or surrender and die. As I see things now, there are so many distractions on the way to the Real Deal, so many strange con games being played.

For example, the distinction between something Authentic and something Cosmetic are worlds apart, but nowadays many of us would rather have the Cosmetic and push the Authentic aside. You know what I'm saying?"

They nodded in tandem. The old man was about Truth, and that's what they came for.

"Early in the game we were exposed to the raw face of reality, Authentic reality, in the South especially, but in the North too. There was no Cosmetic face to study, this was the Real Deal. You're here to talk with an old man about what he sees, what he has seen. And I'm giving it to you straight up.

We were not as confused and messed around by a lot of subliminals. I think it would've been pretty hard to think of yourself as an 'upper class slave' or a 'lower class slave.' I loved Malcolm X for many reasons, but I never felt comfortable with his 'house niggers' and 'field niggers' thing.

Surely there must've been 'house niggers' in the field and some 'field niggers' in the house. Common sense would tell us that. There wasn't a bunch of computers back then, or sophisticated anti-African-American think tanks. Stuff was real primitive back then – shootings, burnings, lynchings. We knew who the enemy was. Everyday was Katrina time.

I wouldn't want to try to pin-point the exact moment in time that we went from the Real Deal to Fantasy. But I suspect it happened somewhere in the '60s, when enough fertilizer had been spread to make people believe that racial justice was going to be achieved. Of course it didn't happen and it's not ever going to happen so long as we continue to buy into the Cosmetic. That may sound like a negative assessment of the situation, but that's what Reality can be like."

The old man paused to take a slow sip of Chivas Regal.

"Grandfather, do you believe our Ancestors, the Spirits are responsible for us surviving chattel slavery, and the aftermath?"

"Daughter, I'll tell you the honest to God truth, I can't point my finger at any other energy source. I've spent many hours of my life trying to discover the secret of our will to overcome, many hours.

And after all the fancy wrappings have been stripped away, we always windup at spiritual benchmarks that were drawn by our Ancestors; don't give up. Don't forget those who suffered for you. Look back, but keep on moving forward. Sankofa.

You know something? I've been disappointed in our intellectuals, our poets and writers, for years, because they've never made a serious effort to tap into our spirituality.

From time to time, one of the more adventurous types will step out a half step, but they never go beyond that. I suspect that they've all been so Christianized and Islamized that they feel that delving into <u>our</u> spiritual history is blaspheming or something.

Kojo, I've taken your Daddy to task about this. I used to ask him – why is it I can go to the bookstores and pick up books on 'Hindi Thought about the Other Side'? 'Japanese, the Sun and Cherry Blossoms,' 'Jewish Thinking on the Jewish Holocaust,' but there's not one book on the 'African Spiritual Conquest of Chattel Slavery.'

He told me that he didn't have any books about this phenomenon because no one has written one. Can you imagine such a thing?! We ought to be swamped with books, pamphlets even, about the spiritual forces that we tapped in order to overcome the nihilism inherent to chattel slavery.

I'll go a step farther and say that we need to have our asses kicked, pardon my French, Akosua, for not having a Holocaust/Diaspora Monument erected in all of the places we were shipped to.

It's absurd that they would have monuments to Lassie, the Wonder Dog, and statutes for every racist snake-dog who ever showed his face, but only a very few serious monuments to the blood, sweat and sorrow that our people have given this country."

"Granddad, do you think a film could be a monument?"

"Let's take a look at it."

$$\text{·} \quad \wp\wp \quad \text{·}$$

"Questions? Do we have any strangers in the house? Anybody here who doesn't know everybody else? Good. However, there is one person I would like to introduce to you; her name is Akosua Ferguson-Brown, my wife."

Kojo looked around the room. Wall to wall talent. Thelma Nagata, D.J. Robinson, Phillip Charles, Sid Burns, Ed Burns, Mac Weaver, Jackie F. Muhammad, Michael Sims, Juna, heavy weights.

"Now then, let me give you the briefest of explanations concerning this project."

Thelma Nagata, the future office manager, pulled out a steno pad and ballpoint. The explanation given, the floor was opened.

"Kojo, you're talking about a film production company that will produce excellent films."

"You got that right, D.J., and with good fortune smiling on us, you'll be the camera man, like Bergman's Sven Nyquist."

"I like your idea of using sound effects, rather than a lot of dialogue, that's never been done with Black films. They usually have us talking too damned much."

"Sid, with all due respect ... we're talking about a whole new ballgame. That's one of the mean things that's been done with us for a long time, we've had the wrong labels slapped on our goodies."

"Sounds like the music is going to be the most important element of this film, 'My Grandfather's Eyes.'"

"Which is why we have asked the inimitable Juna to do the score."

"Were you wondering why I was here, Jackie?"

"Juna, I never wonder why you're anywhere that you are, wherever that might be."

Uhh oh, past hostilities. Akosua slipped in suavely.

"Now, now, now, sisters, we can't have Jackie F. Muhammad, the top p.r. person around and Juna, the top musician-computer around, clawing each other to pieces, can we?"

There was a moment of edgy silence while the people in the room looked at the would be antagonists with disapproving eyes.

"Now then, going right along. I'm going to assume, from this point on that everyone here is going to become a card carrying member of 'Our Production Company.'"

Akosua did a double take and smiled at Kojo's reaffirmative wink. "Our Production Company." Perfect. Better than Kosmic Muffin Productions …

"If we have anyone who wants to get out?"

Ed Burns, assistant director/second unit director on thirty feature movies, cleared his throat.

"Ahhem, I want in, definitely, but I think some serious questions need to be addressed. The first consideration is, of course, 'The Dream,' and you've done a hellified job of laying that on us."

"It's called pitchin', Ed, you know how it's done!"

The group shared "insider's" laughter.

"Right. Now then, after 'the pitch' – let's get to the most important question of all. Where's the money coming from to do 'Grandfather's Eyes'?"

Every eye focused on Kojo. He took a subconsciously aggressive stance.

"Ed, as the politicians say, I'm glad you asked that question. The only answer I can give you at this moment is an honest one. I don't know."

Akosua's jaw dropped with all of the other dismayed reactions in the room. Kojo rushed on to say …

"No, I can't tell you at this moment exactly where it's coming from. But I'm going to ask you to trust me, for at least a couple months, 'til we really kick this thing into gear."

"Mac Weaver here. Kojo, let's say we all trust you and we know we can because you've always been a straight up guy."

"Thanks, Mac."

"Now then, let's say we wind up with a fabulous film, how do we get it distributed?"

"We'll have to cope with that problem when we get to it. I have a sneaking suspicion that we may have to deal with the usual suspects."

Once again they shared "Insider's" smiles. They knew who the usual suspects were.

"Question? Please put your hand down, Thelma, and stop pretending you're in fifth grade."

"Ahh, it was such a wonderful time in my life, before I discovered boys. O well. Question is, do you have any fears that 'Our Production Company' will have a racist flag put on it by 'the usual suspects' because we have no non-colored people in the company?"

"Thelma, I read you loud 'n clear. I've asked the people who are closest to me to participate in this venture. That's all. We may find other people who are willing to go through what we know about and we'll consider their particulars.

You see, what I'm asking for is a very strong commitment from everybody here. I wouldn't consider people I don't know as well as you brothers and sisters.

I know that I'm asking a lot, but I know we can pull it off. We've done it before."

"Kojo, what about office space, phones, all of that madness?"

"Jackie, by the end of next month we'll have office space in a fantastic Quonset sized loft on Slauson and Stanford, a half block east of Main St."

Juna gasped – "That's in south Los Angeles! South Los Angeles!"

Kojo, uncertain of her gasp, whether it indicated approval or disapproval, moved right along.

"By the end of next month, once we've set up, we'll go into a pre-production mode at the end of the following month. In other words, we'll be doing this on a month to month schedule.

Unless something crazy happens, in December we'll start getting into film. I'm going to be asking you brothers 'n sisters to do a lot of stuff for free that the usual suspects would pay you big bucks for. It may come free at first, but I give you my word, we will profit at the end of the day."

There was a heavy moment of silence, broken by Juna's raspy voice.

"Sounds like we gettin' ready to kick some ass 'round here!"

· ༄ ·

I have Thelma Nagata as my secretary-office manager. D.J. Robinson camera man, Phillip Charles, the man who once lit the inside of a barrel, using only a knot hole. Sid Burns for sound. Ed Burns, assistant director. Mac Weaver, assistant director-actor. Juna the musician doing the score. Jackie F. Muhammad, p.r. wizard. Photographer Michael Sims. And Akosua Ferguson-Brown, my co-writer-co-producer wife.

I've got a dynamite group ready and willing to get down with me and I'll pickup more on the way. Why worry? The only problem was money.

· ❧ ·

His landlords, the Chans, were gracious about his moving to his wife's house.

"Well, c'mon now, Kojo, we wouldn't expect for a man to live away from his wife. Best of luck to you two."

October 1ˢᵗ, Kojo was firmly established, doing ten things at one time.

"Kojo, what about this loft you talked about using as an office for 'Our Production Company'?"

"It's a real deal. My friend, John Outterbridge, is getting ready to move back to North Carolina and he's leasing his space to me for a year, with an option to buy."

"What will we use for money?"

"Well, he's giving us the first three months free and after that, 800 bucks a month."

"Man, that's what I call a friend."

"Yeah, John is a gem, always has been."

Stuff started happening.

"Kojo, now you know if you talked to your grandfather it was bound to get back to the family. I think I may have something of interest for you, if you need money."

"Dad, please don't play with my head like this – if I need money?"

"Well, I just wanted to make sure, hahhhahhah. Think you might be able to break away for a meeting with One Hundred Black Men?"

"Your group?"

"Yeah, one of the organizations I joined not too long after we moved out here. How does Saturday morning, about ten a.m. suit you?"

"Ten a.m. is cool."

"Good, I'll pick you about nine thirty. How's Akosua?"

"Busy, Dad, busy."

"Sounds like you guys are onto something dynamite. See you Saturday."

Kojo gently dropped the phone back into the cradle. One Hundred Black Men was one of the few organizations that his father belonged to that he wasn't exactly enthusiastic about. They gave him the impression that they were a collection of good time types, high rollers, professionals with pretensions, jive types.

But I shouldn't jump to too many bad conclusions, after all, Dad's been in the group for ages and I know he's about something.

"Kojo, you want to take a lunch break with me?"

·   &Cß   ·

They sat under the thrift shop beach umbrella in their spacious back yard; ten dollars for hundreds of dollars of shade – "Compare compari" " – and feasted on shrimp salad sandwiches and chilled white wine.

"Akoś, I just got an interesting call from my Dad. He's inviting me to a meeting of One Hundred Black Men on Saturday."

"What's the deal?"

"I don't know yet. He's making little sounds about money but I don't have the slightest idea where it would be coming from."

"Well, I don't want to throw any curve balls at your head or anything, but the sooner we get our hands on a large sum of it, the better."

"Are we bankrupt already?"

"No, sweetheart, not yet. Everything is cool on the home front, but I've been talking with Thelma about office equipment and stuff and she's running some interesting figures at my head. The lady is an organizational genius."

"Yeah, she's really something, ain't she?"

He noticed it as she wedged herself away from the table. Looks like Akosua is gaining a little weight.

"Akoś, looks like we're going to be going on a diet pretty soon, huh?"

She came to pose in front of him, both fists on her hips, a slight bay window blocking his view.

"You don't diet away babies, Kojo, you give birth to them."

He pulled her down on his lap and smothered her face and neck with kisses. It was happening.

· ℘℧ ·

CHAPTER 10

One Hundred Black Men held their Saturday meetings at the Crenshaw Club. They wandered in from early golf dates, tennis matches, aerobics workout, weight lifting, jogging.

Well, I gotta say this for 'em, they're certainly a fitness conscious bunch of dudes.

There were also a number of the One Hundred who offered some evidence of having serious hangovers and Bloody Mary breakfasts. But in the main, Kojo noted, they were a healthy collection of middle aged African-American men.

He recognized a few of the more public figures: Assembly man whatshisname, the three middle echelon actors, six or seven doctors, a few lawyers, teachers, upper level civil servants, a stray airline pilot or two, some real estate guys, the owner of the best stocked and most Africentric book store in Southern California.

"Dad, are there really one hundred men in this organization?"

"More like sixty-five, but someone thought one hundred would sound better than sixty-five."

Enormous steam trays of scrambled eggs, sausages, bacon, white/rye toast and huge carafes of orange juice were spread on a buffet table.

"Brunch is served," someone announced and the men made their way to the food, laughing and joking. Kojo felt trapped. Thought we were supposed to meet at ten a.m.

His father took note of him making a sly study of his watch and whispered, "Kojo, relax, this is the way the brothers do it. Remember, we haven't seen each other since our last meeting."

Breakfast finally finished (11:30 a.m., he noted), it was time for the business of One Hundred Black Men. The minutes of the last meeting were read, an update on the fifteen college aid grants they were sponsoring. The medical bills that they had helped a couple strapped members meet, the situation with the orphanage that they were sponsoring in Accra, Ghana.

Their total financial state of being was put into a transparent perspective by an accountant who made certain that everyone understood that it was his astute expertise that multiplied their funds threefold during the past two years. Kojo was fascinated by the casual manner the business was framed, yet how efficiently it was worked out. He was startled to look and see that his father was speaking.

"So, rather than attempt to tell you what it's all about, I'd prefer that you be given the story first hand. May I present my son, Kojo Bediako Brown."

He felt slightly befuddled for a moment, as polite applause accompanied him to the lectern. What the hell can I say to these guys? It took him a few moments to unravel the tape, to know where to start and where he wanted to wind up. They weren't a difficult group to talk to. In some ways it was like speaking to sixty-five facets of his father.

"I don't have a prepared speech because I didn't really expect to speak to you guys."

"Speak your heart," someone called out from the rear of the room. He decided to go from his U.S.C. film school days: the frustrations, the Eurocentric racism that was so deeply engrained there that the people who were guilty of maintaining it didn't even realize it. It was like a second skin to them, he explained.

The support that his Mom and Dad gave him, the family.

The difficulties of trying to gain creative control of some percentage of the cinematic African-American image. What his recent trips to Ghana and Denmark meant. The heroic story he wanted to tell in "My Grandfather's Eyes," how it represented, in some way, all of their grandfathers. The problems he was facing, trying to take it up. After twenty minutes of heartfelt speaking he dried up. He had let it all out; there was nothing else to say.

The applause surprised him. What were they clapping for? The Saturday meeting of One Hundred Black Men was slowly melting away, the business was just beginning.

Father Brown came to steer him into a room where five members of the One Hundred were seated at a conference table, waiting for him.

"Kojo, this is our preliminary screening committee: This is brother Franklin, brother Castle, brother Turner, brother Settles, and brother Dirkson, our accountant."

He shook hands with the men and stood in place, feeling like a schoolboy in front of the class.

"Have a seat, Kojo. Let's talk about what you need and what we want."

I think I must've stumbled out of the conference room after about forty-five minutes of information-exchange-interrogation. They wanted me to give them some hard edged reasons for granting me the "seed money" for "My Grandfather's Eyes." Our exchange indicated how little they understood above the line/below the line costs, and a few other things about the movie business. But they understood how money can be cloned. And what they were concerned about was whether or not they would receive a decent return on their investment within a reasonable time frame. Brother Dirkson, the accountant, asked the toughest questions and took the most notes.

"Have you identified your core market? How long do you think it will take for you to show us a profit on our investment?"

I had to confess to Dad that I had doubts about whether or not I had come off as well as I wanted to. Dad stroked me out nicely.

"Kojo, it's cool, everything is cool, take my word for it. These brothers have been waiting to jump onto some media action for quite awhile. A couple years ago we were debating about the acquisition of a television station. You're the perfect scenario for us; young, educated at one of the best film schools in the country, got a productive track record, traveled, about to burn the world up with your accomplishments, and you're my son to boot. What're you worried about?"

· ℘℆ ·

"Akoś, did you get the message from your publisher? He seems to be excited about the outline, the excerpt, whatever it is you e-mailed him."

"Got it! Kosmic Muffin Publishing, Ltd. seems to really be in love with me these days. What's happening with the 'Black Men'?"

"Brother Dirkson, the accountant called me this morning and wanted some clarification of what I meant in paragraph six on page twelve. He's a serious dude, that one. What's the word about our bank loan?"

"They're chewing on it. You know how it is when they're asked to loan money for 'artistic purposes.'"

· ℰℛ ·

"Dear Grace,

I've been so busy doing so many things that I haven't had the time to reply/write you. I've gotten married; I may as well be up front about that, in line with our-be-honest-with-each-other policy. The major reason why I got married is something that I have to be honest about too. I had to do it for ritualistic reasons.

No, please don't laugh and change the channel. I've known Akosua Ferguson, now Brown plus Ferguson, for more than two years, and it was time for us to do Something.

I'm telling you this honestly, so please be prepared; my relationship with Asiafo, the man in the forest, was my catalyst for getting married. He was the one who said that I should do it, if I wanted to get what I wanted.

I could lay out the rest of the stipulations, but that wouldn't serve any worthwhile purpose.

Please understand that I will always love you, in all of the ways that we can love and that I wish you the kind of happiness that I'm experiencing. I'm not married to the kind of woman who would become hysterical if I received on occasional letter from Ghana, so, don't hesitate if you feel the urge.

Love, Kojo

P.S. Looks like there's a little Kojo or Akosua on the way, about seven months from now. We won't do any scanning."

· ℰℛ ·

The loft space was opened to them. John Outterbridge had gone back down home to work for awhile. Kojo and Akosua strolled through the Quonset hut sized area.

"We could build sets in here."

"Woww! This place is huge, you'd never have any idea that this was here, entering that ordinary sized front door."

"'Bridge planned it that way. And check out the burglar proofing, all of the grillwork on those windows that look like works of art."

They separated, peeking into odd corners, discovering.

"Kojo! Kojo!"

"I hear you, but where are you?"

"Over here, behind the big panel."

"What is this?"

"It's a mini-kitchen, exactly the kind of thing you'd want to use to prepare midnight snacks."

"Now I'm really beginning to understand what he meant when he said, 'I'm not going to give you a guided tour; I'll let you discover the place for yourself'."

Fourteen anxiety ridden days later, Kojo received a call from his mother.

"Kojo, your father decided to give me a chance to have some of the fun."

"What's up, Mom?"

"Looks like you are, my son, looks like you are."

"I don't understand."

"I'm proud and happy to say that One Hundred Black Men have just granted you a 1.5 million package to do your thing."

Kojo suddenly saw stars flashing through his head. O my God, don't let me punk out here and faint.

"One point five mil? Is that what you just said?"

"Exactly. The information came straight from the accountant to your father. Congratulations! Looks like you're in business."

"You better believe it! Thanks, Mom, talk to you later."

Kojo offered a silent prayer of thanks and tried to pull off a nonchalant stroll into the kitchen.

"Kojo, you want to have a little snack out back, I'm frying eggplant with Parmesan."

"Yeah, yeah, that would be real tasty."

He had to force himself to handle the plate without a nervous rattle. But at the same time he felt strangely calm, as though the news he had received was "natural."

"There's some Chardonnay in the fridge."

"Why don't we have some Champagne?"

She stopped placing slices of eggplant, powdered with Parmesan cheese, on their plates.

"Champagne?"

"Yes, what better ways to celebrate this 1.5 million dollar grant I just got from the Men."

Akosua screamed and raced around the table to give him a gigantic embrace.

"Oh Kojo! That's wonderful! Fantastic!"

"Yeah, we can have Thelma begin to set up the office now, and open up a payroll, we're in business.

· ℘ℭ ·

AN ASIDE

"Yeah, folks, it was a done deal from the minute he told us that he wanted to do a 'film,' not a 'movie,' about my father's vision, his grandfather's eyes. Me and Nzingha talked it over, and we clearly understood that he was not talking about a film that would have automatic acceptance, or maybe no acceptance at all.

"Let's face it, Dad; we're talking about something that might be considered 'an art film.' And it gets 'art film' reception."

But, I pulled his feet as close to the fire as I could; is this going to be an important film, an important statement? Think big boy Michael Moore here … Boy reminded me so much of Grandfather, it took him damned near five minutes to think on my question and give me an answer.

"Yes, Dad," he finally answered, "it's going to be an important film, an important statement."

That was all we needed. Our son wanted to do an important film with an important statement. That was all we needed. "The Black Men" were shocked by the way I lobbied them.

"Look, bro' Dirkson, let's get real here. What is it going to take for 'The Men' to release some funds for my son's project?"

"Uhh, well Brother Brown, we're not as concerned about the objective of the project as we're concerned about how we can capitalize on the project. We'll need some guarantees …?"

It was not about nepotism. Let's get that squared away forthwith. If I had felt that Kojo's project was bullshit, I would've been the first to say that. No, "My Grandfather's Eyes" was about much more than that. And I think enough of "The Men" would've been in agreement with me. And they <u>did</u> agree with me.

They, we saw the possibility of bringing out some stuff that 99% of the movies had never addressed. Probably hadn't even thought about. Who wouldn't want to be a part of that kind of history, if they were "reasonable men"?

Especially if it offered the possibility of making more money than had been plowed into the project. I hammered on that angle. And we, me and Nzingha, offered the house, the store, her jewelry and damned near everything else we could offer up as collateral. We wanted to make certain that the "Black Men" understood that they wouldn't lose their money, no matter what happened.

What were they offering Kojo? One point five mil would barely cover commissary costs for a major league, "mainstream" production. The plus side of the whole thing is that the "Black Men" clearly endorsed creative efforts. Astute types asked questions.

"Brother Kofi, what're we going to understand/relate to, after 'My Grandfather's Eyes,' that we wouldn't've been aware of before the release of the film?"

"Fair question. I saw 'Waiting to Exhale,' by way of example, and the theater was filled up with gray haired African-American women, women who had stopped going to movies because there was nothing for them. They've lost too many sons and daughters to be thrilled by people getting shot up, or blown up. I can't say that I loved 'Waiting to Exhale,' but no one can deny that it filled a niche. Hollywood thought it was taking a very bold step by releasing 'Exhale.'"

It wasn't all that much of a bold step, or a gamble. African-Americans are the most loyal movie goers in this country, especially the young people. And, if you give the older heads something of substance, we'll go to see it.

Of course my son would be able to explain it much better than I'm explaining it, but we both feel that we're at a perfect time in our history to reveal some of the wisdom, humor, common sense, attitude, philosophy, whatever you want to call it, that our male Elders have held onto and passed onto us.

I think "Grandfather's Eyes" would force a lot of our people, especially the younger ones, to relate to their Elders in a different, more positive way. I don't really think that a lot of young people, and some not so young, are even aware of how negative and disrespectful they are to the Elders.

As we all know, one picture is worth a zillion words …

Some really interesting stuff began to happen during the time that the "Men" were debating about Kojo's project. One afternoon three young brothers came into the bookstore looking for Kojo. Between the three of them they could've opened up a jewelry store in the mall, that's how much bling bling they were wearing.

"Kojo isn't here, I'm his father, and can I help you?"

The spokesman for the trio came right to the point.

"Uhhh, Mr. Brown, we hear that Kojo be needing some coins for his project, we wanna help him. Ask him to call me, here my card."

I got together with Kojo a couple days later, told him about his visitors and gave him the card. He came into the bookstore a day later, his face lit up with a big smile.

"Dad, I just came from a meeting with 'Mr. Big Time Woo Woo' and some of his … uhh … business associates."

By the time he got to the "business associates" he was laughing out loud.

"C'mon, Kojo, don't keep the punch line to yourself."

"O.k., let me tell you about it. It seems that 'Mr. Big Time Woo Woo' – "don't you just love that name? – heard about my project. How do you think he got the word?"

"Easy, One Hundred Black Men have one thousand family members plus friends. The info could've come from anywhere. You didn't want to keep the project a secret, did you?"

"Well, not really, but I did find it a lil' peculiar that these guys had all the info they have. What they wanted to meet and talk about was financing for the film, from above the line to 'way below the line."

"Hey, that sounds great, son! What could be better than having the support of your peers? Gotta ask one question though, where are they getting the money from?"

"Same question I asked, Dad. But a lot more diplomatically. 'Mr. Big Time' assured me that it was 'good money,' no taint on any of the green bucks. But he hemmed 'n hawed about the source. I was quite diplomatic and polite about it, but I had to explain to him that it was very important that I had to know where the money was coming from, for tax purposes and all that.

He finally admitted that it had something to do with drugs."

"You know, I didn't want to 'profile' the young brothers, but that's the first thing that came to mind when we talked in the bookstore."

"I don't think he could deal with where I was coming from. It would be incredibly wrong to have to say that 'My Grandfather's Eyes' was made with drug money."

"I think Grandfather himself would be a lil' pissed off about it."

· ℘CR ·

CHAPTER 11

The loft offered them a unique business venue. There was privacy over here and openness over there. Thelma Nagata was in office heaven.

"My God in Heaven, or wherever She is, there's enough space in here to run a train." And within weeks, a creative train was running. Pre-production was on.

"We're going to have to do it as well as it can be done, the first time, because we won't have the resources to do it again. And again."

Kojo and Akosua scouted for locations, after hours.

"Akoś, we're going to have to shoot fast and close. We're looking for all the physical elements we'll need in our script, the actors and actresses are going to have to enlarge themselves, to fill us up for an emotional voyage."

"I get it."

The phones rang.

"Kojo, line #4."

"Kojo Brown here."

"Hi Kojo, Charley Bascom here. So, how's it going, pal?"

Charley Bascom, Bascom Productions. The hyenas have sniffed a scent. Well, if the young drug dealers knew about "Grandfather," why wouldn't Charley Bascom?

"Charley, haven't talked with you in a while."

"Not since you turned down the golden chance to do the jazz series."

Kojo felt confident enough to wedge the blade in a bit.

"Sorry, Charley, but I don't think it was a "golden chance.""

"Awww c'mon, Kojo, that was just one thing on the way to many other things. What's this 'Our Production Company' stuff? You didn't tell me that you were going into business for yourself."

"You didn't ask, Charley, you didn't ask."

He could almost feel the neurotic anger come through the receiver. The man was not accustomed to having his psyche played around with.

"So, I'm asking. What's the deal?"

Kojo, well aware of how accurate and informative the Hollywood Grapevine could be, decided to splash broad strokes into Charley Bascom's ear.

"That sounds great, Kojo, really great! How's your distribution set up?"

"Charley, we'll have to talk about that at a later date. Right now I'm late for two meetings."

"Sure, sure, I understand, Big Guy. Looks like you're onto something hot. Why don't we get back at this, let's say – the beginning of next week?"

"Yeah, beginning of next week, sure thing."

Kojo hung up and smiled into Thelma Nagata's beaming face. You couldn't really call it revenge, but it definitely felt good to give the moguls a little taste of their own medicine.

It was happening. Our Production Company was a 24-hour a day operation. Members of the staff came and stayed to do the zillions of things that are necessary to make a film happen.

Mr. and Mrs. Ferguson came.

"We just happened to be in the neighborhood."

Akosua winked at Kojo. Minerva Ferguson wouldn't be caught dead in this neighborhood. Just passing by? They gave them a tour of the bustling facility. The Fergusons were impressed, Harvey Ferguson wandered off by himself.

"Don't get lost, Harvey."

"I'll try not to, Minerva."

Mrs. Ferguson frowned at his reply. The man was becoming a bit sarcastic in his old age.

"Kojo, Ahkosua, can we go to some private spot in your place?"

They exchanged puzzled looks. "Private" meant being fifty yards from the nearest phone.

"Sure, we can sit over here."

Akosua had put her thrift shopping expertise to work and scrounged a dozen comfortable Danish chairs and three sofas for their studio. Kojo rushed to take a quick call and returned with glasses of pineapple juice.

"Sorry, had to take that one, did I miss anything?"

"No, you didn't Kojo, I waited for you … hmmm. This is delicious."

They were in a flight pattern that Mrs. Ferguson knew nothing about. She made them feel antsy, but they cloaked their impatience with bland expressions. Phones were ringing, machines clicking and clacking. Mrs. Ferguson was playing her scene.

"Ahko-sua, you look perfectly adorable pregnant …"

"Thank you, Mother."

"Uhhh, Mrs. Ferguson, this is like, like in the middle of our work day."

"I understand. Well, to get right down to brass tacks here, Harvey and I were wondering what kind of legal representation you had for your company?"

They exchanged numb dumb looks.

"Hmmm, just as we thought. I've spoken to my attorneys on your behalf; Green, Shafton, Clarke and Rasch."

"Woww! They're pretty much upscale, aren't they?"

"They would be if they weren't trying to earn brownie points for aiding and abetting a couple of fledgling African-American filmmakers."

Kojo stunned her with a juicy kiss on both cheeks. Akosua pulled her mother up from the sofa and gave her a huge hug. Harvey Ferguson wandered in, smiled at the warm tableau.

"Kojo, you need a fifteen-car parking lot out back, I think my firm can take care of that for you for, let's say … $20 or so."

· ❧ ❧ ·

One of those balmy November evenings that only seem to happen in Los Angeles. Akosua and Kojo had decided on a picnic in Griffith Park. They drove up past the golf course, around to the "back side" of the park.

"Kojo, you know something? Life is beginning to have an unreal, almost surreal quality about it with us."

"How so?"

"Well, look at what's happening. We have a fat bank account, all the people you wanted to bring in for our film have come in and more are on the way. You're being granted a serious amount of respect for your creative efforts, me too, things are rolling with Our Production Company, I'm on the cusp of selling another book to Kosmic Muffin Publishing House, we're in love and I'm pregnant!"

He shared her feeling. The snags that occurred were minor and easily resolved. Every obstacle seemed to flatten out after a few minutes. Asiafo …

Would the same things be happening if I hadn't met Asiafo? Is he really the catalyst for all of this?

"Akoś, I know what you feel, believe me I do. Hey, looks like we have this section of the park to ourselves."

"Good. Who else comes to picnic on Tuesday at 5 p.m.?"

They chose a spot under a large, low limbed tree, spread their blanket and settled it. They were having catered goodies from the Nagasaki Café: Bento boxes of vinegared rice, sushi, sashimi, Nori filled with Tempura shrimp, wasabi.

"Oh, Kojo, we forgot your beer."

"I'll get it."

He popped up from the blanket, nibbling on a rice ball and jogged toward the car, parked a hundred yards away. What could taste better than a cold Kirin right now?

He pulled the bottle of Kirin from the cooler in the trunk of their car and turned to jog back to their spot. The scene registered on his brain as a still photo. A large black dirty, ragged man was standing at the edge of their blanket.

Kojo broke into a hard run, gripping the long neck of the beer bottle. He came up behind the man, catching Akosua's eye. What the hell is he doing here, what does he want?

Kojo circled around to the front of the man and almost sighed with relief. It was just one of those wild and crazy guys who were running around in the world these days. He stared into the man's spaced out eyes.

The man's stance at the edge of the blanket disturbed him, but he wasn't armed and he was obviously sick.

Kojo decided to try the sweet approach.

91

"What can we do for you, my brother?"

The man's spaced out eyes stayed on a distant target as he made the hand to mouth gesture for food. Kojo felt a sudden rush of nervous perspiration pop out under his armpits.

He stared into the man's face, trying to glean something from the dead expression. Nothing. Kojo reached down, closed his bento box and handed it to the man. The man opened the box, dabbed a California roll into the nostril stinging wasabi mustard and swallowed it without chewing. He bit into another roll and turned away from them and began to walk in a serpentine fashion, very quickly, as though he was late for an appointment. Akosua moved closer to Kojo and squeezed his neck.

"Kojo, I love you, do you know that?"

"I love you too, baby." He was perspiring heavily.

"That was one of the most unselfish things I've seen in a long time. You gave that man your dinner."

"Yeah, but I didn't give him my beer." He tried to joke it off. He had fed a visitor. Was it the right visitor?

"Kojo, you can joke about it if you like, but there aren't a lot of people who would give away their expensive lil' boxes of Japanese food."

"Well, you know how it is; you have to go with the vibe sometimes. When I see dudes like that, all I can think is – there, but for the grace of God and the Orishas, go I."

"I heard that. Here, have some of my Tempura."

· ෨ൟ ·

92

CHAPTER 12

Invitations started pouring in, attention from the Moguls.

"Dan Dryson here. Sayyy, what's the deal here, Kojo? I've called your office twice awready."

"Sorry, Dan, been meaning to get back to you. So, what can I do for you?"

Bascom had the scent first, now they all have it.

Good. Let 'em pant for awhile. They know the quality of my work, the quality of the people I've pulled in. Good. I'll get to 'em when I get to 'em. How many times have I been put on semi-permanent hold, or held at arm's length for days?

One Hundred Black Men sent them a gold embossed invite to their Winter Ball. "The Men Celebrate."

"Well, of course, we have to make that."

Akosua's latest book provoked public acclaim that she wasn't really prepared for.

"Wow, looks like the 'OUTLAWS' has struck a little literary gold here."

The African-American community wanted to take a closer look at the successfully functioning African-American couple with the supportive in-laws. Publicist Jackie F. Muhammad was right on the stick.

"O.k., Kojo, Akosua, let me make a couple things crystal clear. I'm the best, o.k.? So, go with me. I'm going to promote you guys behind the beyond. I see a somewhat royal touch here: Akosua as queen of the literary scene and you, Kojo, as the African-American 'King of the Cinema.'"

Kojo and Akosua, both somewhat shy by nature, slunk down in their seats as the bold outlines of their p.r. person's campaign was scrolled out for them. Jackie F. Muhammad pulled them back with a well designed pep talk.

"Look, Kojo, you want your film to make money so that you can pay your people well and make mo' bettah films. Right?"

Kojo nodded numbly.

"Akosua, you want your books to sell so that you will be able to call your own publishing shots. I want to live up to my reputation. And the only way we're going to be able to pull any of this off is by extending the current methodologies of publicizing into an African-American realm.

'Dagbladet,' the Danish film magazine will be here tomorrow for an interview and lots of flicks."

"Dagbladet? I'm impressed, how did you know about them?"

"Kojo, I have done a serious research job on you two and I'll be bringing in folks who have your best interests at hear. 'Dagbladet' is, as you know, one of the most prestigious film mags in Europe. That's gonna give the European some idea of who you are.

I've pulled the 'Literary Gazette' in to do a piece on Akosua's father-in-law stocking her books in his store. There are angles, my sister, my brother, and I know many of them."

"Well, you know we start shooting at the end of the week and the time will be tight. We'll only have four months to do what we have to do."

"Kojo, I know the schedule and I know you've engaged some of the heaviest talents in the industry, including yours truly. Now, what I'm saying to you is simple, let's put enough serious, honest publicity out there to guarantee your success. Remember, my friends, in the Beginning was The Word/Publicity."

· ℘ℭ ·

Kojo sat at his desk, outlining some of the visuals he wanted to use in his opening montage.

#1) A series of subliminal shots give us a stroboscopic look at neon-lit city life. Something has a phosphorescent glow. The atmosphere is electric, the activities almost ant-like, but unlike ants these city life activities are nebulous, almost meaningless.

#2) A gang fight between two Black gangs is in progress. Uzi bullets, tracers, small arms fire, lots of blood. The scene is a caricature of a Hollywood "urban action" movie, except that the blood isn't ketchup and the dead do not appear in other movies.

#3) A baseball card collection of authentic African-American folk heroes, half-female/half male. The subliminal effect is to use the faces and names to jar our memories.

#4) A bedraggled, drunk collection of men and women lounging around in a liquor store parking lot. They have reached the desperate stage of not being able to go too far from the source of their pain killers.

#5) African spiritual practices in various parts of the world: Use one ritual and show how it morphs – in America, the Religion or Yoruba. Brazil/Candomblé. Haiti/Vodun. Cuba/Santeria/Lukumi. Puerto Rico/Santos/Santeria. Trinidad/Venezuela/Shango. Jamaica/Obeah/Poco.

#6) Aside from the widespread indigenous spiritual systems of Africa, we'll look at those places in Europe, Asia, and the Middle East that have been greatly influenced by these spiritual systems. The focus will be on Greece and their wholesale adoption/adaptation of the Yoruba mythology.

"Kojo, what time did you tell your Grandfather we were coming?"

"Four o'clock. I'm coming. Just give me a couple more minutes."

#7) Healthy African-American children/sick African-American children/psychologically. What makes them healthy/sick?

· ℘℃℞ ·

During the course of the pre-production madness, Kojo felt compelled to get away for a couple hours, to talk with his grandfather-mentor about a few things. Akosua definitely wanted to explore his thoughts concerning the spiritual elements of the Diaspora/African Holocaust.

"Kojo, Akosua, ahhh young lady, I must say ... pregnancy really becomes you, your whole being is aglow."

"Thank you, Granddad, I think you're the first man I've ever received that special kind of compliment."

"Whoa, hold on here a minute, Akoś, I'm always telling you how beautiful you look."

"Kojo, you know that's just because you've read that lil' book that says – "tell her nice things, if she looks a lil' dumpy.""

"Akosua!"

"She's right, Kojo, we men folks do stuff like that, 'specially if we're sensitive. Hahhhahha."

He ushered them in on a tidal wave of good vibes, exchanging hugs, kisses, and an affectionate pat on Akosua's exploding stomach.

"C'mon in, c'mon in. You just missed your Aunt Rose, Aunt Deborah and Aunt Afiya by about ten minutes."

"Paying you a visit, huh?"

"Killing me with kindness would be more like it."

"Granddad!"

"Just joking, daughter, just joking! Can I get y'all a drink of something? Water, pineapple juice, Coke, Chivas Regal?"

Akosua took the lead.

"Granddad, why don't you pour yourself a drink, I'll get us something from the fridge."

"You know where it is."

Kojo settled himself in his favorite armchair, affectionately gazing at his Grandfather, the neat stack of books next to his low slung "barber's chair," a collapsible chair he had designed for himself.

"Who wants to sit and read in a ramrod position?"

"That's quite a lady you got there, Kojo, quite a lady," he whispered to his grandson while Akosua was shaking ice cubes free in the kitchen.

"I'm beginning to appreciate that more and more each and every day, Kojo whispered back.

Akosua returned with a tray loaded with ice cubes, two kinds of fruit juices. Kojo smiled at the tray and made a snap decision.

"This is an afternoon off for us, I think I'll join Granddad and have some of his juice."

Grandfather Kwame chuckled at the comment and poured two fingers of Chivas Regal into two glasses. Akosua held her glass of pineapple juice up for a toast.

"Here's looking at you two because I can't join you, but there's always next time – cheers!"

"Cheers!"

"Yeahhh, cheers!"

They sipped their drinks silently for a few moments. Grandfather Brown opened the floor.

"So, how's the movie thing going, where are you all at now?"

The flood was suddenly channeled. They had someone who cared, who would listen to their blues without smirking, or being judgmental.

"It's always uphill when you do a so-called independent production. As you know, 'The Men' granted us 1.5 mil to do the thing and we're doing it, but we could use twice as much."

"We're trying to stay away from the usual suspects, in order to get more money, because they will start putting their sticky fingers all over everything."

"We'll have to deal with them when it comes to distribution ..."

"There are so many things to do when you set up an independent production company. All of the busy-busy stuff that would be taken care of by a bunch of gophers in a major league studio has to be done by us, all of us become gophers."

"So, things are going pretty well, huh?"

Akosua and Kojo exchanged smiles. The old man had shuffled them down to the bottom line. Was it happening or not?

"Uhh, yeah, Granddad, I guess you could say that. We start shooting next week."

"Good."

They sipped and relaxed. Akosua loved being in Grandfather Brown's psycho-space. He was a soothing agent. He didn't make them feel as though they were compelled to start jabbering about what they were about. He offered them space and allowed them the chance to shade in the blank areas at their own speed.

"Grandfather Brown?"

"You can call me Granddad, Akosua, you're one of my daughters now."

"Granddad, we're dealing with a recurring theme in our film, the presence of a certain kind of spirituality. We want to talk with you about that."

"Well, let's talk about what you want to know. If I know something about it, I'll tell you everything I know."

They settled back to think for a few seconds. What do we want to know? Akosua led off.

"Do you think that Africans, people of African descent, have a greater sense of spirituality than other people? And, if so, is that a factor in our people surviving chattel slavery?"

The old man pursed his lips thoughtfully, matched sips with his grandson. When he answered her question his voice had taken on a darker texture.

"Akosua, you know something? That's a question I started putting my mind on, about forty some years ago. I used to talk with my wife about it. I'll share the conclusions we reached: Number one, I don't want to dig a grave for myself and say that we have a monopoly on any kind of spirituality. No, I wouldn't want to say that. But I will say this – if there was ever a race of people in the world who were forced to call on reserves of ancestral strength, ancestral courage, to survive, we would have to be #1.

People sometimes forget that we had the Bubonic plagues, the Jewish Holocaust, genocide, slavery, Hiroshima, Nagasaki and colonialism put on us at the same time. Think about that.

Someday someone a whole lot wiser than me will have to explain the why-of-why we've had to go through all of this. But one thing we all know is that steel is tempered, strengthened by pressure.

If we were to take spirituality as a form of steel, then we can certainly say that we are definitely a bunch of sharp swords."

They shared a smile and tipped their glasses against each other in agreement.

"Every where I look around the world and I see people of African descent, I see a certain kind of 'Ancestor Strength' that's being used to help solve their daily problems.

We seem to take slightly different approaches to our ancestral strength, but it all seems to come down to the same thing in the end. We've had to go deeper than a lot of folks because of our historical circumstances. That's quite obvious.

But in answer to your question – was our spirituality a factor in our survival from chattel slavery? I'd have to say yes. When you do a broad sweep with your camera, what do you call it, Kojo?"

"A Pan."

"Hahhhahhah, that's the word. When you do a 'Pan' of the African spiritual scene, you can come away with some very interesting possibilities, psychologically and otherwise. I'll just give you a few examples of what I mean.

Remember Fredrick Douglass and that knock down-drag out fight he had with the so called 'slave breaker'? Remember that a 'bocor,' a roots man, had given ol' Frederick a root that would protect him and allow him to overcome his enemies. What was that all about?

Think about Harriet Tubman and those so called 'spells' she used to have. Think about Nat Turner, Denmark Vesey, Sojourner Truth, and folks like that, and how they were touched by the spirits. Think about Boukman, the priest up there in the mountains of Haiti, the one who really kicked the revolution off.

Toussaint L'Overture may have carried it on but Boukman kicked it off. Think about Zumbi in Brazil and the quilombo of Palmares. All of these things and so many more that nobody could count 'em, tell me we hooked into something quite deep, a loonng time ago."

"What about White people, Granddad, where do we put them on the spirit scale?"

"Much as I hate to say it, daughter, I'd have to say way down, way down, if we used an African scale to weigh 'em. Sometimes I think that the White race got up on the wrong side of the bed one morning, and blamed everybody else for it.

Now don't get me wrong, there are individuals, have always been individuals who could measure up, spiritually I don't have to name names, they know who they are, but on the whole, no go. I see that as the reason why so many young Whites go skipping off into Eastern religions, to African religions, to obscure little islands in search of something that their ancestors didn't give them, maybe couldn't give them.

How would you feel praying to a great great grandfather who had been a brutal slave trader, a serial rapist, a family destroyer, a torturer, a killer, a mad man? I think you would be on pretty bad terms with ancestors like that. Now, your question has to be, how did it happen? How do you wind up with a rogue's gallery of people for ancestors?"

"Granddad, you stole the question right off the tip of my tongue."

"That's as much of a mystery as the reason why we're so often held the dirty end of the stick in modern times. As liberal as we all try to be in our study of the White psyche, we inevitably come to the conclusion that you're dealing with a lot of dis-eased minds, warped mentalities. There's a folk tale that says that the 'It' of the universe deposited growth matter on this planet. The Black growth grew naturally, the Yellow, Brown grew naturally, but the White growth had something happen to it.

Remember now, this is just a myth, but it goes on to identify some of the terrible traits we find in Whites; their rapaciousness, greed, lack of sensitivity, self control, concern for Nature, need to fight all the time, racism, traits that came out of their growth and have been kept alive for centuries."

They were completely silent for a few thoughtful moments.

"I think about the White people I went to school with, there was always something I just couldn't understand about their mindsets, you know what I mean?"

Grandfather Brown took a sip of his drink and smiled at Akosua's comment.

"Yes, I know what you mean, daughter. If you've had a problem trying to figure out where they were coming from, just think about the job that our ancestors had, not even knowing his language, let alone where his head was.

I think that's one of the big reasons why we pray to those super human beings who had to come to grips with this weirdo every day of their lives, and deal with him, their lives depended on how well they 'negotiated.'"

Grandfather Brown's tone was jocular, but the undercurrent was serious.

"Any objections to continuing this while we try to polish off a few pounds of this ton of food these women brought over here."

·   ℰℭ   ·

CHAPTER 13

"Akoś, you awake?"

"Yeah, I'm awake but I don't feel like going with you this morning. I think I'm the victim of something called 'morning sickness.'"

"Can I do anything for you?"

"Yes, go do your exercises so that you'll be able to teach the baby how to do Capoeira."

"I love you, Akoś."

"I love you too, Kojo."

Forty-five minutes later, his playground workout done, he loped up their Echo Park street feeling loose, ready for whatever the day had in store for him.

"Sheila Buttram called, wants to talk with you."

They fell into each other's arms, laughing at the absurdity of it all. If you were bold enough to tell them to kiss your ass, they would pursue you. If you kissed their asses, they would abuse you.

"So, now what do we have? Dryson wants in, now Buttram, they must smell blood."

"Or money; a damned good script is about to be filmed."

They reviewed the structure of the shoot. Kojo had chosen two top flight assistant directors, Ed Burn's and Mac Weaver to be his "wing men."

"I'll be handling the main thrust of the piece while they're doing the peripheral stuff."

"Sounds good to me. That was some heavy drama Granddad laid on us last night, huh?"

"You're used to it, he blows me away."

"Really. Well, it's time for the producer-writer-director to charge off to the office. Thelma and the new girl have been gathering up extras since last week. I need to take a look at that. We also have to get some definites on the trucks, the catering …"

"Kojo, you're running late."

"Aren't you going?"

"Not today, let's say the pregnant woman took a day off."

"You o.k.?"

"Yes, love, just pregnant that's all."

"Well, call me if you need anything."

·   ℰᏜℛ   ·

From the first day's shooting in December, Kojo felt that he was on a plateau of ecstasy. Akosua came back strong after a week of "morning sickness." Each element of the production team was functioning at maximum efficiency. They "gorilla-ed" their way around, dropping off cameras and actors on a corner to do something creative and exciting before permits were requested and acquired.

"I learned how to do some of this stuff from Oscar Michaux, one of our cinematic godfathers."

The actors and actresses, all virtually unknown, but immensely talented, the extras, got into the groove. Once the premise was explained to them, a very un-Hollywood-like thing, they got deeply enough into it to make suggestions, some of them constructive.

Trick bags were opened and goodies sprung forth: the African village-community in South Carolina. Mac Weaver went and shot, using a documentary style. It was happening. Kojo's Our Production Company was shooting a film entitled "My Grandfather's Eyes."

The moguls had re-connected…

"Now look, Kojo, let's not be difficult about this, I wanna help put your movie out there. You know what I'm sayin'?"

"I know you do, Charley, I know you do."

Because you think that we've connected with a nerve that you didn't know anything about. And there's gold in them than theaters.

They were constantly being pleasantly surprised.

"Ah yes, Ah-ko-su, this is your mother, have you forgotten?"

"Oh, Mother, I'm so sorry. You sounded like someone else. And we've been so busy."

"I understand ..."

"Well, what can I do for you? How's Father?"

"Your Father is well and reading the Sunday newspaper from front to back, as usual, but that's neither here nor there ... I think I may have some good news for you."

A half hour later Akosua floated, rather awkwardly, from her workshop space to Kojo's space, furiously juggling scenes and ideas, to the rear of their house.

"Kojo! Kojo? Can you stop for a moment?"

"Akoś, what's wrong, sweetheart?! Is it time?!"

"No, not yet, Mr. Producer, I've got a lil' while to go yet."

"You had me lil' shook up there for a second."

"My mother just shook me up."

"Your Mother? What's her problem?"

"No problem, none at all. The lady has put us in a position to get a few hundred thousands more for 'Grandfather.'"

"What?!"

"You heard me. Seems that a number of the sisters who are married to ONE HUNDRED BLACK MEN felt that they should get into a matching funds number; prompted by my Mother, of course."

"Of course, of course ..."

"So, there it is. She wants you to contact this lady, set up a meeting and pitch! Mother is telling me that the fix is on, it's just purely a matter of going through the forms."

"Well, I'll be damned!"

"That's what I said!"

"Akoś, were going to have to do something real nice for your Mother."

"Kojo, we are doing something nice," she said, patting her "Georgia Ham" rounded belly. "I'm off for a little afternoon siesta, per the naturistic doctor's suggestions; wanna join me?"

"In a little while, I have a few things to straighten out, and the news you've given me has re-charged my batteries."

She sprinkled a wave of her fingers and waddled away to their bedroom. Kojo sat at his desk for a few minutes, discovered that his work energy was temporarily shot, decided to sit under the Campari umbrella in the backyard with a goblet of San Antonio Red.

Los Angeles sprawled beyond the borders of his view. It was

December, winter time, and the air was clean enough to breath. Really weird that people only think of coming out here in the summer when the place is suffocating from the smog.

He leaned back in his chair, umbrella shaded, feeling full of himself. It's happening; my dream is becoming a reality. When it gets to the point where Akosua's Mother starts kicking in, it can't get any better than that.

He glanced at the green and black coil; about ten yards to his left, looked away and then back at the coil. A snake. The coil wasn't moving, the snake's split tongue flicked in and out, but the body was motionless.

Kojo sipped his wine, stared at the thick coils, black bottom, green top. He made a quick mental review of all the zoos his parents had taken him to, the herpetology books, trying to place the snake's color pattern and head shape.

Black and green, what's that? He felt a chilled fascination at the sight of the snake, smothered in centuries of ignorance, fear and myth. He glanced away from the snake to sip his wine and when he looked again the snake seemed to be closer. Was it moving? Is it closer?

Kojo made two quick decisions; if it comes closer I'll throw my glass at it. If it stays where it is I won't bother it, snakes have a right to live too.

The raspy sound of a voice that seemed to come from nowhere froze his blood and made the hair stand up on the back of his head. The only time he could remember having that terrifying feeling was when he saw "Psycho," Alfred Hitchcock's monster thriller – when Anthony Perkins slashed Janet Leigh in the shower with a butcher knife.

"Feed me," the raspy voice said.

Kojo gripped the arms of his chair. O my God, no, this couldn't be the visitor that Asiafo spoke of, this is a snake.

"Feed you what?" He asked, his voice trembling.

"A large rat."

Kojo placed his glass on the table, edged up from his seat, being careful to keep the table between himself and the snake.

"When?"

"Tonight, here," the snake whispered in his raspy baritone and slithered away. Kojo couldn't control his trembling, the sudden film of perspiration that coated his face. He looked around in all directions.

People will think I'm out of my mind, out here talking to a snake.

No, I couldn't've been talking to a snake, snakes can't talk. A large rat. He wants a large rat, that's what snakes eat, rats. The trembling gradually eased as Kojo began to reason with himself. It wasn't a mirage, it wasn't somebody doing ventriloquism, it was real.

A "visitor." I'm supposed to feed a visitor. He didn't say anything about the form of the visitor or the kind of visitor. He thought back to the ragged crazy looking man in the park.

I'm supposed to feed a visitor four times a year, that's the deal. But for how long? I should've read the small print.

A rat. Where can I find a large rat? The Echo Park Pet Shop. Perfect Time. Akosua is napping. The Echo Park Pet Shop, six blocks away. He decided to jog it, rather run the risk of waking Akosua up by using the car.

He jogged easily, his mind tingling with ambivalent thoughts. This can't be real; I can't be running down the street to buy a snake's dinner. The thought stunned him to a shuffling walk. Asiafo has sent me a snake to feed. He revved himself back up to a jog. What will happen if I don't feed the stranger, the snake?

"Yessir, may I help you?"

"I want to buy a large rat."

Kojo felt a sour taste well in his throat, thinking about what he was doing.

"This way, please."

The sales clerk led him into an off room.

"We keep them here so that the children won't come in and harm them. Now then, what did you have in mind?"

Kojo managed to keep his repugnance of rats from showing. White rats with pink eyes, pinto rats, black and gray rats, rats.

"I'll take that large one over there."

"Good choice. Rats are very intelligent, you know?"

"Yes, I know."

Should I kill the damned thing? The thought jarred him. The rat was going to be alive, let the snake kill it. He paid, placed the rat in a large shopping bag and started jogging back home. I hope Akosua isn't awake; I'd have helluva time trying to explain this rat.

· ℰℭ ·

CHAPTER 14

He tiptoed through the house, peeked into the bedroom. Good. Still sleeping. He went to the kitchen, cut a length of string from a ball of twine and tied a noose around the rat's left rear leg. The large gray rat, genetically domesticated, sniffed at the string tied to his leg.

Kojo found a short stick in the yard, staked it in the place where he saw the snake. The rat, tied to the stake, scurried around, obviously looking for food.

So, the condemned rat is hungry, huh? He hurried inside to get a crust of bread and a dish of water. What the hell …

He paused to gulp a glass of wine before slicing the bread, feeling a little shaky, disoriented. What the hell am I doing? If I don't do this I'll cut off my flow … If I don't do this I'll cut off my flow. He stood at the top of the porch steps, horrified, and repulsed at the sight of the rat being swallowed head first by the snake. God, what an ugly way to eat. He backed up, fascinated, feeling as though he wanted to vomit.

It was on; the visitor coming to visit him was a snake and he was feeding it. He threw the bread into the trash, poured the water into the kitchen sink and sat at the kitchen table thinking about the scene in the backyard.

I can't tell Akosua about this, she'd never understand. The phone rang – he heard Akosua answer it – "Kojo, it's for you."

Well, that's enough of that, time to get back to work.

Later that evening, after an afternoon of phone calls and paper work, he strolled out into the backyard.

He picked up the string that was still wound around the stick. The other end of the string that he had tied into a noose to go around the rat's leg had been untied. How does a snake untie a noose from a rat's leg? The mystery puzzled him. In addition, he was beginning to feel a secret guilt. *What if I told Akosua that I married her because it was part of a deal that I made with a man in the forest?*

How could I tell these intelligent people I'm working with that it's all happening because of a deal I made with Asiafo? Is it really happening because of the deal I agreed to?

He stared at the distant stars lights flashing and thought of rebelling against the deal, and quickly shelved it. *How can I rebel against something that's paying off like this? But what is paying off? Would it be happening anyway?* That was the thought that nagged him. *If I had come back from Ghana and jumped on the stick the way I did, maybe it would be happening just the way it's happening. Maybe.*

The last month of the year found them blazing away, creatively.

"It's like a pure distillation, Kojo, like a pure distillation."

"Funny that you would see it that way, I think of it like having a baby."

"Without any morning sickness, I hope."

• ₮℔ •

Once again the snake came. Kojo was doing his morning workout in the Echo Park District playground. He was doing a handstand against the trunk of a tree when he spied the familiar black and green coil. He came down from his handstand and attempted to ignore the snake.

"Feed me," the snake spoke in the now familiar raspy voice that grated against Kojo's nerves, made the hair on the back of his neck stiffen. He looked around the area for a rock or a stick to throw at the snake, but thought better of it.

"I already fed you!" he ground the words out, angry with himself and the gruesome situation.

"Feed me!" The snake's raspy voice demanded.

"Feed you what? Where?"

"A rabbit, in the yard," the snake answered and slithered away. He stared at the disappearing coil of green and black with angry tears in his eyes.

"So, I'm supposed to feed a damned visitor four times a year, right?!

For how many years?! And you're no visitor, you're a damned snake and I've seen you before! You're not a visitor!"

Kojo stopped ranting when he saw the shocked, curious faces of two mothers who had brought their toddlers to the play area, fifty yards to his left.

Bet they think I'm just another nut case on the loose. Who knows? Maybe I am. A fuckin' rabbit.

· ℘ℭ ·

He worked on a distribution deal with the Charley Bascom Company.

"It was either gonna be him or one of the others. They're all the same. The thing about Charley is that he's a bigger asshole than most, and that's what we need."

Busy, busy, busy. The office in the loft seemed smaller with the influx of workers. The phones were ringing constantly.

"Kojo, you think we could ask the sister to back off from the p.r. pistol for a minute?"

"Not likely, she has booked for something or other until you go to the hospital."

A rabbit in the backyard, back to the pet store.

"Welcome, Mr. ...?"

"Jones."

"Well, Mr. Jones, we have the white bunnies here, great for the kids, and the great Belgian hares over here."

"I'll take the bunny."

Where in the hell can I hide a rabbit? The thought of seeing the snake eat a rabbit made him feel nauseous.

Where can I hide a rabbit? He sat in his car, trying to figure out an angle. If I take it to a friend's house, they'll be sure to ask Akosua, one day, what happened to the rabbit?

He drove aimlessly to the ocean. 7 p.m. He left the rabbit on the floor of the passenger's side with a half dozen carrots, a bowl of water, and strolled along the beach.

It was a rare short day, but they had worked 'til midnight, the night before. Damn, what a helluva crew I have. They're willing to do it until it's done right, that's the only way.

The clear December ocean air was brisk, caused him to dig his hands deep into his pockets. How do I do this? Keep the rabbit in the car until Akoś goes to sleep? What? The absurdity of the dilemma caused him to laugh aloud. What kind of madness is this?

He turned away from the ocean to walk back to his car, the problem still unresolved. He opened the door and looked at the rabbit on the floor, content, crunching on a carrot, little black pellets scattered about.

Dammit! Rabbit crap. Now I'll have to get the car vacuumed.

· ℰℭ ·

All of the worrying was wasted. Akosua called his cell to tell him that she was at her parents.

"Mother is holding me captive, Kojo. She's determined to feed me some of Dolores's excellent Mexican food and have me spend the night in my old room. Think you'll be able to make it through the night without me?"

"Of course, sweetheart, don't sweat it."

"See you in the morning."

"Enjoy yourself, give 'em a big hug for me."

"With this belly in front of me – everything I do is big."

"Hahh hah hhah – see you in the morning."

Kojo staked the rabbit and sat on the porch steps to watch him for a half hour. He went inside and, came back out, an hour later, cradling a cup of coffee.

The rabbit was gone. He searched the perimeters of the yard to make certain he hadn't simply escaped. No, he hadn't escaped. The string attached to the noose had been untied. The rabbit had been taken, eaten.

· ℰℭ ·

Following Sister Muhammad's p.r. blitzkrieg, they were interviewed. And interviewed, by magazines, bi-weekly newspapers, tabloids, "show biz sheets," radio.

"Yes, some people will look at the film as though it were some sort of documentary, but that's the risk one has to run whenever one does anything new and unique."

"Can you give your listeners some idea of the basic story line of your film?"

"Actually there are three interwoven stories, and they are viewed through the yes of a wise old man."

"You're listening to 'Family Ties' KPPK, 90.7 on your radio dial and our guest this morning is brother Kojo Bediako Brown, the brilliant co-writer-director-producer of 'My Grandfather's Eyes,' a film that will be released sometime this summer.

This is Rick Sands of 'Family Ties' and we invite your questions for our guest, Kojo Bediako Brown. Ahhah! I see the red light! Go ahead, caller, you have a question for Brother Brown? State your name please."

"Yes, my name is Kwame Sekou Toure the Second and I want to ask the brother if the film he's just spoke about is going to be a Negrocentric thang or a Black thang?"

"Brother Brown, how would you respond to that?"

"I'd simply like to say that the film is an African-American statement, not either one of those other thangs."

Rick Sands winked at him. Amazing how parochial some of the brothers can be, at times.

"Next caller, please state your name."

"Uhh, yes, my name is Latisha Khalidifia and I'm calling to congratulate the brother and the sister for pulling together the way they've done. You know, far too often we have the sad story of the brother who has made it, turning to the White woman as though she represented the pinnacle of some kind of achievement.

I've just finished reading a wonderful story on Brother Brown and Sister Akosua in 'African-American Life,' discussing the sister's literary accomplishments and the success the brother has been having.

I think that, we as a people, must address ourselves to the idea of independent entrepreneurial enterprises, no matter it be wholesale goods, films, or whatever ..."

"Uhh, Sister Latisha, we appreciate your observations, but I'm afraid we must move on to the next caller. Caller? Your name please?"

"Black Jack Knife. My question to the brother is – where do you stand on the no snitch rule?"

Rick Sands, the radio talk show host, rolled his eyes skyward and threw up his hands. Kojo didn't hesitate.

"Let me answer you like this, Brother Knife. As you know, the 'no snitch' rule was strongly advocated during the Bush baby regime, during the business with 'Scooter' Libby, Karl Rowe, Cheney and the rest.

So, in many ways, it was just a code of ethics that slipped right down from the White House to the ghetto.

Personally I don't endorse the 'no snitch' rule; I think it forces our community into a jailhouse ethical mode, a kind of civilian lockdown.

I don't think we're behaving in a reasonable way when we allow bad policemen and the most negative elements in our community to determine what our behavior should be.

Let me put it another way – I would gladly endorse a 'no snitch' initiative if all of the African-American mothers and fathers who have had their children murdered, or lost in some other violent way, were able to have their children returned from the dead."

Rick Sands gave him double thumbs up.

"Uhh, yeah, I hear what you're sayin', my brother, but … uhh …"

"Thank you for your comment. Next caller?"

From the radio station to the office for a meeting with his assistant directors, a quick dozen phone calls to be made/returned. Suddenly the late nights that frequently saw them yawning at dawn were coming to an end.

The middle section of 'Grandfather' had seemed glacial, but they had finally worked past that and the ending was starting to appear at the bottom of a deep well. Akosua had retreated to the office setting, doing re-writes of troublesome sections of the script.

"I can be more useful here; you don't need a pregnant woman on the set."

So far so good. They had pulled the budget belt as tight as it would go, no one had goofed off and the results were almost ready for the editing room.

Kojo left the office-loft feeling euphoric. It's all happening; my vision is becoming a reality. My wife is going to have a beautiful baby and we're going to have a great, profitable film. He made an impulsive stop at Trader Joes in Echo Park.

Be a nice thing to take a good bottle of white wine home. Wonder that Akoś is doing for dinner?

· ଚୀ ଓଃ ·

CHAPTER 15

"Akoś, put it all on hold for an hour, the phones, all of it, we're going to have dinner, sip some wine and lap up the sunset."

"I'm with you all the way, except the vino."

Kojo studied his wife's movements as she waddled out to their table in the yard. Her shape has changed but she's still graceful, in an awkward sort of way. It won't be long now. How many months? Six months? It won't be long now.

"Linguine and clams? How did you know I wanted pasta?"

"I know my man," she answered and gave him a lascivious wink. Linguine and clams, garlic bread, No Business Talk, a good French vin ordinaire.

The lush colors of Fellini's "Roma," the art of Marcello Mastroanni, Giancarlo Giannini, Sophia Loren, Vitorio de Sica, Victor Storaro … flowed through his senses as the flavors of the food mingled in his mouth.

"Akoś, if you weren't an African-American woman, you'd be the best Italian cook in California."

"I don't see any contradiction there."

They exchanged loving smiles. "Bread, love and chocolate." "Dark Eyes." "La Dolce Vita." "Rimini." "Bitter Rice." "Mambo." Wonder what happened to Silvana Mangano? That's what I'd like to do, an African-American-Italian film. Or an African-American-Ghanaian film. Or maybe an African-American-Brazilian film.

"What's the secret little smile about, sweetheart?"

"Oh, I was just thinking about all of the good things happening to us."

Akosua circled the table to drape her arms around his neck.

"Kojo, I love you so much."

He led her around the chair to sit in his lap.

"I'm too heavy."

"No, you're just right."

They had each other. He placed his hand on her stomach. Such a large, tight ball. Akosua nuzzled her nose into his neck. Kojo, looking over her shoulder into the border of flowers, shivered when he spotted the green and black, slithering blur of the snake. For a moment he felt a deep sense of revulsion about the dirty deal he had going on, in order to claim fame and fortune.

I can't lie to myself about it, not after feeding this damn thing twice already, a rat and a rabbit.

"Kojo, I'm going to take a shower and a little nap, you want to join me?"

"Just as soon as I polish off this glass of Vouray."

She planted a solidly erotic kiss on his lips and strolled into the house, winking at him over her left shoulder.

Just look at this woman, six months pregnant and she's sexy as she can be.

The Snake. The Snake. He stared at the flower under bush. I <u>did</u> see it. What the hell is it hanging around for? He sipped his wine and frowned at the setting sun.

·   ℘℃℞   ·

Exactly one month later, into the New Year, while doing his early morning Capoeira workout, the snake slithered casually into view. Kojo froze in place. Now what?

"A small pig."

Was the snake actually speaking or were the sounds coming from his forked tongue by some sort of vibration?

"What?"

"A small pig."

"No! No! I'm not going to feed you again."

The snake slithered away, leaving Kojo in place, trembling, sweating, and the workout forgotten. Why me? Damn!

He draped a towel around his neck and started the uphill jog home. I've already fed the damned thing four times – a rat, a rabbit. Another rat, a baby chicken.

But that was last year, a small voice whispered at the back of his head. Last year, this is a New Year. The New Year meant a few crucial scenes for "Grandfather's Eyes" had to be re-shot, post production work started, arguments happening with Charley Bascom about the final cut.

"Kojo, c'mon man, you've got to admit it's a pretty rare situation we have here, where the guy whose responsible for making the deal of the decade, doesn't <u>really</u> know what the fuckin' movie is about, really, and has no say so about the final cut. This is some crazy shit; you know what I'm sayin'?"

"I asked you to trust me."

"Yeahhh, yeah, but I still think I oughta have a little more say so about the product."

"It's not a product, Charley, remember that, it's a film."

"Yeah, sure, Kojo, didn't mean to piss you off."

· ℠ ·

The music, a really important element, was going straight up, with Juna "the genius composer" and the Earth One musical group.

Yes, it's all coming together, why should I cater to the whims of a damned snake? I'd have to be out of my cotton pickin' mind to do some shit like that.

Time to shower; shave, off to Our Production Company.

"Kojo, Jackie has me scheduled to speak to a women's group this afternoon, she thinks my pregnant tummy will have a positive effect …"

"Smart lady."

"And then I have this literary number to do this evening."

"Hey, don't stress yourself out."

"Nothing like that, no stress marks here. She's made limo arrangements for me, the whole bit."

"Good, I'm glad she decided to focus on your side of the screen for awhile, she was wearing me out."

"She'll get back to you next week, have no fear."

"Does the woman ever sleep?"

"Only when she doesn't have anything else to do."

Agreements made, contracts to read, an appointment with the lawyers, Green Shafton and Rasch, a visit to the hospital to cheer up Thelma Nagata, the super office manager who was recovering from a slight case of fatigue.

Editing, a half zillion things to do. He was backing out of the driveway with all of it on his mind and almost rolled over the three year old.

The mother's scream froze his foot on the brakes. He looked in the rear view mirror at the woman who snatched her baby up into her arms as she scurried across the driveway. They exchanged mean eyed looks.

You almost ran over my baby ... you beast!

You shouldn't let your baby run around driveways, idiot!

He felt unnerved by the experience. God, how would you feel, running over a baby?

The thought caused him to become more cautious at stop signs, drive a little slower through the city streets. He came off the freeway at Slauson Avenue and pulled over immediately to let the screaming fire truck pass. Always something burning in South Los Angeles.

He was surprised to see the truck make a blistering right turn a few streets ahead of him, his street.

He accelerated. What the hell is this?! He turned the corner to find it blocked off, fire trucks and police cars in his way. He backed up, whipped around to the next street for a parking space and ran back to the Our Production Company office-loft.

A crowd of the curious blocked his way.

"Let me through here, I'm the owner."

"Sorry, pal, doesn't matter who you are, you can't get through here."

"Let him through, officer," one of the firemen called out to the overzealous policeman.

"You say you're the owner?"

"Yes, I am – what happened?"

The fireman strolled to the side of the smoking building with him. The neighborhood folks, excitement over, melted away.

"Well, number one, the damage isn't all that great, it's more a case of smoke than fire, luckily."

"Inside, any damage there?"

"Most of the fire happened here, in the rear, looks like an electrical short circuit fire, I'd say, off hand. But we haven't checked the premises closely."

Kojo took a deep breath and released a sigh of relief to find the office and office equipment intact, except for a few large puddles of water.

"You were fortunate that someone spotted the smoke right away and called in."

"Yeah, I really appreciate that."

Efficiently, the firemen cleared the space, rolled up their hoses and cleared out.

"Uh, Mr.?"

"Kojo Bediako Brown."

"Uhh, Mr. Brown, your bill will be sent next month, thanks for your cooperation."

"Yeah, thank you."

A fire caused by an electrical short circuit. He strolled through the space, consciously trying to block certain thoughts from his mind.

Almost ran over a baby. Fire in the office. No, no connection, all just pure coincidences. He sprawled on one of the office sofas, wishing he had someone to talk with.

What's wrong with me? I have hundreds of people to talk with. He fished his cell phone out and called his parents.

"What're we doing? Just sitting here, twiddling our middle aged thumbs, and waiting for you, Akosua and our grandchild-to-be to pay as a visit."

"Akosua is working on something, but I'll be there in fifteen minutes."

"C'mon!"

· ഇൟ ·

"Dad, you were into herpetology at one point, weren't you?"

"Yeah, you know how it is when you own a bookstore; you'll have things grab you for periods of time. Your mother was one of the hippest hypnotists in the country at one time. Nzingha, remember your hypnotic period?"

117

"Make fun if you want to. If I had had more time I probably could've hypnotized you, even."

"Hah! That would be the day!"

Kojo laughed with his parents, the pressures forgotten for the moment. *I'm going to have to deal with the burned up office and all the rest in a little while, but I'll chill for the moment.*

"Kojo, you staying for lunch?"

"By all means."

"Well, let me go whip something together."

"Make it hypnotic."

She spanked her husband's shoulder playfully on the way to the kitchen. *Mom and Dad. I hope me and Akosua are like you two when we mellow out.*

"Now, what's this thing about the snakes?"

"Uhh, well, we're dealing with a couple scenes that concern snakes."

"So, what do you want to know, I've got a few books around here …"

Kojo toyed with the idea of beating around the bush. *No, not with Dad.*

"How often do snakes eat?"

His father gave him a curious look.

"Well, as you know, a lot depends on the size of the snake, the type of snake and the size of the meal. A fair sized anaconda can swallow a monkey and not have to eat again for three-four months."

"So, theoretically, a certain kind of snake of a certain size would only have to eat, maybe four times a year?"

"Right. There's no evidence of greed in snakes, unlike some other species of beings."

Kojo gave his father an attentive look, his signal that he wanted to know more.

"The snake is a very interesting figure in everybody's mythology. We have the Christian thing with the evil snake in the Garden of Eden, of course, and a whole bunch of other cultures have feared and worshipped the snake. I guess it has something to do with their appearance and the way they move.

Did you ever see the documentary of a group of people in Burma, or whatever it's called these days, who make a pilgrimage once a year to a cave where a giant white cobra lives, thing must be at least eight feet long, huge."

"White?"

"White and huge. Anyway, in the documentary a woman was designated to lure the snake out of the cave and kiss it on the head three times. The reason for doing it is to ensure a successful harvest.

Tiny woman, making moves like the snake herself, feints back and forth at the mouth of the cave. The snake lunges out at her. Huge and thick barreled. The snake strikes at the woman and she dodges, the snake strikes, she side steps.

It was like watching a Balinese temple dance. After a few attempts to strike her, they settle into a calm state. The snake, who was holding himself higher than her, lowers his head and she makes the first kiss."

"I never saw this, I'm sure I would've remembered it if I had."

"I'm sure. The second she kisses the snake's head he is aroused and strikes at her. Little sister could move, I'm telling you. Three times she did it, three times. I thought maybe it was trick photography or something.

But no, this was the real deal. After she performed the last kiss she backed off and the snake slid back into the cave. It looked like it had been choreographed.

When they did the close up of the woman you could see venom all over the front of her clothes. Maybe it was a giant species of spitting cobra, I don't know.

Yeahh, that was a helluva piece of film. I think I saw it at one of those herpetology sessions I used to go to, years ago.

Incredible thing about the snake, it's always been considered an evil messenger, even by people who worshipped it, the ancient Egyptians, for example.

I can't think of any record anywhere that offers us a picture of a 'good snake'."

Kojo felt a chill grip the back of his neck.

"But snakes do a lot of good, they eat rats …"

"Right, they stabilize the balance that makes Nature work as well as it does. But once we take the creature out of the desert and the fields, he becomes an evil demon, in league with wicked spirits, stuff like that."

"How do you feel about that, Dad, that the snake is a messenger of evil and all that?"

"Well, I have to feel that there must be a bit of fire in some of that smoke. I mean, let's face it, if people all over the planet have come out with negative stuff about the serpent they must know something. Or they've found out something.

I put a special trust in the so called 'primitive' people, they're the ones living closest to the snake, and they know him. And they have mythologies that stress his evil side as well."

"If you gentlemen can put your gruesome snake talk aside we can have lunch. Kojo, would you like a glass of wine?"

· ℅Ↄ☊ ·

He drove home, belly filled with Mom's old fashioned tuna fish salad, lettuce 'n tomato on sour dough rye, bolstered by a couple glasses of dry white wine. Things couldn't be too bad if they can be repaired. Yeah, that's what they said.

"You were lucky someone called the fire department right away."

"You can say that again."

What the hell, we got some repairs to do. Thank goodness nothing was burned. It could have been worse.

· ℅Ↄ☊ ·

CHAPTER 16

The sight of Akosua sprawled on the front room sofa, a big white bandage on her forehead, almost sent him in to shock.

"O my God! Akoś, what happened?"

"Just a clumsy move, that's all. I was coming in from the backyard and tripped up the steps. The problem is this balloon in front of me, I couldn't see the steps. No big thing, a little gash on the forehead, a warning to be a little more careful."

Kojo folded her into his arms.

"Be careful, sweetheart, please. We don't want anything to happen to you."

I almost ran over a baby. We had a fire in the office. My wife stumbles up the steps and gashes her head. O.k., Snake-Asiafo, you win.

· &ↄↄ ·

He went for his workout a half hour earlier, feeling antsy. The workout was half hearted; he had his mind on half a dozen other things. How in the hell do I communicate with this damned thing, to tell it that I surrender? You want a fuckin' pig, you got it.

He finished his workout, draped a towel around his neck and sat at the base of a tree, waiting.

What if the damned thing is angry with me? What if it doesn't come back? How can I square myself?

After a half hour of anxious waiting he reluctantly decided to pack it in for the day. He looked over his shoulder at the last place he had seen the snake.

Now what? The rest of the day was spent dealing with one small catastrophe after another.

"Kojo! The computers are down, crashed!"

"Be cool, Thelma. Have you called our computer repair guy?"

"He's here now; he says we might be out of business until tomorrow."

"Then tomorrow it'll be."

He replaced the phone it is cradle, tilted his chair back, tented his fingers under his chin and frowned.

I goofed. I should have done what I was asked to do. A small pig. What the hell!

Later that day, after a full day in the editing room and a light dinner of curried red snapper, Kojo sprawled in his backyard chair.

"Kojo, I have some reading to do, you want anything?"

"Nawww, I got a glass of San Antonio Red, that's about all I need for the moment. Don't worry about the dishes I'll take them in. Hey, looks like that cut on your forehead is healing pretty well."

"I'm using aloe vera, miracle stuff for cuts, burns, things like that."

He watched her go into the house, feeling melancholy, blue. He and Ed Burns had carefully studied crucial footage and discovered a number of sophomoric mistakes.

"Damn! How did the mike shadow get in there?" One thing after another. He sat up slightly as the snake slithered across his peripheral line of vision. And sat up rigidly as the snake gathered itself into a tight coil, ten yards in front of him. He seemed to be waiting, his forked tongue flicking in and out of his mouth.

Kojo slugged half of his wine down, tried to avoid looking at the coiled creature for a minute and then, in an irritated tone of voice – "Where, what time?"

"Here, tomorrow, midnight."

Kojo was trembling as he watched the snake curl away. He remained in place, gritting his teeth. Damn! Where am I supposed to find a baby pig?

· ℘Ↄ ·

The clerk at the pet store was willing, but unable to handle the problem on such short order.

"Sorry, Mr. Jones, it would take at least three-five weeks for our supplier to ship ..."

"You have any idea where I can get one? It's my daughter's birthday and we promised her a small pig. This is sort of an emergency."

"Give me a couple minutes to make a call or two; I think I can help you."

He slipped the clerk a folded twenty dollar bill. There was nothing like a little money to grease the skids. The clerk returned fifteen minutes later.

"Mr. Jones, you may be in luck. I called a friend of a friend, you know what I mean?"

"I do know what you mean."

"My friend tells me that he has three baby pigs left, I asked him to save you one, that you would be at his place within the hour."

"I'm on my way – name and address?"

"Mr. Nguyen, 231 Alpine Street, Chinatown."

Chinatown. It took him fifteen minutes to get there and forty-five minutes to find Mr. Nguyen's small pet shop behind several other shops. His place was almost hidden.

The sign said "Nguyen Pets" in English, God only knows what it said in Vietnamese. Quite a few shops in Chinatown with Vietnamese owners, a legacy of the ethnic cleansing that the Vietnamese communist's programs used to rid Vietnam of the Vietnamese of Chinese descent.

Mr. Nguyen nodded pleasantly as I entered, obviously aware of Who I was and why I was there. I browsed the shop while he dealt with a couple who were looking for a chubby puppy. I gathered that from the way they were feeling the rib cages of the dogs they were being shown.

Were they looking for a pet, or for something to barbecue? Hmmm ... A number of snakes in glass cages.

Finally, after having sold them two of the fattest puppies in the store, he came to me.

"Ahhah, Mr. Jones – my friend in Echo Park call me, you want young pig?"

"Yessir, that's exactly what I want."

Likeable, charming guy, Mr. Nguyen, about sixty or seventy maybe, with a series of long hairs sprouting from his chin. He could have been an ol' fashioned Mandarin noble.

"You, come this way," he gestured for me to follow him.

I followed him to a small, squared off, dirt enclosure that looked like a patio. And right there in the middle were three of the cutest little pigs I'd even seen.

"You pick," he suggested, "only three."

I stood there, watching them play around with each other. They seemed more like puppies than pigs. They were comical, fun to watch. I'd never thought about a pig as being funny. And, of course, all kinds of lil' piggy stories came to mind. One Little Piggy, Two Little Piggy; the Three Little Pigs…

"You pick," Mr. Nguyen prompted me.

Randomly, I chose the one closest to me. I had half a mind to buy all three until Mr. Nguyen gave me the price for one.

"$500, I give this reduction because you are Mr. White's friend, regular customer he say."

$500 for a baby pig? What was I <u>not</u> understanding about this transaction?

"Mr. Nguyen, five hundred dollars for a baby pig?"

He gave me that vacant, indulgent smile that the hip always gives to the un-hip.

"Mr. Jones, these pot-bellied pigs. These special Vietnamese pigs. They are many times used for pets. They are more intelligent than dogs."

"Yeahh, but $500?"

"One never knows, your pig may grow up to become a genius."

"I wish that I had time to see that happen."

Mr. Nguyen cut me a strange look as he took my check and three pieces of ID on his Xerox machine.

"I know your daughter will enjoy this pig, it is called 'pot-bellied pig' in English."

"Does it speak Pig latin?"

"So sorry, sir, I not understand."

"No problem, Mr. Nguyen, and thank you very much."

I don't think I'd ever had so many people smile at me as I trotted to my car with this Vietnamese pot-bellied pig under my arm. So, now, I have my pig. What to do with it until tomorrow night?

I couldn't think of one single friend that I could think of who would be open to the idea of baby sitting a pig.

"Uhh, 'scuse me, Mom, Dad, can I leave my pot-bellied Vietnamese pig with you 'til feeding time tomorrow night?"

The Pet Shop. This guy was becoming my partner in crime without even knowing it.

"Mr. White, I wonder if I could leave my birthday pig with you 'til tomorrow evening?"

"Of course, Mr. Jones, be glad to accommodate you. I see Mr. Nguyen has sold you one of his rare pot-bellied pigs, rare in this country. Wonder where he got it from?"

I slipped Mr. White another folded twenty.

"I'll pick my pig up before you close tomorrow evening. Anything to feed this little beast, he seems to be a bit snackish."

"O yes, they love oatmeal and apples, corn, veggies; very intelligent animals. Some tests show that they're much more intelligent than dogs."

"See you tomorrow afternoon, Mr. White."

· ಒಔ ·

The show was back on the road. The film, "My Grandfather's Eyes" was scheduled for a limited Spring-Summer release. Members of his staff called to discuss whatever they were involved with.

Jackie f. Muhammad, the p.r. person, had gone toe to toe with Charley Bascom and won by a split decision.

"Kojo, where in the world do these Neanderthal thinking White men come from? You know what this guy had in mind for our publicity posters? He wanted an Uncle Remus type figure with a little boy perched on his knee, kind of a take of on 'Song of the South.' Can you believe?!

We had to circumnavigate his madness to put things on the proper track. All praises due to Allah."

The law firm of Green, Shafton, Clarke and Rasch ran expert interference in negotiations concerning the money details between the filmmaker and the distributor.

"Mr. Brown, I think you'll be pleased to know that Mr. Bascom has finally accepted our terms. We'll have contracts for you to sign in the coming week."

Contracts, loose ends, endless details. And a small, pot-bellied pig to be staked in the backyard at midnight for the snake's consumption.

A helluva day, that's the official title he stuck on it.

"Uhh, Kojo, are you still with us here, brother?"

"Yeah, yeah, I'm with you…"

Telephone calls, meetings, minor league emergencies – "These people at the African-American Anti-defamation League want to meet with you on Monday, they've gotten the word from somebody that the N-word is going to be used a lot in your film."

"No, it's not period."

"Well, that's what you'll have to tell them. How about 10 a.m. on Monday?"

"O.k., 10 a.m. on Monday."

A helluva day. And finally it was over and he was racing to get to the Echo Park Pet Shop before it closed.

"Ahh, there you are, Mr. Jones – thought you had forgotten about your lil' porker here."

"Not on your life, not on your life."

"We've put a leash on Jonny boy for you."

"Jonny boy?"

"Hahh hah hah, that's what my wife called him the minute she saw him."

"Thanks for babysitting my pig for me."

"Not a problem, any time."

6 p.m. Six more hours before midnight. Akosua. The Almighty cell.

"Hey Sweetheart … how's it going?"

"Busy. Jackie gave me some homework to do. I'm re-writing some stuff to go on Our Production Company website."

"That makes two of us busy, I have to get together with Ed Burns and Mac Weaver to talk about some scenes that may have to be re-done. Don't wait up for me, o.k."

"I'll leave a snack on the bottom shelf of the fridge."

"And a glass of Red?"

"And a glass of Red. Love you, baby."

"Love you too, sweetheart."

Now what? He eased back into his car to stare into the bright little eyes of his pot-bellied pig.

"Bet you'd like a snack, wouldn't you?"

The pig nodded in agreement. He stopped at the nearest supermarket for milk, a large box of cold cereal and a cheap aluminum baking pan.

The pig nuzzled under his thigh when he got back in the car. Friendly little fellow.

"So, you know I got you some goodies for you, huh?"

Once again, the pig seemed to nod in agreement. He drove to Echo Park Lake, parked and led the pig out by his leash. Feeding the animal cereal and milk in the park, in the late afternoon, seemed to attract all kinds of people.

Children came to oooh and ahhh …

"Can I touch 'im, mister?"

"What's his name?"

"Uhh, Jonny Boy."

A couple Asians came over to question him about "Jonny Boy."

"Sir, this is a Vietnamese pot-bellied pig. Do you have others?"

"Uhh, no, this is the last of a litter."

"Are you going to bar-be-que it, or steam it?"

"I hadn't thought of doing either one."

After feeding "Jonny Boy," he sat on a park bench, staring at the water in the lake. The pig lay down under his bench.

Life is a bitch. Life is a bitch … the words kept stabbing him in the head. Life is a bitch …

He felt guilty about lying to Akosua. The whole business seemed to be compounding interest. First I lie to my wife, then I have to tell a lie to support that lie. He stared at the pig sprawled on his side under the bench. O well, a man has to do what a man has to do.

9:30 p.m. The park was deserted, time to leave before the bad guys or the police showed up. He scooped "Jonny" up in his arms, gently placed him on the floor of the passenger's side. Now what? Nothing to do but drive around 'til it was almost time.

He didn't feel at ease driving aimlessly in "El-A." After a certain hour they ought to roll up the sidewalks in this town. He knew he had to avoid the Black and Brown areas of the city, where the police presence was heavy and often oppressive.

And it definitely wasn't a good idea to drive around Beverly Hills or any of the other affluent, largely white sections. He thought about stopping on Crenshaw to have a couple beers, just to kill time, but common sense vetoed that notion.

That's all the police would need – a drunken Black man with a pot-bellied pig in his car. He decided to stay on the freeways, to mingle with the late traffic for a couple hours. For the first time since he had come to Los Angeles he actually welcomed the idea of being caught in a traffic jam.

10:45 p.m., he made a U-turn just above Malibu and kept within the speed limits all the way to Echo Park. He was in a slight panic, driving around the streets near his house.

I can't pull up in my driveway, it might wake Akosua up, if she's not already up, waiting for me. No place to park. Damn!

He was beginning to feel desperate when the parking space, two blocks south of his house, suddenly yawned open for him. 11:39 p.m. Have to be there at midnight.

Have to be there at midnight. He parked, grabbed the pig and trotted up the street. Now, the tricky part. The front porch light was on, but their bedroom light was off. Good. Looks like she has done the sensible thing and gone to bed, instead of waiting up for me.

He felt like a burglar, unlocking the high wooden gate of the driveway. A couple of the neighborhood dogs barked. He froze for a minute. What would Akosua think if she saw me sneaking into the backyard with a pig under my arm?

The thought almost caused him to laugh out loud. What if she called the police and they caught me out here? I can just see the headline now in the California section of the Los Angeles times – "Brilliant young African-American filmmaker arrested in his own backyard with a pot-bellied pig."

The clouds suddenly drifted away from the moon's face. He suddenly felt naked, exposed. He knelt to remove the leash from the pig's neck. Sorry 'bout this, lil, piggy.

Now, something to tie you up with. He was sweating, feeling anxious. Have to improvise. He pulled one of his shoe strings off, struggling a bit with the pig, which was beginning to squirm, to try to escape, noosed the string around the pig's left leg and tied him to the leg of their garden chair.

Have to remember to come out here for my shoe string in the morning. The pig tied in place; he stared down at the animal, feeling guilty, sorry, and very nervous. He backed away from the scene thinking – what if the snake doesn't come? How in the hell could I explain away a pot-bellied pig in the backyard? He sneaked back out of the driveway and jogged down the street to retrieve his car.

Akosua gave him a drowsy – "hi honey" – and turned on her side to continue dreaming. Kojo undressed, put on his pajama bottom, crawled quietly into bed and stared up at the face of a full moon, imagining the scene taking place in the backyard. The snake swallowing the pig. He was up at 6 a.m., pretending a toilet run. It took a glance through the backdoor window to see that the pig was gone. He took a deep breath, a sigh of relief. Going back upstairs, he paused. Maybe the damned thing broke free.

He made a quick trip into the backyard. The shoe string was tied to the chair and the other end, the noose that held the pig was untied. Once again the tried to puzzle that one out.

He prowled the perimeters of the yard, to make certain that the pig was gone, that he wasn't hiding anywhere. He was gone, sacrificed.

· ℘℧ ·

CHAPTER 17

Akosua checked the calendar next to his desk.

"Kojo, what date are we having the preview?"

"The 15th."

Charley Bascom had insisted on at least one preview.

"Kojo, c'mon! gimme a break f' God's sake! I'm the distribution guy of the decade, you're getting the lion's share of the percentages, you have to give me a preview, an idea of what's going to make or break us in 'Granddaddy's Eyes.'"

"'My Grandfather's Eyes,' Charley, that's the title – o.k.?"

"Sorry, Big Guy, no need to get testy about it."

They did ying-yang ying-yang about the location for the preview. Kojo wanted Leimert Park, the Magic Johnson Theatre Complex. Bascom wanted a "traditional Pasadena preview." Bascom won by reminding Kojo ...

"Kojo, Look, I think we can make book on your own people digging 'Eyes,' it's these other folks we have to think about. What kind of crossover audience is this thing likely to draw? You know what I'm sayin'?"

The preview audience was composed of industry professionals, invited guests and people who had heard the buzz and decided to sneak a peek at "My Grandfather's Eyes."

Charley Bascom's people were scattered strategically in the audience. Bascom wanted to make certain, beyond the opinion cards that he was made aware of unusual laugh spots, where sad angles intruded, what effect a basically African-American story would have on a primarily White audience.

The cast and crew of Our Production Company formed a tight core in the center of the theatre audience. They seemed to be saying, with their circle-the-wagons attitude, we did it, now come and get us.

For the first ten minutes Kojo felt like a man holding his breath under an iceberg. Akosua started his breathing back to normal by grasping his hand.

Yes, it was happening, they had put the far reaching vision of the old man's eyes on film. The ways he looked at the world became more than a peek through one pair of glasses; there were facets, sections that were African-American cubistic. They had created a work of art on film, without any artsy-craftsy pretensions, and the musical score that Juna and the Earth One Group played glued it together.

One hour and forty-five minutes later the film came to an end, technically; but it was obvious to all those present that the ending was really just the beginning, a strong point that Kojo wanted to make.

The audience, led by Our Production's people applauded long and hard. Charley Bascom gave Kojo two thumbs up, but most importantly, Grandfather Kwame Brown had a smile on his face.

· ℘ℭ ·

The word was out. A day later the trades were heralding a "latter day Spike Lee."

'They really bug me with this stuff. Why can't they accept Kojo Bediako Brown for who he is and Spike Lee for he was. Why must they always pigeon hole us?"

"You know why. But be cool, sweetheart, you don't want to angry up your amniotic fluid, we've only got a few more weeks to go, right?"

"About three, to be exact."

"So, be cool, let them say what they feel comfortable saying, we know what the real deal is."

Sunday afternoon in the Brown house. A dozen calls to deal with, more details to be ironed out. The business of the business couldn't be ignored.

"Kojo, Jackie wants to set up a press conference in Chicago for the opening there. Are you game?"

"That's next month. Sorry, too close to your time. This is a first for both of us and I'm determined to be on the scene when your 'opening' takes place."

More details.

"Juna called, she's having second thoughts about the last forty-two seconds of the music in the film."

"What kind of second thoughts?"

"They're not really second thoughts, she's just on an anxiety trip."

"Cool her out, I beg you."

"No problem."

"Did you read the Times review?"

"I glanced at it."

"Well, I don't want to burden you with the whole thing, comparing you with Buñuel, Cocteau, Gordon Parks and Fellini ...

What he does get to is this; 'rarely, if ever, do we find ourselves faced with a true trace of Africentricity, which means that a creative person of African descent has traced his root lines to a primeval source, etc, etc, blah-blah-blah.' Crazy, huh?"

"Yeah, you know I think it drives some White people, and some Black people nuts when they realize, after all these years of cultural imperialism, and other kinds of whippings, that we ain't them and we ain't about to become them."

"You do sense a little hysteria there, don't you?"

An hour later, after talking to four members of Our Production Company – "Juna, don't worry, everything is fine. Akosua will be talking with you about this tomorrow."

"Are you sure?"

"Definitely."

"What time?"

"In the afternoon." What a worry wart she is.

Breaking away from the track for a couple hours, Kojo selected "Mississippi Masala" from his collection, settled down for ninety minutes of one Indian director's idea of what Indian-African-American relations might've been way back then.

Hmmm ...not bad, not bad at all. I don't believe it, but it was nicely done. Denzel was his usual good actin' self and the Indian girl with the luscious lips and wild hair made a suitable sex pot.

He was tempted to put one of his Cary Grant movies on, decided not to, poured himself a goblet of San Antonio Red and drifted out into the backyard, feeling egotistical.

We've got a helluva film on our hands, a helluva film.

He sat on the porch steps, leaned back, sipping his wine and tried to see into the future. The spiraling piece of thick black and green rope coiled twenty yards away from him. Kojo felt a sudden chill. Now what?

The snake slithered away. Kojo stared at the slight depression the snake had made in the grass. Now what?

What do I do about this? Talk to Granddad, yeah, he would understand, but how could I even begin to tell him about this madness?

Akosua? No, never, she would feel used. I think I would feel the same way if someone told me that they married me because they had made some sort of supernatural deal.

He wrote mentally, scratched off a half dozen names, friends.

No, I can't take them this burden, this one is on me.

· ℘ℛ ·

Monday morning, Capoeira workout time.

"Akoś, how do you feel?"

"Oh, just a little green about the gills, but not bad."

"Anything I can get you before I make my run?"

"It would be great if you could fast forward this event for me."

They shared a big smile.

"I wish I could, sweetheart, I wish I could." He leaned over and kissed her gently.

"I won't be long; I just felt an urge to go up to the bridle path this morning."

A final wave and off to Griffith Park. 7:30 a.m., the prelude to heavy traffic. Kojo joined the building flow of vehicles, heading north on Riverside Drive, pleased that he wasn't a daily member of the morning-evening migration, that he didn't have to pay dues to the clock.

"Kojo, whatever you do – stay out of the herd. Once you become a labor unit you're dead. You'll b working your life away instead of doing your life's work."

Thanks, Dad, that was the best piece of advice you've ever given me.

He glanced at the man in the next lane, biting his nails. The woman talking on her cell phone and doing her make up, the aura of tension evident beyond the steel frames of their vehicles.

Impatient drivers blew their horns, changed lanes, and cursed other drivers. The streets were electric with hostile vibes. Kojo released a pent up sigh as he drove into the park. Thank God I'm out of that madness for a moment.

He drove slowly up the winding avenue, enjoying the great green trees, smiled at the chubby joggers struggling up the slight incline into the heart of the park.

Poor babies. Well, you gotta give it to 'em for getting out here to make the effort. Power walkers, joggers, people doing the cardio thing to try to stay health. He parked, did a brief warm up and started his run on the bridle path.

He felt strong, full of energy. Damn it feels good to be in good shape. He fell into a comfortable groove, running easily, using his run as a sight seeing tour.

The morning golfers, people with their dogs, horsy types bouncing along on their thoroughbreds. After the five-mile run, breathing easy, he decided to drive to the "backside" of the park, the place where he and Akosua did their picnics.

A couple men with guitars sat on a picnic table one hundred yards over there. Good. They have their thing to do and I have my thing to do.

Capoeira – alone. Shadow movements. The ginga, that basic dance step that has so many variations – Besoa, the front "blessing" kick. Meia lua de Compasso, the spinning half moon compass kick. Au-au-au-the cartwheel-somersault.

Thirty minutes later he wandered over to a picnic table and sat down, a bit sweaty, but feeling good.

He took casual notice of the tree limbs scattered around. They're trimming dead wood from the trees.

Beautiful Spring day in Southern California. He did a slow Pan of the green hillsides, the woodsy atmosphere. Hard to believe that we're in the middle of a big nasty city. It seemed to be one of the dead limbs until the familiar green and black shape slithered toward him.

Kojo froze, feeling scared of this horrible thing that Asiafo had put into his life. The snake coiled ten yards in front of him, flicking its forked tongue out and in.

"Feed me."

The rasping sound grated in his ears.

"I've already fed you."

"Feed me."

The same rasping sound, like hard scales being scraped against metal. Kojo felt the perspiration trickle under his arm pits. He made a quick decision.

I have to do what he wants if I want to keep the flow going, remember what happened the last time. I'm too deeply in the game to back out now.

He felt the words struggle out of his throat, felt himself choking.

"Feed you what and where?"

The snake made a dancing movement with its head.

"Your first born, here, next month."

Kojo leaped from the table, grabbed a length of dead tree limb and began to beat the snake to death; heavy, methodical blows up and down the body of the snake. He felt mad and nauseous, as though he wanted to take revenge on the snake for all of the bad feelings he had caused him. He pounded the snake into a long, bloody pulp.

The guitar players ran to his side.

"Woww! What happened, man?"

"Did it attack you?!"

"Yes, yes, it attacked me."

He threw the tree limb away and walked slowly to his car, pausing to vomit en route.

·   ℰℭ   ·

It took a great effort to keep him from cracking up after the episode in the park. He was disturbed and nervous. Akosua noticed it, talked about him with her mother and mother-in-law.

"You should see this man, he's a bundle of nerves, and you'd think he was having the baby."

Kojo felt compelled to do all of the things he had to do … attend the meetings, discuss the publicity campaign for the film, deal with people and circumstances. But he did it mechanically, like a blind man on a treadmill, with no possibility of getting off.

He nursed the secret feeling that something dreadful was going to happen to him. Or Akosua. Or the baby. He spent hours at the beach, staring at the waves, waiting for something terrible to happen, for some sign. Akosua tried to pull him out of his doldrums.

"C'mon, Mr. Creepy, let's go for a picnic in the park."

The idea of going to the park made his stomach churn.

"Why not the beach? We haven't done a picnic at the beach in a while."

"Suits me, but I won't be able to wear my bikini."

"Don't worry about it."

The letter came to his post office box three days after a false-baby-arrival alarm. It was from Grace and he made a mental note to talk with Akosua about his ex-girlfriend in the Motherland. She's a sweet sister but I don't think she would like for this correspondence to continue. I don't think I would dig it if she was receiving letters from an old flame. He sat on the back porch steps to read Grace's letter.

"Dear Kojo,

Long time, eh? I hope all is going well with you and your work. I'm doing well and trying to do better but, as you know, in Ghana here one must be careful not to cause too much envy.

You recall what degree they will give me? It is called a Ph.D./'pull her down.'

From this point on I will limit my correspondence to Christmas cards. Why? Well, I started thinking of how I would feel if you were my husband and you were receiving letters from some woman in Africa. I hope you can appreciate my feelings about this matter."

Kojo paused and stared up at the clouds for a beat. God, I wish I could've married both of them.

"Now then – the news, as they say on the Ghana Broadcasting Corporation/G.B.C., I went to visit Aunt Eugenia (she thanks you for the cedis) in Tsito last week and she was full of news. The most devastating bit of news concerns that 'Wild Man of the Forest,' Asiafo, the one you made your 'deal' with.

He was found dead in the forest, his skull crushed. There is great suspicion (according to Auntie) that he was killed by members of a family who suspected him of having a 'romance' with the youngest daughter of this family.

Of course the police were called in and they found nothing, nor did they find the person/persons who murdered Asiafo. The consensus seems to be 'good riddance.'

I must say to you honestly, I was a bit surprised when you spoke of your deal with this man. I couldn't come out openly and say to you; Kojo, I think it's rubbish because you seemed so totally taken in by the possibilities that were being offered you.

Well, in any case, at the end of the day, I should like to suggest that whatever obligations that were imposed on you should be considered null and void. The man is dead. As the proverb says, "What sense does it make to put chop in a dead man's mouth?"

Kojo felt the tears sliding down his cheeks before he realized he was crying. All of the weeks of tension, of feeling sick of the "deal" and the terms he had to meet, began to flow out of him.

"I will be traveling to Cuba and possibly the U.S. next year. Perhaps we could make arrangements to meet and 'do lunch,' as you chaps say in Hollywood.

> *'Til then, all my best,*
> *Grace"*

He folded the letter and pushed it down into his shirt pocket. I'm free; I don't have to feed that damned snake any more. He shook his head trying to reason with himself. Was I hallucinating? Did I actually make sacrifices to a snake? Have I been successful, so far, because of the deal? What now? What day was it that Asiafo had his skull crushed? I'll have to write Grace and find out.

More speculations were cancelled by an urgent call from the upstairs bedroom.

"Kojo!"

"Yes?"

"I hate to disturb you but I think it's time for us to go to the hospital! Now!"

· ℘ℜ ·

CHAPTER 18

Grace's reply to his letter came three weeks later.

"Dear Kojo,

Please forgive me or taking so long to reply to your letter, I have been frightfully busy. Ghana is going on, sometimes ahead, frequently behind, but always on. We discover new ways to do old things, old ways to do new things.

Now then – the news, as they say on the G.B.C., from the village of Tsito. I cannot give you the exact date that Asiafo was murdered. It appears that he had lain in the forest for a few days before his body was discovered.

However, I can tell you that there are other developments concerning this matter; it seems that this girl that Asiafo was having his 'romance' with ("man does not live on fufu alone") has disappeared. My Aunt Eugenia, a reliable source, tells me that the girl was pregnant. Now, her disappearance might mean that she was ostracized, banished, exiled from the village. Or perhaps her shame was so great that she ran away. Who can say?

I'm sure you found, during your brief stay in Tsito, that life in a small, conservative place like that can be quite parochial. So, at the end of the day, there you have it. I don't know what else to say. I wish you well,

Love, Grace."

Kojo re-read the note again. The girl was pregnant.

He put the letter in his files, vaguely disturbed by the idea that Asiafo might have a child, somewhere in the world.

· &CR ·

"My Grandfather's Eyes" was scored, edited, distributed, applauded and made big profits. Akosua Ferguson-Brown gave birth to a seven-pound five-ounce boy who was given a traditional West African "outdooring" and named Kofi Brown, after his paternal grandfather. Growing up, he was always called "Lil' Kofi."

Kojo's films, following "My Grandfather's Eyes" – "Secret Music" and "Dry Longso" – removed him from most of the stereotypical White definitions of an African-American writer-director-producer.

"Akoś, listen to this one – 'Kojo Brown's 'Dry Longso,' an almost indefinable word of African origin, appears to substantiate his appeal to people in general, rather than Blacks only. The high level of his art should make all of us appreciative of that fact. He shows all of the qualities that made Bergman and Fellini creative powers in their day.'"

"Still stacking you up next to the White boys, huh?"

"Inevitably. But I can't complain too loud … Fellini, Bergman. That's not bad company to be in."

The Browns were on a roll. Akosuas' books, fine examinations of the finite play between the sexes were critically acclaimed (and sold well) and Kojo was following his five-year plan in his fourth film. Kofi Brown (named after his paternal grandfather) was five years old, precocious and his grandparents were the first ones to take note of the boy's interest in snakes.

"Kojo, notice what happens when I open that big book on reptiles? Kofi stares and points at them as though he knew every one of 'em."

"Close the book, Dad, please. I don't want him to become interested in snakes."

"Hahhhah, that's not like you, son. I thought you wanted your boy to be interested in <u>everything</u>."

"It's a long story, Dad. Please, just close the book, I'll explain it to you one day."

· &CR ·

139

LIL' KOFI ...

"No doubt about it, I really missed my great grandfather Kwame. We had been really good friends. When he died at one hundred and four, and I was ten, it seemed unreal to me, I thought he was supposed to live forever, or at least until I blew into my teens.

The old man's death pulled me into a reality that I had never experienced before. What do you know, what do you think about death at ten years old? I had seen dead animals here and there, but never a dead person, and especially not someone I felt close to.

He was old when he died, but he had never seemed to be one hundred and four when he was alive. Maybe it had something to do with how alert, how sharp he was.

"Kofi, what did you learn in school today?"

He would sit in his favorite chair and quiz me about school, about what I wanted to be in life, stuff like that. He was the first one I talked to about becoming a herpetologist, about my wanting to find a cure for certain kinds of neurological disorders by synthesizing the venom of various snakes.

He never laughed at my naïve views of the world, people, life in general. It took me a little while to come to grips with the idea that he wouldn't be around to answer my questions any more, to play chess with (I never won a single game), to laugh and joke with.

But it wasn't like I was hung completely out to dry by Gramps' death. I still had Mom and Dad, and their parents, my grandparents, to lean on. I thought my Dad's Mom and Dad were some of the smartest people on the planet.

Granddad Kofi (I was named after him) and Grandma Nzingha were as busy as two middle aged people could be, with their book store, their civic activities, and all the other stuff they did. But they always had quality time and <u>original</u> answers for me, no matter how busy they were.

Mom's parents, my maternal grandparents, were/are quite different. They always gave me presents; they're always giving me presents, things. And I love them for their generosity, but there are times when I wish they would back away from the gift shop thing.

Mom reminds me all the time – "That's the way they are, Kofi, that's their way of showing their love."

Growing up I was always encouraged to ask questions.

"Grandson, if you don't ask questions people will assume that you know everything, just like all the rest of the young folks."

That's a good example of my Granddad "Big Kofi's" dry sense of humor.

"Kofi, if we don't have the answer offhand, we'll go to the library and find out." That's Grandma Nzingha.

Grandmother Minerva and Grandfather Harvey have always had a different mindset – "If we don't know the answer, we'll buy it from the best possible source."

Whenever I hear that proverb, "It takes a village to raise a child"; I can definitely say I had the benefits of being "village raised." My Mom and Dad and my grandparents have always been there for me, except for one thing concerning Dad.

"Why herpetology, son?"

"I don't know why, Dad, it's just something I'm interested in."

"Well, son, it's natural to be interested in a lot of things when you're ten years old. Why don't you feel around a bit, explore a few other career fields before you settle into one particular groove?"

Dad's attitude really puzzled me because he was usually wide open to whatever I flung at him. It took a loonng time to find out why he wasn't enthusiastic about my interest in snakes."

· ⁊∵ ·

FATHER KOJO

"My Dad, the bookstore owner, noticed Lil' Kofi's interest in snakes and was always giving him books about reptiles, on his birthday, for Kwanzaa, whenever. I was really in a bind. I mean, how could I tell my Dad, my son, my wife, about my deal with Asiafo the Wizard? And how a snake came to be the main character in the business.

I must've flash backed to the Asiafo scenario at least once a day, for years. I'm forty-six years old now, a successful writer-producer-director, got all the goodies I think I need or want. And it <u>may</u> all stem from a deal I made with a guy in a forest in Ghana, West Africa, twenty years ago."

· ℬℛ ·

LIL' KOFI

"I can't say that I would've been better off having a brother or a sister. I can say that it would've made a difference because all of the goodies, all of the attention would not have been lavished on me.

Being an only child can have its advantages and disadvantages. One advantage is that I didn't have to share a bunch of things with a brother/sister. That doesn't mean that I was spoiled rotten, that I had my way about things. Mom and Dad wouldn't put up with bratty behavior. Like, they had rules …

"Kofi, when you get out of your bed, make it up."

They were the parents and I was the child in the house, they made me understand that very clearly, early on.

"Kofi, there is one father in this house. There is one mother in this house, and one child, you. We are a dictatorship of two, me and your mother, and what we say goes."

I was not oppressed or anything like that, but there were rules to be followed. I could talk with Mom and Dad about anything under the sun, but at the end of the day they made the final decisions.

"Kofi, you don't know enough to make an informed decision about this matter."

It wasn't until I got in my teens, in this elite private high school, that I paid some attention to the way some of my peers were being raised, the relationship they had with their parents, their families. Let me give you three examples of what I'm talking about; I wanted a car or at least a motorcycle. We had a family conference (Granddad Harvey and Grandmother Minerva would've bought me one in a minute).

"Kofi, we've decided that it wouldn't be a good idea for you to have a car or a motorcycle at this time."

"Because, basically, you're just going back and forth to school and public transportation serves that purpose very well."

"Awww, but Dad, Mom, other kids have cars and stuff…"

Man, what did I say that for?! They didn't let me off the hook for an hour, patiently explaining why I should never, ever even suggest that I was supposed to use "the herd" as a validation-support for any argument I wanted to make.

"You must not ever tell us you should be allowed to do this or that, or have this or that because others have it. Or do it. We will not allow you to do the herd mentality number."

"Kofi, you're going to find out, as you grow older and wiser, with our guidance, that a lot of the members of your peer group are just simply blundering around because their parents are not doing their work properly. And they're all going to suffer the consequences."

Check it out. I was not allowed to listen to rap music. My Mom was hell on rap, 'specially gangster rap. Or what some people used to call "hard rap."

"As a writer," she said to me, "I know something about the power of words, how they can be used and misused. Unfortunately, I think that too many of the rappers have misused the words, stepped off on the wrong foot and have no idea that they're out of step."

"I'm not quite sure I understand what you mean, Mom." I was trying to look for an opening, to defend my rap heroes.

"Well, let me put it to you another way; when an immature collection of young men and women decide that they are going to legitimize as many negative elements in our community as they can, then I feel that they're on the wrong foot. Yes, it does have something to do with the hoe-bitch-motherfucker-nigga thing. But, for me, it goes deeper than that. Too many of these young people just simply don't have the maturity, the wisdom to be trying to tell others how to behave.

Do some of them have real talent? You're damned right they do. And they've grown up in rough neighborhoods and been shot, and shot at, but that doesn't give them the credentials to counsel others."

"Kofi, as you know we listen to everything, everybody. I was stunned to discover that the country 'n western dudes, people like Garth Brooks and others were actually saying something. Thank you, Akosua.

I object to two big things in rap. Number one, the sound is much too loud. Eighty-five decibels is the normal, safe hearing range. When it's revved up past a hundred decibels plus that undercurrent sonic boom, it's blowing your ears out. Right now most of your friends have hearing problems, think of what they're going to be able to hear at age forty - fifty. I know, you guys can't even imagine being older than twenty-five. But trust me, my son, it's gonna happen one day. You'll look at yourself in the mirror and say, "Damn! I'm twenty-six years old." That's how fast time flees.

I could spend a lot of time talking about the age/time lapse process. But let's stay with the rap genre for a bit.

Aside from the deafening effect it's having, where are the musicians? The drummers? The Bassists? The pianists? The horn players? When we look at the musical legacy that's been left to us from Blind Lemon Jefferson, Muddy Waters, I'm just going random here, Sidney Bechet, Louis Armstrong, Duke, Count, Nat "King" Cole, Miles, Diz, "Bird"...

I could go on and on, but just let me stop at "Bird," Charlie Parker. How many of the rappers are going to pass along music, sheer music, pure music, instrumental as well as local music that would be the equivalent of the "Bird's" contribution?"

"But, Dad, rap is a different thing."

"But they call it music, don't they? You make music with instruments or/and your voice. I'm simply asking – where are the musicians?"

"We don't mean to gang up on you, Kofi, but that's a legitimate question – where are the musicians? In addition, as a writer, I'd like to ask – where are the poets? The people who are supposed to be responsible for creating the lyrics in their genre."

"Every rapper is a poet, and some, of course, are better than others."

"Without a doubt some are better than others, that's true in anything. But my question is – where are the poets? I'm not talking abut rhymers, I'm talking about people who can write the words of their raps in different rhyme patterns. If they wanted a rap in iambic pentameter, could they sit down and do that?"

"Kofi, do you hear what your mother is asking you? She's not talking about rhyming – eeny meeny minee mo. Anybody can do that. We're talking about complexities, not simplistic rhyming."

I'm not going to say that they fully convinced me of anything on every level, but I paid close attention to what they said. They were not into self righteous preaching, or trying to browbeat me for the hell of it.

Drugs. Dad played it out clear and clean for me.

"Being in the business we're in, we've always had access to drugs, cocaine mostly, but whatever our lil' heart craved.

When I was younger I smoked a little herb and snorted my lines of coke, that's a fact. Didn't we, Akosua?"

"You got that right!"

I must've done a double take Mom 'n Dad smoking weed and snortin' coke?! That sounded unbelievable.

"Kofi, we don't want to dethrone ourselves from Sainthood in your eyes, but we've been there, done that, and have the T-shirts to prove it."

I made a note to use that expression at a later date. Mom sipped her Martinellis apple juice like it was a glass of fine sherry, and took up the narrative.

"It was there, we were adventurous and we did it, simple as that. And that was the end of it."

"What made you stop?"

They exchanged looks, that little psychic/mental shorthand they had.

"Well, as you know, cocaine is addictive <u>and</u> expensive. I mean, who, with any sense, wants to snort up thousands of dollars up your nose? Marijuana is different, it's not addictive, but you can become habituated to it."

"We used to know some people; we won't mention any names, who sat around smoking weed and watching T.V. all day. For most people it's not a drug that promotes active, creative behavior. It alters your perceptions, for most people, in a negative way."

"What about the creative people, the artists, the musicians who say that the herb inspires them?"

Dad could hardly wait for me to finish the sentence.

"Kofi, like I said – for <u>most</u> people it's not a drug that promotes active, creative behavior. There are always exceptions. Let's take "Bird," Charlie Parker, for example. This brother was known to use heroin, cocaine, marijuana and booze ..."

"Wowww!"

"All at the same time, and blow other musicians off the bandstand. One of them, can't think of his name right now, once said, "That 'Bird' created a whole bunch of dope fiend musicians. They felt, they thought, shit, if he can play like that under the influence, then that's the way to go.""

They made the mistake of thinking that they could do what "Bird" did, under the influence. Just for the record I can tell you, personally, drugs will not help you think better, play better or write better. Drugs are crutches that can make you depended, but not more creative, unless you're Charlie Parker and you want to die at the age of thirty-four."

"And besides, there are too many natural highs out here – yoga, tai chi, swimming, jogging, and reading, writing ..."

"Making films."

"But Mom, Dad, you guys drink wine pretty often."

"You're right, Kofi, we do. But you've never seen either one of us get drunk and disorderly."

"Or get a big buzz on just before we get ready to go out, which is what a lot of people do. I'm getting ready to go to this party, so let me smoke this sinsemilla."

"Drink three shots of whisky."

"Snort these four lines of cocaine..."

"None of that madness. First of all, you're putting yourself in danger, and you're a potential accident for everybody else. A glass of fine vino at the end of the day is a real pleasure, especially if it's a special occasion, but there are rules and regulations to be followed. You got to know when enough is enough, and no one can be a better judge of that than you."

My Mom and Dad talked to me, not at me, to me. They didn't always sit me down for family conferences, but if there was something happening that had a lesson in it, they didn't hesitate to point it out.

One day, coming home from school, I must've been about thirteen – fourteen at the time; I gave this ol' wino guy a quarter to buy me a pack of cigarettes. I guess you could say "The Devil made me do it." I can't offer any other explanation. Somehow it just seemed like it would be a cool thing to do. I lit one on the way home, took a couple puffs of this awful smoke – ugh! And put the pack into my backpack.

Mom found them.

"Kofi, are you smoking cigarettes now?"

"Uhh, o no, Mom. These belong to a friend of mine, he put 'em in my backpack and I just forgot ..."

"You're telling me a lie."

Ohhh, you're talking about angry. They hated a liar worse than God hates lil' green apples. I had to back track immediately.

"Well, actually, yeahhh, I guess I did buy 'em but I wasn't planning to smoke 'em."

"Yes, you were – that's why you spent five dollars for them. I see you've already smoked one."

"Actually, I just took a couple puffs and threw it away."

"Well, we can't have you wasting your hard earned money, so it looks like you have a little smoking to do, young man."

We didn't even have an ash tray in our house; Mom went downstairs and came back up with a small, empty flower pot and a package of ol' fashioned wooden matches.

"Here you are, it's five o'clock now. Light 'em up. You have exactly one hour to smoke this pack. I want to see twenty-one filter tips when I come back up to your room at six o'clock or else you can consider yourself grounded for the next three months."

Mom and Dad didn't play around. If they said it, they meant it. I knew she was being extra hard on me because I had attempted to lie my way out of the situation. I had to smoke these awful tasting, gaseous cigarettes or else I would b grounded; that meant no T.V., no basketball, no movies, no walks through the mall to look at the girls, nothing.

It was an hour I'll never forget. I puffed and puffed and puffed. Blue, gassy smoke all over my room. I hated to think of what my room would smell like.

Rather than smoke one at a time, I tried smoking three at once. That was a real mistake, I could feel myself turning green, so I went back to the one by one method. I don't know how I did it, but at five minutes to six I was puffing on the last butt. Mom knocked on my room door.

"Give me the flower pot."

I opened the door to give her the pot and there she was, with a damp cloth covering her nose. I felt so bad. I felt bad physically, but I felt even worse about the problem I had caused for her.

"Twenty-one butts in here?" She asked through the cloth.

"Yes ..."

"Open your bedroom window to let that horrible odor out; we're having dinner in a half hour." That's all she said, and went back downstairs with these awful cigarette butts. A half hour later she called up to me – "Kofi, dinner's ready."

"Thanks, Mom, I'm not hungry right now."

"Awrighty!"

I was sick as a dog, stomach churning, headache, and this horrible taste in my mouth. I had never had a hangover but I'm sure the way I felt was the equivalent of a beastly hangover. Dad was working on a documentary so I didn't see him 'til the following evening, when we sat down for dinner.

"Your mother tells me you gave up smoking yesterday."

All I could do was nod. And that was it. They've never been the types to beat a dead horse. And I've never smoked a cigarette since that day.

My folks had high expectations for me and they gave me responsibilities. I don't think having a brother or sister would've changed that."

· ℰℭ ·

KOJO'S STORY

"Hey, what can I say? Kofi was twenty-one years old and, like most of the people in our family, had decided to make his trip to Ghana. That was, and had been, pretty much a tradition in our family.

It wasn't like a Haj to Mecca, or anything religious. But, for some reason or other, at about twenty or so, all of the members of the Brown family had made, or would be making a trip to Ghana. We even had a family fund for that purpose. So, as you can well imagine, I was not shocked when Kofi came to us and announced; "Dad, Mom, I feel Ghana calling."

(Akosua had made her "Haj' three years after I came back, ranting and raving about the cinematic possibilities that Ghana offered. She spent three months in Ghana and soaked up enough stuff for three books. When Kofi made his announcement, I felt it was time to level with everybody, to tell the truth, basically.)

I made an occasion of it. I gathered Akosua and Kofi to my secret one evening, prior to Kofi's trip. Akosua was as angry/pissed off with me as she had ever been during our twenty-one year old marriage.

"Whoa! Let me get this straight! Are you telling me that you married me because of some weird deal you made with a cursed man in the Ghanaian Equatorial Rainforest?"

"I also made some other sacrifices." Talk about putting your foot in your mouth.

"Damn these other things you did, that's between you and whats-his-name? I'm talking about us. I thought you married me because you loved me?!"

"I did, I do …"

I placed the knee pads at thigh level and tiptoed around on thin ice for a loonng week. Akosua looked at me as though steam was blowing out of her nostrils, and Kofi shook his head as though he was listening to something he didn't want to hear. Exactly a week after I had told them about Asiafo, Akosua confronted me in the backyard.

"Kojo, you know … I've been thinking a lot about this story you told us. Are you pulling off one of your famous practical jokes or something?"

"I wish I was. No, Akoś, this is the real deal, it's something that actually happened."

She tilted her head to one side, to give me her special "skeptical look."

'What proof do you have, I mean, what could you show us that would take this whole thing out of the Twilight Zone?"

I thought hard on it for a few minutes. The letter. The letter from Grace, about Asiafo.

"Akoś, I can give you proof, but it's going to take a couple days, I have to go through my old files."

She folded her arms across her chest.

"I'll be more than happy to wait for as long as it takes."

The challenge was on. An hour later, Kofi passed me in the downstairs corridor, on his way to play basketball, smirking. "Dad, Mom says you're going to give us some proof of this wild man in the forest story."

I wanted to throw something at him, but instead I went up to our attic storage bin. Grace's letter. I prayed I hadn't thrown it away. After all, twenty years is a long time to keep a letter. I got busy.

I started with the boxes on the left side of the attic; I discovered first/second draft scripts of "My Grandfather's Eyes," menus from the Sompun, a great Thai restaurant we used to go to, story outlines for projects that never took off, receipts for this and that, including a receipt from the Los Angeles Fire Department for a fire that occurred long ago in our South Los Angeles office – loft. Needless to say, I felt I was getting warm.

Kofi let me know, very respectfully, that he was still pissed off about me not wanting him to become a herpetologist.

"Dad, just think about it. If I had paid strict attention to your advice, I wouldn't be headed for a brilliant career. I wouldn't have a full scholarship to the University of Florida. I don't know what would've happened to me, I might've wound up on Skid row or something."

"Stop it, son, you're exaggerating a bit, aren't you?"

They had me by the short hairs, I had to admit. Akosua took great pleasure in asking me, at different times of the day – "Found anything yet?"

Filing cabinets loaded with twenty years of stuff that once meant something, whatever it was, at the time. I was filling up trash bags with memories, but no letter from Grace Hlovor. I was beginning to think – well, maybe they are right, maybe it was all something I imagined.

I was about to give up on the whole business and just eat my crow and be done with it, 'til I came across this receipt for the purchase of a Vietnamese pot-bellied pig. I sat there, staring at the Chinese letters on the receipt. "Mr. Nuyen's Pets."

The whole business washed over me; sneaking into the backyard with the pig. Akosua was pregnant. How fearful I was that the snake wouldn't take the sacrifice and that I would be running into bad luck at every turn. I kept fishing.

It was about 8 p.m. of the second day and Akosua and Kofi were beginning to feel a little pity for me, I could tell from the gentle way they spoke to me.

"It's o.k., Kojo, it's o.k., honey, you don't have to prove anything."

"Yeah, Dad. Why don't we just forget about the whole thing?"

The envelope with the Ghanaian stamp with Queen Elizabeth and Prince Phillip (of all people!) on it sat up in front of me. Grace's letter …

I read it three times to make sure I had the right letter. And three folders away – another letter from Grace. I was so nervous the pages shook in my hands.

"Dear Kojo,

Long time, eh? I hope all is going well with you and your work. I'm doing well and trying to do better but, as you know, in Ghana here, one must be careful not to cause too much envy.

You recall what degree they will give me? It is called a Ph.D./ "Pull her down."

From this point on I will limit my correspondence to Christmas cards; why? Well, I started thinking of how I would feel if you were my husband and you were receiving letters from some woman in Africa. I hope you can appreciate my feelings about this matter.

Now then – the news, as they say on the Ghana Broadcasting/ G.B.C. I went to visit Aunt Eugenia (she thanks you for the cedis) in Tsito last week and she was full of news. The most devastating bit of news concerns that "Wild Man of the Forest," Asiafo, the one you made your "deal" with.

He was found dead in the forest, his skull crushed. There is a great suspicion (according to Auntie) that he was killed by members of a family who suspected him of having a "romance" with the youngest daughter of this family.

Of course the police were called in and they found nothing, nor did they find the person/persons who murdered Asiafo. The consensus seems to be "good riddance."

I must say to you honestly, I was a bit surprised when you spoke of your "deal" with this man. I couldn't come out openly and say to you; Kojo, I think it's rubbish because you seemed so totally taken in by the possibilities that were being offered you.

Well, in any case, at the end of the day, I should like to suggest that whatever the obligations were that were imposed on your should be considered null and void. The man is dead. As the proverb says, "What sense does it make to put chop in a dead man's mouth?"

I will be traveling to Cuba and possibly the U.S. next year. Perhaps we could make arrangements to meet and "do lunch," as you chaps say in Hollywood.

'Til then, all my best,
Grace."

And then, the second letter, a reply to the query he made about the day Asiafo was murdered. He felt compelled to know if there was more than coincidence to the fact that he had killed the snake on a particular day, and that Asiafo might have been killed on that same day.

"Dear Kojo,

Please forgive me for taking so long to reply to your letter, I have been frightfully busy. Ghana is going on, sometimes ahead, frequently behind, but always on. We discover new ways to do old things, old ways to do new things.

Now then – the news, as they say on the G.B.C., from the village of Tsito. I cannot give you the exact date that Asiafo was murdered. It appears that he had lain in the forest for a few days before his body was discovered.

However, I can tell you that there are other developments concerning this matter; it seems that this girl that Asiafo was having his "romance" with ("man does not live on fufu alone") has disappeared.

My Aunt Eugenia, a reliable source, tells me that the girl was pregnant. Now, her disappearance might mean that she was ostracized, banished, exiled from the village. Or perhaps her shame was so great that she ran away. Who can say?

I'm sure you found, during your brief stay in Tsito, that life in a small, conservative place like that can be quite parochial. So, at the end of the day, there you have it. I don't know what else to say. I wish you well,

Love, Grace."

So, the girl was pregnant, Asiafo might have a child somewhere in the world. Hmmmmm …

· ℘ℛ ·

I could hardly wait 'til the next morning to share Grace's letters with Akosua and Kofi. I had xeroxed both of them and put inside red folders. I wanted to make a presentation. I thought of how Bill Cosby would have done it.

I didn't want to stand over my wife and son and gloat, but it felt damned good to be able to pull up a couple pieces of evidence to validate what happened, what I had experienced, twenty years ago.

"Akosua, Kofi, now that you have finished your high fiber cereal I would like to present you two with copies of two letters from a Ghanaian lady named Grace. Perhaps they will serve to validate what I've told you."

I would've paid cash money to have a photo of the expressions on their faces when I passed out the red folders.

I felt like a big time poker player spreading his winning hand on the table in front of skeptical opponents. They read the letters slowly. And then read them again. I had just a tinge of feeling about how Akosua would react to a couple twenty-year old letters form an old girlfriend. Not a problem.

Then, to put the icing on the cake, in a manner of speaking, I gave them xeroxed copies of the receipt for the Vietnamese pot-bellied pig. Akosua stepped out of the fog first.

"Who, who else knows about this?"

"Over here, nobody, now that great granddad is dead. As you can well imagine, this isn't the sort of thing you go around bragging about."

"Great granddad, who else?"

"Well, uhh, the woman who wrote the letter, Grace. Her auntie in the village. Maybe a couple other people in Ghana.

It's not a very popular story, by any means."

Kofi's turn. He stroked his chin like he had a full gray beard.

"What happened to the girl who was pregnant, the one who left the village?"

"I don't have a clue. Remember, I was back over here when that scene went down. Not only that, it didn't concern me."

Akosua squinted at me, the way she did when she had a ripe story idea.

"Kojo, wouldn't you like to know what happened to the girl who ran away? The girl who was pregnant with whatshisname's child?"

"No."

"But, Dad, there's a <u>really</u> interesting story here."

"For who? Or should I say – for whom?"

Akosua's squint sharpened. I could tell, she was on to something.

"Kojo, we're not looking at a market here, we're looking at an authentic human interest story. I think the story would have real value if it were only done as an 'African Tarzan' – mystery tale, why not?"

"Dad, we wouldn't even have to bring you and "the deal" into it at all. It would just simply be the story of this wild guy and the relationship he had with this village girl. You know you're always talking about how Hollyweird neglects the stories with African foundations."

"Kojo, I think I would like to write a novel about this, the circumstances are interesting and it fits the Pan-African Occult agenda."

I felt like I had pulled all of it down on myself, while trying to prove a point. It would've been pretty hard to fight Akosua-Kofi's point/ suggestions.

"Well, I'd be a fool to argue that it's not an interesting story, that's pretty obvious. But ..."

Akosua was three jumps ahead of me.

"Kojo, no buts. Look, Kofi is getting ready to go to Ghana in May."

"May, that's the beginning of the rainy season. I looked it up."

"May, that's three months from now. Why couldn't we commission him, ask him to check out a few things for us?"

"Awww c'mon, Mom, you wouldn't have to commission me to do anything, just tell me what you want and I'll go for it."

"Well, what do you think, Kojo?"

I'll never be able to make any concrete accusations, but I'll always feel that my wife and my son did a little deck stacking on me.

"What do I think? I think it, uhh, I think it would be interesting, but what exactly is Kofi going to do?"

Akosua was right on the point.

"He'll do four specific things. Number one, he'll check out the village where the girl came from."

"That's Tsito and Aunt Eugenia."

"Aunt Eugenia?"

Kofi had a pad and ball point right in front of him.

"Aunt Eugenia is, uhh, Grace's aunt, the one who wrote me the letters about Asiafo."

"Got it; Aunt Eugenia in Cheeto. What'sher name?"

"I never knew it. When you get to Tsito, just ask for Aunt Eugenia, if she's still alive they'll direct you to her."

"Number two, we want to know where the girl went when she left the village. Number three, did she have a baby? Boy or girl? Number four, what's her story? What's her lifestyle like those days? And, if you have the time to do it …" Akosua cut a sly look at me, "You might check out this Grace creature that your Dad received mail from. It would be interesting to see what she's up to these days. She might be of some help, who knows?"

"Kofi, that's a very low priority, o.k.?"

He nodded in agreement.

"Now then, Akoś, Kofi, having given you all my deep little secret, I would like for you two to agree to keep this strictly in the family, our deep dark family secret."

We stacked our hands atop each other on the breakfast table.

"Kojo, trust me, I think it's such a bizarre little story that no one would believe it anyway."

"Yeah, Dad, it is a little bit over the top."

"No matter where it is, let's just keep it in the family."

CHAPTER 19

LIL' KOFI …

"My first trip to Ghana, to Africa, to the Motherland. I don't think I had a full night's sleep for a week before my trip.

"Don't let 'em lock you out of Africa, Kofi. Don't let 'em lock you out physically or emotionally, they've been trying to do that to us ever since they brought our people over here."

"That was something Great Granddad Kwame used to say a lot, and it was definitely backed up by Dad's side of the family. Somebody was always going or coming back, usually from Ghana because DNA research had determined that Dad's back ground was Ga and Twi, two of the main tribal groups in Ghana. The research showed that Mom as a descendant of the Fon people, from Benin, south of Ghana.

Granddad Harvey and Grandmother Minerva weren't very much interested in their African roots.

"We would rather spend vacation time in France, wouldn't we, Harvey?"

But that didn't stop them from giving me a thousand dollars book of traveler's check.

"Enjoy yourself."

Grandfather Kofi, Grandma Nzingha, my Dad and Mom had a little going away dinner for me, the evening before my departure.

"What's on your agenda, Kofi? What're you planning to do for a whole month?"

"Well, aside from checking out the snakes," a sly look at Mom and Dad, "I'm just going to go with the flow."

"Good idea! Remember what happened to your Aunt Rose and Aunt Afiya when they went over last year? Both of 'em came back sick, trying to run all over the place and do everything. Go with the flow, that's the way to go."

The next day I was on British Airways, heading for a day's stopover in London, a half hour stopover in Kano, Nigeria, and finally Kotoka Airport, Accra, Ghana, for a month in the Motherland.

I called them "Thoughts in the Air," the thoughts I had during the eighteen-hour trip. Thoughts about the slave trade/African Diaspora. What would've happened if we had simply be left alone? What would Africa be today?

Thoughts about "African-African-American relations." Some Africans think, no matter how poor their countries are, that they're superior to African-Americans, Africans in the Diaspora, because we only have the countries we were transported to.

Thoughts about how strange it felt to be going back to some place you had never been, that was your Motherland.

Thoughts about things that his folks had talked about.

"Kofi, remember, as weird as it may sound – lots of Africans still are into divided, tribal mindset modes."

"No, in the 21st century?"

"You read the newspapers, the magazine articles, the books. There are a group of people over here who would like to get at the people over there. Now don't get me wrong, that seems to be a world wide situation; the Irish Catholics against the Irish Protestants. The Shiites against the Sunnis, the Northerners against the Southerners, those over here against those over there, for some unknown reason.

I guess it's just a little harder to bear because these are <u>our</u> people and we want them to have better lives, lives without violence, war.

I remember a Nigerian brother telling me one day, after one beer too many; "You guys were forced to become Americans, that solved your tribal differences. We are still burdened with ours."

"You think a little latter day, transcontinental slave trading would help you out."

"O Kofi, you are a terrible man, terrible!"

Kotoka Airport, Accra, Ghana.

Everyone of my family members who had been there had given me an idea, a perspective, a vibe, a feeling; but I don't think any conscious African-American could ever describe the emotions that are released when you step on to African ground for the first time.

What with all the chaos of people seeming to go in ever which way, I felt completely cool. I was at home. Outside the terminal, the taxi drivers swarmed on the newly arrived like locusts.

"I am called Kwame," he said very quietly.

"That was my great grandfather's name," I told him. And Brother Kwame became my official driver for the whole time I was in Ghana. I had two pieces of luggage, a small bag and a slightly longer small bag. I had traveled enough with Mom and Dad to know better than to burden myself with a lot of unnecessary stuff.

It was humid at twilight and the sky glowed with pastel colors.

"And where do you want to go, sah?"

"I want to charter your taxi for two hours, just to drive around, and then you can take me to the Green Leaf Hotel in Osu."

Brother Kwame looked across the space separating us in the front seat.

"You have been in Ghana here, before this time?"

"No, this is my first time, but members of my family have been here and they've given me good information. Why do you ask?"

"Because you say, sah, to charter my taxi ..."

"Maybe it was my great grandfather speaking."

He smiled, one of those beautifully open smiles, nothing phony about him at all. We bonded. He looked to be about forty or so, and I could tell from the exchanges he made with the other taxi drivers that he was a regular. I was surprised to see how close the airport was to central Accra, I could've walked downtown in an hour.

Brother Kwame drove me to LaBadi Rd., a hundred yards east of the ocean.

"That way leads to Teshie Nungua, very nice. The other way leads to Jamestown, not nice, not nice at all."

He was the perfect tour guide. He pointed with his chin and said whatever seemed appropriate.

"This is Ring Road east, it goes through Accra. If you go this way, you will be in the neighborhood called Adabraka. There are many wicked clubs and women in Adabraka."

"Up the hill from Danquah Circle is LaBone, very nice. The opposite way is Osu. Osu is poor, but I like it better than LaBone."

"Why?"

"Because of the people, sah, because of the people."

"This is the LaBadi Hotel, very nice, very expensive."

"This is the Novotel Hotel, also very nice, very expensive."

"And the Golden Tulip. Very, very expensive."

It would be hard to say where we didn't go within my two hour "charter time." I didn't realize that until I had been in Accra for a couple – three days and realized that I had some idea of where I was.

And, "at the end of the day,' as I must've heard a dozen times a day, Brother Kwame eased up into the circular courtyard of a beautiful little three story building with a small green leaf carved above the door.

"Green Leaf Hotel, sah, very nice, not very expensive."

Mr. and Mrs. Lartey welcomed me as though they had been expecting me.

"Ahh, Mr. Kofi Brown, your room is 301, the boy will take you there."

Utilitarian room in a cinder block built hotel; a bed, a chair, a table, spacious, but not grand. And not expensive. I was satisfied. I cam down to pay Brother Kwame.

"Sah, you are on to some serious business Ghana here, I will be your driver."

No question about it, Brother Kwame was going to be the man who took me around Ghana.

"Do you know where Tsito is?"

"Sah, my grandfather was born near Tsito, I know it well."

"Good. Give me a couple days to settle in here, get the lay of the land …"

"You say?"

"I'm going to just hang out, just wander around Accra for a couple days, and check things out."

"I see," he said, "so, I will collect you when you have the 'lay of the land.'"

I liked that, the dude was sharp, alert.

"Yeah, a couple days ought to give me enough time to get a lay of the land."

"Sah, just there, down this road is the Country Kitchen, a good place to eat."

I "dashed" him a few more thousand cedis for his info about where to eat. Very important for the traveler, anywhere, to know where to eat.

"So, I will collect you on Thursday morning. You will charter?"

"Yes, I will charter you for a trip to Tsito? Cool?'

"Tsito? Yes, my grandfather ..."

"See you at about 10 a.m. on Thursday? If you're not here by 11 a.m., I will have to charter another driver."

Dad had been very clear about this ...

"Kofi, don't fall in love with people you want to do things for you. Sometimes they will do exactly what you expect them to do, what you want them to do. And then, at other times, the exact opposite will happen. Don't become dependent on anybody just because you like them."

"10 a.m., Thursday morning, I will be here, sah."

"Great! See you then."

The Country Kitchen. I was ravenous by the time I strolled through three "blocks" of guttered "streets." It was night and the humidity was forcing droplets of sweats to flow from my armpits to my wrists.

The Country Kitchen loomed up like a mirage. It was a huge thatched hut, open on all four sides for the breezes, whenever they came, to blow through. Beautiful idea.

"Yessah, I am Emerald, I will serve you."

I was beginning to trip on the formality of the scene, this "sah" business. I took a well disguised look at Emerald. Hmmm. 38-25-38. An Emerald? No, more like a diamond in the rough.

"I'll have the lobster and fried rice, and an ABC Lager beer."

She brought the well chilled ABC to me five minutes later. And twenty minutes later she swiveled back to my table to tell me, "The lobster is finished, sah."

I knew what she meant by that but I couldn't resist joking; "How can it be finished? I haven't had any of it yet."

She simply stood in place, obviously immune to my flirtatious humor. O well, I checked out the menu again.

"Do you have number five, the shrimp fried rice with okra?"

"Yessah." Her bright smile cancelled out all of my negative thoughts.

"I'll have that, and another ABC, please."

"Yessah ..."

Yessah, no sah. It gave me an odd feeling to have someone my age (Emerald looked at least twenty-one), or even older (Brother Kwame, the taxi driver), say "yessah, yessah."

But Mom and Dad had prepped me pretty well on this one.

"Ghanaians are very polite people, Kofi. People don't talk loud, and they're not demonstrative the way we tend to be. You won't see any hugging 'n kissing anywhere, not even amongst the young people.

Basically, I'd have to say, people are quite conservative. You won't see or hear a whole bunch of stuff you've been used to hearing and seeing until they revolt."

10 p.m., the waiters and waitresses were clearing off the tables, time to return to the Green Leaf Hotel. He walked slowly, carefully down the rutted road, bordered on each side by drainage ditches. Where it was dark, it was inky black, and where there was light it was soft and dim.

"Good evening, sah."

"O, good evening." I had spoken to someone I couldn't even see.

Back in 301 at the Green Leaf, he "showered" in tepid water that dribbled from a shower head and sprawled out on his hard, narrow bed, covered by a sheet, the only cover needed in this rainy season heat.

He laid there, thinking, listening. No loud sounds, no drive by audio assaults, no sirens, just the soft sound of voices now and then. He drifted off to sleep with a smile on his face – I'm in Africa.

· ℰℭ ·

CHAPTER 20

Well, if I didn't drift off to sleep with a smile on my face, I definitely woke up with a smile. Someone was singing. Beautiful clear contralto, a female voice that was almost a baritone. I couldn't understand the words but it had to be happy song, it sounded like one.

I tiptoed to the door. It was coming from the hallway. I opened the door just as the singing maid was pulling the sheets from the bed of the room across the hall. She looked up, startled, and stopped singing.

"O! Sorry sah, I didn't mean to annoy …"

"You're not annoying me, you have a beautiful voice, don't stop singing."

I closed the door on an expression that was a mixture of shyness, "puzzlement" and delight. But she had stopped singing. O well …

My room had a large whirly bird fan in the ceiling which kept the air reasonably cool, but I could look out of the window at the glistening, sweating faces of the people trudging up and down the road in front of the hotel to see that it was hot out there.

"Good morning, sah, you slept well?"

"Like a top."

"You say?"

"I slept well."

Have to watch that, these little "Americanisms" that I've never paid any attention to, the expressions that make people say, "You say?"

He stood at the side of the road in front of the Green Leaf Hotel, watching the people and an occasional car pass, trying to make up his mind about where to go and what to do. The Country Kitchen. Of course. A nice breakfast and let the flow begin.

Once again he walked down the rutted, sewer drainage bordered road. He was struck by the smiles turned his way, by the fact that no one was trying to hustle. *If this were Tijuana, Chicago or New York, I'd have people clinging to me by now.*

"Kofi, the Ghanaian is a funny kind of being. They're very warm, outgoing, and friendly. But they have a long tradition in trade, so they will never hesitate to try to get the better of you in a deal. Beware."

Thanks, Mom, gotta remember that. The Country Kitchen wasn't open yet. No hours posted, he gathered this info from a tall dark man passing by with a briefcase under his arm, obviously a bureaucrat or a businessman.

"'Scuse me, sir, can you tell me what time the Country Kitchen will be open?"

The man studied his watch for a few seconds.

"O! They will be open at eleven or so. You are wanting your chop yes?"

Who told me that the Ghanaians didn't have a pidgin, like the Nigerians, for example?

"Uhh, yes, I wanted to have breakfast here."

"So, 'tis nine-ish now. You can wait for two hours more or you can come with me for waakye."

I didn't give it a second thought, my stomach suddenly started rumbling.

"Uhh, o.k., I'll go with you."

And down we went, into the main stem of Osu, called for some reason, "Irene."

"My name is Andrew Aboage."

"Kofi Brown."

"You are an American."

He said it with such a definite sense of being correct Kofi felt no need to argue for "African-American."

"Uh yes, I'm an American."

Have to write Mom and Dad about this, the first time in my life I've ever been called an "American."

There was a surge of people on the broken sidewalks that went back and forth. Many people going one way or the other, but not one was rushing, he noticed.

"This is what we call Osu."

Mr. Aboage led him to a snack stand on a busy corner. "They have excellent waakye here."

Kofi took instant notice of the open drainage ten yards away from the waakye stand.

"So, what is waakye anyway?"

Mr. Aboage laughed – "Oooo! You do not know waakye? I'm sorry!"

"That's o.k., just tell me what it is."

Mr. Aboage turned from his question to place his order. "You will see."

The man placing black eyed peas and rice on a small banana leaf asked, "Egg? Spaghetti? Pepper?"

Mr. Aboage nodded enthusiastically, Kofi simply stared at the pile of peas and rice on the banana leaf. Black eyed peas and rice, mixed. A bit of spaghetti, a boiled egg and a large dab of homemade chili on the side. Mr. Aboage paid

"Please, allow me, Mr. Brown."

"Well, thank you, Mr. Aboage."

Waakye. It was good, no sign of meat in the mix at all. And it cost only a tenth of what he would have paid for breakfast at the Country Kitchen. But the proximity of the drainage ditch bothered him.

The waakye stand owner gave them small finger bowls to wash their hands after the meal.

"Medase," Mr. Aboage thanked the man, "So, how long will you be in Ghana here, Mr. Brown?"

"I have a month."

"Well, as we say – akwaaba/welcome. Here is my card. I must be off."

Kofi shook hands with his benefactor and studied the card. "Henry Aboage, Barrister. 2648 Abresem Way, Accra, Ghana, Specialist in import/export law."

Nice guy. Export/import law. Better keep this, it might come in handy. He meandered down the street, checking the people and the scene out.

Woww, if it weren't for the colorful clothing, the women's head wraps and all, it could be the Westside of Chicago, or Watts, during one of our festival days. A barbershop. Yeahhh, exactly what I need, a haircut.

"Mane-ly men Barbershop." It could have been a barbershop on Crenshaw, except that the sport pictures on the walls were of soccer players. And one spectacular photo of Serena Williams whacking a tennis ball.

Kofi noticed that there was a subtle shift of language, from Ga and Twi, to lightly British English.

On my account? Well, that's a nice thing to do.

"So, my brother, how is it?"

The barber, a short version of Snoop Dog, offered him the finger clicking West African handshake. Kofi felt surprised that he was able to do it.

"Everything is everything," he replied, recalling an ancient piece of music by the late, great Donny Hathaway.

"Everything is everything," the barber repeated after him. And suddenly his chair was horse shoed by the usual suspects who hang out in barbershops. They wanted to talk with him, get to know the latest American slang.

Kofi, never a great user of slang ("Kofi, learn how to speak standard English before you start trying to do patois"), couldn't offer them many linguistic windows to jump out of. Ardent hip hop fans, they knew the names of more rappers and their stories than he did.

"What's up with Ten Cents?"

"Did Lil' Woo Woo get married to Bee Bee Honey?"

"How long have you been in Ghana here?"

"How long will you stay?"

"Are you famous?"

He strolled out of the barbershop with a haircut-style he had never considered before, and the good wishes of everyone in the place.

"Akwaaba to Ghana!"

The sun hit him in the face like it was the glare from a furnace. Damn, it's hot out here. 11 a.m., time for a siesta.

· ∞☾ ·

"Dear Mom, Dad,

I've spent my first day and a half in Accra, in Osu, actually. And I'm lovin' it. It's about high noon now and I promised myself I would take a little siesta, but I'm too excited to sleep. The people around me, the vibes, the atmosphere are really intoxicating.

I keep telling myself, from minute to minute, you're in Ghana, in Africa, where your ancestors came from.

Impressions: Everybody is working. I haven't seen any evidence of anybody "hanging out." People carrying things on their heads are both a delight to see and a mystery. Where does that kind of ability to balance come from?

It's a bit startling, to say the least, to see a man turn to a wall and relieve himself. It's even more startling to see a woman do it.

Mom, I know you told me about this, but it's still a surprising sight. Sister is walking down this back street near my hotel, a platter of something on her head, a baby tied to her back (how?) and she pauses over the open drain at the side of the road, lifts her long skirt slightly, reaches under to pull the crotch of her panties to one side and lets fly – straight down into the drain.

Seems that I was the only one to pay attention to this, and I was very discreet. It makes perfectly good sense, when you think about it … where would you go to pee or whatever, if there are no outdoor toilets?

"Relatives," I've had to stop myself from asking half a dozen people, just ordinary folks passing by – "'scuse me, are we related?" In this short space of time I think I've seen a look alike for every member of our family. I've seen great Granddad Kwame at least twice.

(I've engaged a taxi driver named Kwame to take me to Tsito on Thursday. I hope he shows up.)

People are quieter, on a whole. There is almost none of the loudness that you would associate with a big city. Pleasant to have that kind of atmosphere, instead of everybody's car bumpin' 'n thumpin'.

Could I live in Ghana here? (That's what everybody says.) My emotional reaction is yes, yes, yes. But my realistic answer would have to be no. Life is hard here, I can see that. When you see little kids pushing, pulling carrying heavy loads in the hot sun, you know they're doing it out of necessity.

The people are poor, no doubt about it. But I see a lot of the same kind of fire and joy that I've seen in the ghetto in "El-A," New York, Chicago, New Orleans, Mexico City …

Going to take a nap now, preparation to see what the night life is like here –

Love, Kofi"

· ℰℛ ·

10 p.m. … The Zebra Club

Kofi stared at the women dancing the Electric slide. Never seen anything so beautiful in my life. His eyes roved through and over the dozen women performing the steps of the dance – step to the front – shimmy-shimmy to the side – take a step back – work the hips right 'n left. Beautiful. Gorgeous. A new form of "tribal dance."

"Would you care for another drink, sah?"

"You say?" Listen to me; I'm beginning to sound like one of the locals.

The waitress's question managed to penetrate the layers of thick, bassy sound that flowed out of the speakers in the Zebra Club.

"Would you like another drink?"

"Yesplease." He had noticed that people placed "yes" and "please" together, as one word. The Zebra Club in Adabraka, it has been recommended by one of the Green Leaf Hotel workers.

"Uhh, 'scuse me, my brother. I'm getting ready to go out and have a few beers, maybe dance a little bit. Where would you go, if you were me?"

"You say?"

"Where do you, when you got out to have a few beers and dance?"

"O! I go to the Zebra Club in Adabraka, it's very lively." Big smile validation.

Kofi "dashed" his "informant" a couple thousand cedis, a piece of advice his father had laid on him.

"Kofi, don't be careless and foolish, but a little judicious "dashing" will give you great dividends."

"What's 'dashing'?"

"You'll find out."

He had been in town almost two days and discovered the power of the "dash." Brother Roxy's advice (the hotel worker) to go to the Zebra Club in Adabraka was worth ¢10,000. What was that? A dollar. But a dollar/¢10,000 could feed a family of four for a day. Or more, if they stretched the soup a bit. And, he could tell, from the brother's sincere smile, that he had created an ally, and maybe a friend.

Roxy was right, the place was lively. But, he thought, in a conservative way. He couldn't detect any of the aggressive flirtation that he would normally find in one of the Crenshaw night spots, West Los Angeles, the Main street set in Santa Monica.

Men outnumbered the women three to one, but the men were cool. They drank their beers, made eye to eye contact with the women on the scene, but there was no hint of frenzy. So far as he could tell, it was definitely a Ghanaian scene. He looked around.

I must be the only obruni in the house …

·   ❧ ❧   ·

CHAPTER 21

"Kofi, you're going to hear the word used to describe you, sooner or later. Don't trip. It means, literally, 'a European'. But it carries another kind of baggage: a person from the outside, someone who doesn't know the scene. I equated 'obruni' to 'square' when I found out what it meant."

"I don't agree with your father on this one. I resented being called 'obruni'. If that's supposed to identify Europeans, all well 'n good. But I don't think it should be applied to Africans in the Diaspora. I think the Ghanaians, Africans in general, should find another name for us. You mean we went through all of what we went through, all of what we're going through, and they still want to think of us as 'Europeans', I can't get with that."

The woman holding her hand out to him didn't speak, she was inviting him to dance with her. He didn't hesitate. She was one of the Electric Slide dancers that he had admired so much.

The music had morphed from loud, snap-crackle-semi-rap to a style he couldn't identify.

"I like this music, what is it?"

"It is high life."

It only took him a couple beats to make a surreptitious study of the dance movements to get it down.

"What's you name?"

"Salena Sarpong."

"I'm Kofi Brown."

"You have danced the high life before?"

"Sort of. I like dances that give you a chance to hold the girl."

She snuggled a little closer to him and smiled. He glanced over her

169

shoulder to look at her girlfriends making animated conversation. And looking at them.

"Looks like your girlfriends are talking about us."

"Oh! They are just jealous."

"Jealous of what?"

"That I'm dancing with you."

Kofi held her at arm's length to check out the expression on her face. This gorgeous, chocolate colored woman with this beautiful head wrap on is telling me that her girlfriends are jealous of her dancing with me?

"Salena, I'm not quite sure I understand …"

"One of them, all of them wanted to dance with you but they were too shy …"

"But, why me? You got lots of guys up in here."

"Because you are an African-American, and African-Americans dance well."

Kofi puffed his chest out a bit and added a little more zip to his hips. Well …

"And besides, if you ask the Ghana boy to dance he will think you are a loose woman."

Kofi did a mental-cultural review of his social life at home. Would a woman ask me to dance? More likely a White girl than a sister, but it was not an unknown thing. Would a brother at home think the sister was "loose" because she asked him to dance? Maybe.

But then, there were some brothers who thought that <u>any</u> woman, in any club, that was not with a man, was a "loose woman."

The music came to an abrupt end, followed by a stream of inane disk jockey-commentary.

"Okay! Everybody! Let's put our dancing shoes on for this next one! This is the one you're all been waiting for …"

"Salena, do you think we could go someplace a little quieter, I'd like to talk with you about Ghana that I don't know anything about."

It wasn't necessary for him to pretend to be sincere, he was.

She did a close up face reading.

"We could walk out back; they have a large garden area there."

"I was thinking of another place, some place with soft music. Have you had dinner?"

She shook her head and laughed. What's funny?

"Did I say something funny?"

"No, not really. I was just thinking of how different we are. In Ghana here, a strange man would never suggest that he take me out and pay for my chop, unless an 'agreement' had been reached. Where do you propose to go?"

"I thought maybe you would know some place, I just got here yesterday…"

"I know a place you might like. I'm coming."

"I'm coming"/Mi Ba. That's what Mom and Dad were always saying to each other, when one or the other was waiting for the other. He watched Salena weave her way through the once again dancing bodies, retrieve her purse and have a few words with her girlfriends.

He tried to keep his smile from becoming a smirk. Hey, if y'all were jealous abut her dancing with me, what's going through you now? He couldn't resist a quick military-type salute to the girlfriends. They cut their eyes in his direction.

"O.k., I'm ready, we can go. I told them not to worry about me, that you would bring me home," she flashed him a warm, trusting smile.

"Not a problem, not a problem."

He took a deep breath and stared up at the stars sparkling in the dark blue sky. Beautiful night, Ghana, a beautiful woman at my side.

"Are you mobile?"

"Uhh, no, we'll have to take a taxi."

Taxis were lined up at the curb, the drivers waiting anxiously for customers. Salena approached one and began to palaver. After a couple minutes of gestures and frowns, she announced, "This man is offering us a fair price to LaBone."

"Well, let's go."

Kofi took note of the new familiar landmarks being driven west on King Rd.

"So Mr. Brown …"

"Please call me Kofi, Salena."

"So, Kofi, you have been in Ghana two days now?"

"Got in Monday evening."

"You are having a good time here?"

"Now I am."

They sat next to each other, feeling each other's warmth, the vibes.

"What brings you to Ghana?"

"It's almost a tradition in my family for us to come here. We started doing it years ago. It's not exactly a 'Roots' thing, although my Dad had some DNA research done that proved his people are Ga and Ashanti, my mother found her tribal DNA in Benin."

"Hmmm, very interesting I am Ashanti."

He stared at her profile. No, Salena, you're a Queen. An Ashanti, but definitely a Queen.

3rd Norla Lane/LaBone. "Susan's Place."

"This is it. You wanted soft music, you will find it here."

Hip set. That was the first thought that popped into his head. They were welcomed into a huge, loft designed room by the proprietor/designer/artist/entrepreneur, a small framed beige colored, very attractive woman that everyone simply called Susan.

"Ahh, Salena, my goodness! Where've you been?! I haven't seen you in ages! And who is this very polite, very handsome African-American gentleman?!"

No one had to tell Kofi that he was in the presence of a dynamic, well connected member of Ghanaian society. And he could tell Good Taste when he saw it.

"Please, Mr. Kofi Brown, Ms. Susan. She is our host."

Ms. Susan stood back to take a harder look at Kofi.

"Your parents are Kojo and Akosua?"

"Yes, do you know them?"

"I met them when they came to Ghana here, when was that? … Oh, please excuse me, my maitre d' is calling me, he has a problem. Please, make yourselves at home."

Wowww! This is unreal. I'm in the home of someone who knew, someone who knows my parents. He loved the homey, yet sophisticated atmosphere of "Susan's Place."

Subdued lighting, tables for two placed diplomatically/strategically around the large space. A bar at the opposite end of the room, gorgeous music spilling in from discreetly placed speakers, "Susan's Place." Susan moving quietly and efficiently from table to table, charming, witty, caring.

"Do you have everything you want, Dearie?"

"Yes, Susan. Thank you."

"Jakob, please take another cold beer to table six."

"Yes, Mr. Brown, as I was saying – I met Kojo and Akosua some time ago. As I recall, they were separate packages, in a manner of speaking. Kojo was here first and then some time later, Akosua came. She explained that he wanted her to experience her <u>own</u> Ghana, without his interference. I thought that was quite an interesting way to go about it.

How are they? O please excuse me, I have to see these people off. Please make yourselves comfortable, your waiter will be with you in a moment. Zacarias, see to those people, please."

"Yessirr Madam."

Yessir Madam?

The waiter, a very lean, dark skinned man with a humorous twinkle in his eyes, stood at attention next to their table.

"Uhh, may we see a menu please?" Kofi asked.

The waiter looked puzzled. A menu? Salena solved the problem.

"One doesn't need a menu here, order what you like and if they don't have it; you'll order something they do have."

"I was thinking about food …"

Salena took up the cause.

"We'll have two ABC Lagers and a little something."

"Yes, Madam."

Salena smiled in his direction.

"As I understand it, Susan wanted to create something unique, a sort of home away from home, with a romantic foundation. I think she has succeeded, don't you think?"

Kofi glanced around at the people at the other tables; the place was three fourths full at 11 p.m., but there were no loud conversations, nothing to indicate that they were in a commercial establishment. Not even menus.

Their waiter returned with two frosted bottles of ABC Lager and three bowls, two for washing their hands and one filled with finger sized bits of grilled beef, veal and chicken, "a little something."

"Umm, this is delicious."

"If it wasn't Susan wouldn't serve it."

"What's her story? She's a very interesting woman."

Salena nibbled on a nugget of chicken, took a sip of beer.

"Well, her Dad is one of the richest men in Ghana, he's an Ewe man, her mother is English, but Susan is 100% Ghanaian. Her Dad offered her some property to do something with and she did. She created the first Montessori School in Ghana."

"Really?"

"Yes, the school buildings are just there, behind this structure. As I understand it she uses the revenue from this business to fund her school. What with the high fees she charges the elite, and these funds, I suspect she's quite in the red. Incidentally, all of her servants, the waiters and waitresses have their children in the school on scholarship. She's quite a remarkable lady."

"You can say that again."

Susan drifted back over to their table after shaking hands, smiling and hugging a couple couples out into the night.

"Uhh, Susan, may I ask you a question?"

"Shoot!" She answered with a bit of Americanese. And a big smile.

"A few minutes ago, when our waiter answered you, he said 'Yessir Madam', that's a real puzzler for my little U.S. raised brain. Is that a special title or something?"

Salena and Susan gave each other high fives and burst out laughing. Kofi looked from one to the other, waiting for his answer.

"Kofi, I've been asked that question before. Let me explain – Zacarias, your waiter, is a devout Muslim from Burkino Faso, quite chauvinistic, and an excellent chap. He had one tremendous difficulty dealing with me when he first came to work here, he just didn't want to accept the idea that he was working for a woman and, since I'm a modern Ghanaian woman who wears slacks occasionally, he discovered a way to save face, by calling me 'Sir Madam'."

Kofi joined the joke.

"Woww, that's really saving face the hard way."

"Now then, having explained who I really am, 'an honorary man', so designated by my head waiter, I am going to call an early evening of it, I have a bunch of admissions applications to study and an early day tomorrow."

"I've told Kofi about your school."

"It's my reason for being."

"Mind if we take a peek at the classrooms?"

"Salena, dear, you're at home – you know where everything is situated. Mr. Brown, I hope to see more of you during your time in Ghana here?"

"Most definitely."

And she was off, smiling, exchanging bits of wit with people at nearby tables, pausing to discuss something serious with a couple of Kofi Annan look-alikes.

"That lady is smooth, real smooth. Thank you for telling me a little bit about her, introducing me to her.

Now, tell me a little bit about yourself, about this Ghana that I don't know anything about?"

"Did you say that you wanted to see the classrooms?"

"By all means – lead the way."

They strolled through the room, nodding pleasantly at people who seemed to be friends. Zacarias was there to hold the screen door open for them.

"Medase."

"You are welcome, Madam."

The night air and the chalk white moon fell on them like an exotic blanket. Kofi stared at the sky and mumbled, "I'm in Africa, the Motherland."

"You say?"

"Oh, just mumbling to myself. Seems that every time I step outside, no matter if it be day or night, I'm suddenly aware that I'm in Africa."

"I felt the same way during the whole four years I spent in Chicago."

"Chicago?! That's where my family came from, from Chicago to California. What were you doing in Chicago?"

They strolled on a well defined path, paved with large white flagstones, buildings that were designed like African village huts/thatched, on either side of the path. Fringed by low, spreading palm trees.

"I got a scholarship, through the Rotarians of America – believe it or not – to go to the University of Chicago."

"Great school, I've heard a lot about it."

"Great and very expensive. My scholarship didn't cover very much, so I had to work very hard, but as you can see I made it."

"You got your degree?"

"Masters, Sociology. I'm teaching at the U. of Ghana, in Legon."

"Funny, I'd never have guessed that you are a teacher."

"Well, what then, tell me?"

Kofi was tempted to tell the truth. I had no idea what you were about, and I didn't really care, I just saw you as a gorgeous African woman.

"C'mon, Kofi, tell me the truth – you didn't even think of me in a profession, you just looked at my face, my breasts and my hips."

He was stunned by the way she laid it out for him.

"Hey, you don't fool around, do you?"

They sat on one of the small white benches bordering the path.

"Life is too short for games …"

"Is that something you learned in the States?"

"No, I don't think so. It was already part of my thinking before I left Ghana here. I'm sure you've been here long enough, even if it's only been a couple days, to see that life isn't for day dreamers, people who can afford to live on illusions."

They were silent for a few moments, listening to the night noises of Accra and the music filtering out to them from "Susan's Place." "What's Going On?" the classic by Marvin Gaye was playing. Kofi held his hand out for Salena to dance with him. She floated into his arms.

· ಋ಄ ·

CHAPTER 22

Kofi woke up with a smile on his face. The singing maid was at work. He sprawled out in his bed, stretching, yawning, and feeling indulgent. He laced his hands behind his head and stared up at the slow whirling fan in the ceiling, mentally reviewing his evening with Salena. After "Susan's Place," a taxi to Salena's apartment in another section of LaBone.

"I would invite you in, but I must confess frankly, the place is a mess. And my neighbors would be scandalized to see me receiving a male guest this late."

"Well, what they don't know won't hurt them, will it?"

"Kofi, you don't know Ghana. By now everyone in this neighborhood knows that we have just left 'Susan's Place,' that we have had several beers, that we've enjoyed each other's company …"

"So, we're adults, what's the big deal?"

"In some places it wouldn't be a big deal, but in Ghana here – it is a big deal. When my parents gave me permission to have my own apartment, I promised them that I would not create a scandal. Would you like to kiss me good night?"

Kofi squirmed around in bed, remembering the kiss. And the aftermath.

"So, you are going to Tsito on Thursday on a research project. Then what?"

"Well, I don't know. A lot of what I do after Tsito depends on what happens there, what comes out of that."

He hadn't felt comfortable with the idea of revealing the Asiafo-Kojo story to her, yet.

"So, how long will you stay in Tsito?"

"O, I'll just run up and back, maybe get there in the morning, come back in the evening …"

She laughed at his time table.

"Kofi, you don't know Ghana. This is the rainy season; roads that were somewhat reliable may not be reliable at all. So, I would say, if you are going on Thursday, and all goes well, then you should be back in Accra on Sunday."

"Sunday? I didn't have any plans to hang out in this place."

"That doesn't mean a lot to Mother Nature. Remember, you're in West Africa. Rain has a real meaning here."

"So, when will I see you again?"

"Here is my card – call me. If the phone doesn't function properly, hire a small boy to deliver your message. And if I'm out and about, I will come to your place. Oh, one more thing, do you want me to be your girlfriend while you are here, or do you want many girlfriends? You can have it either way; you are a man in Ghana here."

Kofi squirmed around in bed, folded his arms across his chest, locking all of the ambivalent thoughts he had about Salena into place.

"Yes, of course, I would like for you to be my girlfriend."

"O.k., but no sex, I'm 24 years, almost an old maid, but I'm saving myself for my husband."

Once again, Kofi squirmed around in his bed. Mmm, if we kiss like that more than once, then we are definitely going to have a problem with her virginity. Woww, a 24-year-old virgin. Well, let's see what the flow has in store for us.

· ℘ℭ ·

Thursday morning, 9:38 a.m. He re-checked his backpack for essentials and non-essentials. The mosquito net essential. The last thing I need is a case of malaria.

10:30 a.m. He was thinking about going down to the front desk to have someone grab him a taxi when Kwame, the taxi driver, tapped on his door.

"Sorry, sah, I had to collect my wife's mother to take her to Makola market for goods."

"Your wife's mother?"

"Yessah, she is a trader and collects her goods at the market on Thursday."

"What time ..?"

"Oh, she goes to the market at five in the morning."

This is a busy man; he's already put in a half day's work.

"Well, shall we get on?"

"Yessah."

· ℘℃ℛ ·

It only seemed that they had taken a few left and right turns before they were out of the city. Kofi settled back in the passenger's seat, feeling a little ill at ease without a safety belt across his chest. O well ...

"Uhh, brother Kwame?"

He noticed a huge smile crease the driver's face. He likes that – Brother Kwame.

"Yessah?"

"I didn't have a chance to check the map, is Tsito very far?"

"Tsito is not near and it is not far. We should be there in three, maybe four hours."

Nothing to do but take in the scenery. Beautiful, picturesque country side. Reddish clay roads, like they have in Georgia. Neat rows of pineapples, plantains, cassava, mud wattled village huts a few hundred yards to the left and right of the road, people doing what their ancestors did centuries ago.

What <u>my</u> ancestors were doing centuries ago. The country side whizzing by, the gentle motions of the people carrying enormous loads on their heads ...

"Brother Kwame! Look at that!"

The driver glanced at the two small, wiry muscled men strolling along the side of the road with a six-foot log on their heads. Men carrying a log on their heads, what's exciting about that?

"O! I see, sah."

Kofi saw the humor of the moment. O.k., I get it. You've been seeing people carry logs on their heads all your life, but it's a first for me. The heat of midday made him very thirsty.

"Brother Kwame, you think we could stop for a drink, I'm very thirsty."

"Yessah, just ahead, there is a village to the left."

They made an exit from the two-lane highway into what looked like the 17th century. A small village, maybe ten huts clustered around a village circle, a "general store."

"What would you like to drink, sah?"

"Water would be fine, but a cold beer would be better." His father's words rang a bell in his head.

"Kofi, I know you're a sober young man, thank God! Akosua worried about that a lot when you were growing up. We were praying that you wouldn't fall into that alcohol-pot bag that a lot of your friends fell into, but when you go to Ghana, drink beer rather than water. The beer has been pasteurized, the water can be problem."

"A beer, sah? I'm sure they will have."

Kofi strolled the few yards from the taxi to the "general store," suddenly surrounded by a dozen little curious children, their eyes glowing from the excitement of seeing a stranger. One of the five-year-olds, bolder than her peers, reached up and grabbed his hand. Kofi was tempted to pick her up and cuddle her in his arms, but decided not to for fear that he might be violating a cultural norm.

It's o.k. for her to cozy up to me, but they might not like the idea of me treating her like a little teddy bear or something. Brother Kwame shooed the children away.

"Go 'way, leave this man alone! Go 'way!"

Kofi waved goodbye to the children as he entered the store. He had to conceal his surprise at the sight of a middle aged White man standing behind a long wooden counter. He was a bit swarthy, but a White man nevertheless. The man walked around the counter to shake his hand.

"Akwwaba, welcome ... I heard the commotion outside. What can I do for you? You are an African-American, are you not? We seldom have visitors here, as you can well imagine, being such a small place."

The man spoke in short, clipped phrases, his words literally rolling off of his tongue. He was obviously glad to see a new face.

"In answer to your first question, I would like a cold beer. Do you have a cold one?"

"Yes, my wife is in back, she will bring it." He turned to call out, "Nana, bring the cold ABC, it's at the top of the 'fridge!"

"In answer to your second question, yes, I am an African-American. And yourself, where are you from?"

His wife, an African woman, brought two beers on a wooden tray, with frosted glasses. Kofi took note of the affectionate smiles that the couple exchanged.

"Ahh, my wonderful wife, this is Nana, my wonderful wife. See, she has brought me a beer also. May I join you?"

"Yes, of course. But first, let me check on my driver, to see if he wants anything?"

Kofi found brother Kwame carefully posed up against the edge of the porch, his back to the wall, sound asleep.

Well, I guess he's getting what he needs most. He went back inside the store to find the owner had pulled a small wooden table into the center of the store and placed two three-legged stools for them to sit on.

"Please, please be seated, Mr. ..?"

"Kofi Brown."

"Ahh yes, a good Ghana name. I am Sardun Al-Bayati."

Kofi sat and chugged a full glass of beer down. It tasted unbelievably good. Dad was right; water couldn't touch beer in Ghana here.

"Ahh, that's really a thirst quencher."

Mr. Al-Bayati beamed at him, pleased to be his host.

"There are others, almost as cold as that one. Now then, you ask where I am from? I am from Iraq ..."

Kofi took another large sip of his beer, perked up a bit by the word "Iraq."

"Most people think I am Lebanese because there are many Lebanese in West Africa, traders, and store owners like myself."

"From Iraq to this small village, that's a big jump."

Mr. Al-Bayati stared at the sunshine streaming into the store through the screen door. He looked sad.

"Well, I went to England before here. I had lost my wife, three children; other relatives in the war ... The Americans killed them. Those Blackwater security people."

The beer suddenly tasted a little bitter. The scenes of the Iraq quagmire flashed through his mind.

"I did not like England, it was so cold all of the time. So, one dark, windy day, I decided to come to Africa, to Ghana here. I had no desire to go anywhere in the Middle East, with all of the violence and the divisions between the people: the Shia against the Sunni, the Wahabi against everything."

They shared a smile.

"You know the Wahabi, Mr. Brown?"

"They're the fundamentalists in Saudi Arabia, aren't they? The guys with the fashion police, the ones who don't like the idea of women driving cars, like the Taliban in Afghanistan."

"Yes, exactly that. Not at all like we have it in Ghana here. I found all of the freedom I could not have in my own country. If I don't want to go to the mosque, no one will give me a problem. If I don't want to pray five times a day, no one will call me bad names. But best of all there are no bombs, no one killing themselves, or anybody else. I love it here."

After a second beer, Kofi had to pull himself away from Mr. Al-Bayati's grip on his arm.

"Mr. Al-Bayati, I <u>must</u> go. I have an appointment to keep."

"Ahh, but Mr. Brown, you have not eaten. My wife is a wonderful cook; she is preparing groundnut stew with chicken. We can have another cold beer."

"Next time, Mr. Al-Bayati, next time. I'll be coming this way again in a few days ..."

"You <u>must</u> come, we will talk more about the world, o.k.?"

"By all means - as salaam alaikum."

"Wa alaikum salaam."

Kofi thought he saw the beginning of tears in the man's eyes when they exchanged the Muslim greeting/wish for "peace unto you." He quickly placed the cedis on the low table for his beers and walked quickly to brother Kwame, waiting in his taxi.

"Brother Kwame, would you like a cold beer before we get back on the road?"

"No, sah, I never take alcohol while I am driving."

Kofi settled back in the passenger side seat. Good man, don't drink and drive. He nodded off, lulled into sleep by the beer and the steady drone of the car's engine.

· ৪০ঙ্গ ·

CHAPTER 23

He woke up from a sweaty, soggy nap an hour and a half later, feeling slightly disoriented. Where am I? O yes, Ghana.

"You slept, sah."

"Yes, a good sleep. Where are we?"

"Tsito is not far."

Kofi yawned, stared out at the people in the fields bordering the road.

"What're they planting here?"

"They are planting ground nuts, very nice."

His mind flickered back to Mr. Sardun Al-Bayati. Poor guy, he may love the peace and quiet of this place but he must miss his home, his roots. Exile, expatriation must be one of the hardest things anyone would have to deal with, emotionally. Wonder how that would factor into the African-American psyche?

"Tsito, sah ..."

3 p.m., a sluggish time of day. They drove through a hard dirt packed "main street." A post office, a church, a general store, a few open front shops, cinder block houses with corrugated tin roofs. A relatively prosperous looking place.

"Brother Kwame, how many people do you think live here?"

"O, I would say, maybe three thousand, maybe five thousand."

Three-five thousand? How do I go about locating somebody named Aunt Eugenia in a place with thousands of people? He felt a sudden sense of helplessness. Damn!

"Brother Kwame, where would I go if I wanted to find out where someone was living?"

"To the police, sah," he answered without hesitation.

Yes, of course, the police would know. The police knew where everybody was. And they did know.

"Oh, Auntie Eugenia, she lives in 'Old Tsito'. Tsito is divided, you see. This is New Tsito. She is in 'Old Tsito', it is just there, about ten minutes fast walk down this road."

"Thank you."

Brother Kwame whispered, "You should dash him, sah, for the information, police do not earn much money in the small town."

"How much?"

"O, ten thousand would be nice."

The policeman accepted the dash gratefully, and walked them back to the taxi.

"Auntie Eugenia is a crusty old sort, but she makes very good banku and okra stew … hah hah hah."

· ℯ)ℳ ·

"Old Tsito" was thatched, mud wattled huts. Clean and arranged in a circular patter, rather than the straight rows of "New Tsito." It took only one inquiry of an old woman sweeping her front yard with a bundle of cut twigs to find Aunt Eugenia.

She shifted her chewing stick/tooth brush from one side of her mouth to the other, and silently pointed at the house/hut across the road from her.

Kofi had the feeling that he was approaching a relative that he hadn't seen in many years. The woman chopping wood behind her hut turned to face him as he turned the corner of the hut. She shaded her eyes from the afternoon sun.

"Ahh, Kojo, my son, you have come back to see your old Auntie Eugenia?"

"No, m'am, I am not Kojo, I am Lil' Kofi, Kojo's son."

The old lady, he guessed that she was seventy or so, dropped her hatchet and walked past him into her hut. Her movements were strong, energetic. A moment later she emerged from the hut with a tray. Two glasses of water, a few nibs of fresh coconut and two ears of corn.

She directed them to sit on a bench in the shade of the thatched hut.

"You are welcome, please sit-sit-sit!"

"This like ol' times," Brother Kwame whispered.

Following Brother Kwame's example, Kofi dribbled a few drops of water on the ground before drinking it. O no, water. Water from where? O well ...

Once again, following Brother Kwame's example, he nibbled on the coconut and ate all of the kernels from the fresh, rich tasting corn cob. Aunt Eugenia pulled a stool up in front of them and watched them as they ate.

The eating finished, she took the tray back inside.

Brother Kwame took the opportunity to whisper more "cultural advice" into Kofi's ear.

"Sah, here in Tsito your business cannot be done quick-quick, you must stay awhile."

Salena was right on the money – "So, I would say if you are going on Thursday, and all goes well, then you should be back in Accra on Sunday evening."

Aunt Eugenia came out of the hut with a futon draped over her shoulder, and a carry-carry bag of personal items. She strutted across to the house on the other side of the road. She had a short, animated conversation with the woman who had been twig-brushing her yard. And returned with a bright smile.

"I will stay in my sister's house while you are here, come – I will show you where your father slept."

Kofi liked her definite way of doing things. The guess work was gone. Your father slept here, this is where you're going to sleep period. She beckoned for him to follow her into her hut with the hand pulling down motion that he had seen other people use. He came to the entrance of the hut and stared inside.

There was order, neatness, everything in its proper place. She hasn't done this because she was expecting visitors; this is the way she lives.

"Kofi, you father slept here, this is where you will sleep."

The random thoughts about where to find cheap hotels in Tsito were immediately kicked to the curb. Look closely, boy, this is where you're gonna be while you're up in here, dig?

He stared at the elevated mud sleeping platform, the various woven bags of whatever hanging on the walls of the hut. Nice. It would definitely merit a home beautiful tag, if they had enough sense to recognize what good/utilitarian homes were all about.

He could sense that Aunt Eugenia was delighted to see him, felt good about his presence, but was cool. That was the Tsito way.

"Auntie, my friend, this young man from Amerika, has questions to ask of you. May I speak more?"

Kofi stared at Brother Kwame and felt like hugging him. Wowww, this dude is really on it. And he was deliberately speaking English to make certain that Kofi understood what he was saying.

Aunt Eugenia nodded her head back and forth, indicating that she wasn't sure she wanted to respond to these questions. There was a long pause. This is not Amerika, things take time here.

Brother Kwame, understanding the protocol, stared at the ground until his Elder chose to respond. Aunt Eugenia nodded yes, please continue.

"Auntie, my friend, Kofi, the son of Kojo …"

"I knew this one," the old lady interjected.

"Kojo's son wants to know something …"

"Eh heee."

And there was silence for a few beats. Brother Kwame leaned over to whisper – "She will speak with you. But not today. Maybe tomorrow, it is late in the day now."

Kofi felt momentarily at sea. So now what?

"Kofi, my son, I am going to prepare your evening meal. Would you like to take a bath after your long journey?"

"Uhh, yes m'am." What else can I say?

Brother Kwame shuffled his feet, changing his stance from one foot to the other. He was obviously anxious to leave. Kofi walked to the taxi to retrieve his backpack and to pay the driver.

"Brother Kwame, I'm a little new at all this. So, what happens now?"

"Well, sah, Auntie will give you a nice chop. You will sleep. And then tomorrow, perhaps, you may begin to ask of her what you wish."

"O.k., I understand that part, but how will I get back to Accra?"

"I will collect you."

"When?"

"Oh, let us say Sunday morning."

"Sunday morning: I hadn't planned to spend two days here."

Brother Kwame smiled. "In Ghana here, one must exercise patience and remain flexible."

He paid the driver and returned to the hut. Brother Kwame drove slowly away. Aunt Eugenia snatched his backpack and hung it on a stake in the wall of the hut.

"The water for your bath is there ..." She pointed to a wooden stall in the back area. An outdoor bath, never had one of those before. He took a hard look around the neighborhood. Most of the huts were within eye range of each other. Over there a woman was stirring a pot of something. A woman sat on a stool, getting her hair braided.

Four old men sat under a large tree over there, drinking from wooden cups. Bet it's palm wine, have to try some while I'm here. Aunt Eugenia had hung a large towel with the logo "Las Vegas" on it onto a stake at the side of the "bath house."

Kofi undressed inside the stall, hung his clothes on the back side/ outside and went inside for his bath. He had to smile at his own feelings. Suddenly I'm buck naked outdoors, everybody knows I'm in here ... the thought drove his smile to a giggle. Woww, this is funny. Wonder how Dad felt when he did this?

Two full buckets of water and a bar of soap. It took him a couple seconds to figure out the drill. Pour the whole bucket over my body, soap and then rinse. Or splash some water on myself and soap up. More water to rinse off the soap.

He decided to splash, soap and rinse. O my God what a good feeling. The water was sun warmed-tepid and the evening air, just barely filled with breezes, was a giant caress. The water splashed over his body from the buckets prolonged the caress.

He toweled himself off and reached for his clothes. Gone. He felt around for a frantic second, saronged the "Las Vegas" towel around his waist and opened the door of the "bath house," peeking out shyly.

Aunt Eugenia gestured to him – come. Kofi felt a little self conscious walking out of the "shower" with just a towel on. Aunt Eugenia gestured again – there! Flip flops.

He snuggled his toes into the made in China flip flops and tried to stroll across the distance separating them without feeling self conscious about being out in public with only a towel draped around his waist.

"I have soaked your clothes, all salty-sweaty, they will be washed. You have more clothes?"

"Yes m'am."

"You say … 'm'am.'" What means 'm'am'?"

She stood in front of him, her fists on her ample hips, asking a very reasonable question. What was it the policeman said, "Auntie Eugenia is a crusty old sort, but she makes very good banku and okra stew …"

"M'am." What the hell does "M'am" mean? Obviously it's a contraction of something. Maybe an American adaptation of the French "Mam'selle." Maybe that's it. But "M'am" is something that I've always heard used when folks were addressing older people.

"M'am, let me say this … I don't really know what 'M'am' means, other than as a way to address someone you want to show respect for."

The old lady clapped her hands three times and laughed aloud.

"Eh heee, you are your father's son."

"Now tell me this, m'am, what does 'eh hee' mean?"

He thought he was going to have to pick the old lady up off of the ground; that was how hard her laugh convulsions took her. Finally, she gained control of herself and told him why she was convulsed with laughter.

"Kofi, my son, you must be very careful about how you say – 'eh hee'." It is <u>very</u> funny."

"O.k., what I say may be very funny, but what does it mean? You didn't answer that."

He was beginning to get a positive grip on the old lady's grasp of things. If you couldn't track with her, she would simply write you off as a poot butt. Kofi was beginning to feel right at home. She stared at him and smiled; a lustrous, full teethed smile, no white sugared cavities showing anywhere.

"I am making groundnut stew and fish for you, M'am."

Kofi smiled at the old lady's back as she went to stir the ground nut pot. "M'am?" "Yessir, Madam." Maybe, like Master Thich Thien Long used to say, "It is all One."

· ෨෬ ·

Awaking up by a rooster crowing. In Accra, at the Green Leaf, it would be a hotel maid singing; here it's a rooster crowing. But not just one rooster crowing, there were several roosters answering. Hey guys, you don't have to challenge who is going to be the sunrise guy.

He yawned and stared up into the thatched roof. Have to ask what kind of snakes they have here. He sat up on the side of the hard mud packed bed stand, covered by a thick futon. Hard, but good to sleep on.

Damn that stew was good last night. He had eaten two full bowls of the groundnut stew while Aunt Eugenia simply sat and watched.

"Aren't you having some of this, Auntie?"

"I had my chop at one o'clock, I eat one time a day only."

Hmmm ... no wonder you still have that chorus girl figure.

He dug down into his backpack for a T-shirt and short khaki pants. Now, let me get out here and see what's happening in Tsito. Aunt Eugenia, in concert with the other women in the neighborhood, was twig-sweeping the area in front of her hut.

"Good morning, Auntie."

"Good morning, my son, there is water for your bath." She smiled briefly, barely glanced up at him as she continued sweeping, a toothbrush chewing stick firmly clenched in the corner of her mouth.

Kojo looked around. People in "Old Tsito" were bathing in their "bath houses," sweeping, eating breakfast, tending small garden plots, doing the things they did every day, maybe for generations. On the way to the "bath house" he took note of his clothes, his shirt and pants had been washed and hung out to dry. She washed my clothes, by hand. Have to thank her for that. May be I should "dash" her. No, I don't think so. She's the type who would be insulted if I offered her a tip.

The bath water was slightly cooler in the morning, very refreshing. He toweled off and was relieved to find his T-shirt and khakis still in place.

Aunt Eugenia sat next to her coal pot, stirring something around in a small pan.

"Kofi, come – I have made your breakfast."

"I thought I would wait and have food later, in the afternoon."

"Sit-sit-sit, you must eat. You are young you need more food, I am old I don't need so much food."

He could see the logic of her reasoning. No sense trying to argue with her, she's right. He sat in his usual place, in the shade of the thatched hut. She gave him a bowl with — "grits!"

"No, this gari, with ground nut sauce.'

"It might be garri here, but back home we call it grits."

"You like?"

"I've always liked grits … mmm … this is good."

After his gari-grits with ground nut sauce he leaned back against the wall of the hut. I feel like I've been living in this place a long time. The rhythms of life are so simple here. Nobody rushes to do anything. No bus to catch to go here, there or anywhere.

He stared up at the clear blue sky. No pollution, not even a cloud. But it was getting hotter by the minute.

Aunt Eugenia marched past him with a large basket of ripe tomatoes on her head. Kofi jumped up to help her.

"Here, Auntie, let me give you a hand with that."

She stared at him. Foolish boy. How can you help me?

"Can you carry this on your head?"

"No, I couldn't carry it on my head, but I could carry it on my shoulder."

He knew, from the moment he struggled to lift the basket from her head that he wouldn't be able to carry the basket full of tomatoes anywhere. But he tried, for a few yards, before he struggled to lower the basket from his shoulder without dropping the load.

"Uhh, where are you going with these?"

"Up the road to New Tsito. I have two people who will buy all I bring."

Mysteriously, the neighbor across the road was there to help Aunt Eugenia place the basket back on her head.

"This is my sister, she is younger."

Kofi smiled and bowed, the woman nodded and stuck out a work worn hand to give him a very limp hand shake. Ahhh, so that's where you went last night, to your sister's house.

Aunt Eugenia was in stride with two steps.

"Kofi, I will go and come, if you need anything, call my sister, her name is Patience."

· ෙ ·

CHAPTER 24

"Dear Dad,

I am now in this small place where you once stayed, with Aunt Eugenia. I don't know how old she is, but she has twice as much energy as I have.

She has just marched off down the road with a basket full of tomatoes on her head, which I could barely lift. She's a bit gruff, but very nice, very sweet. I like her.

The taxi driver who drove me here is named Kwame, Great-Grandfather's name. The man is rich source of cultural info. He will be "collecting" me on Sunday morning. Today is Friday. I've been here overnight and I feel as though I've been here for weeks.

There is a great natural rhythm here. You wake when the roosters crow and you go to bed when it gets dark. It may sound like a cliché but it's so quiet, I can literally her myself think.

I am staying in what is called Old Tsito, the village that you once stayed in Old Tsito looks like something from an issue of National Geographic, with the thatched huts and old stuff. New Tsito, a couple football fields away, has cinder blocks and corrugated tin rooftops; I imagine it's quite hot inside of one of these dwellings.

I haven't broached the subject of Asiafo, the girl who left the village, or any of that, upon the advice of Brother Kwame, the taxi driver. He suggested that I give it all a chance to come out as it comes out, not to force anything. I'm cool with that.

It's close to midday-noon and the sun seems to be directly overhead. It's hot and humid, but the civility of the scene makes everything cool.

I don't know when I'll be able to drop this letter into a mail box, but I thought I would write it anyway, just to let you know, to let you and Mom know that I'm having a great, interesting time, and that I thank you both for preparing me for this adventure.

Love, Kofi"

· ℰℂ ·

Aunt Eugenia returned in the late afternoon, about three o'clock, the tomato basket filled with store wrapped goods.

"It has been a long day. Leave me have my bath, we will eat and then rest for a little while."

He didn't see any reason to dispute the schedule she outlined in a brief sentence. He stared at the "bathhouse," knowing that she was splashing herself with a well deserved shower. After she finished, marching past him, she called out, – "Kofi, water is there – go."

She didn't have to urge him. What could feel better than a refreshing shower at late midday? She changed his clothes while he was in the shower, replacing his shorts and T-shirt with the pants and shirt he had worn when he arrived. When did she iron these things?

Stepping out of the shower, feeling fresh and almost dapper in his freshly ironed shirt and pants, he found the answer to his question across the road; sister Patience had ironed his clothes. There, there it was, full blown, that African cooperation syndrome. It would be great if more African-Americans were into this kind of thing, beyond Kwanzaa.

They sat down in the shadow of the hut to eat a delicious meal of kenké and smoked fish that her sister brought from across the road on a large covered tray.

"Kofi, I must warn you, the sheetaw, the pepper sauce is hot."

The sheetaw was very warm, but it wasn't hot. Aunt Eugenia took note.

"Eh hee ... the sheetaw does not cause you a problem."

"Auntie, I grew up on habaneras and Scotch bonnets, 'cause that's what my Dad likes."

"Eh hee ..."

Work, food, eat, sleep. He lay on the hard mud packed bed, thinking a jumbled number of things. How do I go about asking this woman the questions I want to ask her? Better put this mosquito net up before I go to dreamland.

He woke up to the sound of drums in the distance. Wonder what that's about? He was surprised to see several people from nearby huts assembled in Aunt Eugenia's backyard.

"Kofi, come."

Aunt Eugenia was obviously refreshed from her bath, her "chop" and her nap. She and her neighbors were seated around an old fashioned star fire. She beckoned him to a medium sized, hand carved stool at her right side. They had wooden cups. There were drinking.

"Kofi, I have something you can take." She pulled a fifth of Grant's Scotch from the basket at her side. He stared at the label for a second. Woww ... this is the serious time.

"Uhh, Auntie, what're you all drinking?"

It seemed that all eight heads in the circle swiveled in his direction.

"Akpeteshie," she answered, and pulled a bottle of white liquid out of the basket.

"I'll have some of that."

She seemed to be a bit contrite as she poured him a large drink in a small wooden cup.

"This is akpeteshie, it's the poor man's drink, but we like it."

He dribbled a few drops on the ground before taking a sip, which earned him approving glances. Eh heee, Aunt Eugenia's son knows how to behave proper. Akpeteshie. He had tasted freshly made moonshine in the South a couple times; the akpeteshie had that kind of kick, plus the aftertaste of a good gin. He smacked his lips with approval. The man to Auntie's left made a comment in Ewe.

"My neighbor says you are a rare obruni, most do not like akpeteshie."

Kofi shook his head, smiled at the man, and took a more generous sip of the drink. Can't get away from this obruni thing, no matter what you do.

・ ஓౡ ・

Two hours later, with Indonesian mosquito coils wafting up mosquito-protection curls of smoke, Kofi, Aunt Eugenia, her sister and the man who had made the comment about him, stared into the fire, pleasantly drunk.

"Auntie, what is that drumming all about?"

"It's a funeral. A big-big man has died, they are playing for his funeral."

Now was the time, he could feel it.

"Auntie, I want to ask you a few questions ..."

"Eh hee."

"About a man named Asiafo."

No one had to tell him that he had struck a chord. Another bottle of akpeteshie suddenly appeared, was passed around, libations and prayers offered.

"What do you want to know of this wicked man?"

"Well, as I understand it, he was killed, right?"

He felt it would be better to lay a little groundwork before jumping right into it. The three people sitting around the small fire with him nodded their heads in tandem.

"Yes, he was struck down over there," Aunt Eugenia pointed in the direction of New Tsito, "When all of that land was forest land. So ...?"

"I'm just curious. My father told me many times that he had spoken with Asiafo, he told me that this man possessed strong powers, maybe magic ..."

They sipped from their cups of akpeteshie, were silent for a few moments. The drumming from New Tsito had gone from staccato to slow, deep bass notes.

"I told Kojo, your father, to stay away from that wicked man. But he disobeyed me. I feel that he is very lucky that something very bad did not happen to him."

Aunt Eugenia's sister Patience and the man sharing the akpeteshie with them agreed.

"Eh heee ... he was very wicked!"

"This Asiafo could turn himself into a serpent."

Kofi's ears perked up at the word "serpent."

"What kind of serpent, uhh, what kind of snake?"

The man's eyes rolled around a couple of times before he answered.

"A big-big snake," he answered. And they all laughed. And sipped more akpeteshie. Kofi was beginning to feel a bit loose headed. He felt it wouldn't be long before he would feel the need to either go to bed or vomit. But he was also determined to get the information he needed.

"Auntie, your niece wrote my father a letter, years ago, telling him that Asiafo had a girlfriend from the village. In the letter she says that after Asiafo was killed, this girl was banished from the village …"

Aunt Eugenia's sister spoke, slurring her words slightly.

"She was not banished, she ran away from Tsito because she was pregnant with Asiafo's baby."

Aunt Eugenia ended the conversation by pouring the dregs of her drink onto the dying coals of the fire. The fire flared up briefly and then died.

"It is late now, time for us to go to sleep," Aunt Eugenia announced. And strode across the road to her sister's hut. Kofi struggled to his feet, shook hands with sister Patience and the man (her husband? boyfriend? friend?) and staggered into the hut. Wonder what kind of snake Asiafo turned himself into?

· ₮ℓ ·

The roosters crowing wake him up. He opened his eyes slowly and gently placed his head between his hands. Good, no hangover. He had felt certain that he would wake up with a hangover. Good, no hangover.

Aunt Eugenia sat on a stool in the shade, peeling and slicing vegetables. He recognized onions and okra.

"'Morning Kofi."

"Good morning, Auntie."

The fleeting smiles that they exchanged were self explanatory. We tied one on last night, didn't we? He took his splash-shower-bath and strolled back to the cool bench by the side of the hut. Aunt Eugenia placed a large bowl in his hands – "Fufu, light soup. Good for you."

It <u>was</u> good, but by the time he finished eating with his right hand, pinching off a small wad of the cassava-plantain fufu, stirring it around in the goat flavored soup and putting it in his mouth, he had dribbled quite a bit of it down the front of his shirt.

"Kofi, give me your shirt, there is soup on the front."

"There is also soup inside of me too."

He stripped off his shirt and went inside the hut to dig into his backpack for another T-shirt. Aunt Eugenia had placed his shirt in a pile of other clothes to be washed.

"Kofi,' she signed to him, "Come – sit-sit-sit."

He sat on the bench near her, checking out the expression on her dark brown face. She looked off into the distance, in the direction of New Tsito for a few moments before speaking.

"Kofi, my son, we do not like to speak of unhealthy things before we go to sleep, it can arouse bad spirits in our dreams. Are you getting me?"

"Uhh, yes m'am, I understand." She turned to face him and removed her chewing stick – toothbrush from the corner of her mouth.

"Yes, Kutu ran away from Tsito because of the shame she felt and because she refused to take the herbs that her mother, her father wanted her to take, to stop her pregnancy."

'That was the name given her after she left. In your language it means 'pot'."

'So, why would they call her 'pot'?"

Aunt Eugenia took her chewing tick and pantomimed stirring something around in the palm of her hand. A stirring something about a pot, Kutu, I get it.

"This happened many years ago, when women and girls did not have anything to do with men before they were married. Now it is different."

"So, where did Kutu go?"

"No one knew where she was for a long time. But then one day a woman from our village told us that she had seen Kutu in the market place in Osu ..."

"That's where I'm living right now, at the Green Leaf Hotel in Osu."

"Eh heee. She was seen in the market place with a baby on the back."

"Asiafo's baby?!"

"Maybe that one or some other man, who knows?"

"And no one else has seen her since that time?"

"O yes, someone will see her now and then. You must remember, in Ghana here, it is not easy to disappear or keep a secret, especially in Osu.

There is a saying – "Reveal yourself in Kumasi today and they will know about it in Osu tomorrow."

Kofi reasoned that Aunt Eugenia was saying that Kutu was living in the section of Accra called Osu, but indirectly.

"So Auntie, let's say I wanted to find this person in Osu – who would be likely to know where she is?"

"I am a village woman, I don't know the city. Perhaps my niece will know."

"Grace? Can you give me a number for her?"

"You say?"

"Can you give me an address?"

"Eh heee. She lives in Kanda, not far from Osu on King Road."

"I know it, my driver showed it to me when I first arrived."

"That is all I will say about this now, I must pull weeds from my garden before it rains."

"Huh? Rain? Where?"

Kofi stared up at the bright blue sky.

"There, over there," she pointed.

·   ℰℭ   ·

"Dear Dad, Mom,

It's raining here in Tsito. It's like somebody had opened a faucet. The rain is coming down like that. Aunt Eugenia pointed at a distant cloud this morning, which I couldn't even see, and predicted rain.

Three-four hours later the wet stuff happened. The thunder and lightning that goes with this downpour is enough to make you believe that there is a Shango, if you didn't already believe.

I'm quite dry, however, in my little thatched hut (Auntie's house), writing, reading, eating. Auntie is across the road at her sister's house, but she's been back 'n forth about four times today: to bring me my "chop," to make sure that I hadn't gone stir crazy and finally, to bring me an old fashioned coal oil lantern.

I think I have gotten the info I need to find this girl who had Asiafo's baby. Auntie explained what the moral climate was like back then, and offered a reasonable explanation of why the girl (she was named "Kutu"/pot because she had been "stirred" around inside) ran away from here.

I have been in Tsito since Thursday night, today is Saturday and my taxi driver, the cool brother Kwame is scheduled to "collect" me tomorrow morning.

Aunt Eugenia has played with my head a little bit by telling me – "Sometimes, like now, it will rain for one day or one week. The roads become very muddy and many children are conceived."

Well, I don't have to worry about any children being conceived, but I'm crossing my fingers and praying that the road won't be too muddy for Brother Kwame to get to me.

This is the second letter I've written, that I haven't mailed. I'll go to the post office as soon as I get back to Accra.

Love, Kofi"

· ဆဃ ·

CHAPTER 25

Kofi lowered the wick inside his lantern and stared out of the window at the storm. How long can it rain this hard? Midnight. He sprawled on his bed, listening to the hard rain splattering on the thatched hut.

Incredible design, the thatched hut. He could see huge rivulets splashing down the window pane. I've never experienced anything like this. But there were no leaks.

For a few minutes he felt afraid, but it passed because he couldn't identify the cause of his fear. Am I afraid of the thunder, the lightning, the rain?

A long roll of thunder that started off as a bass drum beat ended with a trillion volts of lightning. He laced his hands behind his head.

It would be very easy to understand how and why a man would feel humble before Nature, why a man, a human being, would find reasons to worship this kind of energy.

I have to dig a little more deeply into this, have to find out more. He drifted off into a storm driven sleep.

His dreams were vivid, almost psychedelic. He felt himself running across wide stretches of land, chasing some sort of deer-like animals, with a large stone bound to the end of a stout stick.

There were other men running with him. They were chasing the animals, corralling them, herding them toward a steep cliff. They shouted and waved their clubs to make the animals run over the edge of the cliff.

Finally, after the last animal had jumped, or was pushed by his companions, the men came to stand at the edge of the cliff. They were shouting and dancing, celebrating. Now, after many hungry weeks, they had meat, food. The women who had been following them finally caught up and followed the men down the steep trails to the ground beneath the cliff, their sharp stone knives ready to skin the animals and cut up the meat.

The men wandered through the herd of animals, clubbing those to death who had not killed by the fall over the cliff. A few of the men and women used flint and dry moss to start fires, they wanted to roast and eat some of the meat on the spot, they were hungry.

Aside from that, they could use the fire to frighten the other animals away; the giant wolves, the giant hyenas, the other beasts who craved meat, who were beginning to assemble on the fringe of their kill, lured by the smell of blood.

Kofi tasted the barely roasted meat, he looked at the gleaming eyes beyond the peripheral areas of the man-made fires. We managed to survive because we had fire, but who made the thunder and the lighting?

The crowing of the roosters sounded slightly soggy, but it was there, nevertheless. Aunt Eugenia made her dynamic appearance soon after sunrise. She called from the door way.

"Kofi, my son, you are there?"

"Yes, m'am, I'm here."

"So, come out and see what God has done to His world."

Kofi lowered his midnight wick, pulled on a black T-shirt and stumbled out to a world of muck and goo. All of the thatched huts in old Tsito had weathered the storm well, but the ground all around was like shallow red quicksand.

Aunt Eugenia and her neighbors were energetically pushing and pulling at the plants in their gardens, checking on the thatch of their huts. They called out to each other as they worked. Kofi couldn't figure out what to do. Aunt Eugenia, sensitive to his helplessness, called for him to come and help her straighten up the corn rows in her garden.

"Understand them, my son, know where they want to grow, don't try to bend them to your will, eh heee …"

Kofi thought – yeahh, that Japanese planting/raising technique – Bonsai – and went in that direction. Hours later, Aunt Eugenia complimented him – "Kofi, you did not do badly. It is time for us to go to church. Please wear your long pants and your long shirt."

Kofi felt his head spinning. We've just been rained on, to the point where you could swim through some of the puddles, people have been up since dawn trying to square their lives away, and the sister is talking church? O well.

Brother Kwame put in a miraculous appearance a half hour before the church service.

"I know you would be anxious, sah, so I started my journey to collect you quite early."

Aunt Eugenia took charge …

"Ahh, Brother Kwame, you will go to church with us and after that you will enjoy omo tuo. And then you will go back to the city to do his work with this one."

Kofi had no idea what Aunt Eugenia had said to Brother Kwame, and Brother Kwame confessed, later, that he was not sure of what she had said – "I do not always hear the Ewe correctly, it is very difficult. But Sister Eugenia made it quite clear that I was not to leave before we had chopped on omo tuo."

· ℰℛ ·

Brother Kwame drove them to the church in New Tsito, very carefully. A seasoned mud driver, he stayed on the hard edges of the road, away from the gushy middle. They made it. Kofi was surprised to see a packed house.

There were lots of muddy feet to be washed in three large basins at the entrance of St. Michael's Episcopalian Church, but everybody's clothes, he noticed, were clean, starched and pressed.

The choir of six men and six women sang a gorgeous selection of songs in Ewe. Kofi settled back in the straight back pew to take it all in. By the time the priest, with his white dog collar, came to the pulpit, the church was beginning to broil.

The priest gave his loong sermon in English. Kofi leaned over to ask his driver; "Why is he speaking in English?" Brother Kwame wrinkled his brow, thinking hard on the question before he replied/whispered back.

"Maybe it is difficult, sah, to talk about Christianity in Ewe."

The priest took a long time to explain that they were all sinners, that God was punishing them every day for their sins. He reassured them that they would suffer the sulfurous fires of eternal damnation. And on and on.

Kofi stifled a yawn and stared up at the corrugated metal roof. God, if we stay in here much longer we'll all be cooked, we won't have to burn in hell. Aunt Eugenia sat rigidly, sound asleep. Finally, the ordeal was over. The collection basket had been passed twice and the congregation was limp from the humidity and being chastised. The priest, a small, pot-bellied, stiff necked black man, stood at the exit, shaking hands and offering more advice to the sinners.

"Joshua, I have not seen you in church for the past month. Why?"

"I've been busy working on my farm …"

"That's no excuse, you should always remember that the most bountiful harvest comes from being in the house of our Lord and Saviour, Jesus Christ."

Kofi dreaded his encounter with the little self righteous moralist. One long sermon was enough to make him dislike the man.

"Ah hah, the American that everyone has spoken of. I am glad to see that you came to share the Lord's blessings today. Have you found Jesus?"

"Not yet, I'm still looking."

There was something in Kofi's tone of voice that alerted the priest to the fact that he had a sinner in front of him.

"And tell me this, my boy, how long will you go on looking for what is obviously right in front of you."

"Well, you know how it is, Reverend, sometimes you can't see the forest for the trees."

Aunt Eugenia ended the beginning debate by nudging Kofi's back and mumbling to the priest as she passed, "Very good sermon, very good."

In the taxi going back to Old Tsito, Aunt Eugenia made one remark that seemed to sum up the whole morning.

"That man likes the sound of his own voice too much."

· ℰᏋ ·

After the delicious goat stew with large molded balls of rice ("omo tuo"), washed down with a cold bottle of Club beer, they were ready to make the trip back to Accra. Aunt Eugenia fussed over him like a mother hen.

"Kofi, you have the number for Grace?"

"Yes, m'am."

"Your clothes are there, all clean and proper. You will tell your father and his wife to come visit me before I die?"

"Yes m'am."

"Here, take this omo tuo for you and Brother Kwame to eat as you travel, you don't want to starve to death before you reach Accra."

"Yes m'am."

Finally, the exchange dried up and they simply stood in place staring at each other. Brother Kwame looked from one to the other, wondering how the scene would end.

Kofi reached down and gently swept the old lady into his arms.

"Thank you, Auntie, thank you for everything."

When he released her, she took a step back from him, shading her eyes from the sun.

"Kofi, my son, you are tall," she said.

"No m'am, I'm not so tall, you are very short."

"Eh heeee eh heeee eh hee ..."

He popped into the taxi, registering her huge smile in his memory. Brother Kwame waved good bye and slowly maneuvered to the hard edge of the road.

"Your Auntie is a good woman, sah."

Kofi stared into the side view mirror at Aunt Eugenia, standing in the middle of the road, a chew stick-toothbrush in the corner of her mouth, both fists jammed onto her hips.

"Yeah, you're right, she is a good woman. I left her a hundred thousand cedis under the pillow on her bed, just as a little gift, not a dash."

Brother Kwame almost slid over the edge of the road as he looked at Kofi and blinked.

"A hundred thousand cedis, sah?"

"You think I should've left more?"

"O, no, sah, a hundred thousand in Tsito is serious money, she will be very happy."

One hundred thousand. What's that? $12.00! I should've left two hundred thousand.

· ℘ ℘ ·

The sun didn't take long to bake the road almost back to its former hardness. Kofi was damp with perspiration. The road ahead seemed to be filled with mirages, the heat waves shimmering up from the baking earth.

"What is America like, sah?"

The question came from the driver's mouth, but it sounded very strange. What is America like? Kofi's immediate impulse was to say, "I don't know, I haven't been there in a few days."

"What is America like? Is that what you asked me?"

He thought hard on the question. I have to be honest with this man.

"Brother Kwame, you know something? When I was younger, let's say twelve-fifteen, something like that, I would've been able to answer your question without hesitation.

I could've said – America is my skateboard. Or America is this rapper that I like. Or it's a milkshake or this girl next door. Or something like that.

But now that I've gotten older, I'm twenty one now …"

Brother Kwame smiled in his direction. So young. Kofi returned the smile. Yeah, I know, twenty-one isn't very old at all.

"But now that I've gotten older, and taken a harder look at things, I can't honestly say what America is like. There are so many Americas. There is a White America, a Black America, a Yellow America, a Native American America, a White rich America, a White poor America, a poor Black America, and a rich Black America.

There are different kinds of Whites:" Russians, Germans, English, Irish, etc., etc. Different kinds of Blacks: Cubans, Puerto Ricans, Brazilians, mixtures of all kinds. Different kinds of Yellows and Native Americans too.

There are layers and layers of America, like a giant cake. That's just dealing with the people. And you have to start with the people because they are the ones who make the place what it is.

There are people who think things should be done this way, others who think that things should be done that way. People who like this, other people who hate that.

Some people say that America is a big melting pot, others say the opposite. And maybe they're both right. Or wrong. It all depends on your point of view."

"I'm getting you, sah."

"You are?"

"Yes, I am. America is complex."

"Yes, yes, that's the word I was looking for. But complex like what? Like the inside of a watch? Maybe. Like the inside of a human body? Maybe. Maybe it's all of the above."

They both laughed.

"Brother Kwame, you've made me thirsty. Let's pull over somewhere and get something to drink. I'll tell you more about what America is like later."

"Your friend's village is a few miles ahead."

"My friend?"

"The Arab man."

"Ah yes, let's stop there, I told him I would drop in on him on the way back to Accra, but we'll only stay a half hour, I have stuff to do."

·   ℰℛ   ·

CHAPTER 26

The children who surrounded him on his short walk to Mr. Al-Bayati's store were not laughing, bouncing around. They seemed very solemn, almost sad.

He opened the screen door and walked in. The table and stools were still in place, the ceiling fan still whirling slowly.

"Mr. Al-Bayati!"

A woman's voice answered, "I'm coming."

He stood in place, looking around at the shelves of canned goods, the rolls of bright cloth, buckets of odds and ends. Mrs. Al-Bayati came in through the rear door, holding a sleeping baby in her arms.

Kofi didn't want to stare at her, but it was hard not to stare. Mrs. Al-Bayati looked like a charcoal carving, with almond shaped eyes. About five feet five, he estimated, and gorgeously shaped, not too much of anything anywhere.

"Uhh, your husband, Mr. Al-Bayati? Is he here? I told him I would drop in on him on my way back to the city."

The woman stared at the floor for a moment before speaking in a soft voice.

"Sardun, my husband, was buried yesterday night."

Kofi felt like walking out of the store and coming back in, for a different version of the scene.

"I don't understand ... your husband is dead?"

Kofi felt stupid asking such a dumb question, but he had to make certain that he was hearing right. The widow nodded yes yes yes.

"How, I mean, what happened? I was just here on Thursday..."

"Yes, I remember."

She looked so sad and helpless.

"Please tell me what happened?"

Once again, in a soft voice, but with just a tinge of anger in it.

"Some of the people in the village, who were jealous of his success with this business made juju on him."

Kofi was prepared to hear her say that the man had had a heart attack, that he had been bitten by a poisonous snake, a scorpion maybe, but "juju." What did that mean?

"Juju?"

"Excuse me please, I will bring you a cold beer."

He thought that she had done an extraordinary thing, to think of what he wanted, with so much on her head. He squatted on the stool. Juju.

She had put the baby in his crib and stood at the side of the table with her hands clenched in front of her.

"Please, Mrs. Al-Bayati, please sit. I don't want to annoy you with a lot of questions but I'm very curious about this juju."

She sat on the edge of the stool, unclenching and clenching her hands.

"Are the police on this now? Are they looking for the suspect or the suspects?"

He was surprised to hear such a hard laugh come from someone with such a soft voice.

"Hah hah hah ... the police in this place cannot deal with juju, they are afraid of it themselves."

The beer was cold and went straight to his gut.

"Please forgive me for asking you this, but what is juju? I don't know what it is."

She stopped clenching her hands and placed them in front of her eyes for a few moments.

"Juju is evil, mister, it is evil. And those who do it are evil people, wicked people."

Kofi could sense that he was not going to get much more than "evil people, wicked people." He wanted the components, the philosophy, if there was one, the stuff that went into the making of it.

She sat very still, staring at the floor. Kofi guzzled his beer, unsure of what to say. He felt like an intruder on her grief.

"My husband was a good man, a decent man. He came to our village from far away, this E-raqi place. He tried to learn our language and he helped many when they needed help. He loaned many people cedis. He gave credit. Some paid him back, some did not. He said, 'Allah is great, He will reward me in Paradise.'

And then the jealous ones made juju on him."

He wanted to ask her – "How do you know it was juju that killed him?" – but decided not to. He stood, overpaid her for his beer and turned to walk out.

"Thank you for returning, Mister, my husband would like that."

"Thank you, Mrs. Al-Bayati."

They had driven five miles from the village and the tragedy in the store before Brother Kwame asked; "So, you want to know about juju, sah?"

"Brother Kwame, you're reading my mind. How did you find out what happened?"

"I spoke with the older children, they told me."

"So what is this? I've heard the word before but I don't think I've ever known anybody, personally, to be harmed by it."

Brother Kwame pursed his lips thoughtfully, easing around a wagon loaded with melons.

"Sah I think juju is like America. There are many layers and I think they are all wicked and evil. I have never heard of good juju."

"But what's it made of, how is it done?"

Once again, Brother Kwame pursed his lips, rubbed his chin.

"I can only give you one example that came in the newspaper last year. An Ashanti man wanted to make some serious money for his export/import business. He went to the juju man. The juju man says I will make it possible for you to have this serious money you desire.

You must bring me three new born boy baby hearts."

Kofi cringed involuntarily.

"Three boy baby hearts, sah. Are you getting me?"

Kofi nodded yes, feeling repulsed and disgusted.

"You must bring me the left hand of a young woman who has recently died. You must bring the eyes of a black cat. And three hundred thousand cedis. And within ninety days I guarantee you that you will receive serious money for your business."

"Well, did he get the money?"

"Yessah, he did get the money, but he got caught smuggling drugs into the country and the police made him confess to his deal with the juju man."

"How did they make him confess?"

"Oh, this is Ghana here, sah, the police have their ways to make the criminal confess."

The hustle and bustle of Accra was beginning to envelope the car. Wonder what Salena is doing? I've had enough juju for one day.

•   ⁊Ɔʁ   •

The hotel staff greeted him like a long lost relative.

"Mr. Brown, good to see you back, we were praying for your safety. The rain was very bad in Tsito, eh?"

"Hard for me to say, first time I've ever experienced anything like that."

"You have a message here."

He could tell, from the sneaky look in the hotel clerk's eyes, that he had opened the small envelope.

"Dear Kofi,

I was passing the Green leaf and decided to leave this note for you. Call me when you return. I miss you now.

Kisses,
Salena."

"May I use your phone?"

"Oh, sorry Mr. Brown, the telephone is spoiled; we can send a message with a small boy, if you like."

Easier and simpler to send a young man in a taxi, rather than use the phone. Well, that's one way to solve the problem.

"Dear Salena,

Just as you predicted. It is Sunday afternoon and I'm back. Would you like to join me at "Susan's Place" this evening for a cocktail or two?

I will be there at 8 p.m.—

Mo' kisses,
Kofi..."

Remarkably easy to send a messenger.

"Yessah, I know LaBone, I locate this person."

"But how? I've only given you the name of the street she lives on."

"No problem, sah. Her neighbors will know her."

"And while you're at it, drop these letters at the post office for me."

A generous ten thousand cedis dash-tip made the desk clerk click his tongue with disapproval.

"The boy does not deserve so much, Mr. Brown."

"But he has to take a taxi, doesn't he?"

"He will not take a taxi, he will run. He is halfway there now."

· ℘℃℞ ·

Kofi sprawled on the bed in his room, resting and sorting a few things out in his head before going to "Susan's Place."

Al-Bayati. Mrs. Al-Bayati, juju. I guess it would be possible to kill someone physically.

O well, whatever. He's gone now. Tsito, Aunt Eugenia. Seemed unreal that I was there. I'll remember that time for the rest of my life. The storm. The aftermath. Asiafo. The girl's name is "Kutu."

The girl is a well grown woman now. Twenty some years ago. The baby she had must be about my age now. What a helluva world we live in, for all of this kind of stuff to be happening.

Asiafo was a juju man. Dad had dealings with a juju man. You give me what I want and I'll make certain you get what you want. That's enough of that, time for a little power nap. Hope the small boy was able to deliver my note to Salena.

· ℘℃℞ ·

"So, how is it, handsome?"

"Good evening, Susan. And I must say you're looking quite gorgeous yourself..."

210

"It's all done with smoke, mirrors and make up, believe me. 'Scuse, have a little problem to solve in the kitchen. Make yourself at home."

Kofi strolled through the half filled room, responding to the pleasant greetings from the tables en route.

"Good evening."

"Good evening."

A pleasant nod here, a smile there. One of the hippest friendliest places I've ever been in. Usually, if the place has a hip reputation, the clientele tends to be a bit snooty, but that's not the case in "Susan's Place."

He sat at a table next to the wall, near the rear exit, a spot that gave him a fish eye view of the scene. A beautiful mix of people. A few beautiful women who also looked interesting and intelligent, not simply beautiful. A fashion plate here, a buffed up type there, all looking sophisticated.

"May I take your order, sah?"

"Your name is Zacarias, isn't it?"

"Yessah, you have a good memory."

How could I ever forget "Yessah, madam."

"Zacarias, I'd like a little something to munch on and a nice cold daiquiri …"

"Yessah."

He sat back and admired Salena's entrance, the way she paused, placed her left hand on her beautiful hip and coolly surveyed the room.

"Ah! You are hiding over here!"

She gave him a little peck on the lips before sitting across from him. Kofi was stunned by the intricately wrapped gelé, the iridescent skirt and blouse, her lovely face, the subtle perfume.

"You look absolutely gorgeous, you know that?"

"For now, wait until you see me twenty years from now."

"I think I would like to see you twenty years from now."

She gave him a curious look as the waiter placed his daiquiri and an oval plate with Scotch eggs in front of them.

"Oh, Daiquiri and Scotch eggs, that's an interesting combination, especially the Daiquiri. May I have one please?"

"Zacarias, do you think we could have another one of these?"

"I will bring it, sah."

Salena took a healthy bite out of a Scotch egg. Kofi stared at the meat coated egg.

"I don't think I've ever had one of these."

"Try one, they're delicious."

Susan swept through, passed at their table to greet Salena with their cheeky-cheeky kiss.

"It appears that we'll have to keep Mr. Brown in Ghana here, Salena, it would give us the opportunity to see you more often."

Salena cast her eyes down demurely, pleased with Susan's remark. And then Susan was off to take care of other business. Kofi and Salena sipped their daiquiris.

"Mmmm ... now that's the way a daiquiri should be."

They clinked glasses in a silent toast.

"So, how was it in Tsito?"

"Warm, feeling, caring, delightful and, at the end of the day, muddy as hell."

"Yea, we got a little rain here too, but it never seems to be as bad as it is in the villages."

Miles Davis playing the "Solea" cut from "Sketches of Spain" grabbed Kofi's ears.

"That's one of my Dad's favorite pieces of music."

"I don't know it at all."

"All you have to do is listen to it once and you'll know it forever."

He reached his hand across the table to hold her hand while they listened to Miles blow. Kofi whispered, "Look around, we're not the only disciples in the house."

Most of the couples in the place had stopped their conversations to pay attention to the music. Two more daiquiris arrived at their table – courtesy of Susan, who gave them a thumb's up and a big smile from behind the bar.

The "Solea" was followed by something less mesmerizing, giving them a chance to carry on their conversation.

"Kofi, I missed you ..."

"I missed you too, Salena."

"I told myself that I didn't want to miss you, but I missed you anyway."

He wanted to ask her why she felt so ambivalent about him, but he felt he understood because he felt the same way.

I can't think of anything that I would like to do more than make love to this gorgeous woman. But then what? She's already made it plain that she's "saving" herself for her husband. She wants a commitment, a relationship. Am I ready for that?

Ready or not, I still want her because she looks so delicious, so feminine, so desirable.

"Kofi? Kofi?"

"Yes, I'm right here."

"I asked you if you had a girlfriend in the States?" Debra, a girlfriend? No, more like an interim sex partner.

"No, I don't have a girlfriend at home."

"You lie."

Yes, a lie – why alienate you by telling you the truth? And besides I think it would be too difficult to explain what a "sex buddy" is. Debra's words ran through his sub-consciousness.

"Kofi, look, I don't want to mislead you or anything, but I have to be completely candid with you ... my career comes before anything else. I want to have sex with you and we <u>will</u> have sex, but it will have to be a monogamous thing. You know what I'm saying?

I cannot run the risk of contracting any fatal doses of anything."

"I can promise you that you'll be my only sex partner. Can you make that promise?"

"I can, definitely. And we'll give each other advance notice, with no malice aforethought, if we decide to change that status quo. Agreed?"

"Debra, you're going to be a great attorney, I can feel it in my bones."

"Me, too. Now what were you saying to me about these world class condoms you have?"

"I'd rather show you than tell you ..."

"Well?"

Debra Ashley, would be world class criminal lawyer, sex partner. Sometimes they joked about it.

"Kofi, you know I think we must be the only couple I know of with a pre-sexual agreement."

It was working. They were into their third year of mutually satisfying sex. Would it develop into more than that? He had doubts. It's good for what it is, but who wants to delude himself into thinking that sex, and sex alone, was the foundation for anything concrete? No, dear Salena, I wouldn't be able to explain my "sex buddy" to you.

"Salena, let's take a little stroll."

They took their daiquiris and walked toward the rear exit. Zacarias was covering their Scotch eggs up with large white cloth the minute they left their table.

· ᔓᘖ ·

They strolled the path between the palms, sipping their daiquiris.

"Kofi, I said that you lie about having a girlfriend at home – you didn't dispute it."

Several other couples passed them, arm in arm, his arm around her waist, whispering little jokes, enjoying the atmosphere.

"No, I didn't dispute it. And I didn't give you a yea or a nay because I don't think the question is relevant to our circumstances in Ghana here."

They sat on the small white bench bordering the path.

"What is that croaking I hear? Are those frogs?"

"Thousands of them, they are always out after a big rain."

Salena took a long sip from her glass and placed it on the ground near the bench. She reached over and gently lifted his glass from his hand.

"Kofi, can you kiss me? I like the way you kiss. I don't want to quarrel."

· ᔓᘖ ·

CHAPTER 27

Ahhh yes … the singing maid. If she only knew how lovely that makes my day begin. He did a slow body stretch in bed. Have to find some place to do a little workout; I'm beginning to feel stiff.

Salena Sarpong. The thought of her made him smile.

Lady was full of surprises. Kisses and a slow dance in the school room at "Susan's Place." More kissing. An impulsive taxi ride to the ocean.

"Kofi, let's charter a taxi for an hour, I would like to take a walk on Labadi beach with you."

"You got it!"

Body warm breezes, the ocean softly slapping against the shore. He had to explain what made him cry…

"O! Kofi, you are crying? Why are you crying?"

"I just felt a very strange feeling. It was almost as though I could feel my ancestors being herded onto ships from this beach, maybe from the very spot we're standing on."

Salena scuffed her toes around in the warm sand, silenced by what he told her. And then they kissed again. She pushed him away, held him at arm's length.

"We must stop this kissing so much; you are making me feel very hot."

"You're the boss, sweetheart, you're the boss."

"But we don't have to stop immediately …"

Kofi stared at his erection as though it were an appendage between his legs that he had no control of. Let's see how this plays out.

Riding away from the beach he had given her a basic outline of why he had gone to Tsito, and the detective work he was going to have to do.

"This is very interesting, very interesting. So, you are going to see this auntie's niece?"

"First thing tomorrow."

"And then what?"

"Hopefully, she'll be able to tell me where to find this girl, the woman who ran away from the village because she was pregnant ...'

"And then, later in the evening, at about six o'clock you will go with me to a performance of the National Dance Ensemble of Ghana?"

"I would love to go with you anywhere."

"We'll meet here at six. Can you kiss me some more?"

·   ℘ℂℛ   ·

Kofi had discovered a vital element of the "Osu telegraph system," the taxi drivers.

"Do you know Brother Kwame?"

"There are many Kwames in Ghana here."

He gave a beef sheet description of his favorite driver. The taxi driver knew him.

"O, Kwame Asiedu, I know him well."

"Please let him know that I would like to see him at the Green Leaf Hotel tomorrow morning, about ten o'clock."

"I will pass the word for sure."

Two thousand extra cedis, the "dash," was almost a guarantee that Brother Kwame would receive the message before the end of the day. Taxi drivers were better than tour guides.

"My directions say that the person I'm looking for lives behind a large green gate, the third house from the corner."

Aunt Eugenia had given him the best address she could describe.

"I will give you also her post office box, but it will be easy for you to find her house. She lives in Kanda."

And it <u>was</u> easy. The large houses in the area were protected by "guards," men who sat on little benches beside the house gates all day. What a boring job that must be.

His taxi driver only had to ask one of the guards for the information he needed.

"This man says that madam is just there, at GBC." GBC, the Ghana Broadcast Company. Wonder what she's doing there. Five blocks east.

"Good, let's go to GBC."

Kofi felt at ease with the drill, after having gone through it so many times with his father. The approach to the gates of the studio, a question from the utterly serious guard with the baggy uniform and the cap that was too large for his pin head.

"The person you wish to see, sah?"

"My name is Kofi Brown; I am an African-American producer here to see Ms. Grace Hlovor."

"Do you have an appointment, sah?"

"No, I do not have an appointment, but she is expecting me and she will be very disappointed and annoyed if I'm prevented from seeing her."

Kofi had noticed that the Ghanaian response was quickened by the judicious use of four words: "annoyed," "dash," "proper" and "African-American."

The guard studied his clipboard and nibbled on the eraser of his #2 pencil for a moment. Kofi debated "dashing" him, but decided not to. Either he'll let me in or he won't.

"Uhh, Madam Hlovor-Adjei is there, around the corner of this building and then the first building on your left, the second floor. She is very busy … your taxi must wait outside."

His current taxi driver, he hadn't asked his name, was already backing into a convenient space.

"I am parking here."

"I shouldn't be long."

"You say?"

"This won't take a long time."

The driver was already slumped in his seat, a handkerchief covering his eyes. It didn't matter, he had been "chartered" for two hours.

Kofi took his time strolling through the studio. So, this is the media nerve center of Ghana. People were moving faster on the GBC studio lot than he had seen people move during the two weeks he had been in the country.

Looks like the media is the media is the media is the media wherever you go. People with briefcases, or scripts in hand, with ballpoints tucked behind their ears, seemed to be oblivious of him, the walls around them, or anything, other than their immediate goals.

"Oopps! Sorry, ol' boy!"

The man bumping into him, and the completely English-English that erupted from the man was almost funny. No doubt where he learned his English. And judging from his pipe, old school tie and tweed suit, where he learned how to dress.

First building on my left, second floor. The name neatly stenciled on the door – "Grace Hlovor-Adjei, Producer."

The secretary, a large framed brown girl painting her fingernails, looked up at him as though she had been ambushed.

"Who are you, what do you want?"

It wasn't the secretarial greeting that he was used to, but he had been on the scene long enough to know how to deal.

"My name is Kofi Brown, an African-American producer, and Madam is expecting me."

The secretary placed her nail kit on the floor underneath her desk, stared at him for clues, and took three barefoot steps to the door behind her desk. She tapped gently and opened the door.

"Mrs. Adjei, there is this African-American man here who says that you are expecting him."

Suddenly, through a wide crack in the door, he was being studied by Mrs. Grace Hlovor-Adjei. He would always recall the blinking eyes, the door suddenly thrown up, the woman's warm embrace –

"Ahh Kojo! Come in! Come in! I'm so glad to see you! You could've been my son you know; if I decided to marry your father. Just think of it, I could've been your mother ..."

"And I could've been your son. But I think it all worked out pretty well anyway, don't you think? And the name is Kofi, not Kojo."

After the initial excitement, witnessed by the barefoot secretary, Mrs. Hlovor-Adjei sat Kofi down in a chair, pulled another chair in front of him and studied his features for a long minute.

"Perhaps our son would've been a shade darker, but no big thing, eh?"

Kofi felt that he was in the presence of a dynamic personality. And she's a fine woman, he thought. I thought African women were supposed to be breast 'n butts. This lady has got some legs too. I wonder if I'm being blasphemously incestuous here, after all, this could've been my mother.

Evidently the thought intrigued both of them, because they felt an instant bond.

"Kofi, I was about "to do lunch," as you say it in America. Would you like to join me?"

"I'd be privileged to join you."

Kofi smiled, watching the familiar producer wrap up just before lunch; The Producer on the phone.

"Michael, I'm not going to say this again … if you can't shave seven minutes from your program, then I will have someone who can. Are you getting me?"

"Yes, Afua, my dear, I have read your script and I find it not quite up to GBC standards. I would suggest that you go back through it and carefully orchestrate some of the more attractive elements. What are these elements? You tell me, dear, I'm simply a dumb producer."

"Hello, Daniel. Yes, I did receive your script and I loved a couple ideas in it. My suggestions are many, so I won't try to give them all to you at once. I would suggest that you re-read your script and make a determination, based on the core-audience-base that you're trying to reach, as to what will work and what won't work. Yes, call first."

Finally, they were ready "to do lunch."

"Maria, please take messages for me, after you've finished doing your nails."

"I will take the messages, Ms. Adjei.'

"Be sure that you do, because if I find that you have missed one of them whilst you were decorating your nails, you will be sacked. Are you getting me?"

"Yes, Mrs. Adjei, I understand."

"Come, Kojo…'

"Kofi."

"Yes, of course, Kofi. But you look so like Kojo. Come, we have an hour to talk about a lot of things. How about the Afrikiko Gardens? They have a great fufu with plantain there. And the beer is always cold. Are you mobile?"

"I have a taxi waiting."

"I like that, one should always be prepared."

· ℘℃℞ ·

AFRIKIKO GARDENS

A large outdoor restaurant, twenty-five tables and busy, bustling waiters and waitresses. "Yessah, Madam."

"As you can see it's mostly a media bunch," she informed him as she smiled at this one, waved to that one, and gestured to a man for him to call her. Kofi saw a scaled down Hollywood/Beverly Hills scene. Maybe they call it "Ghanawood" or something.

And Mrs. Hlovor-Adjei was definitely in the mix. She was one of the few people in the restaurant with a cell phone.

"Please excuse me, Kofi, I must take this call, it's quite important."

"Ah yes, Mr. Yankah, so good of you to return my call. Yes, yes, yes, I can assure you that I'm quite prepared; GBC looks forward to broadcasting your documentary about the effect of global warming on Ghana here. I will be in my office this afternoon, say about 3-ish, if you would like to pay me a visit, to look in some of the tail ends of this venture.

Tomorrow? Yes indeed, tomorrow at 3 would be fine. And thank you for your prompt response. 'By 'by ..."

Grace Hlovor-Adjei turned back to Kofi with a wide smile. She looked like a soccer player who had just scored a goooaaaal.

"Well, Mrs. Adjei ..."

"Oh, please call me Grace!"

"Well, Grace, you look as though you've just scored the winning goal."

"In a way I have. I've wanted to produce one of Mr. Yankah's award winning documentaries for a loonng time and now he's giving me the opportunity. I'm elated. What're we having? Waiter!"

Kofi had to smile at the lady's bursts of energy. She seemed to be in motion even while she was seated. And her conversation was equally energetic.

"So, tell me, Kofi, son of Kojo. We would've been an excellent match, if I had wanted to go to America. Of if he had decided to stay in Ghana here. But one cannot chew meat from bones that are twenty some years old, can one?"

"I don't think so."

"Now then, abut this business of tracking down this girl who left Tsito with Asiafo's baby in her belly. It was years ago, but that's no problem for Ghana here, some things remain the same for years. Are you having the fufu and goat stew, it's excellent."

"I'll take your recommendation."

"And waiter, please make the ABC Lager cold, we want it cold."

Dynamic, forceful, driven. Kofi couldn't imagine her as his mother. The contrast between his mother; a cool, dynamic, but laid back lady, was clearly distinct from this woman who might have been his mother if circumstances had been different.

"Grace, let me ask you – where would I find this girl, this woman that they named 'Kutu'?"

"So you know that too. Of course, Aunt Eugenia remembers everything."

She paused briefly, studying her well manicured nails.

"I was told, some time ago, that she was seen in the Makola market, here in Osu."

"Yes, that's what I heard."

"But she was not living in Osu then, or now."

"How can you be so sure?"

"If she lived in Osu I would know of it, Osu has no secrets. Now then, logically, since she was not affluent when she left Tsito to come to Accra, she would not be living in LaBone, Kanda or any of the other upscale areas here. She would be living in the poorest section of Accra."

"What's that?"

"Jamestown."

"Jamestown? That doesn't sound Ghanaian at all."

"You're right, but in some ways it's more Ghanaian than a whole bunch of other places. Ahhh! Our food and beer have finally arrived. Bon appetit!"

Lunch with the woman who might've been his mother was delicious; both the fufu, goat stew, cold beers and the quicksilver observations and conversation he had with Grace Hlovor-Adjei.

"Kofi, I think that the story you're pursuing would make a perfectly delightful and legitimate two-part program but, unfortunately, I'm not dealing with people who see the real value of such stories.

Isn't the goat stew fabulous?! One of the reasons I could never leave Ghana is that I would starve to death elsewhere.

If the powers that be, here at GBC, had enough imagination, they would be all over a story like this. I would love to produce it. But they have a tendency to think lightly of stories about the real Ghana."

"But I heard your conversation with Mr. Yankah ..."

"It's going to go forward for two reasons – number one, I fought tooth and nail to have the green light on his documentary. And secondly, since Mr. Yankah is a member of a very prominent family, the studio heads felt compelled to meet me halfway on this project.

Ghana is locked into the who-you-know/what-can-be-done syndrome. Matters are changing slowly, but not fast enough to suit me. I'm having another beer, will you join me?"

After two beers each and the delicious fufu/goat stew, Mrs. Hlover-Adjei announced, "I have lined the walls of my fortress, I'm anxious to get back to battle."

"Well, I feel sorry for whomever you're going to do battle with, because they will definitely be at a disadvantage."

When they deposited her/when she came down in front of the GBC gates, she erupted from the taxi and reached back inside to hold his face in her hands. Inches away from his face, she whispered, "I loved your father, Kofi. I will always love him for the joy and intelligence he brought to my life. I have two children now, a successful marriage, and a successful career. But I tell you, your father was the one true love of my life. You may tell him that."

"I will tell him that."

"Concerning this matter of Kutu, I must warn you that there may be juju involved."

There it was again, juju. But what the hell were they talking about?

"All I can say is – thank you for your advice."

"If I can help you in any way, don't hesitate to contact me."

· ℘℃℞ ·

CHAPTER 28

Later that day ...

A quick daiquiri at "Susan's Place" with Salena and a bit of advice from Susan.

"Kofi, I would be very careful about going into Jamestown, it's not one of the nicest sections of Accra. 'Scuse me, Zacarias is signaling his 'yessah, madam' for help with something."

"How did she know I was planning to do business, to go to Jamestown for something?"

"Did you not say that you had met with Grace Hlovor-Adjei at the Ghana Broadcast Corporation today?"

"Yes ..."

"She and Susan are good friends and, after all, it is the GBC, are you getting me?"

"Well, live and learn. It's 5:30 ... don't you think we should be on our way?"

Salena laughed ...

"The performance is scheduled to begin at 6, but I doubt if it will start on time. In any case, the auditorium is on a few minutes away. Kofi, you know something? I'm beginning to like you too much."

·　ℰↄℭ　·

"Dear Dad,

Yesterday night, as they say in Ghana here, I paid Mrs. Grace Hlovor (Hu-Lovor, I discovered) Adjei a visit. She is a producer at GBC and a dynamic personality.

223

We "did lunch," as they say in Hollywood and she told me a number of very interesting things, I'll save them for my return. She also gave me an interesting lead concerning "Kutu," the girl who ran away from Tsito.

News travels like lightning here. I met with Mrs. Hlovor-Adjei and two hours later, at "Susan's Place," Susan was almost able to give me a blow by blow accounting of what we talked about. Today I'm going to do a little overdue shopping at the National Culture Centre.

And so it goes. But the big news, so far as I'm concerned, happened yesterday night when I went to a performance of the National Dance Ensemble of Ghana with my girlfriend (her official designation) Salena Sarpong. We got to the theatre at 6:15 p.m. for a program that was supposed to begin at 6 p.m.

Promptly, at 7:15 p.m., the curtains opened on this bare, football sized stage and from that point it was "on." The bare stage became, during the course of the two hours that followed, a small village nestled in a valley near a waterfall. It was the scene of two opposing armies fighting to determine who should become the next king. It became a forest filled with ghostly trees that tried to bring harm down onto the errant lovers who were having a romance in their shade.

A full-fledged soccer game! Never seen anything like it. Soccer-dancers, playing in time to the rhythms of some of the most intricate drumming I've ever heard in my life.

The score was tied one-one when the soccer-dancers danced onto the sidelines, opening the door for a dance about a wedding abduction party from Northern Ghana.

My favorite was the story of the young man who is trying to court two of the village cutie pies at the same time, and loses both of them because he spends so much time in the local bar, boasting about himself.

There was much, much more — the stilt walker-dancers alone would take all of the pages I could give them. And the acrobats who gave me the impression that they were flying through the air. A beautiful evening of songs, dances, scenes, drumming.

I'm definitely enjoying myself in Ghana here. This afternoon,

*after my little shopping spree, I'm going to Jamestown to check out a
lead on the girl from Tsito.*

Love, Kofi"

·   ℘ℂ℞   ·

"Brother Kwame, good to see you."

"Long time, eh?"

"Well, not really, but it seems that way. Let me explain what I need.
I want to divide my day into two parts with you. This morning I want
to go to the National Cultural Centre for a little kente cloth shopping,
they tell me that it's the best place to go for kente."

"Very good, sah, very good."

"I'll come back to the hotel, rest for a couple hours and then I'd like
to go to Jamestown."

He felt a little elitist telling the taxi driver that he was going to rest
after shopping, while the driver was going to be out in the hot sun,
driving here and there.

"Jamestown, sah?"

"That's where the trail seems to be leading."

"What time should I collect you?"

"Uhh, let's say about six."

Kofi got the distinct impression that brother Kwame was not
overjoyed at the prospect of tripping to Jamestown. But he was a pro,
and if Jamestown was on the agenda, then so be it.

Three hours later, Kofi dropped ten pounds of kente cloth in the
corner of his hotel room, worn out from trying to hold his own with a
succession of kente cloth sellers.

Damn, I never knew they had so many different kinds of kente.
Brother Kwame had walked through the narrow aisles of the kente cloth
section with him.

"Mr. Brown, I speak five Ghana languages but I cannot help you here,
I know nothing of kente cloth."

He was certain that he had been cheated in all of his transactions,
but what did it come to? The difference between $5 and $6.

"Brother Kwame, 6 p.m., o.k.? I'll need you for 2 hours."

"I will be here, sah."

Time for a shower, a nice long siesta.

· ℰᴏᏟᏋ ·

"How far is Jamestown from Osu, brother Kwame?"

"It is just there, sah, not far at all."

"But everybody makes it sound like it's a long way."

"O, not so far. We take this road, it goes along the ocean, we go through the Accra Centre and just there is Jamestown. You will see."

"Now then, let me ask you this …"

"Yessah?"

"If you wanted to find someone, someone like the person I'm looking for, where would you begin?"

Brother Kwame pursed his lips, a familiar expression when he was thinking hard.

"I would begin in a popular drinking bar. You must ask the person who owns the bar what you wish to know, and then return later for the answer."

"Like fishing, huh?"

"Yessah, like fishing. News travels faster in Jamestown than it does in Osu."

"That's pretty fast. I'll double up on the speed; I'll go to three bars."

"That's a very good idea."

Looking at the sunset on the ocean, with the magic pastel shadings, made him wish that he had brought a camera with him. No biggie, it'll be in mind forever.

"What is that awful smell?"

"Jamestown, sah, Jamestown. It comes from there, the slaughterhouse."

A huge, grim building blotted out the sunset and the streets narrowed. The drainage ditches stank and, Kofi noticed, the people seemed dirty, an unusual thing for Ghanaians who always seemed to be bathing, or about to bath. But it was the stench from the slaughterhouse that made the biggest impression.

"That must be a horrible way to start your day, smelling something like dead, rotting rats."

"If you live in Jamestown, you would not be aware of it."

"Guess you got a point. Where would you suggest I make my first stop?"

"There, sah, the big outdoor drinking bar. I will remain in my taxi to prevent problems."

The expression – "Like a virgin in the prison exercise yard" – came to his mind as he stepped out of the taxi and walked the ten steps to the entrance to the "Pito Bar."

The place was half-filled with men and women who looked as though they lived there. No one paid him any obvious, overt attention, but he couldn't help but notice that the loud conversations became muted as he entered the bar and took a seat against the wall.

Well, if they're going to stick a knife in my back, they'll have to climb up behind me.

He could see brother Kwame through the open side of the bar. He wasn't power napping as usual, whenever they stopped somewhere for longer than ten minutes. He was clearly on the alert, carefully checking out the streams of people going back and forth on the rutted road.

The man standing in front of his handkerchief-sized table gave no indication that he was a waiter. Kofi took a chance.

"You have ABC Lager?"

"We have, but the bottle is not cold, the fridge is spoiled."

"I'll take it."

The man strolled away, not at all like the brisk walking waiters and waitresses he had become accustomed to. Kofi studied the people passing the "Pito Bar." They were obviously the dregs of Accra: large numbers of handicapped people, polio victims who scuttled along like giant crabs on their elbows and knees. Wonder what kind of polio that is? People without noses, fingers, toes. Leprosy. The thought jarred him. Leprosy, they have leprosy here.

Little children with bloated bellies and reddish colored hair, nutritional deficiencies. Clots of young men who looked mean and evil. And they flowed past as though they had no destination.

Inside the bar, as the conversations started up again by a few decibels, he heard the word "obruni." Well, at least I've been recognized officially. He had decided to sip a glass of beer before approaching the fat man behind the bar, who gave the impression of being the owner.

"Three thousand cedis," the "waiter" announced as he placed the unopened bottle on the table. Well, it was usually two, but I guess the one more is my "obruni tax." The man produced a bottle opener and popped the cap off of the bottle after he gave him a five thousand cedi note.

Smart man. If I didn't want to pay they would put the bottle back in the warm place it came from. No harm, no foul. The warm beer wasn't bad. It was liquid and it quenched his thirst. He thought about taking brother Kwame a soft drink, a Maltina maybe, but decided against it.

"May I sit with you?"

It only took a glance to see that the lady was a prostitute. The slit up the front dress, the low neckline, the loud, cheap perfume, too much lipstick and her attitude said it all.

"You may not sit <u>with</u> me, but if you want to sit in the chair across from me, be my guest."

He knew it was important to establish the perimeters right away. No, honey, I'm not looking for love in all the wrong places. She sat on the edge of the chair and pouted her full bosom out at him.

"Will you buy me a beer?"

"No, but I'll share this one with you." He signaled to his waiter with the hand down, pulling motion that meant come. The "waiter" approached the table with an evil grin on his face.

"Yes?"

"Uhh, would you please bring me another glass for my friend here?'

The prostitute frowned and the waiter's grin disappeared. That's right; understand who I am right now, a cheap obruni who is out looking for information, not sex.

He noticed the eye to eye exchange between the waiter and the pro. What's with this one? What do you make of it? Why is he here?

Kofi filled the lady's glass and poured himself a half a glass – "What's your name?"

"I am called Daphne."

"Well, here's looking at you, Daphne."

He click-toasted his glass against hers, took a sip. She took a big swallow, eyeing the rest of the beer in the bottle.

"Now then, Daphne, let's get down to the reason why I'm here."

She pouted her breasts out a little more, viciously eyeing a couple rivals who had occupied a nearby table.

"Yes, let's get down to your business."

"I'm willing to give you a small dash for some information."

"You will dash me for information? What information?"

"I'm looking for a woman named 'Kutu'. She may have a child about my age. And she may have other children also."

It suddenly occurred to Kofi that he didn't know whether "Kutu' had a male or a female child. And after so many years, how many more? He slid the two thousand cedi note across the tiny table into her eager hand. Well, here we go.

"Kutu? Kutu? I don't know of this person. Maybe my friends will know. 'Eh Betty, Mabel!"

Daphne's two friends rushed to their table, smelling obruni money in the air. The other patrons looked on with great amusement, making comments in their corrupt, Jamestown Ga.

"What do you think, the obruni has three pricks?"

"Who can say, a rich obruni <u>might</u> have three pricks."

Daphne blindsided Kofi with her comment.

"My friend here wants to know where he can find this woman named 'Kutu', he is willing to give 10,000 cedis for the correct information."

Kofi gave her an approving nod. The "correct information" was the clincher. Betty and Mabel stared at Kofi as though he were a piece of raw meat.

"Ten thousand cedis, you say?" Mabel asked to have the amount verified by him.

"Yes, ten thousand for the correct information."

Betty and Mabel stood to leave them.

"Let us see what happens," Betty said as they strolled away, looking for more immediate prey.

"Thank you, Daphne. How do you say 'thank you' in Ga?"

"Oiwaladonne."

"Oiwaladonne."

He poured the rest of the beer into her glass and stood up to leave. She held his wrist.

"You are a strong young man, you only want to buy information? She let the split in the front of her dress open a bit.

"Information only, Daphne, information only. Oiwaladonne."

He nodded to the regulars as he strolled out. A nice bunch, they look as though they could slice me into sections and sell me, if someone offered them the right price for my body.

·   ℘ℛ   ·

CHAPTER 29

"The Whatever Bar." Get to the table against the wall, survey the landscape, decide who would be the most likely person to have the info I want. He pretended not to notice the man in the ol' fashioned seer sucker suit and canary yellow, pointy toed shoes who eased into a seat a few tables away. The waiter clasped his hands behind his back as he stood in front of Kofi. The expression on his face said it all. Are you lost?

"Do you have a cold ABC Lager?"

"You wish to have a cold ABC?"

"If you have one."

"Yes, we have."

Kofi and the man in the yellow, pointy-toed shoes casually eyed each other as the waiter strolled away to get his beer. The waiter returned with the beer, as warm as the one he had sipped in "The Pito Bar." The waiter overcharged him and made an oblique movement back to the bar.

The yellow shoes guy made a super casual movement to Kofi's little table.

"Please excuse me, sah, but I will like to ask you if you are of the African Diaspora?"

Kofi almost choked on his sip of beer. Of all the approaches ...

"Well, yes, as a matter of fact I am of the African Diaspora."

"Ahh hah, just as I thought"; he slid into the chair on Kofi's left, offering him a clear view of the bead hung entrance, "just as I thought, an African-American."

Kofi decided to enjoy the moment, after all this might be the information source he was looking for.

"That's a brilliant deduction, that I'm an African-American."

"I make these deductions all the time, fortunately."

He looks like an African version of that ol' fashioned character in the movie "Casablanca," the weasel type. What's his name? Peter Lorre. Peter Lorre, that's who he looks like, with yellow, pointy-toed shoes and a wash 'n wear seer sucker suit.

"Incidentally, I am to introduce myself, my name is Mister Charley James Kotey. I am of royal blood, my great grandfather was almost a king."

"My name is Kofi Brown and I am not of royal blood. What can I do for you, Mr. Kotey?"

It was getting late and he wanted to hit one more spot before he called it a day. Aside from the fact that brother Kwame was behaving in an antsy fashion.

"Ahh hah! I like what you ask, Mr. Brown. What can I do for you? I like that. But I must say that perhaps there is something I can do for you."

"Oh?"

"Mister Charley James Kotey" looked over his left shoulder, looked over his right shoulder as though he were checking the area around him for spies. He reached into the inside pocket of his suit and gracefully pulled out a handkerchief that had been white, once upon a time.

He hunched his upper body over the dirty, neatly folded handkerchief, to prevent any curious types from peeking at his treasure. Kofi worked to conceal/stifle the smile he felt coming to his face.

He made a Houdini-like production of unfolding the handkerchief. In the center of the handkerchief was a ring with one of the worst gold settings Kofi had ever seen.

"This was taken from my great grandfather's finger just before he was buried, Lord bless his memory."

The "gold" was beginning to turn green and the ring itself looked like a narrow cut of copper pipe. Kofi studied the ring before making his assessment.

"Hmmm, looks a little tarnished, don't you think? What do you plan to do with it?"

"Kotey" made a theatrical production of blinking with surprise. "I'm going to sell it to you, my African-American Diaspora friend, for only ... 50,000 cedis."

"Why so cheap?"

"You say?"

"Kotey" was obviously not up to Kofi's level of sarcasm.

"I'm asking you why you're attempting to sell me such a shoddy piece of jewelry so cheaply."

The sarcasm finally registered, and acted as a spur for "Mr. Charley James Kotey's" next item for sale. He reached inside his jacket again and pulled out an envelope.

"Mr. Brown, my African-American Diaspora friend," he whispered.

"I have here the last will and testament of my great grandfather, who was poisoned by his third wife. Before he died he told me that he had buried a box of valuables in the hills just outside of Kumasi.

I have only to go there, unbury this box and I will be a rich man. Whoever helps me to get there will also share in the wealth…"

"So, how much does it take to get to Kumasi?"

A shrewd gleam appeared in both of Mr. Kotey's eyes.

"O, not very much, my Diaspora African-American brother, not much at all. I would charter a taxi. It would cost perhaps … 20, 30,000 cedis."

"Well, don't look at me, my African-Ghanaian slick brother, I'm not the one to sponsor your trip."

"Mr. Charley James Kotey" looked seriously disappointed.

"However, I'll dash you a couple thousand for a little information, it's about a woman."

"Mr. Kotey," the bi-polar hustler, immediately perked up.

"O ooo! I know many women, my African-Diaspora brother, I will go for one of them at this time!"

"No, no, stop. I'm talking about a specific person, her name is 'Kutu'."

The hustler frowned, rubbed his chin thoughtfully, chewed on his bottom lip.

"It seems that I have heard of this name … mmm."

"Well, tell you what, I'm going to give, dash you a thousand cedis. If I come back here tomorrow and you have the correct information about this person, I will dash you three thousand more. Are you getting me?"

The shrewd gleam reappeared in "Mr. Kotey's" eyes as he folded

Kofi's thousand cedi note in a neat square and pushed it down into his inside pocket.

"You can count on me, my African-American Diaspora brother from America." And then he slithered away from the table.

Back to the taxi, Brother Kwame.

"Mr. Brown, sah, it is getting late. I think I must be getting home to my wife and children."

"Just give me one more stop, brother Kwame, just one more stop."

"Just one, sah, o.k.?"

"Just one."

"Sir Lord's Bar" was painted on the tired sign half hanging above the entrance to the small bar, across the drainage ditch. Kofi barely had time to sit down at the back table before the owner; a large round faced Black man in a bright red shirt approached him. He reached out to give him the middle finger popping West African hand shake. Kofi felt a sense of accomplishment at being able to do it.

"Welcome to Sir Lord's Bar, my friend. What would you like please?"

"A cold beer and a little information. Are you the owner?"

"I am, indeed. A cold beer? No problem. Kuahena! One cold beer now! The beer is coming. Now, sir, the information part? You will dash me, eh?"

Damn, news does travel fast, doesn't it? He slipped a thousand cedis out of his pocket.

"Uhhh, it would be bettah if the dash was two thousand."

Kofi was feeling a little ragged. Why argue over a half a dollar? The beer was as warm as the previous bottle at the "Whatever Bar." Guess the electricity was spoiled. Listen to me, spoiled. I'm beginning to sound like a local.

"Now then, sir, what is it you would like to know?"

"I'm looking for a woman named 'Kutu'."

"Kutu, an unusual name. But you have come to the right place."

"You know this woman?"

"She was here, about twenty minutes ago. She lives not too far from here. I can send the boy for her if you like?"

Another thousand cedis, of course.

"Ask her to hurry, I don't have a lot of time."

Kofi suspected that a little stuff was being rubbed into the game when the man gave the messenger instructions in Ga. He could understand only one word of the order – "obruni." O well, here we go again.

The big man paced back and forth as they waited for "Kutu," flashing fishy smiles in Kofi's direction. Ten long minutes later, the messenger led a young woman into the bar. Kofi judged her to be about twenty, plump, a vacant shoe button look in her eyes. Was she retarded?

"Ahhah, beautiful Kutu, come let me introduce you to a new friend."

"Sorry, Mister, this is not the Kutu I'm looking for. The woman I'm looking for has a child that's about twenty some years old."

"Hahh hahh hah, this one has two children, ages six and eight, that adds up to thirteen … hahh hah.'

Kofi made a bee line for the door. No need to waste any time here.

"I'll be back," he called over his shoulder.

· ⁐⁒ ·

NEXT DAY …

Salena was not pleased that he wanted to spend another evening in Jamestown, rather than go dancing with her at the Zebra Club.

"Kofi," she pouted, "why must you go to that dreadful place? There are many wicked people there."

"Salena, there are wicked people everywhere."

"Well, I don't like it."

"Salena, look, one of the reasons why I came to Ghana was to check this out."

"But why?"

"Why? Because my mother and father are curious about what happened – why don't we? …" (Click)

Well, I'll be damned, she hung up on me. O.k., if that's the way you want to be. 5:30 p.m., time to take a shower and get ready for the "wicked folks" in Jamestown.

He chose a dark green T-shirt to wear. Maybe it'll make me a little less conspicuous. Strolling through the lobby, the desk clerk ran over to him.

"Mr. Brown, a small boy delivered this for you a few minutes ago. Sorry the telephone is spoiled again."

"Dear Kofi,
    Sorry we were cut off. I didn't mean to sound annoyed with you, but I am so worried that something might happen to you. Please be careful.
    Tomorrow we will meet at "Susan's Place" and then go to the films. 7 o'clock?

Faithfully yours,
Salena Sarpong"

He felt relieved. So, it was a dropped call, that I can understand. "Can I have a pen and paper, please?" He scribbled,

"Dear Salena,
    7 o'clock at "Susan's Place." See you then.

Best wishes, kisses,
Kofi"

"The boy will deliver it straight away, sah."

He gave the messenger five thousand cedis, five less than the last time. The desk clerk smiled his approval. The obruni is learning how to dash proper.

Brother Kwame pulled up fifteen minutes late, looking a little sheepish.

"Ahh, Mr. Brown, I want to take you to do your work, but my wife says no. She does not want me to go to that place in the evening."

"Brother Kwame, no problem. I'll just charter another taxi. Can you collect me tomorrow morning? I have a few errands to do."

"What time, sah?"

"Ten a.m. would be fine."

"I will be here, sah."

Kofi stood on the steps in front of the Green Leaf Hotel, watching brother Kwame's taxi pull away in a cloud of dust and gravel.

O.k., my brother, if not your taxi then somebody else's taxi. He strolled out onto the road in front of the hotel. Every empty taxi that saw him screeched to a stop and then made an immediate get away when he announced, "I want to charter your taxi for two hours, to take me to Jamestown."

The irony of a Black man being unable to get a taxi to take him to a "Black" part of town made him smile. This is like what it's like in New York, trying to get a taxi to Harlem. Or from downtown to 47th Street on Chicago's South Side at midnight.

A half hour later, a driver was persuaded to make the trip; "but I must double the charter rate and I must be paid now."

Kofi was beginning to feel impatient, it was close to twilight.

"O.k., pal, you got it."

He didn't have to be told when they had arrived in Jamestown, the balmy breeze carrying the slaughterhouse stench did it.

"You know Jamestown?"

"I know how to get to three places in Jamestown; the 'Pito Bar' right up the road here. And then we will go to the 'Whatever Bar' and then 'Sir Lord's Bar'."

The taxi driver, a wiry little man with tribal scars on both cheeks, looked up into his rear view mirror at Kofi. Why come all the way to Jamestown to drink beer? The ways of the obrunis were very strange.

The regulars in the "Pito Bar" seemed to be in exactly the same places he had seen them in, the day before. The Afro-Beat music was louder than before, forcing people to argue louder. The man who didn't look like a waiter came to his table with a warm ABC Lager.

"Thank you, just what I needed, a warm beer."

The man's smile looked like a grimace of pain.

"Four thousand cedis."

"It was three thousand about this same time yesterday."

"O sorry, I made a mistake, three thousand is correct."

Kofi slapped the money down on the table, feeling a little bit pissed. You brothers are beginning to get to me a little bit.

"Where is Daphne?"

"Daphne is not about."

"I can see that, how about Betty and Mabel?"

"They come and go, they go and come."

Kofi took a sip of his warm beer and smiled to himself. What else do prostitutes do but go and come, come and go. Or is that their job? He checked his watch. I'll give this fifteen minutes. He noticed two men at the corner of the bar checking out his watch. If there was ever any such thing as two dudes looking like hyenas on the prowl, it would be those two. Time to move.

"Eh! You have more beer in your bottle."

"It's for Daphne, save it."

Leaving the bar he felt as though he escaped from a quiet mugging. The taxi driver was also feeling uneasy.

"This part of town is not nice."

"And we're not going to be here long either, I just need to stop at two more spots. The one just around the corner here – the 'Whatever Bar'."

"How do you know of these places?"

"It's a long story. Why don't you park right in front of the place? I won't be longer than fifteen minutes."

"It will be dark in a few minutes."

"I can see that, my friend."

Kofi took his table against the wall. Looks like they've reserved this one for me. The waiter seemed a tad friendlier than the day before.

"It will be a very warm night, eh? You would like ABC?"

"ABC cold, please."

The waiter smiled at his request. Where do you think you are, in one of the posh hotels? This is the Whatever Bar in Jamestown.

Kofi glanced around the dimly lit bar. It could be a jook joint somewhere in deepest Mississippi. Thank God the music isn't too loud. The waiter sat the beer on his table, popped the top off and accepted his payment.

"Oh, where is Mr. Charley James Kotey, is he about?"

"Yellow Toes."

"Is that what you call him?"

"It is what everybody calls him. Don't worry, he will be here as soon as he hears you are here."

Kofi wanted to ask another question, but the sudden darkness cut him off. The waiter announced, "The electricity is spoiled again."

"Uhh, how long will it be spoiled?"

"Who can say? Maybe all night, maybe all week. You want to buy a candle for your table?"

Kofi glanced out of the bar at the sight of the taxi driver easing away. You dirty low down dog ... you ...

"Yes, how much?"

"Five thousand."

"Bring it."

He sat in the darkness, studying the glowing cigarette ends. Were they moving closer to him? The bar had quieted down to guttural whispers and an occasional laugh. Outside, a few vendors along the road had set up small lanterns, barely casting enough light to show what they were selling.

The waiter lit his candle and placed it in a cut off milk can. It was the only light in the bar. Kofi tried to appear nonchalant, but his brain was working feverishly. Don't panic, be cool. Don't panic, be cool. Gotta figure the way out of this. If I get up suddenly and try to run out of the door, they'll think I'm scared to death. And where would I go when I got out of here? I've only seen two taxis since I've been in this section and I was in one of them.

While he was feverishly considering alternatives, he could see the outlines of four men enter the bar. Two of them groped their way to the bar, one of them seated himself in a dark spot near the entrance and the fourth man walked into the light of his candle.

"My name is Ananse, my mother's name was Kutu. I have been told that you are asking of her, why?"

The man in front of his candle looked like someone out of the jungle. His hair was nappy and wired out, his open shirt torn on the front and the sleeves, and his eyes were glowing like hot coals.

"Ananse, sit down, we have stuff to talk about."

· ℘ℂ ·

CHAPTER 30

An hour later …

"This is a very good story you have told me, Mr. Brown."

"Call me Kofi, man. You make me feel like your grandfather or somebody when you call me 'Mr.'"

Kofi studied Ananse's bright white smile. I guess that comes from not eating candy, refined sugar all the time.

"So, Kofi," Ananse paused to light his second joint in the candle's flame. "You are telling me that your father's success as a filmmaker and all that came from a deal that he made with my father?"

Kofi sensed an undercurrent of anger in the question, or was it just the spooky atmosphere of the Whatever Bar?

"No, my brother, that is not what I'm saying. My father would probably have been successful at any rate because he is a very talented man. What I <u>am</u> saying is that there was a connection formed between us, because of my father knowing your father.

Whatever happened way back then is what happened; we can't chew meat off of bones that are twenty years old."

He could see a shrewd look on Ananse's face. This guy is sharp, smart. Ananse passed the finger sized joint over to Kofi.

"No thanks, bro. Just smelling it is enough to get me high."

Ananse laughed, a low pitched rumble.

"It's a wise thing to know what you should do and what you shouldn't do."

"Who told you that?"

"My mother.'

"How is she?"

"She died from the malaria ten years ago."

"Sorry to hear that."

They were silent for a few beats, Ananse sucking on the joint, Kofi thinking of what next?

"Kofi, you want to take a walk on the ocean? It's just there. I enjoy smoking my wee on the ocean."

"Sure, let's go."

He felt a slight sense of relief leaving the paranoid atmosphere of the Whatever Bar. He stumbled along beside Ananse, feeling insecure, vulnerable. Damn, I don't even have a pen knife to defend myself. Well, what would it matter? The odds are stacked against me a hundred to one.

The streets were charcoal black, with a dim candle here and there. But it didn't seem to prevent the people around them from doing what they wanted to do.

Children were playing in the middle of the road, chasing each other in the dark, doing the childish things that children do all over the world. Lovers were taking advantage of the darkness to exchange kisses and caresses. The pungent smell of marijuana hung heavy on the air.

"Ananse, I thought smoking marijuana was illegal in Ghana?"

"It is," he answered, and took a deep hit on his joint.

"What would happen if the police caught you, if you got busted?"

Once again, that deep, rumbling laugh.

"The police do not often come to this section, and if they dared to arrest somebody they probably wouldn't make it out of here.'

"Oh, like that, huh?"

"Exactly like that."

They skirted a full fledged soccer game on the beach, the full moon making a ghostly thing happen with the players. Kofi hadn't noticed the three men following them through the black streets but now, on the moon lit beach, he became aware of them. So, that's the way they're going to do it; Ananse has set me up.

The ocean is calm and I'm a damned good swimmer, that's what I'll do as soon as they make a hostile move. I'll run into the water.

"Don't mind them, they're with me. They have my back, as you say in America."

"Oh, I didn't know that."

"Yea, we have to look out for each other here."

The three men trailing them never came closer than fifty yards. Kofi began to relax a bit. Ananse paused at an outcropping of rocks.

"One of my favorite spots, let's sit here."

They sat on the rocks, not saying anything for a few minutes. The moon light on the water and the soft lapping against the shore was hypnotic.

"Ananse, when did you come to Jamestown?"

He pulled out a lighter and re-lit the joint. Kofi could see his homies, sprawled out on the beach to their right, were firing/'em up too. Wowww, these guys smoke herb like cigarettes.

"I was born in Jamestown."

"And you've lived your whole life here?"

"And I've lived my whole life here. When my mother was forced to leave the village because of her relationship with my father, she came here. Where else could she go? She had nothing but the clothes on her back."

I'll have to write Grace Hlovor-Adjei a thank you note for steering me in the right direction.

"What was life like for you here, growing up in these conditions?"

O God, I hope I don't sound like some sort of interviewer on one of the magazine shows. Here's what I asked the feral child. And here's what the feral child answered.

"You see how it is here. It was worse for us, me and my mother because there were only the two of us. We were the only family we had. In Ghana here, it is very hard if you don't have family."

He paused for a long hit on his joint.

"We lived in the streets and we slept on the streets. And very often out here on the beach ..."

The familiar laugh rumbled out spontaneously.

"What's funny?"

"I was just thinking of the story my mother told me of how we almost drowned, sleeping on the beach. She said that the first time we came here, I was a baby, she went to sleep, covering me with her shawl and she woke up to find the water about to cover us up.

She didn't know anything about ocean tides and stuff like that.

Sometimes I think it was a blessing that she died because it meant that she wouldn't have to struggle any more. She wouldn't have to struggle to find food for us, to find a place to sleep, she would no longer have to do some of the things she did to keep us alive."

"I can understand how you feel. But let me ask you this honestly, it's something my Dad wanted to know … What did your mother tell you about your father?"

Ananse stared at the horizon for a long time. Kofi had the feeling that he didn't want to answer the question, or maybe he didn't hear the question. Finally he spoke, very quietly, very simply.

"My mother told me, when she was dying, many things that she had never told me before. She told me that she had met my father in the forest beyond her village. And that they fell in love.

In that place and in that time people were not supposed to 'fall in love.' Marriages were arranged by the families.

When she met him there in the forest, she knew he was 'different,' but it was only later that she found out why he lived in the forest. And that he had unusual powers."

"Did she tell you what those powers were, and whether or not they could be passed along?'

Ananse cuffed him on the shoulder playfully.

"Eh! You want to know everything!"

"That's why I'm here, Ananse," Kofi said in a serious voice.

"Yes, I know," he answered in the same serious tones.

"Powers? Well, let me see. She told me that he had the power to make himself different."

"Like going from a man to a snake, for example?"

"She didn't say that. She talked about him amusing her by becoming a tree. Or suddenly moving from one place to another. The kind of things a magician can do. There are men here in Jamestown who can do magic tricks like that.

You have to remember, my friend, my mother was a simple village girl. She would not know how certain things are done."

"But, Ananse, let's just say, for the sake of argument, that your father was a man who had learned supernatural secrets in the forest …"

"And you want to know if I have this magic also?"

"Do you feel that you do?"

Once again, a long pause.

"I've never thought hard on this, but I can think of times when I have managed to avoid danger, serious problems, in ways I don't quite understand. Whether that is my father in me or not, I cannot say."

"Can you give me an example?"

Kofi spotted several large rats scurrying across the rocks to their left. He shivered at the sight.

"Don't mind them, they won't come close to us because they know we would catch them and eat them. An example?"

Ananse turned to face Kofi.

"Yes, I can give you an example. Last month me and my crew, those over there, were stealing from a big big man's house in LaBone."

He paused to gauge Kofi's reaction. Kofi deadpanned; o.k., you're telling me you're a burglar. I'm not the police.

"Suddenly, we realized that the big big man had come home with a large party of people. My crew ran out the back way, but I was upstairs looking around for valuable jewelry.

There were bars on the upstairs windows, as well as downstairs, so I couldn't get out of the windows. And by now the house was full of people.

I heard the Madam call out – "We have had thieves in the house! They may still be here!"

The big big man, I think he was a Minister of something or other, called to his servants and the others – "I have arms in the den! Arm yourselves and search the house. If you find someone –shoot to kill, I will pay for your fine."

All I could think was – I'm done or, they're going to kill me. I wished very hard, I'm telling you, I wished very very hard that they would not find me. And then a great calm settled over me. I can't really describe it completely.

I opened the door of the room I was in and strolled out; I walked right past these men who were going from room to room with pistols at the ready. And out of front door.

My crew is still talking about my miracle escape."

"You became invisible?"

"I can't say that. I don't know. Maybe these people were so anxious to kill me that they just overlooked me."

"Can you think of other examples?"

The joint was smoked down to the roach level, Ananse stuck it in the corner of his mouth.

"Sometimes, I tell you, there are times when I think I can tell what another person is thinking."

"Like when you knew I was concerned about the rats over there?"

"Yes, things like that. But I wouldn't want to say that I am reading someone's mind."

"What would you call it?"

"Kofi, you are a rich obruni from America, you have no idea of what it takes to live on the streets of Jamestown."

"You're right about that, but what's that got to do with reading someone's mind?"

"A lot. If you are not able to figure out what the other person is about, what those other people are going to do, you will not survive in Jamestown. I've lived my whole life in this lousy place, I have figured a few things out."

"I bet you have. But why don't we put this conversation on hold for awhile, I'm getting awfully sleepy.

Where can we go to rent a room for the night?"

Ananse laughed.

"There are no rooms to be rented, this is our bedroom."

Kofi took note of the increase of rats.

"I don't think I would sleep very well on these rocks."

"Well, if you go to the beach someone will surely rob you, and maybe do much worse."

"Well, I guess this is it."

·   ෨ᘓ   ·

Morning, no maid singing ...

Kofi wedged himself out of the rock crevices, every bone in his body sore, aching. Ananse was no where in sight. Kofi panicked and felt for his money belt. It was still in place. Well, I'm still alive and I have money, now how in hell do I get outta this ghetto?

He yawned himself fully awake, stretched and climbed down from the rocks. It was 8 a.m. and the sun was already scorching hot. He felt dirty, wrinkled, funky. And his mouth had a bad taste from the warm beer he drank in the Whatever Bar.

Shuffling through the garbage littered beach, to the road that bordered the beach, he heard his name being called – "Eh Kofi! Eh Kofi!"

Ananse was running to meet him. He held a half coconut in each hand.

"Here! Coconut water, it's fresh!"

He didn't need a second invitation. He guzzled the water.

"Mmm, that's good, thanks, man, really appreciate it."

"We thought you would like it. Hurry with me, we have transport for you back to Accra."

Funny, he says "Accra" as though Jamestown is in another sate. Or maybe another country.

They came to a corner where people were being loaded into a converted Volkswagen bus. The bus would normally accommodate sixteen people, four in each of the four seats, but twenty were being stuffed into the tros tros.

"They call this one the beggar's tros tros."

Kofi didn't need an explanation; he could see the amputated limbs with the pus oozing through, the lepers with the missing fingers and toes, the blind, and the grotesquely crippled.

"Ananse, we need to talk more. Can you hook up with me tomorrow, about six o'clock?'

"Where?"

"Uhh, let's have dinner. How about the Country Kitchen Restaurant. Do you know where it is?"

"I know where it is. I will be there."

Kofi stared out of the window at the filthy drainage ditches, the shacks lining the rutted road, Ananse giving him a phoney British military salute as the tros tros jerked into gear. He did everything to try to avoid looking into the face of the woman seated on his right, who had a black socket where her nose used to be.

· ℘Ↄ ·

"Dear Dad, Mom,

I hooked up with Asiafo-Kutu's son yesterday night. His name is Ananse. If my memory serves me well, I think Ananse has to do with the spider. In any case, we got together on a pitch dark night in Jamestown. A letter won't really do the trick; I'll have to save the details for my return.

He gave me the whole story of him and his mother surviving on the streets of Jamestown. I shouldn't say "streets," that's a serious misnomer. Rutted paths would be more like it.

The brother is twenty two years old, his mother died and he has been living by his wits all of his life. When I think about his life in Jamestown and the level of poverty he has survived, is surviving, it makes me mad to think about our "celebrity-poverty stricken-rappers," who want to glamorize the gangsta life style. They ought to try a week in Jamestown.

Ananse is a thug, I don't doubt that. But I think he can be "saved." We're having dinner together tomorrow evening in the Country Kitchen, to talk about some stuff.

I'll update you. Meanwhile, I'm going to have to explain my absence from the scene last night to my jealous girlfriend. Life goes on.

Love, Kofi"

∙ ⁊ʒ ∙

CHAPTER 31

THE ZEBRA CLUB, 10:30 P.M.

"Kofi, I thought we had an agreement. You said that I was going to be your girlfriend while you were in Ghana here."

"And you are."

"But I stopped at your place yesterday night to leave you a message and they told me that you weren't in."

"I wasn't in, I was in Jamestown."

"I stopped by a little later and you still weren't there, I wanted to take you to Susan's for Sundowners."

"I spent the night in Jamestown."

"O! You are annoying me with this! You don't know anybody in Jamestown!"

"I slept out on some rocks on the beach with Ananse because, as you know, there are no taxis going in and out of Jamestown after a certain hour. Wanna dance?"

He hated to admit it, but he was enjoying this little spat. It gave him a different look at the usually cool, laid back Ms. Sarpong.

"Yes, I want to dance but I also want you to tell me the truth. It's very important, you know, to tell the truth. What if I told you that I spent the night out, sleeping on some rocks in Jamestown. Would you believe me?"

"If it was the truth, I would have no choice but to believe you." They were in the center of the dance floor.

"Oh! You men are all alike! You say anything to achieve your goal."

He pulled her into his arms as they danced, making her feel his desire/urge for her.

"So what do you think my goal is?"

She made a neat pirouette out of his arms and made her own moves at a safe distance.

"I have my own ideas about what your goal is, but I would like to remind, Mr. Brown, that I am not a small girl."

"I know you're not a small girl, Salena, I can see that with my own eyes."

She spun herself back into his arms.

"Kofi, you don't think I'm getting stout, do you?"

He was tempted to laugh and joke about her insecure question, but decided not to. I'm in enough hot water already, no need to add any more fuel.

"No, Salena, sweetheart, you are definitely not becoming stout. As a matter of fact, your shape has become more beautiful in the short time I've known you."

The music went into low for a few minutes, while the d.j. made an effort to be funny.

"So, there I was, standing on the corner of Abresem and Irene and there is this beautiful gurl standing next to me, waiting for a break in the traffic. So, I say to her – "Pardon me, Madam, but it seems that your future is behind you. Are you getting me?! Your future is behind … you … hahhahhah. Now then, going right along! Our next cut features the voice of the late, great Marvin Gaye – "What's goin' on?!"

Kofi and Salena slid into each other's arms. She whispered to him, "Remember this? This is the first time we danced close at 'Susan's Place'."

"I never will forget it."

The would be hassle had been leveled low by Marvin Gaye, there was nothing to do but enjoy each other's company for the rest of the evening – with a few obstacles to be cleared.

"Kofi, I don't care what you say, I still find it extremely difficult to believe that you slept out of doors, on some rocks, near somebody named Ananse …"

"Would you believe it if I introduced you to Ananse, Kutu's son? If he verified what I'm saying?"

He was calling her bluff and she met the challenge.

"If you can produce this Ananse person and he tells me that what you're saying is true, well, I would have to apologize to you."

"Good. I'd like to hear your apology. I have a dinner appointment with Ananse tomorrow evening at 6 p.m., at the Country Kitchen, you're invited. Will you come?"

She felt trapped.

"Of course I will come. I will look forward to it."

They shared the dance floor a couple more times and decided to call it a night. The taxi ride to Salena's place in LaBone was filled with warmth, surreptitious touching, under current feelings. Tonight, maybe?

Salena told the taxi driver, in Twi; "Wait a moment; this man will be going away."

Salena opened the door, beckoned him inside for a long, passionate kiss. And then, abruptly terminated the developing heat by announcing, "I would invite you to sleep here, but you prefer the rocks in Jamestown…"

· ℘℃₨ ·

DINNER WITH SALENA AND ANANSE

Kofi sat at his favorite table, number 15, in the east corner of the Country Kitchen restaurant, people gazing. Such an interesting mix. The quartet of Germans caught his eye; they were obviously attempting to follow the local custom of eating with the right hand only. However, he could see it wasn't working out very well for them, they were dribbling stuff everywhere.

The "sugar daddy" and "baby sweets." He was torn between trying to pretend that she was a relative, and a sexy young thing that he had seduced. They were spending lots of time staring in opposite directions.

The two African-American couples, who had obviously been on the scene before, were acting like "Ugly Americans."

"Waiter! I dropped my spoon bring me another one immediately!"

"Waiter! I asked for potatoes, not rice. Can't you get anything right?"

They were probably frustrated because they weren't back in Philadelphia. Or Boston, or wherever they came from.

Kofi felt like going over to their table, to whisper in their ears – "This is Ghana, guys, you gotta go with a different vibe here."

"Long time, eh?"

Ahh yes, Emerald, the 38-35-38 diamond in the rough.

"Oh, you remember me?'

"Yes, you want the cold ABC before you order dinner?"

"You're right on the money. I'm expecting a couple other people, I'll order when they come."

"Very good, sah."

Kofi made a surreptitious study of Emerald's back as she swiveled away from his table. What was it my friend Herb used to say to women built like Emerald?

"They are ample testimonies to our background."

The place was bubbling with good food smells, exotic perfumes, and unusual people. That guy must be seven feet tall; he's got to be a basketball player. And that gorgeous trio of Ghanaian women over there. Black is beautiful, no doubt about it.

"Good evening, Mr. Kofi Brown."

He popped up from his seat to play the old school gent with Salena.

"Good evening, and welcome to table 15."

She gave him a nice little hug and pecked him on both cheeks.

"Thank you, kind sir…"

Emerald was at their table before Salena settled into place.

"You would like to order now?"

"Not yet, we're expecting one more. How about a beer for you, Salena?"

"Yesplease, make it Guinness."

He stared at her as she propped her elbows on the table and took a hard look around. God, what a gorgeous creature she is. Dark chocolate with reddish undertones, the most kissable lips on the planet, a shape that's only an inch or two from being a diamond in the rough, another Emerald.

"Salena, what're your measurements?"

"What are you talking abut?"

"Your shape, you know, the dimensions of your body."

"I don't know, but I can tell you that they don't come close to our waitress, that girl has a helluva turdcutter on her, don't you think?"

He laughed so hard he attracted amused attention to their table. Salena was chock full of surprises.

"Well, hahhah, I don't think I would've put it in those words. You know you say some very surprising things at times."

"So, a spade called by any other name is still a spade."

He studied her profile as she waved to an acquaintance.

"Salena?"

"Yes?"

"You ever think about letting your hair grow naturally, you know, just let it be?"

Her reply was interrupted by their waitress placing her Guinness Stout in front of her. Salena poured herself four fingers and took a healthy sip.

"Kofi, look about you. Do you see any Ghanaian women with naturals here?"

Kofi's eyes roamed from table to table.

"Ahhah, there! What about those two?"

Salena gave a disdainful glance at the two teenagers having dinner with their parents.

"They are small gurls, not proper women. Ghanaian women who can afford it always want to have their hair straightened, permed, relaxed, whatever."

"But wouldn't you say that perming your hair is symbolic of self hatred?'

Salena looked startled.

"O! You think I hate myself?"

"I'm not saying that, but don't you think that some African women show self hatred by trying to look like White women?"

"Nosir, I won't agree with that atall. I think there are more White women who want to appear African, than the other way around. They admire our skin, our lips, our bodies, our rhythm ..."

"Your hair, your natural hair?"

She cut a malicious smile in his direction.

"No good, Mister Brown, I'm not going to let you lure me into a nebulous conversation about cultural values and all that sort of business.

You're trying to put up a smoke screen for the time you spent with another woman yesterday night."

"Salena, not true – I told you, I spent the night in Jamestown …"

"Yes, snoozing on some rocks on the beach with this Ananse fellow."

"Yes, that's right."

"Well, it's 6:45, where is he?"

Emerald, the waitress saved the day. She made a discreet approach to Kofi's left side.

"Pardon me, sah, but there is a man here, at the entrance … he says that he has an appointment with you."

"Salena, hold your point, be right back."

A couple Ghanaian weight lifters, "muscle boys," were positioned on each side of Ananse. Security.

"He's o.k., he's my guest, please let him in."

The "muscle boys" stepped away from their captive, sneering at the Jamestown boy. Kofi took Ananse by the arm and strolled back through the upper class establishment as though they were old friends. Yeah, I can see what you see.

Ananse's hair wasn't dreadlocked, it was simply uncombed and showed evidence that he had been sleeping in a place where there was hay. Or maybe mattress ticking coming out. The unpressed pants, the weirdly phosphorescent shirt and the canary yellow shoes were grave indications that he didn't know how to dress. Or had very few clothes.

The canary yellow shoes seemed familiar. Last time I saw those they were on Mr. Charley James Kotey's feet. Maybe they made a trade. And the fragrant aroma of recently smoked marijuana left in their wake was ample testimony that Ananse was fully loaded.

Kofi tried to make the introduction as civil as possible – "Mr. Ananse, Ms. Sarpong. Ms. Sarpong, Mr. Ananse" … but it was wasted. Salena didn't like Ananse on sight and the vibe was swiftly returned. They didn't shake hands. Kofi, the designated mediator, plowed right ahead.

"Now then, what're we having for dinner? I'm starving."

He signaled to Emerald, now is the time.

"Ananse, we're already a beer ahead of you. What would you like?"

"I will take the same as Madam."

Uhh ohh, we're getting into caste and class here, I can feel it.

"Too bad they don't have your akpeteshie and pito here, isn't it?" She cracked at Ananse.

"Yes, Madam, it is too bad."

Kofi recognized the insult connected to her reference to cheap, home brewed brands of what they would call "moonshine" in the Southern states of the U.S.

The waitress stood down wind of Ananse, joining the silent anti-Ananse people at nearby tables. Kofi took careful notice of their turned up noses, their vibes. Wowww, they really don't like this brother being up in here.

The waitress gave Salena and Kofi their menus, dropped Ananse's menu in front of him. He picked it up, upside down. The brother can't read. Ananse can't read. The revelation was a surprise.

"What're you having, Salena?"

"The banku and okra stew are usually quite good. I'll have that, and another Guinness."

"Ananse?"

"I will chop whatever you chop."

Salena and the waitress exchanged knowing glances – this bumpkin can't read.

"Well, then, we'll have the fufu with plantain and ground nut stew. And keep the cold brews coming."

"Yessah."

The table was completely silent for a moment. Salena opened up with an acidic question.

"What is your last name, Mr. Ananse?"

"Kutu, my last name is Kutu."

"Hmmm, rather unusual name isn't it?"

"Yes, Madam, it is an unusual name because I am an unusual person."

"I would be the last one to doubt that."

Kofi cut through the developing hostilities.

"Uhh, Ananse, I was telling Salena about my night in Jamestown the other night."

"O, I'm sorry about that Kofi, I have made arrangements for you to have transport when you come again."

"Why would anyone want to go to that place?"

Salena and Ananse glared at each other. Kofi could see that dinner was not going to be a huge success, but Ananse had validated his claim.

"Well, Salena, do I get an apology?"

"Yes, you get an apology and, if I had a medal, I would give you one for surviving a night in that place."

Ananse's eyes seemed to blaze out at Salena.

"Yes, Madam, Jamestown is a hell, but it was man made, not natural. If the so called upper classes in this country cared about those who were poor, those who are poor, we wouldn't have a Jamestown."

"That's so typical. One is always able to find a reason for being unsuccessful and lazy."

Kofi broke it up again …

"Aha, our food is here. I don't know about you guys but I'm hungry!" There. Maybe that will cool them out for a bit. The people at the table on their left paid their check, ground their chairs loudly and grumbled something about the "riff raff" coming into the Country Kitchen Restaurant.

Ananse didn't have exquisite table manners; he gulped his beer and burped loudly. And he dug into his fufu and ground nut stew as though he hadn't eaten in a while. "Mmmm, this good! Very good!"

"You can have more, if you like?"

"Thank you, Kofi, I would like another bowl of this."

"Uhh, Emerald … My friend would like another fufu and ground nut stew. And beers all around."

Maybe that'll do it, keep 'em "lubricated." It'll all be over in a little while. Salena sipped her beer and glanced at Ananse's head-in-the-bowl-pig-in-the-trough eating style with disgust.

"Kofi, are we going out tonight?"

Ananse looked up, ground nut stew splattered on his thick black mustache and beard.

"O! Where are we going now?" he asked.

"I said we, not you!" Salena snapped at him. Kofi felt trapped. This guy probably saved my ass from being robbed, and possibly worse, the other night. He gave me all of the hospitality he was capable of, even if it meant sharing the best place on the beach to sleep. And he gave me fresh coconut water the next morning. I can't treat him like an outcast.

"Ananse, you can go with us, if you like?"

"He can go with <u>you</u>, if you like. I'm going home."

Salena pushed her chair back, stood up and glared at Ananse.

"It is <u>not</u> nice to have met you, Mr. Ananse Kutu."

Ananse made a half bow while seated.

"Yes, Madam, I am in complete agreement."

"Kofi, will you walk me to the roadside for my taxi?"

"Yes, of course. Back in a minute, Ananse."

He felt as though he were walking through an obstacle course. You are leading your lady out and remaining with that dreadful chap, how could you? The eyes and expressions on both sides of the aisle were accusing him of doing the wrong thing.

They stood at the side of the road, waiting for the inevitable taxi. Kofi was steamed.

"Salena, let me tell you something … I do not like the way you behaved toward that brother in there."

She looked startled.

"That's right, I don't like it. And to tell you the truth I'm highly pissed at you. I don't give a shit about what kind of caste and class problems you might have with that brother, that doesn't concern me. What concerns me is that he came here at my invitation and I think it's wrong for you to insult him the way you did."

"But, Kofi, you don't know these people the way I do …"

"Maybe I don't, but I do know that guests should not be insulted."

The taxi skidding to a stop ten yards beyond, and backing up, cancelled out a possible argument.

"Kofi, will I see you tomorrow evening? I would like to."

"I don't know, I'll call you. Or send a message."

She quickly pecked him on the cheek and hopped into the waiting taxi. Kofi waved goodbye and did an about face. Now, time for me to rag Mr. Ananse a little bit.

· ℘℃ℛ ·

"*Dear Dad, Mom,*

Ghana is definitely opening some doors for me, for my consciousness. I haven't seen a snake since I've been here, but I've been so busy I don't think I would've noticed if I had seen one, in any case.

Let me pull the blinds back a bit; had a dinner at the Country Kitchen yesterday night with my girlfriend, Salena, and Kutu's son, Ananse. I had to do it to keep jealousy at low tide. Salena thought that I had betrayed our monogamous agreement and I had not. Ananse was my witness.

The two of them didn't like each other from the git-go. I felt it was a caste/class thing. Ananse is from way down there, she's from way up here. In any case, at the end of the day, as they say here, our dinner didn't go well but Ananse validated my claim that I had spent the night in Jamestown with him.

It didn't matter a helluva lot, they still snarled and spat at each other. The final round happened when Salena asked me if we were going out. And I suggested that maybe Ananse would like to trip with us. I felt I had to do that because I didn't feel it would be right to simply have dinner and then dump the brother.

Salena rejected the suggestion and decided to end the evening. I was feeling a bit pissed myself at this point, so, when I walked her out to catch a cab I downloaded on her a bit.

Then I went back into the restaurant and yanged Ananse a little bit. I had to let him know, number one, that we couldn't be friends, we couldn't hang out together if he was going to be high all the time. The brother smokes wee (that's what they call it here) all the time. I'm truly amazed that he can be as logical as he is.

He told me that I could 'go fuck myself'; that's what the man said. His thing to me was – "You can't suddenly come into my life and start telling me what to do, how to behave. You don't know what my life is like, what I've suffered, what I am suffering. I need something to ease my pain."

I came back at him with what might be called "a Black liberal's response," but it's what I was feeling.

"Look, fool," I told him. "I can help you."

"You can help me? How?"

Well, I told him, I can help get you out of the ghetto. I'll never know what made me say it, but that's what I put out to him.

"What do you want to be, what do you want to do in life?" I asked him. He must've thought about my question for five minutes.

"I want to be a doctor, a healer; I've always wanted to be a doctor."

So, that's where we are. I asked for a project and I got one. Now I need your help. This guy is smart, full of energy and got lots of heart. I told him he would have to reach certain bench marks, if he really wanted my help. Number one, he would have to give up the gangsta life style (burglary, dope), get a legitimate gig (I told him I would contribute to his income), get in school, learn how to deal with the "outer world," etc, etc, etc.

He agreed to all of my stipulations. In addition, he apologized for telling me to go have intercourse with myself. I accepted his apology, of course.

So, that's where that is. Now I'm turning to Mom and Dad for help. As you know, stuff is relatively cheap here, which means that a hundred dollars a month could handle his school fees, clothes and housing. So far as I know he's living in the streets right now.

Please let me know what you think of my project as soon as possible. I'm going to try to get a month's extension of my visa to put this firmly on track, which isn't always easy, so they tell me.

Ananse is about a year or two older than I am, but I think about how different our life styles have been. But, as they say; there, but for the grace of God, go I. You can write me, c/o The Green Leaf Hotel, P.O. # 2896, Accra, Ghana.

Love, Kofi"

· ෨ඥ ·

Kojo passed the letter to his wife.

"Here, read this …"

Akosua read the letter twice, slowly, reading between the lines.

"Well, let's start with first things first. What do you make of this thing with Miss Salena?"

Kojo smiled.

"Looks like the boy's nose is open, if you ask me."

"Sounds like it, doesn't it? It'll be interesting to see how that plays out. I get the feeling that that visa extension request may have something to do with her. So, what about this Ananse project?"

"Kofi is one of those sons that everybody should be privileged to have. He makes me feel so proud of him. How many young brothers would be willing to help somebody else, anybody else, do something with themselves?"

"Yeah, he is unique and I'm not just saying that because he's my son…"

"Our son, Daddy, our son …"

"That's what I meant. So, what do you think about helping Ananse? I'm sure I could get a grant from the Hundred Black Men …"

"O no, this is our party. I wouldn't want to try to explain your relationship to this guy, due to your connection with the juju man, what was his name?"

"Asiafo."

"Asiafo, I wouldn't want to have a screening committee probing into that."

"But, Akosua, it's not like I'm indebted to anybody for anything."

"Kojo, you told us, sitting right here in this room, how you made a deal with this Asiafo, and that everything worked out alright because of the sacrifices you made to this snake and all that. Isn't that true?"

"Yeah, but …"

"No buts. We can handle these ourselves out of the slush fund. No need to go to anybody else for anything. If the burden gets to be a lil' too heavy for our wallets, we can always go to my mother and father. You know they're always anxious to help Kofi do anything he wants to do."

"You got it all figured out, huh?"

She strolled over to drape her body onto his lap.

"You better believe it. That's why you married me, remember? Because I had a beautiful brain and a gorgeous body."

"Akosua, you're outrageous, simply outrageous."

"I know, I know."

· ෙ෨ ·

Kofi literally felt his heart skip a beat when he recognized Salena's elegant scrawl on the face of the envelope. The hotel clerk smiled at his reaction.

> *"Dear Kofi,*
>
> *This will be a long note; I hope you have the patience to read it. To begin with, I must offer you my sincerest apology for my boorish behavior of the other evening. And I think you were quite within bounds to make me sit up.*
>
> *I can assure you that it won't happen again. Concerning Ananse; he said something the other night that has been resonating in my consciousness. "Yes, Madam, Jamestown is a hell, but it was man made, not natural. If the so called upper classes in this country cared about those who were poor, those who are poor, we wouldn't have a Jamestown." That's what he said.*
>
> *A few hours of honest reflection forced me to acknowledge the truth of his statement. I do want, above all else, to be honest with myself.*
>
> *I tried to give him a hard time because he seemed to fit the profile of the slum dweller. I regret that and, if I should ever see him again, I will tell him that.*
>
> *Aside from his hair and his outlandish costume, he appears to be quite an intelligent chap, perhaps one could spiff him up a bit and something could be made of him.*
>
> *Now then, having purged myself of all negative vibes, I wonder if you would please join me for a cocktail at "Susan's Place" this evening? 7-ish?*
>
> *Faithfully yours,*
> *Salena"*

Kofi glanced at his watch – 3 p.m. What will I do with myself from now 'til 7 p.m.?

· ℘ℭ ·

The soft lighting, the chartreuse, form hugging suit, her intricate gelé and the dark chocolate skin moving toward him made him think of a dream.

"Salena, you look like a gorgeous dream."

"O how nice of you to say something like that."

"It's true."

Susan darted from the kitchen straight to their table.

"Well well, so pleased to see you both – back in a minute!"

They smiled at her hummingbird movements – first here, then there, then back over here – back over there again.

Salena signaled to Zacarias, the waiter.

"We'll have two of those splendid daiquiris, please."

"Just exactly what I had in mind.'

They were quietly listening to the always interesting music spilling into the room.

"Mmm ... what strange music. Never heard anything quite like it."

"If I'm not mistaken, it's Ali Akbar Khan playing the sarod. It's Indian music."

"You know this music?"

"I can't say that I <u>know</u> it, but I've been listening to it for years."

"What an interesting fellow you are.'

They sipped their daiquiris, soaking up the good vibes in the room, the sensual music.

"Kofi, about the other night, my letter ..."

"Your letter said it all, that chapter is finished."

They clinked glasses to toast the moment.

"There was a point you made in your letter that I've already jumped onto."

"What was that?"

"The thing about spiffing Ananse up, to make something of him. After you left, I went back into the restaurant and had a soul brother's talk with him. I made him a proposition he seems to be interested in."

Salena's eyes lit up after he took her into the details of his "project Ananse."

"Kofi, that's a wonderful thing for you to do. And may I say to you, sir, that you're sitting in exactly the right place to make it all happen – the visa extension, Ananse, all of it."

"How's that?"

"That lady over there, Susan can make it all happen."

"She can?"

"You better believe it, if we can hold her in one spot for five minutes."

It took them five minutes of eye and hand signals to get Susan to return to their table. They had agreed to have Salena spool out the details of Kofi's deal with Ananse because she was a fast talker, an essential skill in dealing with Susan.

"Yes, dears, wot can I do for you? I could see you signaling frantically from out of the corner of my eye …"

Kofi looked on with frank admiration of Salena's rapid announcer explanation. Susan signaled to her head waiter at the conclusion of Salena's spiel.

"Zacarias, I'm going upstairs to my office for a half hour. I will be unavailable."

"Yessah, Madam."

"Come with me, kiddies, we need to get a little deeper into this without interruptions." And they were suddenly hustling to keep up with her quick flow upstairs.

"Come in, come in, this is what I call my inner sanctum, where I can kick my shoes off. Make yourselves at home."

They looked around at a quietly luxurious room; three comfortable leather chairs, a long leather sofa, a desk, African tribal masks on the walls. Susan grabbed a legal pad from her desk and sat across from them on the sofa.

"Now then, let's pin the general picture down, we can work out the details later. You want to sponsor this young man to his education?"

Kofi nodded numbly. Dealing with Susan was like dealing with someone who was moving twice as fast as other people.

"He can't read or write? No problem, he can be whipped into the alphabet quite sharply. I know a couple people who are experts at that.

Seems to have a few asocial habits? Well, being from Jamestown and all, I suppose one should expect some negatives to be in his baggage.

Wants to be a doctor, you say?"

"Yes, that's what he told me and I believe him."

"Smart, energetic, you say? Not lazy?"

"Not at all."

"Very good, very good."

She scribbled furiously on her pad for a few seconds.

"Now, here's what we can do immediately. I can bring him aboard; we're always in need of people to do work on the grounds here. And it'll give me an opportunity to evaluate his behavior. If he doesn't measure up I will sack him straight away. Kofi, when you meet with him, you must make him understand that. Are you getting me?"

Kofi felt tempted to say – "Yessah, Madam" – but simply nodded instead.

"I'm not overwhelmed by his educational deficits, as Salena can testify, I've brought village boys and girls into my Montessori school, and people who were wearing their first pair of shoes, and taught them how to teach in the Montessori Method in six months.

The important thing is that he should be self motivated and willing to learn ..."

"Susan, I'll tell you what he told me – if you don't have the survival skills and the smarts, you'll never survive in Jamestown."

"I can believe it, that's a dreadful place. Now then, I believe you said you would be able to sponsor his school fees, etc."

"How much do you think it'll cost?"

"In Ghana here, probably less than a $100 a month. If he manages to make it to the secondary level, it'll be a little more. And then, of course, university. But we can scan for scholarships all along the way. Ghana needs doctors."

"I'll sponsor him."

"Good, that takes care of that. Bring him 'round as soon as you can and we'll get cracking."

"Oh, Susan, one more thing – Kofi wants to get a month's visa extension. He needs it to ... uhh ... put this business on track."

Susan smiled slyly at Salena's explanation. Kofi looked from one to the other. How could the saloon proprietor/Montessori head mistress get his visa extended? Susan scribbled again.

"Kofi, ol' man, I'm giving you a note to give to Mr. Joshua Okine, head of the immigration. It says, "Give this young man a visa extension, or else you will not be allowed to visit 'Susan's Place' for the rest of the year." He'll understand and you will have your extension. Now then, if there is no other business?"

"Susan, I really appreciate your help, and I'm sure Ananse will also."

"He had better appreciate it, if he has a brain cell working. But, on the serious level, Kofi, this is one of the big reasons why I decided to make a grand success of 'Susan's Place,' so that I could fund my school and other projects. You're calling this "project Ananse," I like that."

On the way back down to the main room, Kofi and Salena exchanged warm eyed looks.

· ℘ᘓ ·

CHAPTER 32

The next day ...

It took Kofi an hour to find a taxi driver who was willing to cope with Jamestown at high noon.

"I want to charter your taxi for a two-hour trip to Jamestown."

"Sorry, I don't go there."

"Charter, two hours, Jamestown?"

Zooommm!

"Jamestown, two ..."

"No!"

Finally, a desperate little guy who needed the money more than the others agreed to the charger, for an exorbitant rate. Where are you, brother Kwame?

"I'll pay you half when we get there, and the remainder when you bring me back to my hotel."

That's my guarantee that you won't run off and leave me like the last guy did. Off to the ghetto.

Jamestown in the middle of a humid, rainy season afternoon.

"This is supposed to be the middle of the rainy season, it hasn't rained for quite a few days now. Why?"

"O! I think it is because the weather is changing, because of this global warming thing. It always used to rain in this time."

The stench told him that he had pierced that smelly curtain that hung around the area. The driver glanced up into his rear view mirror. What business would an obruni have in this part of Accra?

First stop ...

"Wait here, I'll only be a minute. Don't go anywhere."

The Pito Bar. A few of the regulars turned to check him out. The obruni is back again, but he's cool, he's Ananse's friend. Kofi went straight to the bartender.

"Tell Ananse that I'm here, I'll meet him in 'Sir Lord's Bar' within the hour."

The bartender continued polishing glasses but he nodded agreeably. Next stop, the Whatever Bar.

"Tell Ananse that I'm waiting for him in 'Sir Lord's Bar,' I'll only be there for an hour. Tell him that I have good news for him."

Next stop, "Sir Lord's Bar." The Don King haired owner wasn't on the scene and the ABC lager that was brought to his table was surprisingly well chilled.

"The fridge is in order again."

He sipped his beer in a pleasant haze, a bit zapped out by the humidity and the overwhelming poverty surrounding him.

These people don't have a snowball's chance in hell to make it up out of this. He tried not to stare at the people walking, limping, crawling past "Sir Lord's Bar." A few of them came inside for a tot or two of akpeteshie, the home made liquor that was like gin. And then back out onto the heat stroked road.

Where in the hell are they going? Within a half hour's time, he had seen some people pass back and forth a couple times. Where in the hell are they going? Where in the hell are they coming from? It was a scene from "Seven Beauties," the film directed by Lina Wertmüller, with Giancarlo Giannini, that showed the horrors of a concentration camp. A scene that captured the endless drudgery of the lives of the inmates.

Ananse staggered into the bar, flanked by his "entourage," who took up their designated positions; one at the bar who could see who was coming in, and one on each side of the entrance. The positions seemed casual, but they occupied strategic points.

"So, Kofi, how is it?"

He banged his right hand against Kofi's outstretched palm and gave him the middle finger snap that made Kofi feel that his finger had been snapped out of joint.

Kofi could tell, from the sour grain smell on his breath that Ananse was drunk. And from the fragrant aroma in his bushy hair and his tattered clothes that he had been smoking wee. He decided to cut straight to the heart of the darkness.

"Ananse, listen to me closely, I'm only going to say this once. As you can see, the meter on that taxi there is running on me …"

"O! Don't worry about that. I told you that transportation would be available for you when you came again. You can send that man away!"

The grandiose drunk, how many of these have I seen in my short life?

"No, I'm not going to send him away; he is going to drive me back to my hotel as soon as we have finished our business …"

"Look at you, you have a beer. I want one! Eh Charley! ABC, o.k.?" He shouted to the bartender.

"Mi ba," the bartender responded, and was at their table with a frosted bottle of ABC a minute later.

"And give my homies the same, o.k.?" Ananse demanded.

"Yesplease," the bartender answered in a shaky voice. He was obviously not pleased to be supplying free refreshments to the neighborhood thugs.

"Ananse, I'm going to be straight up with you about this. I can see that you're loaded and all that, but that has nothing to do with what I'm about. If you want to be a clown and blow a golden opportunity – no problem. Remember, my brother, there was a time when I didn't know your po' ass and I can very easily go back to that time. Are you getting me?"

Ananse took a big swallow of is beer, shook his head from side to side, as though he was trying to get rid of cob webs from his skull, and answered, in a super sober voice.

"Yes, Kofi, yes … yesplease."

"Are you sure you're with me?"

"Yes, yesplease."

Kofi took a sip of his beer and took a deep breath.

"Alright, here it is … I can sponsor you, that takes care of the school fees, etc. I've written my parents, who love Ghana, and asked them for their support. I'm 100% certain that they will give me everything I'm asking for. Now then, Susan, of 'Susan's Place' …"

"O! You are talking about Susan Amegashie, the lady with that school with the funny sounding name!"

"I never knew what her last name was, but she has agreed to help you …"

Kofi decided to ignore the tears that slid down Ananse's cheeks.

"Now, here's the way it's going to go. Listen to me closely 'cause I'm not going to repeat myself.

Susan is willing to take you on, working on the grounds at her place. That will give you a little income. But I have to warn you, she is very strict and will not tolerate any bullshit …"

Ananse held his head in his hands, allowing the silent tears to flow between his fingers.

"I have often prayed for this help …"

"So, that's it. I gotta go. I want you to meet me at 'Susan's Place' tomorrow evening, let's say 7-ish? We can work out the details then, o.k.?"

Ananse answered, "O.k." And carefully placed his head on the table and started snoring.

· ℠℣ ·

Next stop, immigration, same day …

Kofi sat in one of the uncomfortable plastic chairs lining the corridor that led to the immigration office. He had determined, early on, that it would be to his advantage to "dash" the woman who was passing out the numbered cards that would decide who was going to be fifth, or fifty.

"I want a low number," he whispered to her as he slipped two five thousand cedi notes into her hands. The blasé Ghanaians who witnessed his action nodded their approval. The obruni knows how to get action.

The people who had probably been there hours before him didn't voice any objections. If they had the cedis, they would do the same thing. The woman who was passing out the cards gave him #20.

"You won't have long to wait, not long atall," she whispered back to him.

A half hour later his number was called. A snooty looking little woman took his card and asked, in very crisp British English.

"Tell me precisely why you are here?"

"I've come to extend my visa for one month."

"That's only done for special circumstances; you'll have to see Mr. Okine."

"That's exactly the person I would like to see."

"Follow me, please."

Kofi followed the quick marching little bureaucrat through a large office space, into a section of the space with individual offices.

"Please be seated, Mr. Okine is busy at the moment, he'll be with you shortly."

Once again Kofi sat in one of the uncomfortable plastic chairs, waiting to be called. He could hear Mr. Okine speaking in a loud, crude voice to someone.

"Now just tell me, who the hell you think you are?! You have overstayed your visa by three months already, and now you want to extend for another month.

Hah! You think because you are White that you can come to Ghana here and break our laws, do what you damn well please!"

"No sir, I ..."

"Shut your mouth while I am speaking! Just because we don't have the man power to go out and check on all the foreigners for overdue visas, it does not mean that we are not concerned about this situation. Why didn't you go home before your visa expired?"

"I intended to, sir, but I was doing archeological work up north."

"Poor excuse, we don't need your kind in Ghana here. All you're interested in is getting whatever you want out of my country, in any way, shape or form. I'm going to deny your extension and, if you're not on a plane back to the U.S. by this weekend, I'm going to have your arrested. Are you getting me?"

"Uhh, yessir."

"Very good, you are dismissed!"

Kofi looked at the tall, lanky White man with a Van Dyke beard and khaki pants and shirt shuffle out Mr. Okine's office. He looked as though he had been whipped.

"Next!" The voice inside the office boomed out.

Kofi stood up, took a deep breath and took the five steps into Mr. Joshua Okine's office. Big fellow, heavy, but not fat, a grim expression on his dark brown face, brusque.

"Hah! An African-American. Sit down sit down! Now let's hear your sad-sad story …"

"Well, sir, I'd like to get a one month visa extension."

"Has your visa expired?"

"No sir."

"Let me see your passport."

Kofi handed the man his passport. Wonder why he's so pissed off? About what?

"So, your visa has not expired but you want a month's extension. Why?"

"Well, sir, the reason is a bit complicated and somewhat personal. I would like …"

The man behind the desk seemed to swell up with anger.

"What the hell are you talking about?! Complicated?! Personal?! Those are not reasons for a visa extension! How dare you? …"

"Maybe this will help explain." Kofi unfolded Susan's note and laid it in front of Mr. Okine's eyes. He glanced at it and then picked it up to read. Kofi was surprised to see a warm smile spread across Mr. Okine's face.

"So, you need an extension?"

"Yessir."

"And you shall have it."

He reached into the top drawer on the right hand side of his desk, pulled out a rubber stamp and ink pad, slammed "One Month Extension" on the proper page in his passport book and reached across to shake his hand.

"You should have told me that Susan sent you when you first come in here."

"I tried. And thank you, sir."

"Be sure and tell Susan that I gave you proper treatment."

"I will, sir, I will."

"Next!"

·   ℘℧   ·

Good. Now that that's been done I can relax a bit.

A soft knock knock knock on his door forced him off of his bed, to drape a towel around his naked body.

"Yes?"

"Telegram, Mr. Brown." He opened the door a few inches.

The messenger boy held out a Western Union envelope to him.

"Just a minute," he left the door with the telegram to get the messenger a tip/dash for delivering the telegram. And to give him a message to delivery. He scribbled …

> *"Dear Salena,*
>   *Susan's at 7 tomorrow?*
>
>   *Affectionately yours,*
>   *Kofi"*

"You know where this person lives, right?"

"O yessah, I know, I have been there before."

"Good, take it to her." He peeled off ten thousand cedis.

The boy looked at the cedis with greedy eyes.

"Thank you, Mr. Brown."

He closed the door and sprawled back on the bed, the towel saronged around his waist. Thank God for this fan in the ceiling, the place would be like an oven otherwise. He ripped the Western Union envelope open.

> *"Dear Kofi,*
>   *Sounds like you're having a very interesting time in Ghana. Concerning the Ananse project. We are 100% behind you. We'll help you do whatever needs to be done. Give our fondest regards to your friend, Salena.*
>
>   *Much love,*
>   *Mom and Dad"*

Kofi sprawled on his hard bed and stared at the slowly whirling fan. What a helluva place this is, this Africa. It feels unreal to be here, to be back here after all of these centuries.

I'm going to work for reparations for African-Americans, for us, when I get back home. Maybe we could use some of whatever we get to help our people over here.

The irony of thinking about the place where his ancestors had been shipped to as "home" and his ancestral home as "over here" made him smile.

Wonder what life would've been like for me if Dad had married Grace and I had been over here, in Ghana here? It would've been a helluva lot different, I can see that.

He sat up on the side of the bed. Wonder why we don't have more stories about what happens to an African-American's head when he comes to Africa? His Grandfather had given him a few notions to consider, as an Africentric bookstore owner.

"Think about it, Kofi. There are books by African-Americans, not a whole bunch, but they are there. In my opinion, they tend to come in several categories: Number one, although I'm not framing this in any kind of order of appearance, or status, dig?

Number one; there are the 'romanticists.' These are the people, male and female, who trip off to Ghana, Nigeria, Angola, maybe even to Egypt and Kenya, and return, all aglow with the 'wonderful cultural experiences' they've had. 'Specially if they've gone to Egypt. They will punch you in the head with the fact that Egypt is in Africa.

That one has always puzzled me. Why would anyone find it necessary to argue with some racist history books or some stupid racists about Egypt being in Africa? I mean, look at the map. Egypt is in the northeastern corner of Africa, obviously.

O.k., I have to cut them a little slack, after all, when you've been programmed all of your life to believe that you came out of the hear of darkness, 'the Dark Continent,' then I can understand why a little pride in building the pyramids and all of that is understandable.

Then we have the 'axe grinders,' the polemicists who have their weirdass little points of view, who use Africa to justify whatever theory, or theories they've come up with. Sometimes, I think, some of them are honest about what they believe, what they want to promote, but there are charlatans in the woodpile too.

Then we have the Ward/Thomas people. These are the ones who can't wait to return from Africa, to write and speak about why they're so overjoyed that their ancestors were fortunate enough to have been enslaved.

I'm so much pro-speech that I think that all of these points of view should be herd and read. The problem, I think, is that we have too few creative writers who write about the subject, and too many bad writers who write so badly about the subject.

When I look at how well so many Jewish writers have written about Israel, the Italians about Italy. Check out Luigi Barzanis 'The Italians.' Solzynitzen about the Russians, at a particular time, the French about the French, the Danes about Denmark, the English about England and, yes, the Africans about Africa – Soyinka, Achebe, Sembene, Oyono, Clark, others, and then we get to the African-Americans on Africa and the subject becomes purely academic.

Maybe it's my family background, but I don't want only academic revelations. Nor do I want to have 'B' class hacks, who write about whatever with equal passion. I want to have genuine, soul feeling people, hones African-American writers give me an honest appraisal of their emotions, stuff that they've really experienced, what happened in their guts.

Sometimes, when I've read stuff written by African-American writers, journalists, whatever they choose to call themselves, I get the feeling that they've simply read the Travel Section of the LA Times, thought about how they could blacken up that piece on Senegal, Liberia, Zaire, Kenya, Uganda, wherever, and embroidered around that base.

I'm not whipping my brush across everybody's back, of course, but I do know that what I'm saying is true, I own a couple bookstores, I have a finger on what the deal is."

Kofi stepped into his tepid shower stall, thinking – too much thinking makes Kofi a hungry boy.

· ౸ౙ ·

CHAPTER 33

Dinner at the Country Kitchen.

"And where is your lady friend this evening, sah?"

"Oh, she had something else to do this evening. I'll have the ABC, of course, and the palm nut stew with fish."

"Thank you,"

Table #15 offered him a perfect fisheye view of the restaurant; the big men, who swaggered in, trailed by their wives, girlfriends and/or children. The quartet of women who sat at one table and their husbands at the next table. Clearly a cultural thing, the separation of the sexes.

Not too many young couples. Maybe they can't afford the prices. Here and there, a stray European. People from one embassy or another. His attention was drawn to the African-American couple with the young son and daughter, seated three tables away. The children seemed to be about eight and nine or somewhere close to that. And bored.

The African-American couple wore strings of beads around their necks, African designed clothes and seemed to be out to make an impression with their Africentricity. The man even had a fly whisk.

"Sit up straight, Sékou, you're in Africa, in the Motherland."

"Aisha, don't put your elbows on the table like that, that's considered bad manners in Africa."

Somehow the couple seemed to be talking to the general public, and were using their children as sounding boards/demonstration pieces – "See, we're in Ghana, West Africa and we know how to behave."

Kofi sipped his beer and smiled to himself. *I wonder if they have any idea how pretentious they sound. No wonder the kids look so bored. I* bet they've been dragged around to every so called "cultural thing" their parents could think of.

Thank God for Kojo and Akosua, for my parents. They could've dragged me off to Africa too, at that age, but instead, they gave me the opportunity to come to my own Africa when I got ready. We'll have a lot to talk about when I get back.

Emerald, the divinely sculpted waitress, blindsided him with the palm nut stew and urgent request.

"Perhaps you would not mind sharing your table with this couple, sah, as you can see we are full just now."

"No problem."

A Ghanaian man and his European wife. They shook hands as they took seats at his table.

The man was almost ebony dark and his wife was pale white, with freckles across the bridge of her nose. It didn't take him long to determine that they were a dysfunctional couple.

"Basil, why must we always come heah for dinner? Certainly there are some English restaurants in Accra."

"My wife," Basil explained, "is from London and she finds the restaurant choices to be too limited to her taste."

"Well, if what I've experienced thus far is any example, then I must say you're right, dearie."

"I take it you two haven't been married very long?"

The couple exchanged looks. How long has it been?

"It's been six months now, officially, but we had an 'Informal' period in England that lasted for two years before we got married."

Basil, the African man, stared down at his menu. Why does this woman talk so much?

"I was in school when I met Dianna ..." he added, a bit sheepishly. Kofi felt no urge to probe, but it seemed that his presence alone was enough to provoke the couple into giving him more information than he needed; the woman was quite outgoing, the man, less so.

Kofi finally placed the woman's British accent. She sounds like a female Michael Caine from the movie, "Alfie." A cockney, not one of the upper classes in any case. The language situation became a bit more ripe after they had each drank a bottle of Star beer.

"I don't know, it seems that we got on much better in England, d'ya know wot ah mean? Maybe it 'ad something to do with the fact that we weren't surrounded by all of these big assed women."

Kofi dipped into his stew, sipped his beer and tried to tune the errant couple out. The stew was too good to need a side show, but they were relentless.

"Are you married, Mr. … uhh …?"

"Brown, Kofi Brown. And no, I'm not married."

"Well, I can tell you," the man said, "it may not be the most desirable state to be in."

"That ain't wot you said back 'ome, when I was seein' t' ya needs 'n makin' certain that ya 'ad enough kipper on your plate, dearie."

Kofi ate and enjoyed his stew, refusing to be drawn into the domestic mine field across from him. It didn't take a lot of imagination to put their scenario together. He, the African man, was going to school in England, had never had anything to do with any White woman, or perhaps any other woman, and along comes Dianna. She gives him an unusual time in bed (freckled white skin, blonde hair), "loans" him as many pounds as possible, irons his shirts and, at the end of the day, asks for marriage as a reward for all of her "sacrifices."

He marries her out of sheer gratitude and they return to Ghana, where she is clearly unhappy.

"I've never been to America, Mr. Brown, is it as 'ot there as it 'tis 'ere in Ghana?"

"In some sections of the south, 'specially in the summer." The stew was almost finished, the beer half done. Time to be moving on. If they have another beer I won't be able to understand a word this woman is saying.

"Dianna, I think you just feel the heat more because you're not used to it."

"Who cud ge' used t' this bleeding' eat?! I 'ate it!"

There, the stew is finished, a few swallows of beer left to cope with and I'll be moseyin' on down the road.

"Well folks, looks like it's time for me to call it a day."

"You're not leaving, are you? I thought we could have another beer and talk about America a bit, I'm completely fascinated with the place."

"Uhh, maybe some other time, I have another appointment to make."

"Give 'im one o' yer cards, Basil; y' can ring us up."

Kofi signaled frantically for Emerald to bring his check, he had the feeling that he was going to be invited to a ménage á trois from the way the English woman was gripping his thigh.

His bill paid, he casually brushed the woman's clammy hand off of his thigh and stood up.

"Nice to have met you folks, I gotta run." He glanced at the card as he passed the table where the African-American family was enthroned. They nodded pleasantly to each other. The children, he noticed, were looking at their fufu and goat soup as though they wanted to puke. Poor kids, they're dying for a couple Big Macs …

"Basil K.S. Lartey, Professor, Economics, University of Ghana, Legon. Telephone 776-268 Fax 7740942."

He walked a few hundred discreet yards away from the restaurant before he tore the card in half and dropped the pieces into the roadside drainage ditch. Thanks, but no thanks, the last thing I need is some "Who's Afraid of Virginia Wolf" stuff in my life. He strolled carefully through the gutted roads leading back to his hotel, his stomach pleasantly filled with delicious food and brew, his senses alert for everything.

What's that smell? Corn, they use a lot of corn here, for the kenkey and banku. And other odors, a bit more ripe. He couldn't restrain his curiosity, passing two small boys feeding a small bonfire.

"Hey, what're you guys burning?"

The oldest answered shyly, "We are burning the toilet paper, sah."

"Oh…"

He had noticed an odd plumbing feature while visiting the Ghana School of Journalism, when directed to the men's room; the toilets didn't flush and after a bowel movement, the soiled toilet paper was tossed into a convenient corner. O well.

The road was dark, but he felt no sense of danger. People that he could only see as silhouettes said, "Good evening," as they passed him. He felt that the darkness offered him a wonderful cover, an opportunity to gaze into people's lives, into their homes, without being seen as an African-American, as an obruni.

African-Americans bring a lot of emotional baggage to the Motherland. He thought about the African-American couple and their children in the restaurant. Looks like some of us try just a bit too much, too hard.

I wonder if I'm doing that. I hope not. Well, I can think some more about this tomorrow, right now it's time to get some good African sleep. Too bad we don't have a night maid singing …

·   ℰ⊃𝒞ℛ   ·

Ten a.m., the next day.

"Yes, Mrs. Grace Hu-Lovor-Adjei, please."

He was trying, for the third time, to get through to the producer-lady, to let her know that he had hooked up with Ananse, and that they were on a fast track. The hotel desk clerk, Mr. Lartey, spoke softly – "One must exercise patience, Mr. Brown, one must exercise patience."

Kofi nodded, acknowledging the man's advice, but he still felt frustrated and a bit pissed at not being able to telephone an executive at the Ghana Broadcast Corporation. After a series of strange clicks –

"Mrs. Hlovor-Adjei here."

"Hello, Grace, this is Kofi."

"Ah Kofi, so good to hear your voice. So, how is it?"

Before he had a chance to answer the sound was blotted out for a few moments.

"Sorry, Kofi, I had to give my secretary some instructions, you were saying?"

She was obviously busy, as usual.

"I just wanted to let you know that I've hooked up with Ananse and it appears that he'll have a chance to get out of Jamestown, get an education, with Susan Amegashie's help."

"O my goodness! You've pulled Susan in on this? You're really dealing with the heavyweights now."

"She's really a gracious lady."

"Quite so. I'll have to make it to her place soon."

"Well, that's it for the moment. She was also instrumental in getting me a visa extension."

"Good ol' Susan. Well, I must go, I have a meeting. Drop 'round when you have the time."

"I'll do that."

"Ta ta ..."

"Bye."

Things to do, always something to do. A few post cards to friends, to his ex-girl friends ... Margo and whatshername? Well, I'll just put her on hold for a bit.

Time for a siesta. He felt guilty about sleeping in the middle of the afternoon until he wandered down into the lobby of the hotel and found <u>all</u> of the employees flaked out.

"Uhh, Mr. Lartey, sorry to disturb you, but I need some more bottled water."

"The boy will fetch it. Eddi! Watah for Mr. Brown!"

A siesta at high noon made a lot of sense. Who, in his right mind, would want to be doing anything under the face of a blazing noon day sun?

The late afternoon shadows brought in the coolness that he was beginning to appreciate. Africa, everyday, in every way, Africa.

Shower, stagger back to the bed, a towel saronged around his waist. Time seemed to have a different value in this place.

He tried to imagine himself in an earlier era. Imagine what it must've felt like to go from this indulgent life style, food dropping off the trees, fish hopping out of the sea into your skillet, no ice, snow, Arctic winds whistling down on you from anywhere.

I think that must have been the greatest shock of all, to be taken from underneath the warmth of the Equatorial sun to, to New York and other cold ass places.

I can understand why the Afro-Brazilians and those who were taken to the islands; Cuba, Jamaica, Barbados, Martinique, Antigua, Cape Verde, could feel something nationalistic about those places, they were warm, at least.

No, that wasn't the greatest shock of all. Being enslaved would be the greatest shock of all, being told that you and your descendants would be chattel slaves forever. That would have to be the greatest shock of all.

He rolled off of the bed to pour himself a glass of water and stare down at the people on the road. Some walked briskly with loads on their heads; others trudged along as though they were weighed down with more than they could carry. Mothers with loads on their heads and a baby on the back. I wonder how they do that.

An endless procession of poor people. They're poor because they're walking, or maybe they're walking because they're poor. In any case, they wouldn't be walking unless they had to; those who can afford it are riding.

Wonder if this place, this Ghana here, would be as poor as it is if there was no history of enslavement? Gotta talk to somebody about that.

I wish it were possible to do a magic carpet number and bring a few, just a few of our big time ghetto whiners, the habitual bitchers, over here for ninety days.

Wonder how they would cope without running, drinkable water, no flush toilets, no portable color TV's, none of the stuff we've all been accustomed to? Yeah, that would really be a trip.

Could I live here? The thought had bounced around in his head several times ...

Yeah, I could live here, but it would take a whole lot of mindset-restructuring. The idea of not doing things on time disturbed him. But, what the hell, I would just simply have to make some adjustments. Yeah, I could live here, someday.

6:30 p.m. Time to get ready for my date with Salena. I hope Ananse remembers that he had an appointment with me and Susan, it would be a shame if he didn't show.

· ℘ℛ ·

CHAPTER 34

"Susan's Place," 7 p.m. Kofi strolled in, tastefully dressed in a mustard colored sports shirt, beige slacks and walnut shaded Moroccan loafers. "When you're looking good, you feel good," Granddad Kofi always says.

Susan dashed up to welcome him with a friendly kissy-kissy on both cheeks – "Welcome! You know where your table is, where's Salena?"

"She should be along in a few minutes." He exchanged civil nods with a few of the regulars as he occupied his wall side table. Good, thank God she didn't ask about Ananse. What could I say to her? I told him that we had an appointment, but he was a bit whacked out at the time. Hope he remembers ...

Zacarias oozed over to his table with a perfectly concocted daiquiri.

"Zacarias, you're a gem."

"Thank you, sah, would you like a little something?"

"You better believe it, I'm hungry as a big dog."

"Uhh, you say?"

"Yes, I would like a little something."

Zacarias released a big smile in his direction and slid away to bring back "a little something."

Kofi gazed at her over the rim of his daiquiri glass.

Damn this sister is fine.

He took in the full photo of Salena, pausing at the entrance, glancing around to locate him. Look at her style 'n profile, as though she doesn't know where I am. Maybe she doesn't, maybe she's near-sighted or something. He felt like shouting, "Hey baby! Hey baby! I'm over here!"

281

A gorgeous vision in ivory white, from gelé to Italian sandals. She finally spotted him and made a bee line to their table.

"Aha! So, you are here. I didn't see you."

"Salena, do you wear glasses?"

She looked down, curled her mouth in fake tragic fashion.

"Yes, yes, I do, but not on all occasions."

What was that supposed to mean? Zacarias broke up the momentary introspection with a daiquiri for the new arrival, and "a little something," Thai stuffed chicken wings.

"There is no pork stuffed in the chicken wings, sah, none at all."

For a few moments they sipped and took bites of their chicken wings. Kofi was really affected by the food.

"You know something? This is the first meal I've had today."

Salena looked stricken.

"O you poor man! I didn't realize you were starving there in your hotel."

"Well, not starving. But when we get beyond ordering beer, it's best to go to the Country Kitchen. I didn't go there today."

Midway into their third bites of stuffed chicken wings and second sips of their daiquiris, before they had a chance to begin to talk to each other, Ananse literally stumbled over to their table, his white shirt drenched with sweat.

"So sorry, so sorry, I couldn't make it at 7 pm."

Salena looked shocked, Kofi took note of his greedy look at their clustered chicken wings. And his neatly trimmed head.

"Well, you're here now, that's what matters. Please, have a little something?"

Ananse forced his eyes to focus on a distant point.

"Thank you, Kofi, I have chopped before I came."

Kofi and Salena exchanged conspiracy glances. Hmm… Hmm…

"Well, would you like a drink? You look de-hydrated," Salena suggested.

Ananse swallowed hard a few times, pulled the sweat drenched shirt away from his front and back …

"A beer would be nice, very nice, indeed."

Kofi took notice of this British-Ghana play out. Everybody has to play his role well, in order for it to play well. Of course he wanted a cold beer, but he couldn't jump up 'n down and do seal-circus claps about it.

The beer came, they sipped their daiquiris and just as though it had been scheduled, Susan floated next to their table and announced, "Now then, that I see that all of the principal figures have arrived – upstairs we go." She signaled to Zacarias – "Not available, forty-five minutes."

"Yessah, Madam."

"Kofi, Salena, Ananse, refresh drinks please …"

· ℬℭ ·

Upstairs to the inner sanctum. Susan ushered them to sit on the sofa, grabbed her legal pad, ball point, sat down in front of them and became "Mr. Madam."

"Now then, we know why we're here – Ananse, why are you so wet, did you swim here?"

He looked down sheepishly and mumbled, "No, Madam, I borrowed a friend's bike …"

"And you pedaled here, from Jamestown?"

"Yes, Madam."

Susan exchanged looks with Kofi and Salena. Is this guy serious or not? She popped from her set to go to the door.

"Jakob!"

"Yes, Madam."

One of the waiters ran up the stairs. Susan whispered to him and stood at the door waiting for him to complete his errand. He ran back up the stairs a few moments later with a white waiter's jacket.

"Thank you, that'll be all. See that the people at table six are served. I see that they've been there for at least two minutes already."

"Yes, Madam."

She came over to give the jacket to Ananse.

"Please go over there in the corner and put this on, we can't have you sweating all over the furniture, now can we?'

"No, yes, Madam Susan, thank you."

"Madam Susan," the die was set. She was to be "Madam Susan" to him from this point on.

"You can hang your shirt on that hook there. Good. Now then, as I was saying, we know why we're here, so let's get cracking. Kofi has agreed to see to your school fees for the immediate future. Needless to say, your performance will determine how far this aid can be carried.

I understand that you're not completely literate, is that correct?"

"I am not reading or writing well, Madam Susan, that is correct."

"No problem. I've spoken to one of my colleagues about you and she assures me that you can be brought up to standard rather quickly. You're a bright chap, I can see that. Other tests will be made in the coming week to determine where you are. Are you getting me?"

"Yes, Madam Susan."

Kofi and Salena stared at the exchange. Susan, the head school mistress and Ananse Kutu, the neophyte student.

"I'm bringing you aboard here, your official title will be third assistant gardener, which means that you will be low man on the totem pole for awhile, meaning that you will be doing a good deal of fetching and carrying for the second assistant gardener, the first assistant gardener, the head gardener and myself. Are you agreeable to that?"

"O yes, Madam Susan."

"We'll discuss your salary later, privately. Now then, let me ask you, are you homeless?"

"Uhh, well, there are places where I can sleep …"

"So, in effect, you are homeless. I have made arrangements for you to have hut number three back there in what our English rulers used to call 'boy's quarters.' Always hated that expression – 'boy's quarters.'"

They laughed at her sarcastic humor.

"Ananse, I like your spirit, I really do, but I run a tight ship here and I will not tolerate an ounce of bullshit. Are you getting me?"

"Yes, Madam Susan."

"Very good. Now here are the rules. No illegal drugs, none whatsoever. They will <u>not</u> be tolerated period. If I determine that you have used an illegal drug, or that you are using an illegal drug, you will be sacked straight away. Your education will be terminated. There are no second chances and I'm not open to excuses, none whatsoever.

<u>Moderate</u> drinking is permitted. After all, I am a salon keeper and we <u>are</u> Ghanaians, we must have our beer."

"Yes, it's true." Ananse nodded in agreement.

"Having said that, I must add that all and any drinking must be done off duty. You may come into the bar here, dine, if you wish, but there is a dress code. You would not be allowed inside with a sweaty shirt, for example."

"I understand, Madam Susan, I understand."

"You're not married, but I take it that there is someone?"

Ananse looked slightly bewildered for a moment.

"Ahh, yes, Madam Susan, there is someone."

"Good. I know you are a bachelor and all that, but I will not permit a succession of women to be brought upon these grounds. I've made my own rules concerning these matters because this is, at the end of the day, my fiefdom. Meaning, I am the ruler here and my word is law."

Ananse, Kofi and Salena took sips of their drinks. Was this the happy-go-lucky-hail-fellow-well-met-person they had always seen? Obviously not, this was the official Susan of "Susan's Place."

"When I am introduced to your girlfriend, or whatever you choose to call her, I will explain to her that she will be the only woman allowed 'overnight privileges' here. Whatever, however you do whatever you do beyond the boundaries of my authority will be your own business. Do you have any questions at this time?"

Ananse stood up. The white jacket looked elegant on his spare frame. He bowed slightly to Susan, Kofi and Salena.

"I would like to say that I am grateful for being given the opportunity to have a new life, I will do everything necessary to make it happen. I, Ananse Kutu, have spoken."

And he sat down. The trio looked at him. Do you want to say more, is that it?

Ananse nodded to each of them, a solemn expression on his face. That's it.

Susan broke the silence – "So, there we have it. It's Saturday night and I must return to the money part of my business. But I must add one more thing. Ananse, we have a seven-hour work day, from 7 a.m. to 2 p.m., six days a week.

Tomorrow is Sunday. I would like to suggest that you pedal back to Jamestown, to get your affairs in order so that you can be ready and available for duty Monday morning, will there be a problem?"

"No, Madam Susan, there will be no problem whatsoever."

"Very good. Well, then, that's that. Kofi, as the sponsor of this situation, would you like to say a word or two?"

Kofi stared at Ananse.

"No, I think it's all been said."

Salena slowly curled her hand up. Kofi felt the spirit of Obatala that was/seemed to be manifested in her all ivory white outfit. Susan pointed at her as though she were in a class room. Kofi was surprised to see his girlfriend rise and bend down on her right knee.

"I want to ask Ananse's pardon for being so judgmental and bitchy, the first time we met. I want to say that my friend, my African-American friend, Kofi Brown, has shown me that I should be more supportive of our Ghanaian brothers and sisters. I pledge my support for this – 'Project Ananse.' I promise that I will do everything in my power to help Ananse. I promise that."

Ananse bowed his head in response. Susan took it to the next level.

"Very good, very good indeed. Now I must return to my business. Ananse, you're off to return the bike. I will expect to see you at 7 a.m., Monday. I will have a uniform with your name printed on the front and back."

"Yes, Madam Susan."

"Kofi, Salena, you're on your own – we'll talk later."

They shook hands all around, and it was over/done. Susan shot back into her mode, Ananse pedaled away with the white jacket on, used to boast of his new status, and Kofi and Salena sampled their fresh daiquiris out on the grounds, on their favorite white bench.

· ₰)ѓ ·

They sat next to each other, sipping their fresh daiquiris, staring up at a full moon and listening to the music from inside "Susan's Place."

Marvin Gaye's classic, "What's Goin' On?" spilled out on them. They stood to dance and melted into each other's arms.

"Salena," Kofi whispered into her ear, as they moved slowly together, "You once told me that you were saving yourself for your husband. I think you've found him."

Salena stopped their slow dance and leaned away from him, to stare into his face.

"Kofi, do you know what you are saying to me?"

"Yes, I'm saying that I love you and that I want you to be my wife."

"O my God! I don't know what to say!"

"Say yes …"

"O yes yes yes yes …"

They kissed for a record length of time before she held him at arm's length again.

"Kofi, you know I fell in love with you when we first met."

"No, I didn't know. Why didn't you tell me?"

"How could I tell you? Maybe you would've rejected me."

"I can't imagine me rejecting you, no matter what the circumstances."

"Well, one never knows. When would you like to meet my parents, to ask for their permission?"

"Well, we could go see them right now if you want to?"

"O no no no, that's so American. And besides it's late. How about tomorrow evening, Sunday?"

"What time?"

"They'll be home after church, let's say four-ish?"

"Four-ish? Fine. Why don't you pick me up at my hotel?"

"Yes. I will. Please hold me. You have made me a very happy woman tonight."

They held each other close and swayed in rhythm with the music.

· ෨ ෬ ·

CHAPTER 35

"Dear Dad, Mom,

I haven't written you guys for a couple weeks because I've been so busy. It's taking a lot for me to control this ballpoint; there is so much I want to say at once. Let me take a deep breath … and let it out slowly. There.

First things first. I got married last week to the woman of my dreams, Salena Sarpong. She is now Mrs. Salena Sarpong-Brown. You may have guessed that there was something happening when I first wrote to you about her. I can tell you this; no one else was even in the running after we met. I knew she was the One when we first met.

I was amazed to learn that she felt the same way, but that didn't come out 'til after I had proposed. I met her parents (they remind me so much of Grandfather Harvey and Grandmother Minerva) and they gave us their permission and blessings.

"As you can see, Mr. Brown, we've always trusted our daughter to make the big decisions in her life."

"Yessir, I can see that."

"Some of our friends were quite upset with us when we gave Salena permission to have her own place."

"Yes, indeed. They thought we were opening the doors for bad behavior. We couldn't see that at all. After all, if you've done a proper job of raising your child there will be no problem."

"None at all."

Long distance, I would like to introduce you to your new relatives – Mr. John Wesley Sarpong and Mrs. Kwabena Appiah-Sarpong.

288

They will be e-mailing you pretty soon, if they haven't done so already.

We had the wedding at our friend, "Susan's Place." The reason for the rush "to the altar" had to do with my visa extension running out. And, of course, school starting in September. I've missed my snakes.

Being married will make it much easier for Salena to get her exit visa. And then there is Susan in our corner, which helps matters immensely. We'll have another ceremony when I get home, but I have to give you a capsule account of the one we had over here.

(We have lots of wedding photos.)

Lots of people came to our wedding at "Susan's Place." It's unbelievable how many people you can get to know in a place like this; people from the hotel came. My favorite taxi driver and his family (six kids), the immigration chief, Mr. Okine, folks I had met here and there. Plus a huge number of Salena's relatives.

Ananse was my best man. Let me tell you about this brother. This is a story that comes from Susan, his new employer, or I should say, his first employer because he has never had a job before. She took him on as a "third assistant gardener," a purely fictitious job that she created 'specially for him.

Anyway, she told us that this is what happened at the conclusion of his first day on the job.

"Zacarias comes to me and says – "Madam, sah, come, the new boy is crying."

"Whatever in the world for?"

"I do not know, Madam."

I went straight away to Ananse's quarters and there he was, sitting on the side of his bed, crying his eyes out. I couldn't believe it and I certainly couldn't understand it.

"Ananse, ol' boy, what seems to be the problem?"

It took him a few minutes to collect himself, to tell me what he was crying for. Well, first off, I thought he had gone 'round the bend, gone bonkers. But it wasn't quite that. The poor chap was crying because he had never cried before.

Are you getting me? During the course of his rough twenty-two-year-old life he had never been privileged to cry before, it was one of those emotional indulgences that the circumstances of his life wouldn't allow. And now he was making up for lost, stifled emotions.

The tears continued to flow as he told me about his life as the illegitimate son of Asiafo, the man in the forest. I presume you are aware of the details, I found the story completely fascinating. The rotten life of an abandoned child on the streets in Jamestown. I shouldn't say abandoned, he was left out there because his mother died and, as you well know, if you don't have family as a safety net in Ghana here, you're up shit's creek without a paddle.

He was also crying, he told me, about the things that he knew about in Africa, in the world. Can you imagine someone being so sensitive about life that he would be weeping about the great tsunami that happened a few years ago, about Rwanda's genocide, about Dafur, about the horrible Mugabe regime in Zimbabwe, about the Bush-Chenney regime's lies that cost so many lives and injuries in Iraq/Afghanistan, and elsewhere?

He paused to dry his eyes for a bit and then went on again about the AIDs epidemic in the world, poverty, global warming, for God's sake! It was all I could do to keep myself from crying along with him.

Needless to say, we managed to get through that first day, but I can say to you – every day since then has been a revelation. I sent him up to my friend, Dr. Dennis OkakuFore, educational psychologist, at the University of Ghana, for aptitude testing and all that sort of thing. Dr. OkakuFore's conclusion, after a two-day battery of tests is that Ananse's intelligence is at, or beyond the genius level.

Apparently, he has a photographic memory and has taken to the computer, to technology, like a duck to water. He will be computerizing my Montessori School operations in the coming quarter, something I've been threatening to do for ages.

I asked him how he learned to read so quickly. He told me, "It was easy, after I learnt the alphabet."

Of course he has lost his job as "third assistant gardener." I'm appointing him "head of technological resources," or some such thing. I don't think we need be too concerned about Mr. Ananse Kutu, all he needed was a bit of a push and I'm quite good at that, pushing."

So, there it is about Ananse, he's on his way. And we'll be on our way this Tuesday, July 6th, after a honeymoon weekend at this Oceanside resort called Kokrobite. I'm sure you know of it from your time here.

I'm sending Grandfather Harvey and Grandmother Minerva, Grandfather Kofi and Grandmother Nzingha a letter somewhat like this, but with no details about Ananse, I don't think they would understand. Well, folks, that's it for the time being. It's raining here right now, making it impossible to go lay out on the beach, but that's not such a hardship, as you can well imagine for a freshly married couple. Smile.

Love always,
Kofi and Salena"

· ℰℭ ·

Meanwhile, on the spacious back terrace of Mrs. and Mr. Harvey Ferguson's home.

"Harvey! Harvey! Put your paper down! Please, put your paper down!"

Harvey Ferguson peeked over the top edge of the Sunday Edition of the L.A. Times. Now what?

"What is it, Minerva? You look like you've seen a uhh, a ghost."

"This, this letter from Kofi, from our grandson. Have you seen it?"

"Have you forgotten, Minerva? I'm only allowed to read the newspaper and monthly bills."

Mrs. Minerva Ferguson pressed her lips tightly together and frowned, clearly annoyed with her husband's sarcastic answer. He's becoming a grumpy ol' man in his old age.

"Don't try to be funny, it doesn't become you. I'm trying to show you this letter we've just received from Kofi …"

"Well, what about it?"

"The poor boy has gotten married, over there in the African jungle."

"Minerva, Kofi is <u>not</u> poor and will never be, so long as we have money. And he's not a boy. When I last checked, he was an adult. And you could hardly call Ghana an African jungle."

"But don't you see? He's gotten married over there to someone we don't even know."

"I don't think we need to be too concerned, I'm sure he married someone he knows."

"You want to treat this lightly, what if he has gotten married to one of those native women with slash marks all over her body. Or a, a very dark one. What do you think about that?!"

"If she's very dark, he won't be able to see the slash marks very well in the dark, will he?"

"You're being difficult again, think about the children, our grandchildren, what will they look like?"

"They'll probably be black as the ace of spades and have slash marks all over their bodies," he delivered his lines like a stand up comedian and lifted the newspaper back up to eye level hiding a malicious smile. Uhh ooh, here she comes.

Mrs. Minerva Ferguson came from her side of the table, ripped the newspaper out of her husband's hand, plopped down in his lap, grabbed his face in both of her well manicured hands and gave him a solid kiss on the lips.

"O you! You comedian, you! Sometimes I just don't know what to do with you!"

He draped his arms around her waist and spoke in his lowest Barry White baritone … and winked salaciously.

"Stay on my lap like that for a couple more minutes and I'll think of something …"

· ЄОСЯ ·

On the other side of town, in the section re-named "South Los Angeles," but still known as "South Central" to just about everybody.

Mr. Kofi Brown, "Big Kofi" sat in the upstairs office-loft of the family book store – "Pages of Afrika" – scribbling titles of recently released books to be ordered from various publishers. He heard the familiar, quick moving steps of his wife, Nzingha, rushing up to the loft.

"Kofi! Kofi! Read this! It just came, I rushed over here. I knew you would want to see it yourself."

Granddad Kofi adjusted his bifocals and read his Grandson's "wedding letter."

"Well, I'll be damned! That's great, wonderful."

"I thought so too. Call it feminine intuition or whatever, but I had a feeling that he was involved, that he had fallen in love, when he kept mentioning this name – 'Salena this, Salena that' in his letters."

"I thought it was because she wouldn't give him none."

They shared a common laugh.

"You men are all alike, no matter how many books you've read."

"Maybe reading helps ..."

·   ℰℭ   ·

Kojo Brown stepped out onto the back porch of their Echo Park home, stared at Akosua's head bent over the outline pages for her next novel. A gorgeous summer day. He glanced at the spot where he had fed the snake, years ago.

No need to focus on that story, it's over and done.

He tiptoed up to his wife and brushed a little kiss on the back of her neck. She shivered with delight.

"Oh, it's you."

"You were expecting Michael Jackson?"

They smiled and kissed, toasting one of their favorite jokes. He held Kofi's letter out to her. She recognized the handwriting and snatched it out of his hand. She read the letter and burst into tears –

"Oooh, look at me, crying."

"Happy face tears, right?"

"O yes yes yes. I'm so happy for him, to find someone you love. That's a blessing in itself."

"Tell me about it."

"Isn't life incredible? I had no idea he would go over there and fall in love."

"I'm sure he felt the same way.

They were silent for a few seconds, just thinking on the idea of their son being married, to an African woman.

"What's that line from Shakespeare? All's well that ends well."

"In this case I think the old West African proverb would fit the circumstances better."

"What's that?"

"What comes around, goes around."

ꙮꙮ

EPILOGUE

Kofi gazed out at the fluffy gray clouds, midway over the Atlantic, and then turned to study Salena's sleeping face, his mind slipping from one thought to another.

We were taken away in chains, came back centuries later on credit cards. And now I'm flying back with Africa by my side.